By the same author:

ISBN: 978-1-988908-17-5

First published by Underhill Books in 2020.

Underhill Books
4183 Murray Harbour Road
Grandview, PEI C0A 1A0
www.underhillbooks.com

BLACK CURRANT FOOL

Greenwing & Dart
Book Four

VICTORIA GODDARD

Underhill
Books

Grandview, PEI

2020

Various Invitations

It was precisely twelve and a half days since I had learned my father had returned from the dead for the second time.

I had spent many evenings with my friend Mr. Dart since my return to Ragnor Bella at the end of September, engaging in activities ranging from conversation with an Imperial Duke to illicit attendance at dinner parties, and this particular Wednesday was no different.

Until the past weekend my university friend Hal (said Imperial Duke) had been staying with me, while his great-uncle Ben, my father's friend and former commanding officer, stayed with the Darts, but now that Hal and Ben had reluctantly left to return home to Fillering Pool, Mr. Dart seemed to feel more interest in spending time with his brother than he had previously.

I suspected part of the lure of indoor activities was that Mr. Dart didn't want me to thoroughly trounce him at Poacher or other card games; he certainly did not want to discuss philosophy of magic or our respective futures. As I in turn did not have his relish for real-life poaching, especially in sleety late-November weather, did not really want to have heart-to-hearts regarding my own emotional state, and was bored of housekeeping, I had accepted the invitation to play at being proper young gentlemen.

I regretted it now. Master Torquin Dart, the Squire and Mr. Dart's much older brother, and his lover Sir Hamish were soundly respectable men whose idea of a good evening was a good dinner with good wine followed by excellent port, more-or-less legal whiskey, and cards. The dinner I had no problem with, as the conversation had kept to the logistics of my father's return, but the after-dinner pursuits led us—or perhaps it was just me—into dangerous territory. I had placed myself firmly next to the fire, but that merely delayed the temptation.

"Jemis."

I started and stared at my father, who had called my name. He rubbed his eyes lightly, whether in exasperation or pain or pleasure that he had finally been able to remove the eye-patch I wasn't sure. I said, "What can I do for you, sir?"

The 'sir' slipped out. He frowned, but did not call me on the formal address. I had called him 'Papa' as a boy, and 'my father' in my head, and 'Jack' when I first met him again as an adult. 'Sir' was about all I could manage with any hint of naturalness in conversation. It was what I had called my stepfather.

"We were thinking of a round of cards," the Squire said, fanning out a deck with a satisfying soft thwacking noise. "Will you join us?"

"No, thank you," I replied, trying to smile pleasantly at them. I indicated the envelopes on the couch beside me. "I've some letters to answer."

"We could play Lotto or Fish," the Squire said coaxingly. "It doesn't need to be—"

"Really, I'm fine," I interrupted, more sharply than I meant. A flash of something crossed my father's face, gone too quickly for me to decipher it.

Sir Hamish put his hand on my father's arm. The Squire glanced at them before fixing me with an intent look. "Very well. Do let us know if you change your mind."

"Thank you. I will," I promised, and met Mr. Dart's amused eyes. I relaxed slightly when I saw that he betrayed no unnecessary concern for my lack of enthusiasm for *proper gentlemanly pursuits*.

I work in a bookstore, I wanted to say. Until a bare few months ago I thought I'd failed university, failed at romance, failed at being everything my father might have wanted me to be. I'd been trying as gracefully as possible to accept I was sliding out of the class to which I'd been born into one somewhere well below it.

Having a title and a fortune and a family thrust upon me in short succession had not helped as much as one might think. One's life could change in an instant. One's heart and mind and entire character did not necessarily transform so easily.

I sighed and returned to my letters as the four of them settled at the table. After a muted discussion they started playing Bridge, with my father and Mr. Dart partnered; Sir Hamish and the Squire were together, of course. I relaxed a little more when I realized what game they were playing, glad (if also stupidly chagrinned) they weren't playing one open to a fifth player.

The bidding washed over me. The fire crackled, sending a burst of applewood-scented smoke into my face. I sneezed once, and only once, as anyone might, and then inhaled the scent with appreciation. Two weeks ago I wouldn't have stopped sneezing for five minutes after a face-full of smoke.

I sipped my wine and shook my head at Sir Hamish—evidently dummy this round—when he offered me the decanter. Not wanting to talk, I unfolded my first letter and pretended to peruse it intently.

Not though I didn't have all three of them practically memorized by this point.

An invitation to the very newly instated Viscount St-Noire to the wedding of the Governor of Orio City, which suggested someone in the Governor's office was paying close attention to the Kingsford chancery records, as that was the only place it had been announced outside of Ragnor Bella. According to the *New Salon*, this wedding was to be the social event of the early Winterturn Season and, by extension, the year. Only the even-more-exclusive New Year's Ball to be held by the Imperial Duke of Fillering Pool would be more glittering and magnificent.

I had a verbal invitation to the latter from Hal, with the promise of a formal letter to come once he was home. My own status as Viscount St-Noire was of too recent a date for his mother to have put me on the list of attendees. Jemis Greene, Hal's friend from Morrowlea, was not in the first tier (no matter how much Hal proclaimed his mother had liked me in the spring); Jemis Greenwing, Viscount St-Noire and son of Mad Jack Greenwing, however, was.

Second was a letter from the Faculty of Laws at Inveragory enquiring whether I had had the chance to make a decision regarding their offer of a place for my second degree.

And the third was a note from the Chancellor of Morrowlea, thanking me for my portion of her entertainment during the 'most interesting week' she had spent in Ragnor Bella at the beginning of November. She informed me that the dragon carcass I had donated to my alma mater was in the process of being cleaned before it could be wired for display. Finally, as if an afterthought, she wrote that a student interested in a second degree might write to the scholars he most admired and ask about their current projects. My tutor, Dominus Nidry, she wrote, had mentioned that there was a professor at the University of Tara who worked on the puzzle poetry I had found so fascinating. To that end, in case I should be interested, she had enclosed a letter of introduction to the Chair of Classical Languages and Literature.

I took another careful sip of my port, holding the liquor in my mouth to savour its complexities. It was a game I played with myself, trying to name all the nuances of flavour. This vintage was a tawny port from West Noon, smooth, hazelnutty, almost buttery.

A flurry of laughter distracted me. A round finished, I deduced, smiling when my father caught my eye but shaking my head again at the clear invitation in his face.

If he was hurt by my repeated refusals he didn't show it, instead taking up the deck to shuffle with dramatic flourishes. Everyone laughed and teased as he dealt the next round. I felt awash in their pleasure and apart from it at the same time, deeply embedded in their careful if unspoken efforts to draw my father into the life he'd lost so long ago.

It really didn't seem fair that seven years as a pirate slave was easier to slough off than half a year of unsettling revelations and overcome curses.

I returned to staring blindly at my letters, three invitations to lives I ought to want.

My name caught my attention. I looked up, startled, to find them all laughing at my distraction. Mr. Dart was standing beside me, holding out his hand of cards.

"Here," he said, thrusting them at me, "play for me. There's a special messenger pelting up the drive and it's the staff's night off."

There was no polite way out of it, as he well knew, so I set my letters aside and took his place as he exited the room.

I fanned out my hand. Twelve cards—but no, there were none yet on the table—ah. An Ace stuck slightly behind the Three of Hearts. I peeled them apart, careful not to show their faces, and looked at the three men watching me. "Any bids so far?"

"One Heart," Sir Hamish said, pointing at my father, who was playing North. "Tor passed, Perry said Two Hearts, and I Two Spades."

I contemplated my hand again, wondering why on earth Mr. Dart had bid Two Hearts. Even if he'd missed seeing the Ace, he still had two Kings and three Hearts. With the bid he'd chosen my father had to have a strong hand.

"Very well," I said, voice deliberately unenthusiastic to counter the emergence of the faint, familiar, perilous thrill.

One hand was not fateful, surely.

I firmly suppressed the thought that the bidding was the part I liked best about Bridge.

My father considered me for a long moment. I kept my face as neutral as possible, as if I were bored, hoping I didn't also look petulant. He had taught me how to play (Bridge, and Poacher, and half a dozen other games of skill and chance). He had also warned me …

"Three Hearts," he said.

Despite my resolve not to get drawn in my mind immediately began to calculate probabilities and possibilities.

"Pass," said the Squire.

Three Hearts meant my father had at least six Hearts, suggesting his hand held at least eighteen points.

I didn't need to glance at mine again. "Four Hearts."

I felt, rather than saw, Sir Hamish's surprise as he said, "Pass."

He had Spades, but couldn't have that many high face cards, I thought vaguely.

My father's eyes were intent. "Four No Trump."

"Pass," the Squire said after a pause, as if puzzled by this, though I was sure he knew bidding conventions at least as well as I did.

Four No Trump was asking how many aces I had. "Five Diamonds," I replied, since I had one.

"Pass," said Sir Hamish. His voice was also a little odd.

I ignored him, watching my father, revelling in the buzz of excitement, the sense of purpose and clarity that came when risk entered my life. Bidding at cards was only a shadow of what could be, I knew too well, and I knew also that even so it was dangerous to let myself enjoy it too fully.

"Five No Trump," my father said, his expression unfathomable.

"Pass."

Mr. Dart came back in the room. He stood at my shoulder, and I could feel his astonishment when I replied, "Five Hearts." This indicated—to my father, at least—that I had two Kings in my hand, that I knew that between us we had all the Aces, all the Kings, and nine Hearts.

Go for it, I thought, as Sir Hamish said, "Pass," in the same odd voice, and my father, meeting my eyes thoughtfully, said, "Seven Hearts." As the rest of us passed on further bids I smiled at him in delight that we had partnered so easily.

"You're going for a Grand Slam?" Mr. Dart cried.

I laid out my cards for the dummy hand. "You need to work on your bidding, Mr. Dart."

"If you ever played with us, perhaps I'd learn."

"You have a master to learn from," I replied, gesturing at my father. I kept my voice light, not wanting any of my emotions to spill out.

Why couldn't I have had a boring hand?

Not that there was such a thing as a boring hand when one played with a master.

Said master took easy control of the play and, despite Sir Hamish and the Squire's best efforts, quickly trounced them. I permitted myself to watch, admiring the way my father drew out each remaining high card and trump before winning the last hand with my Three of Hearts.

As the Squire took the deck to shuffle, he said idly, "Won't you play this next round, Jemis? Now that Perry has a letter of his own to ponder—it is for you, I take it?"

"So the address indicates."

"Well, then, Jemis?"

I felt my face stiffen involuntarily. "No, thank you, sir."

There was a pause. I disdained the coward's way out, though my heart was fluttering miserably, all thrill from the game extinguished. Why could they not let well enough alone?

—I met my father's slight frown and exhaled.

Well, for exactly the same reason I badgered Mr. Dart about the wild magic he was still refusing to acknowledge possessing.

"I had thought," Sir Hamish murmured, "that perhaps you had taken a dislike to playing, or that you did not feel your skills were, ah, adequate."

I snorted softly at that, unable to prevent myself. The Green Lady had given me the gift of skill at cards—and the White Lady all the weaknesses that might come of it.

"So what is it, then?" the Squire said, still shuffling the cards. "Your words say you don't like the games, but your face said otherwise."

"I do like playing," I blurted at the unexpected edge in his voice, and went on before I could quite make myself stop. "Too much."

The Squire's hands stopped in the middle of a movement. Cards scattered everywhere, across the table, fluttering to the floor, the Jack of Spades landing face-up on Mr. Dart's letter, as if in mute instruction. With the way Mr. Dart was suppressing his magic it might well have been. I sighed again when my father leaned forward intently, far too much understanding in his face. "Jemis. Tell us, please. Did you have trouble at university?"

"Not with cards," I admitted, knowing I was flushing, ashamed to the root of my soul that this conversation was happening, that it had to happen.

My father looked at where I'd been sitting before, at the half-full glass of port I'd been nursing all evening. My mouth twisted with wry amusement. "No, not liquor either."

"If not gambling or drinking—how much of a habit are your death-defying stunts?"

"You're one to talk," Sir Hamish muttered, and even as my father gave a bark of laughter I felt my stomach fluttering again with the terrible aching emptiness that such thrills were never going to warm, and everywhere, like a sticky cloud engulfing me, there was the loathing that I had let it all happen to me.

"Drugs?" he said softly, face dismayed, eyes boring into me. "Oh, Jemis—"

Mr. Dart suddenly thwacked me on the side of the head with his letter, sending the card into my lap. I flinched belatedly, earning a glare from my friend.

"Honestly, Jemis, anyone would think you thought it was your fault! Jack, an unscrupulous wizard decided the best response to him preferring her friend was seduction, enchantment, and drugging him with wireweed to the point where it's frankly amazing he survived, let alone came First at Morrowlea."

I opened and shut my mouth several times before any sounds came out. "I—I—"

"Is this true?" the Squire said, his face thunderous. "How long were you given it?"

I shrank in on myself. "Er, nearly three years."

They stared at me in appalled silence. In their eyes I could see that they knew (as I had not) what unscrupulous wizards used wireweed for, and what almost invariably happened to their victims.

Not that I thought of myself as a victim, exactly. I'd been so *stupid*.

I really did not want to go into detailed explanations. I took a deep breath and carefully and consciously relaxed my hands and shoulders.

"In answer to your earlier question, Master Dart, yes, I like playing cards. However, even though it was not intentional on my part, I am living with the after-effects of the wireweed. I have no intention of letting myself be controlled by anything that promises to fill the—the space left behind by the drug." I had to stop there to take a breath through my nose before I could bring myself to meet my father's stern gaze again. "You cannot deny there is ample precedent in my family for a tendency to destructive addictions."

A grandfather who had gambled away his inheritance, an uncle who had conspired at murder to hide the fact he had done the same to mine, a great-grandfather whose liver had given out on him at the ripe old age of forty-seven—

No one spoke for a moment. I waited until it was clear they would press me no further this evening—I knew better than to even hope that the topic would not be raised again another time—and turned meaningfully to Mr. Dart.

"Anything you'd like to share from your missive? Why was a special messenger sent to the Darts on a cold November night?"

Mr. Dart, Lady bless him, grinned first at me and then at his brother. "It seems to be an elaborate prank. Unless, of course, you actually do have a secret wife and daughter you've never mentioned, Tor."

There was a very peculiar silence. Master Dart and Sir Hamish stared at each other.

And then Sir Hamish said, "Good heavens. Ingrid."

CHAPTER Two

In Which Various Requests Are Made

As far as distractions went, this was superb.

I was grateful that Sir Hamish clearly already knew about the Squire's secret wife and daughter, for that meant I could focus my attentions on consoling Mr. Dart. I was vaguely miffed to discover that Mr. Dart was far from needing consolation. Indeed, he was almost indecently delighted with the whole thing.

The Squire explained, painfully and with much embarrassment, how he had come late to the discovery that he preferred Sir Hamish's company to any woman's.

Mr. Dart interjected, "Even your wife's?"

I would have been sympathetic had he said that with commiseration or solemn understanding or any appropriate emotion. As he was nearly burbling with mirth, I acted as any friend ought, and kicked him in admonishment.

The Squire explained, even more painfully and with even deeper embarrassment, that in the more permissive age of his youth such experimentation had been common, but that it was his folly that he had not undertaken proper precautions—

"Hence your daughter, or possibly whence," said Mr. Dart, before scooching his chair away from me.

The Squire explained, with lugubrious pride, that he and the lady in question had decided to marry, just in case the child were a son and would therefore inherit the Dart estate.

"But of course, now that they're changing the inheritance law, she will anyway," said Mr. Dart, beaming at his brother so brilliantly even Master Dart noticed.

"Perry—oh, Lady, Perry, I never thought! I'm so sorry—"

"Think nothing of it," Mr. Dart replied, waving his hand dismissively. "I quite understand how you could forget the existence of even a wife and daughter after, what, twenty years?"

The Squire winced. "Perry …"

Sir Hamish laid his hand on his lover's knee. At least this explained a minor mystery of the barony, I thought numbly, namely why the two of them had never performed the ceremony of commitment. Rondelan law provided no such ritual for two men or women in a relationship, but Astandalan law had, in its byzantine complexity (covering as it had the diverse cultures of five worlds). But although polygamy was permitted in certain demesnes, Northwest Oriole had never been one of them. The horrified response to the discovery of my own mother's accidental bigamy had made that exceedingly clear.

"Shall I read the letter aloud?" Mr. Dart said, even more brightly. "Or leave our dear friends to their not unjustified confusion?"

The Squire winced again. Sir Hamish said, with commendable restraint, "Perry. Please."

Mr. Dart made a show of shaking out the letter. "'My dear Sir—' a most restrained opening, I must say. The meat comes quickly, however:

'My dear Sir—

It has been many years since we last corresponded, for which I apologize. I must presume this finds you well, for in the wake of the unrest that has followed the capture of the Blood Eagle, I find myself in sore need of sanctuary for myself and our daughter. The pirate blockade is closing in around the Reaches even as winter draws near, and there will be few opportunities after this to escape ere the spring, and I fear there will be no safety for us if we delay so long.

Please believe I would not be so importunate if I had any other recourse. I know you are an honourable man and will not deny us this sanctuary. I cannot wait for any written reply, but we will await you for the evening in the Old Pear Tree Inn of Orio City on the last Monday in November. From all accounts the city is yet safe to travellers.

Your wife,

Ingrid Ingridsdottir Dart'

We all sat there for a moment to digest this. After a moment my father said, "The *Blood Eagle* was my ship." I stared at him, shocked by the memory of the dream-vision I'd had of that ship's capture. He misunderstood my expression and smiled wryly and with little humour. "It was the premier pirate ship of the North." He looked at his friends, who were gazing intently at the letter. Mr. Dart had turned away to stare at the fire.

"Right," said my father, clapping his hands for attention. "This has been a most unexpected development. Jemis and I shall leave you to your deliberations—"

The Squire and Sir Hamish both protested this plan. While they were remonstrating with my father about needing his advice now more than ever, Mr. Dart scooched his chair back over to me and beckoned me to lean close, which I, with an internal sigh of resignation to whatever mad plan he'd managed to concoct in the past few minutes, obligingly did.

"My brother's Acting Magistrate this session and the Assizes have barely begun. Hamish recently started a major commission for the Duchess, and I think he's under a bit of pressure to get it done promptly. Your father's just returned and needs to deal with the estate and things."

Things, in this case, ranging from the arrest of my uncle for conspiring to commit murder to all the legal and social tangles involved in clearing one's name of treason and one's status of being considered dead.

I contemplated Mr. Dart's eager eyes and the value I placed on our friendship, and the fact that the last Monday of November was this Monday coming.

"When do you want to leave?"

* * *

Having received permission to relay the story to my employer, Mrs. Etaris, I did so with some eagerness to hear her response. Over the two and a half months or so of my employment at her bookstore I had come to have the greatest respect for her judgment.

"How intriguing," was her first response. We were sitting in the comfortable chairs beside the wood stove, which was burning merrily to ward off the November chill. Mrs. Etaris' cat Gingersnap lay on his back in my lap, purring madly as I stroked his chest. Outside it had started to snow, large picturesque flakes.

Mrs. Etaris glanced out at the market square. "It is not, alas, the best weather for travelling. Fortunately it is not the worst, either; it could be late January. And if the ladies in question feel it necessary to brave the Northern Sea in storm season to throw themselves on the Darts' hospitality, it behoves one of the Darts to make the effort to meet them."

I sipped the cocoa we'd made earlier. Gingersnap batted at my cuff in annoyance that I'd stopped petting him.

"Of course, it will have to be Mr. Dart who makes the journey. Equally of course you wish to accompany him."

"I do not wish to leave you in the lurch, Mrs. Etaris, especially so close to Winterturn. This must be a busy season for you."

"Naturally," she murmured, smiling with an air of mischief I did not really understand. "Nevertheless … let me think a moment. You see, Mr. Greenwing, after all the excitements occasioned by your return to Ragnor Bella—"

She paused there, presumably to let us both reflect on said excitements. I squirmed a bit in my chair. Gingersnap rolled over and began kneading my thigh in protest.

My initial return had been poorly enough received to cause a quarter-year's worth of gossip, and that was before the criminal gangs and the mermaid—let alone the dragon and my maternal inheritance—and that didn't even begin to touch on the cult to the Dark Kings and my father's second return from the dead.

Mrs. Etaris smiled at me almost triumphantly. "The lead-up to Winterturn is always my busiest time, as you've so cleverly noted, but this year the autumn was quite remarkably busy, what with one thing and another."

Half of Ragnor Bella and the surrounding barony coming in to see for themselves what Mad Jack Greenwing's son was making of himself, and buying books as poor camouflage, that meant.

"Indeed," Mrs. Etaris went on, "I find myself in serious need of stock to ensure I have enough for the Winterturn season. I would count it a great favour if my assistant would be willing to hazard the roads and attend the Silverheart Book Fair in Orio City."

***

Once Mrs. Etaris had given me a mission it occurred to me that there might be others in the community who had hankerings after items only to be found in the 'big city'. It only took me an hour to begin to regret this idea.

"And just how do you think this will all fit into our carriage?" Mr. Dart asked when he caught up with me just outside The Ragnor Arms adding Mr. Fogerty the Fish's request to my list. He leaned his chin on my shoulder to read what I'd written so far. "What are grains of paradise?"

"Some sort of spice, apparently," I replied.

"Pity your friend Hal's gone back to Fillering Pool already. I'm sure he'd know—and have a carriage sufficiently grand with which to convey them."

I smirked at Mr. Dart. Hal had left the week previous, when the letters from his mother had become too importunate to bear. He'd showered me, my father, and Mr. Dart alike with invitations to spend Winterturn with him, but though the coming-of-age ball of an Imperial Duke had its appeal, I had wanted to spend the holiday with my father.

There was also the small but pertinent fact that Hal had also assured me that I was well on my way to becoming the second-most eligible bachelor in Northwest Oriole, after himself.

"Why are you smiling like that?" Mr. Dart demanded. "Not from your list—egads! What's this about a hundredweight of turnips? *Two* hundredweight of cabbage? Fifteen barrels of butter?"

I took my list back from him and stowed it in my pocket. "Be grateful for that section of the list, Mr. Dart. It's for St-Noire village. They missed summer, you may recall."

"Three summers," he murmured, abashed, at this reminder of the cursed village in the Woods Noirell. "They must be down to their last stores. I retract my comments."

"They've had a hard time since the Fall, since no traffic goes through the Woods now. I'm going to use some of the money from my stepfather to get supplies."

"And apart from greatly admiring your dedication to duty, I am to be grateful because … ?"

"I hope it will persuade my grandmother to lend us the use of her falarode."

Mr. Dart looked at me. "That black monstrosity? The one she borrowed from Lady Death?"

I grinned.

***

Thursday noon found me tidying my flat. Mrs. Etaris had given me the day off to organize myself, but once I'd written to my grandmother with the question of the falarode and been given the requests of various friends and what felt like all the small tradesmen and artisans in the barony, I had nothing much to do.

I was in the midst of sweeping when a knock on the door interrupted me. I looked up, for it was the inner door, to find my father standing there watching me.

"Sir—Papa," I said, clutching at the broom-handle.

"Jemis," he returned, a slow smile lighting his face. "May I come in?"

"Of course!" I stepped back, straight into my pile of sweepings, flushed, and added, "Please sit down. I'll—I'll just finish this."

He continued to watch me with amusement while I found the dustpan, re-swept my pile, and finally removed sweepings, broom, and dustpan to their various homes. I washed my hands before returning to the parlour. There in the mirror was the earnest young gentlemen of straightened means, though his clothes were not quite such to suggest the need to clean for himself.

Appearances could be so deceiving. I had only the one winter-weight suit, hastily finished less than a fortnight ago for the reading of my stepfather's will, and a few extra pieces bought subsequently to eke out a week's laundry. Another suit was on order, but my father had returned home with nothing, and took precedence. Both the rival haberdashers of Ragnor Bella were working on our wardrobes, but they had already been busy with their usual pre-Winterturn commissions and had promised nothing but the most basic pieces for my father in the next fortnight.

My father was looking at my bookshelf when I came in with an ewer of water for want of any better hospitality. He had taken already his book of haikus, which had once held pride of place, but not the great golden pectoral of the Heart of Glory, saying he had no fit home for it yet, as he continued to reside with the Darts.

I found myself wishing we could return to the dower cottage my mother and I had lived in (and my father when he was home from campaigns), but I supposed he would want the Manor itself, once the situation with the Arguty estate was settled.

He turned to see me hovering awkwardly, and actually laughed, the rumble I remembered so well from my childhood. "I've not come to scold you. May I sit down?"

"You don't need permission," I blurted. "You're welcome any time."

He sat down in the chair Hal had used when he'd stayed. "Thank you," he said gravely, answering the words with solemn meaning. I sank more slowly down into my chair opposite, wishing I'd done more than sweep. At least the fire was burning well, throwing off a good heat into the room.

"Are you prepared for the journey?"

"I believe so."

He hesitated, then spoke slowly. "Jemis, I am very proud of you."

My uncomfortable admission of the night before hung heavily in the air around us. I swallowed dryly, all the knowledge of the many ways I'd failed the examples he'd set me almost physically present in the room. Even the room itself, the little flat I'd been so pleased to call my own, was symbolic of it. If it had been a little flat in Kingsford or Orio City (or Astandalas, once upon a time), it would have been understood as a stepping-stone to greater things, to a place in the courts of the king or the governor. Here, in Ragnor Bella?

He sat back. "You don't believe me."

I forced myself to meet his gaze. We had had conversations over the past twelve and a half days, of course, even a few long ones.

But for the first week Hal and Ben had been there, and my father's company had been overwhelmed by all the people in town who wanted or needed to speak to him, with the initial statements given to constabulary and lawmen. The last five or six days he'd been closeted with the lawyers, spending many hours with the tangled paperwork involved in his return.

I had gone back to work at the bookstore, and gritted my teeth as I had all autumn and smiled and responded politely to all the good gossips of Ragnor Bella.

Finally, when the silence had gone on far too long, I said, "You cannot be proud of what I said last night."

He met my eyes, his brow furrowed. His injured eye was brighter than the other; it produced more tears as part of the healing process, he'd said. I did not look down, though I felt an indistinct bright shame. I did not know how to put any of this into words. My classical poets were no help; serried ranks of them in the library at Morrowlea gave no voice to the muddled emotions I felt looking at my father whom I'd always loved so much.

"You seem to have a very strict idea of what I approve or disapprove," he said. "I don't know what I did when you were young to give you this idea that I am so harsh."

My eyes flickered unintentionally to the Heart of Glory on the wall, awarded to him by the Emperor himself.

He followed my glance, holding himself very still for a moment, and then let out his breath in a deep huff. "My finest hour," he murmured. "Do you hold yourself to that standard, Jemis? I cannot hold myself to that standard."

I stared at him. What could he mean? Of course he could: of course he *had*. This was the man who had once held a border; who had gone alone into a fortress of the enemy on the far side of the mountains at Loe; who had come home after the Fall; who had come home after his captivity among the pirates despite knowing the reception he had received on his first return. His courage was quite literally the stuff of legend.

He leaned forward. "Jemis, please tell me what you are thinking."

Mr. Dart and I, excellently educated modern gentlemen that we were, danced around our emotions. The blunter approach of those who had come of age in the final days of the Empire always confounded me.

I could not formulate words for what I felt. I could feel my face burning with embarrassment, and looked down to my hands, interlaced on my lap in some parody of a maiden's deportment. "I am sorry, sir," I said at last. "I don't wish to disappoint you."

He slumped, the disappointment with this response all-too-evident, then smiled crookedly at me. "I can see that. Try not to throw yourself into death-defying situations without thinking them through a little first, eh?"

"I'll do my best," I promised, breathing more easily at this familiar instruction. What long conversations we'd had so far had mostly centered around my tendency to embroil myself in danger. I was aware that it would have been hard to accept counsels of prudence from anyone other than him.

"Here," he said, reaching into the deep pocket of his coat and drawing out a small knife in a sheath. "I have something for you."

I felt something relax in me, knowing that we were moving on from the quicksand. Albeit I did not quite understand why the conversation had felt so dangerous in the first place.

CHAPTER *THREE*
We Borrow the Falarode

MY PREVIOUS EXPEDITIONS had been leaving Ragnor Bella to go to Morrowlea and leaving Morrowlea to come home via a tour of most of the kingdom. Morrowlea was one of the Three Sisters—or the Three Rivals, if one preferred that name for the three greatest universities of Alinor—but unlike Stoneybridge (Mr. Dart's alma mater) or Tara (the Honourable Rag's), Morrowlea was known for its radical politics and a policy of equality for all its students.

I had, therefore, not been required to bring more than myself and what I needed for the actual journey to South Erlingale. Mr. Dart, preparing at the same time to go to Stoneybridge, had required two trunks and numerous other containers; I did not like to think what the Honourable Rag, then (since I had not yet been acknowledged by my grandmother as heir to the Imperial Marquisate of the Woods Noirell) highest ranking young man in the barony, had decided it was necessary to bring with him to Tara.

Leaving Morrowlea heart-broken and ill for a walking tour with Hal and Marcan, I had taken with me a rucksack containing numerous handkerchiefs, my few changes of clothing, a notebook, and a copy of *On Being Incarcerated in Orio Prison* I had not been able to bear looking at the whole length of the trip.

Getting ready to go to Orio City to fetch the mysterious Mrs. and Miss Darts, as many interesting books as I could acquire for the princely sum of five hundred bees, and a quantity of other items large and small, I filled that same rucksack with the spare elements of my winter-weight outfit, a smaller quantity of handkerchiefs than I'd ever left home with before, a fresh notebook, and, finally, that same copy of *On Being Incarcerated in Orio Prison.*

I had hated the poem—on which I had written my final paper for my degree—all summer as a reminder of what I had lost in the spring. Now that I knew I had, in fact, not totally failed my degree, I was inclined to return to the poem and see if I could tease out a more coherent paper than the one I had written while falling apart physically, mentally, and emotionally from an overabundance of wireweed. And it had to be said that I revelled in the idea of being able to see Orio Prison with my own eyes.

At least from a distance. I had had a brief experience of being incarcerated myself, in Yellton Gaol, and had no interest in comparing and contrasting rural gaols with the most infamous prison in the world.

Most of my earthly belongings packed by Thursday noon, after my father left to meet again with the lawyers, I went for a run.

***

When I had first returned to Ragnor Bella at the end of September I had tried my best to keep my head down and be as unremarkable as possible. Unfortunately, there is a totally unfounded but nevertheless strongly held belief that nothing of interest ever happens in Ragnor Bella except for matters to do with the Greenwings. As the last—or so it was believed—of the family name, therefore, my life was a matter of considerable interest to the good gossips of the barony.

I arrived to find that everyone thought I had missed my step-father's funeral on purpose, and opinions devolved from there until they did an abrupt volte-face with the arrival of a dragon, my subsequent acclamation as Viscount St-Noire, the unexpected reclamation of my father's reputation from being arraigned as the Traitor of Loe, and his even more unexpected return to life.

On my initial return I had thought I could not bear any more *comments* and had therefore tried not to go running. By the end of my first month back so much else had happened that my going running was merely the least of my eccentricities. I tried not to feel too cynical about the fact that a title and a prospective fortune made of unfashionable and peculiar habits acceptable eccentricities, but it nevertheless annoyed me.

It was getting late in the season for running, anyhow, I thought, as I loped down the old Astandalan highway towards the Woods Noirell. The Tillarny limes in the Woods had ceased flowering and now stood arrayed with stiff petticoats of dim gold leaves, pale gold bracts, and small round nutlets. The famous bees of the Woods had gone into their winter quarters, forming softly vibrating balls of warmth around their queens.

I stayed on the road once I passed through the Sun Gate and entered the Woods proper. There were strange magics in the Woods, and on a misty day Fairyland felt especially close.

I couldn't pretend I had never wanted to cross that Border and see what adventures I might find in the Kingdom between the Worlds, but after the autumn's excitement that seemed a bit *too* much adventure. It was not even a fortnight since I had nearly been sacrificed to the Dark Kings, after all.

I cast a jaundiced eye at the silent, gold-carpeted woods on either side of me, half-expecting a supernaturally wise fox or a mysteriously beautiful woman to appear. In the stories the Good Neighbours were more usually active in the spring. I could but hope.

I reached the village without anything odd happening, which was a first in my experiences of the Woods Noirell. The villagers were busy preparing their homes for the coming winter, and though they greeted me as I passed, no one stopped to chat.

I didn't much mind, as all I intended was to go up to the castle and find out whether my grandmother had decided about the coach. She kept changing her mind, sending a succession of amused villagers to town with notes for me, all filled with dire mutterings about the fates and the fey and the shortening of the year.

As I cut across the village green I was hailed by Mr. White, the innkeeper. I stopped, immediately glad to put off seeing my grandmother a little longer, and shook my head inwardly at my foolishness. The recovery from the curse with which I'd been afflicted seemed to be causing me to have widely swinging emotions.

"Mr. Greenwing," the innkeeper said, nodding his head.

"Mr. White." I bowed back politely, making him grin. I liked the innkeeper a great deal, though I had yet to spend much time with him. He kept laughing at my deliberate refusal to act the 'grand gentleman' (much to my grandmother's annoyance), but seemed to have no problem whatsoever in treating me as an equal.

He was not local by birth, I knew, but rather one of those travellers who had passed through St-Noire back in the days when it was on the road to Astandalas. He had fallen in love with the innkeeper's daughter, and stayed to learn to run the inn, and that was all I knew about him so far.

"Was there something else you've thought of that you'd like me to get?" I asked, presuming this was what was on his mind. He was the *de facto* leader of the village, and had been the one most concerned with getting sufficient staples for the winter.

Mr. White nodded slowly, his eyes on the mist-cloaked buildings across the green from us. He sighed after a moment. "It's probably too long of a shot …"

"I'll do my best," I said recklessly, meaning it. "I don't mind having an odd mission in Orio City." I rather liked the idea of exploring the city by means of searching out the various items requested, in fact.

He smiled. "It's not you, lad. You know I'm not from here?"

"People say you came along the road from Astandalas and fell in love with the innkeeper's daughter."

"Aye. I'm not from Astandalas, though."

"No?"

"I had a cousin there, in the Imperial Service. He was the one who wanted to come here, to go to a cheese festival in Yrchester."

He snorted at the memory; I chuckled at the thought of the surprising intricacies of fate. Presumably the cousin in the Imperial Service had not expected to introduce his cousin to the love of his life because of going on a holiday to the Yrchester Blue Cheese Festival.

"Where are you from?" I asked curiously, looking at him again. He was dressed in ordinary clothing—breeches, waistcoat, shirt, coat, neckerchief—his colouring an equally common mid-brown. His features were not pure Shaian, but that was common enough across Northwest Oriole and, I presumed, the rest of the old Empire. There were only a few families of pure Shaian lineage outside of the Upper

Ten Thousand. Mine certainly was mostly pre-Imperial Alinorel, even on my mother's side.

"Zunidh," he said, startling me out of my thoughts. I was fairly certain I'd never met anyone from that world before.

Although, I thought a moment later, then again I'd known Mr. White for over a month and obviously he'd always been from there.

"Oh! Is there something from—from home you'd like me to see if I can get for you? I don't think anyone's trading there any more … not since the Fall."

"I expect not," he said grimly. "It's more that I have hopes there might have been some letters. It's a long shot, as I said. Probably nothing's come through, even if anyone survived back home. I just thought that given that we were under the curse so long, there might have been letters gotten stuck somewhere …"

"I'll ask at the post offices in Yrchester and in Orio City," I replied promptly.

"Thank you, lad."

"It will be my pleasure."

"Don't spend too long about it," he warned. "It's just that I would regret not trying at all, and I can't go myself at the moment."

"I'll send the supplies as soon as possible," I promised, and took my leave to find that, indeed, Mr. Fancy the coachman was to accompany us on our expedition to Orio City, along with the six black horses and the ancient falarode.

"Ain't nobody going to catch us," he said smugly, surveying the contraption. He'd obviously spent some time over the past fortnight working on it, as all the leather components were oiled, the metal polished, and the wood freshly painted.

All black, of course, with the exception of one singular white bee in the centre of the crest. Bees were in general an emblem of the Imperial family—hence their presence on our coinage—but some ancestor of mine had been granted the use of the symbol along with the Marquisate itself. At some point I would have to find out the rest of that story.

"Excellent," I said, becoming aware that Mr. Fancy expected a response. "It looks very well, Mr. Fancy. Shall we race back to town?"

He laughed indulgently. "You afoot, and me with my six Ghian-dor horses? Nah, thanks. I've to collect the rest of the supplies. I'll meet you at the White Cross at sunset."

I sighed. "Very good, Mr. Fancy." He touched his cap with one gnarled hand; I gave him a half-bow (for Viscount St-Noire my grand-mother might insist I be, but I was not going to let go all of my radical politics for her), and lifted my feet back into a steady run.

I was working on getting over my dislike of the White Cross. Now that I knew for a fact my father had not been buried under it at midnight with a stake through his heart—the appropriate burial practice for a traitor and a suicide—there was no longer any reason for me to feel disgust at that particular crossroads, but I did.

Perhaps the fact that I had been abducted from there for nefarious purposes had something to do with it. Or that someone, we still did not know who, had buried there the bones of a bull, a stag, and a boar in false semblance of my father's corpse.

Why we had to leave at sunset I was still unclear on. Mr. Dart had wanted to leave as soon as possible, which I was in favour of, but when we had acquired use of the falarode Mr. Fancy had insisted we ought to leave at sunset.

I had argued for dawn, but Mr. Dart had, surprisingly, backed up the coachman. When I confronted my friend in private later he had had no reason beyond an inkling, he said, that Mr. Fancy knew whereof he spoke.

Mr. Dart was concealing a gift of wild magic that was starting to spill out into daily life. He had already saved my life twice with it, most notably by preventing me from being entirely washed away by the Magarran Strid in full flood. When he stood there, every inch a young gentleman of means and property, his eyes were bright blue and guileless, and I had said, "This is your journey, Mr. Dart."

When magic moved in him his eyes flashed other colours. As far as I knew no one other than Hal (who had been the one to first identify the magic) had noticed this, but then again, there were an awful lot of things about Ragnor Bella that no one mentioned out loud.

***

"'Tis a very pretty stick," Mr. Dart said, settling himself in the seat next to me and indicating the potted Tillarny lime sapling I was bracing between my leg and the side wall of the carriage. "Is it a requirement of the coach, the coachman, or the Marchioness?"

"It's a birthday present for Hal. Since we will be passing not too far from the turn to Fillering Pool ..."

"Somehow this simple journey to fetch my relations has become a convoluted plot for you to do errands for half the barony. I am glad that at least one is for yourself."

"I trust I am not entirely selfless."

He laughed and knocked on the front wall of the carriage with easy familiarity. I heard Mr. Fancy cry, "Ho and away, my beauties!", quite as if he truly did inhabit a fairy ballad. With a groaning protest the antique falarode was off.

I sat back, contemplating what I might expect of my life if it were actually a fairy ballad in the process of composition. It could hardly be much more bizarre and adventuresome than the past six months had already proved.

"What of Mr. Cartwright?" I asked, belatedly realizing Mr. Dart's valet was nowhere to be seen.

"He felt self-conscious that you had no one to attend you that he might gossip with."

I glared half-heartedly at him. He grinned. "No, though you might want to think of it along the way. He's ridden ahead to have a day or two at home. We'll catch him up on the other side of Yrchester."

He paused. I wondered whether Mr. Dart had wanted him out of the way, and, if so, why.

"I presume," he went on, fiddling a little with the tassel on his boot, "that you will not entirely object to assisting me? Cartwright has not seen his mother these past nine months, you see, and she's not getting younger."

I glanced at the stone arm that Mr. Dart had received protecting me from ensorcelment. "Gladly," I replied, hesitated myself in turn, and then deliberately turned my attention out the window at the rapidly darkening woods. I had decided to see how long Mr. Dart could take an insistent lack of questioning before he cracked.

We were naturally waylaid by highwaymen long before.

It was done in the classic manner.

The distinctive whistle of a crossbow shot sounded out in front of the carriage, a cry of "Stand! Stand and deliver!" boomed forth, and, as I saw when I looked out the window past Mr. Dart, there was visible at the edge of the woods a carefully posed silhouette of swirling dark cloak, an exuberantly feathered black hat, and a mask.

Mr. Dart and I both looked out the window and then back at each other. Mr. Fancy had reined in the horses but otherwise seemed calmly awaiting instructions or further developments.

"Well?" said Mr. Dart, raising an eyebrow at me.

"I don't know *every* highwayman in the Arguty Forest," I replied, flushing at the almost immediate niggling sense that the silhouette was familiar.

Mr. Dart, obviously noticing this, grinned and indicated I should switch seats with him. Outside we could hear Mr. Fancy expostulating and the highwayman replying, both in nearly impenetrable accents—

Accent, I thought, things clicking into place.

"It's the Hunter in the Green," I said out loud, remembering an instant too late that Mr. Dart was far more religious than I. His eyes started to shine and he stopped in the process of sliding over.

"Get off," I said, pushing him into a seat—any seat. "Come, Mr. Dart, I told you of the Forest camp where Ben and Jack and I spent the night—"

Outside Mr. Fancy's voice rose up, saying something about geese, or possibly a geas. The Hunter in the Green laughed, quite as if he had not just held up the coach.

"This is foolish," I muttered, and at Mr. Dart's enthusiastic nod I opened the carriage door so I could participate in what was going on.

Given that I already knew someone had a crossbow and that the Hunter in Green had a perfectly fine band of fellow outlaws hidden away in a cavernous hideout somewhere in the Arguty Forest, this was not particularly sensible. Then again that is never anyone's first adjective of choice when describing me.

"Good evening," I said, affecting nonchalance. I felt I was improving rapidly, given all the practice I'd had of late.

The Hunter in the Green and Mr. Fancy both swung around to look at me, though neither dropped their weapon. The Hunter had both hands on a long quarterstaff, Mr. Fancy a crossbow.

I paused as that registered and took a moment to analyze the situation. My father, although impressed (he said) with my spontaneous responses to dangerous situations, had also spent a considerable portion of our limited time together in the past twelve days impressing upon me the need to *think* before I acted.

The importance he attached to this lesson—and the fact that acting without thinking had not ended up with me dead only because of the Hunter in Green's timely warning and Mr. Dart's wild magic— had led me to trying hard to put it into practice.

I therefore did a careful survey of the surroundings before doing anything further. The road just here passed through a narrow cleft between two well-thicketed bluffs. Well, I say narrow; Mr. Fancy had taken us along the old highway, which was built in the Empire's heyday as the main route from Northwest Oriole to the capital, and so even in the 'narrow' section there was plenty of room for another horse and rider to pass even the vast bulk of the falarode and its six horses.

Apart from said six horses jingling their tack a little and a slight brush of wind in the thickets, there was no indication that the Hunter in the Green had brought any of his men with him.

I returned my attention to him. In the dim twilight he stood foursquare and broad-shouldered. He was holding a quarterstaff with both hands; a short sword was belted at his waist, along with the horn I had last heard belling warning of the Turning of the Waters on the Magarran Strid. His warning had saved several lives besides mine on that occasion.

Mr. Fancy sat slouched on the bench, reins looped around a stanchion. He was enveloped in a huge black cape and a huge black hat against the coming night's cold. He held a stripped crossbow steadily, its black-fletched quarrel centred on the Hunter's torso.

All this I saw in a quick comprehensive glance, grateful for my father's lessons both old and new, those of the defense tutor at Morrowlea, and my own strange gift for acting calmly in the face of mortal danger.

I did not feel more than a slight tug into the calm clear world of mortal danger.

I had several thoughts in quick succession: one, I had definitely heard a crossbow bolt; two, the Marchioness of the Woods Noirell's falarode was quite possibly the most distinctive vehicle in the barony; and three, all presentiment of danger was coming from the coachman.

And four, Mr. Fancy was the one who had insisted we leave at sunset to go through the Arguty Forest, infamous haunt of highwaymen, smugglers, illegal distillers, and the scofflaws of half a continent.

I raised my eyebrows. "Mr. Fancy, dare I ask why you have waylaid this gentleman of the road?"

The crossbow never wavered, but after a startled moment the Hunter in Green began to laugh. "Never say you can't draw a true conclusion from strange evidence!" he cried once he had recovered somewhat. "What makes you think I'm not the one on the wild lay?"

"I daresay you've spent enough time on the wild lay to know not to waylay the extremely distinctive coach-and-six of one of the few openly practicing wizards in the barony without, at the very least, a long-distance weapon."

He inclined his head. "Smart lad."

"Mr. Fancy?"

"He's hardly an honest sort, playing at costume games."

"How do you know he's playing?" I asked, genuinely curious although I did not, myself, believe that this was actually a divinity. Although that was not to say I thought it utterly impossible. I would have liked to believe in logic and reason and rational explanations, but the circumstances of my life did not wholly lend themselves to it.

Mr. Fancy snarled but did not actually provide me with an explanation, rational or otherwise.

The Hunter in the Green said carefully, "I had indicated, I admit, that I wished the coach to stop."

I thought back to the beginning of the adventure. The Hunter might have said 'Stand!' and the coachman, in a snarling sarcasm, retorted with 'Stand and deliver!' I shrugged. "Was there a particular reason? You've met me already; you know my father; you know that at present I have little of value to deliver."

"It was not your belongings I wished delivery of, but rather myself."

"Meaning, in this instance? As you do not seem presently incarcerated, for instance. If it is ensorcelment I'm afraid I do not have my grandmother's skill."

He made a broadly dismissive gesture. "No, no, you mistake me. I wish to be delivered—to Yrchester, in point of fact, or as close thereto as possible."

I glanced at Mr. Dart, who was grinning happily and nodded firmly in response to the silent question. I looked back at the Hunter. "There seems no objection to that. I feel I ought ask, for the sake of forewarning, whether we should expect any company to be joining us this night?"

"Not on my account," replied the Hunter. "I go on business of my own, of no interest to authorities here or there."

I very much doubted that, but decided that there wasn't very much harm in having him join us. Mr. Dart obviously still did not want to talk about his wild magic or newly-acknowledged relatives; though, mind you, on that point I could well sympathize. I did not really want to talk about my father's return or my slow recuperation from curses and wireweed. And, well, I owed the Hunter in the Green hospitality, from that night in the Forest, and at least a portion of my life.

"Very well," I decided, and gestured to the open door. "After you, sir. Mr. Fancy—"

"I've been coachman these forty years and more," he growled.

"Don't you be telling me my business, lad. I know what to do if we meet the Red Company or their ghosts."

Something in the way he said that piqued my curiosity, but it was truly getting dark and I did not particularly want ghost stories to accompany us through the heart of the Forest. "To Yrchester, then."

"Aye, if the night holds fair."

We made it nearly three-quarters of an hour before the next encounter.

***

Mr. Dart and the Hunter in the Green spent about three minutes in polite discourse before launching into an enthusiastic conversation about various stories and legends to do with the Hunter in Green and the Lady of Summer. Nothing the Hunter said totally precluded him from being the divinity, though nothing precluded him from being an ordinary human being in disguise, either.

I decided not to worry about the fine theological distinctions Mr. Dart was delving into between "the Hunter in Green" and "in *the* Green," and, given said Hunter's ambivalence about the matter, also not to worry about how I went back and forth between the two appellations in my own mind, and sat back to stare out the window and ponder.

They were comparing a legend from South Fiellan to its variant from the north when three sharp shrieks, like a grey jay's alarm call, sounded out from three points around us. I sat bolt upright while Mr. Fancy reined in the horses.

The Hunter in Green tilted his head, as if listening; three more calls rang out, from three different placements. His gloved hands tightened on the quarterstaff he'd leaned against the corner. Mr. Dart looked at me. In the last light of the evening his face was ghostly pale, though not, I was fairly sure, with fear.

"You're blushing again," he said accusingly, then laughed. "Who's this, then?"

"Myrta the Hand's gang," I said, "and I'm guessing that this is why Mr. Fancy wanted to come this way at sunset."

"How do you come by that?" the Hunter asked.

I had my hand on the door. "He didn't spring the horses, and there haven't been any … theatrics."

"You wound me."

"You made a very classic silhouette."

"That's better."

I grinned and opened the door, to find a pair of women I knew immediately outside it. I bowed as best I could while half-folded in the doorway. "Ma'am. Red Myrta."

"Jemis," Red Myrta said, sighing extravagantly. "Why is it always you?"

"Myr," her mother said warningly, then smiled at mc. "It's good to see you again, Mr. Greenwing. I see your sangfroid has not entirely deserted you."

"Is there anything I can do for you this evening?" I asked, deciding to pretend I didn't know very well that they were very definitely engaged on the wild lay. The distinctiveness of the falarode as a mode of conveyance still held, after all.

Myrta the Hand regarded me steadily, smiling slightly, then leaned to glance past me. Mr. Dart nodded with a good degree of natural courtesy; the Hunter in (the) Green had one hand up against his face, as if to hide a smile already hidden by his mask, but he lifted the other hand in greeting.

"This is our second adventure of the night," I said brightly.

"And I see that the first left you with an addition, rather than a subtraction." Myrta the Hand nodded solemnly to Mr. Dart and the Hunter in Green. "I shall follow suit. We have a dozen barrels to be delivered to a safe house east of Yrchester."

While I did not normally condone smuggling, I knew well that there were at least four other people from the Whiskeyjack gang around, and most likely many more in the shadows.

"Is there any information you might convey along with the barrels?" I asked.

Myrta the Hand considered me a moment, then made a gesture to one of her people. A soft cry was the response, along with the sudden illumination of a dozen lanterns no longer kept to a smuggler's darkness.

"The opportunities are not as they were," she said at last.

I resolutely refused to let my skin crawl as it wished, and hoped my voice was steady. "Disruption, disaster, delay?"

"Death," she said softly, "though whose is not yet named."

Well, thanks, I thought, and then, somewhat sardonically, said. Myrta the Hand smiled crookedly. "The waters have turned, but the world has not, yet," she said enigmatically. "All the signs are towards change. In the meantime—travel safely."

Ironic words from a highwaywoman. I bowed, not bothering to hide my sentiment, and, seeing that the barrels had been loaded and tied upon the luggage rack with great expediency, withdrew inside the carriage again.

"You were saying?" Mr. Dart said.

***

It was only an hour later that Mr. Moo of Nibbler's gang accosted us and foisted upon our unwilling selves half-a-dozen kittens he couldn't bear to see drowned and was too allergic to keep for himself.

"Don't say anything," I warned.

"Wouldn't dream of it," Mr. Dart replied, rather too brightly for someone who ought to have been asleep these hours since. "It will no doubt greatly assist in your future legal career to be on speaking terms with all the barony's gentlemen—and women—of the road."

CHAPTER *FIVE*
Yrchester and Surrounds

Even laden with half the Arguty Forest's contraband, the six black horses trotted smartly into Yrchester town square at an hour after dawn with no hint but their steaming flanks that they'd had a long and much-interrupted night's travel. Mr. Fancy wheeled them to a halt in front of the post office, a choice of location that seemed brazen in its insouciance, given said contraband.

I struggled awake out of confusing dreams to find myself with a lap full of kittens and a sound-asleep Hunter in Green snoring against his quarterstaff. I regarded him thoughtfully, petting the tiny kittens absently. They made an extraordinarily loud purring for their size.

One did not fall asleep so easily in front of enemies. I personally found it hard to fall asleep so easily in front of minor acquaintances, too, and had consequently passed an uncomfortable and mostly sleepless night listening to the kittens and other men breathing.

The Hunter slouched, head crammed between corner and staff, feet braced against the seat between me and Mr. Dart. He hadn't taken off his mask or his gloves or even his hat, and in the dim dawning looked like nothing so much as someone sleeping off a night's debauchery.

Mr. Dart was also still asleep, though he'd had the forethought to pad his head with some voluminous garment I didn't recall seeing earlier. At some point between his obviously dream-troubled earlier sleep and my pre-dawn doze he must have woken up to fetch it out of his bag. I shivered, chilled despite the warmth in my lap, and buried my hands into the small quivering masses. The purring, if anything, increased to a mad frenzy.

It was at this point I realized we'd halted. I debated waking my companions, then decided that I should perhaps find out from Mr. Fancy what his plans were. We were not nearly well-travelled enough, Mr. Dart and I, to know what the rest and refreshment requirements were for a coach-and-six. I had not even determined whether we would be changing the horses, which was normal for smaller carriages. How expensive would it be to replace *six* with post-hires?

And how was I to pay for such things before we reached Orio City? Until I could access what I'd been left out of my stepfather's will I had only what I'd been paid by Mrs. Etaris for my work at the bookstore, which was hardly enough for more than the travel.

A faint whiff of coffee decided me. I scooped up each ball of fluff and deposited them in convenient nooks of Mr. Dart's posture—he had one knee bent against the quarterstaff, supporting his stone arm at the wrist. After a moment's hesitation, I then nestled the smallest and most absurd kitten, a powderpuff grey, into the crook of the Hunter in Green's arm.

With any luck he'd fall immediately in love and take it off our hands. The midnight accedence to Moo the Bandit's pleas seemed, in the cold grey light of morning, a great folly indeed. How on earth was I to find homes for half a dozen kittens while travelling between Ragnor Bella and Orio City?

Coffee, I decided, coffee would help. All things seemed brighter in the morning once coffee was involved.

Mr. Fancy had already fetched himself a cup and was now leaning up against a post watching the horses investigate their nosebags. I nodded at him and stumbled into the post office, which did not answer my need, and back out again so I could enter the coffeehouse next door. The proprietors of both had been standing in the doorway, watching, I realized when I approached. The woman at the coffeehouse laughed pleasantly at me.

"Ah, good morning, sir. A cup of coffee, I reckon? Perhaps a sausage roll or two?"

"One for me and half-a-dozen to go, please." I thought of the kittens. "Do you have a pint of milk I could buy, as well?"

Her eyebrows raised as she turned to the coffee maker. "A pint of milk? You're young to be travelling with a child, sir … a sister?"

It was too early in the morning to be the subject of gossip. "No. Kittens. You don't happen to want a cat, do you?"

"Good mousers, are they?"

I covered a yawn. "I expect they'll be able to hunt the Moon's rabbits, once they're full grown."

"Not too bad for first thing in the morning," she said judiciously, passing me a demi-tasse. "Start there, sir. The rolls will be a jiffy."

I sipped the coffee and slowly felt my faculties rouse. The last time I had come through Yrchester had been three months ago, on my unwilling but hasty return home to Ragnor Bella after news of my stepfather's death had finally reached me in Ghilousette. On that occasion I'd been taking the public mail coach and had been called *lad* by everyone who felt the need to address me, and *sir* only in jest.

I leaned against the counter, catching a glimpse of the monstrous black coach. Well, there was the difference. That and the fact that my winter suit was perfectly suitable for a young gentleman of means, better than my travelling clothes had been by that point of the summer. Wear the right clothes and be conveyed by an antique falarode of enormous distinction—one did not need to be beautiful to achieve either note or notice—and one was, by default, assumed to have the substance behind the appearance.

I wondered how long it would take for me to become resigned to being the Viscount St-Noire and, courtesy of my step-father's bequest, a man of substance. How considerable a substance was something I needed to determine in Orio City.

There would be enough, I was fairly confident, for the supplies the villagers of St-Noire needed for the winter. I hoped there would be enough to assist my father with the rebuilding of the Arguty estate. Before Hal had left he had begun organizing the account-books for my father, and although much remained to be seen, it was clear the overall estate was in poor heart. Only my aunt's involvement with the cult to the Dark Kings and its various enterprises had kept my uncle's gambling debts and exotic fish collection from utterly ruining him.

The coffee mistress gave me a warm package of rolls, a bottle of milk, and a roll wrapped in a cotton napkin. "One and six," she said. I finished the coffee and fished out the change from my pocket. "Thank you, sir," she said, when I made a gesture for her to keep the change. "Whither do you travel?"

"East to Orio City," I replied, figuring that safe enough and a little disconcerted by her correct use of 'whither'.

"Then I will say, travel safely," she said firmly.

It was really far too early in the morning for gnomic pronouncements. "Is there anything we should look out for?" I hazarded.

"It's the grand old highway," she said, turning to fuss with jars of cookies and confections on the counter behind her. I contemplated the jars thoughtfully, noticing the double B sigil embossed on glass and cork. My stepfather had been a genius at devising containers; each of those jars represented some fraction of a penny of the fortune left to my stepfamily and me.

"Yes," I replied evenly, "and in other days I would not have needed to ask the question."

She smiled slightly. "You've come from the Woods?"

"Through the Forest and along the River," I replied without thinking, the words from my mother's stories.

"Then I will say to you, beware what the sea brings, and be doubly wary of those who sell what should never be bought."

I stood there with my hands full of sausage rolls, rumpled after a night in the coach, wondering abruptly how much kitten fur was sprinkled about my person, and stared at her. "What—" I wasn't sure at all how to phrase my question. "Can you name it more plainly, ma'am?"

She gave me a most disappointed glance, like Mrs. Etaris when I was being particularly slow. "Sir, *you* should know of what I speak, unless I am much mistaken. Now go, there are those who come for coffee who you won't want seeing what you've got tied so openly on your carriage."

All that contraband whiskey ... I swallowed an oath, made a deep, grateful bow to her, and took my sausage rolls out to where Mr. Fancy was already readying the horses to leave.

Mr. Dart, the Hunter in Green, and all the tiny kittens were still sleeping.

I settled into my corner, nibbled at my sausage roll, and turned over the enigmatic message in my mind. Something about my appearance suggested I should know what the coffee mistress spoke of … something that people sold that should never be bought …

I knew I was not physically prepossessing, especially after the illness in the spring and the long process of recovering from wireweed …

Wireweed, which wizards could use to steal magic.

Wireweed, which the Knockermen—one of the continent's two main criminal gangs—had been growing in Ragnor Bella, only for it to be stolen by the other.

Wireweed, which was as destructive as it was addictive even without adding unscrupulous wizards to the mix.

***

The Hunter in Green woke up an hour on the other side of Yrchester when his kitten meowed in his face. He had shifted position so that his chest provided a sufficient platform for the creature to perch on. I was privately much gratified by his wide-armed flailing as he surfaced to the waking world, though Mr. Dart, who was buffeted by the quarterstaff in the process, seemed less amused. Mr. Dart is not much of a morning person, though I have always thought he ought to be.

"Weeaugh," the Hunter said, in an intriguing range of vowel sounds, before clearing his throat several times and seeming to recall where he was and who with. Though face and therefore expression was concealed by his mask and hood and hat, his demeanour clearly indicated the shift from puzzlement to recognition.

He cleared his throat again—to settle his accent?—and detached the kitten from his shirtfront.

"It seems to have to taken a liking to you," I said, not even pretending it wasn't with ulterior motive. "There's a sausage roll or two for breakfast."

"Coffee?" he asked hopefully.

"Alas, you slept straight through our coffee break in Yrchester. It's nearly nine and we're just coming up to Boldbury Newtown, if that orients you."

"Boldbury … Hell! I must be off." He cast around for his hat, which had fallen off in all the flailing, crammed it back on his head, grabbed the quarterstaff, and banged on the front carriage wall. Mr. Fancy shouted something indistinct back, the Hunter cursed again, and banged harder.

Mr. Fancy responded with a whipcrack. Mr. Dart said, "I believe he is misinterpreting your request …"

"Bah!" cried the Hunter, and without further ado leaned past me, undid the latch of the door, and flung himself out.

I watched as he did a perfect somersault through a patch of grass, the quarterstaff held at such an angle as to not impale either himself or the ground. "Impressive," I murmured.

"Especially as he managed to keep the kitten," Mr. Dart replied, leaning heavily on me so he could reach for the banging door to close it.

My last glimpse of the Hunter was to see him reaching up to settle his hat, the grey wisp of a kitten perched proudly beside the curling feather.

***

We managed to rid ourselves of another of the kittens when we picked up Mr. Dart's valet Cartwright from his mother's house. It appeared that Mrs. Cartwright had a neighbour with a little girl, and that said little girl had been promised a pet if she managed not to start any fights at school before Winterturn. Mr. Dart declared that any little girl with such self-possession deserved a kitten won from a highwayman, and so we left the bemused Mrs. Cartwright with the fiercest of the bunch.

"Leaving us four … or really three, for surely you'll be keeping one, Mr. Greenwing. Which appeals to you? The tabby stripe, the orange, the other orange, or the other grey?"

"Other grey … oh, to the one we donated to the Hunter in Green?"

"I believe the word is dedicated."

"To the god?"

"Or to the cause."

"Of waylaying people in the Forest?"

"From your own accounts most of his activities appear to be the rescue and succour of lost parties, not waylaying *per se*."

"True," I replied. "Do you think a lift and a kitten repays a portion of the debt I owe him?"

"I do not need a kitten, and I do not consider you in my debt, Mr. Greenwing."

"The other grey seems smitten with you."

He groaned and changed the subject to what our plans were once we arrived at the city. Mr. Fancy had informed us at our midmorning rest stop that he did not drive anything but Ghiandor horses, and Ghiandor horses, given the right feeding regime and the right driver, could draw a mere coach-and-six farther than to Orio City.

This did nothing but make me more convinced that Mr. Fancy was one of the Good Neighbours. While I was fairly good with horses—riding them, tending them, that sort of thing—I was by no means an expert in breeds or training. The six black horses were very well matched heavy horses, with thick arching necks, alert ears, brilliant eyes, and black feathering on their fetlocks. Whether there was a slight viridian gleam to their flanks in full sunlight was something I did not want to enquire about too closely.

I had been raised on stories of the wariness one ought display in the face of the Good Neighbours. I had more recently discovered that there was Fairy blood on my mother's side, source of my own gift at magic, which was inconsiderable compared to the feats achievable by Astandalan Schooled magic, but not quite so insignificant that it hadn't managed to waken a dragon to test me.

If Mr. Fancy believed it best to drive the horses through the night and the following day, well, let him. My grandmother had made it clear that the loan of the falarode was dependent on Mr. Fancy's willingness to be the coachman.

I settled the three kittens who were less interested in Mr. Dart more comfortably in my lap. Mr. Dart was facing me, stone arm resting out of its sling on a cushion. With most of its length concealed in his coat-sleeve it was easy enough to pretend he was wearing a white glove on that hand.

CHAPTER SIX

On the Great Eastern Road

It generally took three days to make the traverse from Yrchester to Orio City. Yrchester was an old military city, founded during the conquest of Northwest Oriole to maintain control of the ancient trade routes that met there. Our own River Rag (by this point one large river; the arms that bracketed Ragnor Bella had their confluence just south of the Arguty Forest) was there joined by the Etta coming down from the eastern range.

In pre-Imperial days, or so Mr. Dart informed me, most trade had occurred by river. I found it curious that the Astandalans had so privileged road-building over the surely more immediately efficient river-barge system already in place, but then again I had learned in History of Magic that the great highways had been laid with magic to bind the Empire together. As a key encampment in the nascent province, Yrchester boasted an anchor-pin for the network of Schooled magic. This took the form of the Great Waycross at the centre of the original camp, the subsequent city, and the two highways that crossed there.

We'd come up the Great South Highway, which led straight past Ragnor Bella, through the Woods Noirell, and now ended unceremoniously in the middle of a field, but had once led across the Border between worlds to Astandalas the Golden itself. Outside the Yrchester post office Mr. Fancy turned the horses east, and off we went along a road nowhere near as well-sung but, in these lesser days since the Fall, of more evident appeal and use.

Once we'd picked up Mr. Cartwright from his mother's house, Mr. Dart and I planned out our trip to the provincial capital. Neither of us had been there, but we had our own interests along with our missions.

"I'd like to speak to the Chair of History," Mr. Dart said around midmorning of the day we'd left Mrs. Cartwright's hospitality. "Are you going to speak with someone in Classics?"

I shifted uncomfortably, glad of the kittens for something to occupy my hands and eyes. "Or Magic," I murmured at last, after the silence dragged on too long. Then I cursed myself for caving so easily. I was never going to get Mr. Dart to open up if I couldn't be patient long enough.

"It's Tara," he said after a moment. "From all I hear fashion is basically the new religion there."

"Still, they call themselves the greatest university in the Nine Worlds ..."

I trailed off as we both started to smirk at each other. We had, after all, gone to the two rivals of Tara for that claim.

"I confess to some small curiosity abut the reality behind the reputation," Mr. Dart offered.

"It's Domina Minarey for Classics, but I'll have to ask around to find out who holds the Chairs in Magic. At Morrowlea they had Theory of Magic as a key part of the curriculum, but History of Magic was an unpopular course of study and Practical Magic, as you say, unfashionable."

"We didn't even have Theory available, just History, and they hadn't any money for research. I think there were only three students, poor things."

Both Stoneybridge and Tara were considerably larger than Morrowlea. Even the most popular disciplines at my university, Political and Economic History and Rhetoric, hadn't had more than a dozen students across all years, and there were only two of us, Violet and me, in Classics.

Thoughts of Violet made me sigh, and then shift uncomfortably again as the events of our last encounter came crowding to mind. The past fortnight had pushed them away, and we'd left so precipitously (and been so immediately accosted) that I hadn't thought through it, but now that I had …

"Erm," I said, and cursed my nerves. "I have been reminded of the fair Violet …"

"As the only other student of Classical Literature at Morrowlea? Jemis, we've spoken of this. She is a rare creature, I'll grant you that, of brains, beauty, and character, but she's also in up to her neck in nefarious business."

"Which is based in—"

"Orio—Oh."

"Indeed.

***

"I'm surprised your Mrs. Etaris didn't raise an eyebrow, at least, in warning."

I squirmed in my seat, causing one of the kittens to tumble off my lap. I picked it up and petted it distractedly. "Well, yes, perhaps she presumed I had a plan … or that I need to learn from my own mistakes."

"Could be a fatal one," Mr. Dart pointed out, far too complacently.

"Do you mind? I thought you my friend!"

"Your friends amongst those on the wild lay said it was quiet on your front."

"Except for the potential for death."

"Oh, I'd forgotten." He paused, then offered: "It didn't seem to be yours."

"And of course we believe them unreservedly."

"Of course."

"One might nonetheless question the wisdom of baiting the tiger in its den."

"One would not need to worry about the proverbial dragon, naturally."

"No …"

We regarded each other sidelong for a moment, before Mr. Dart turned to look out one window and I the other.

I felt quite perishingly foolish, and not at all certain how to go about extricating myself from my folly. I did, actually, want to see what the possibilities were at Tara; I did rather need to go to the banking house to sort out the money left there by my stepfather; I did want to see the governor's palace-prison (from the outside); and then there was the book fair and all the little errands I'd undertaken to run. To say nothing of Mr. Dart's sister-in-law and niece.

Mr. Cartwright was sitting on the driver's bench with Mr. Fancy, having a conversation that occasionally sounded forth in loud if unintelligible snatches. They seemed satisfied in their argument, from what I could tell at the rest stops, and withal I was glad to be alone with Mr. Dart. Yet somehow their boisterous conversation accentuated our silent contemplation of how idiotic it was to make a mortal enemy of one of the Indrillines.

Mr. Cartwright collected broadsheets with lurid accounts of their vile dealings. I presumed the broadsheets were somewhat exaggerated, but given the melodramatic nature of my own life, I also had my doubts.

"It's not as if I propose going into any of their haunts," I put forward weakly. "No gambling houses … or money lenders … or …"

"Wireweed dens?"

I shuddered. "Perish the thought."

Mr. Dart tilted his head in wry acknowledgment of the fact I had admitted to his brother and my father that I could not, quite, make that thought perish, much as I wished to.

"A point," he said suddenly, after a glum silence had ensued for what felt like several miles but probably wasn't.

I roused. "Yes?"

"The perfidious Lark knows you as Jemis Greenwing, son of— my apologies—the infamous Major Jack Greenwing."

"Yes."

"Has there been official acknowledgement of your new title as Viscount St-Noire? Beyond what the Kingsbury lawyers gave at the Assizes, that is."

"They officially recorded the accedence to the title. In the absence of the Emperor that's all that gets done now. Hal said there's some sort of conclave held every three years by all those holding Imperial titles, to meet and greet and mingle, but the next one isn't for at least another year. In the absence of any formal court held by the Lady, that's about it."

"It hasn't come out in the *New Salon* yet. The news, I mean."

The *New Salon* was published weekly, but the actual 'new events' section was always at least a fortnight out of step with the events in question. This was to give the writers time to find out what had happened, I presumed, although Mr. Dart had a sort of suspicion that the delay had something to do with precluding any sort of immediate response on the part of the readership.

"When is the next one due to be published?"

I considered. "I'm not sure when they're actually printed, come to think of it. We get them on Fridays for delivery, but that must be after a delay for transport."

He considered. "They're printed in Orio City, I take it? That's eighteen hours at least for the postal run."

"So, Wednesday first thing."

"Or Tuesday afternoon, perhaps."

"Likely enough we've got a few days, anyway?"

I sighed. "Most likely. Why?"

"That would give us a day or two in Orio City before the news comes out."

"I fail to see your point."

"At this point there well may be gossip about the investiture of a new Viscount St-Noire—slaying a dragon at a fair to prove your claim being a flashy sort of thing to do, you know."

"I do," I replied, sighing. Everything in my life was always so much more *extravagant* than anyone else's. "I've received an invitation to a wedding already. They must have heard something about it in Orio City."

Mr. Dart grinned, then grimaced. "If you're lucky it will be overshadowed by the return from the dead and triumphant rehabilitation of Mad Jack Greenwing. Not to mention all the drama—"

"Melodrama."

"—Surrounding your uncle and aunt."

"Melodrama, definitely. Your point?"

"My point being that people are likely aware that the Viscountcy has been filled but not that said Viscount's name is Jemis Greenwing. You do not, if you'll forgive me for saying it, have particularly distinctive physical characteristics. 'Shortish, lean, and brown-haired' applies to approximately half the population. If you don't do anything truly stupid, like go for a long run through the streets of Orio City, you should be fairly safe in introducing yourself as Lord St-Noire. Act like a proper high noble and no one will recognize you."

"Dear Lady," I said, "you've managed to propose the enactment of one of my nightmares."

***

Feeling like a fool made me snappish. Mr. Dart's refusal to talk about any of the matters conceivably affecting him—a digression I had, at first, high hopes for—did not improve my temper any. Neither did the weather, which turned cloudy and cold in the afternoon. In an effort not to be an entirely unpleasant travelling companion, I took out *On Being Incarcerated* and forced myself to think in Old Shaian.

It was slow going at first even to make the letters make sense. I frowned at the text, teasing out tenses and declensions. I had not tried to read Old Shaian in six months, but surely I could not have forgotten it so quickly?

I had a spent over a year on this poem; some passages I must have read dozens of times. Some passages I had spent weeks of time and scores of pages on, describing and disentangling allusions and layers of meaning.

I flipped to one of my favourite lyric passages, the soaring account of finding peace, a home, in the prison. This was one of the passages often excerpted and anthologized, even in works not solely dedicated to the period. I had read it over and over again for its own sake even before I had realized its significance for the esoteric meaning of the poem.

It took a lot more work to read it than I expected. I found myself wishing for a wordlist to assist me. This was particularly galling, as I prided myself on my Old Shaian vocabulary. The letters Mr. Dart and I had exchanged on the Gainsgooding conspiracy had led me to a solid, even (so had said my tutor) excellent command of the language.

"You are frowning sternly," Mr. Dart commented at one point, when I lifted my attention from the book to stare blindly out the window instead, at rain-drenched green fields dotted with black-faced white sheep.

I rubbed my temples. "Wishing I hadn't neglected my studies for the past six months."

He raised his eyebrows in polite disbelief. I glanced down at the text and sighed. Last year's brilliant insights seemed not so much to belong to someone else as to seem the false brilliance of a vivid dream. No wonder my tutor had ripped up my final paper. It had probably been true gibberish.

After a moment Mr. Dart lifted his own book. "According to this author, the stretch of highway through Lower Ederdale, between Middleton and the beginning of the hill country, is notable for being the site of the Battle of Yoxley, where the last independent Duke of Fiellan was defeated by the Duke of Ronderell under the aegis of the Astandalan Grand Duke of Damara."

"Why is it called the Battle of Yoxley if this stretch of highway is known as Lower Ederdale?"

"It's the name of the marshes yonder," he replied, putting the book in his lap so he could gesture vaguely northeast.

"Silly place to have a battle," I murmured.

"It wasn't by Duke Rinald's choice, hence his loss."

"Mm," I said, and returned stubbornly to my book.

***

By sunset that evening I had determined that my 'insights' had probably been a side effect of the wireweed, and therefore not to be trusted in the least, but, more happily, that I was nevertheless not entirely wrong.

Ariadne nev Lingarel had left, like a broken branch followed by a disturbed stone, the barest hint of a trail. Whether it was truly the key to the architecture and secrets of the palace-prison of Orio City, or a hitherto-undiscovered part of the Gainsgooding Conspiracy, or an elaborate hoax played on posterity by a bored prisoner, or some other possibility I had yet to uncover, would have to wait for further study.

I imagined spending time studying the poem. That was—well, not easy, for each line reminded me of Violet, of Lark, of my mind and emotions being not wholly my own—but it was not unappealing, the idea. I could imagine myself with papers spread out on a table, pen in hand as I unfolded allusions and cross-references and delicately distinguished signs and significance and sense.

The carriage rolled along. I watched the hawthorn and hornbeam hedgerows give way to stone walls as we slowly moved from the flats of the lower Etta valley to the narrower and rockier hill country. I could picture it so clearly: the fire burning cheerfully, hot chocolate and gingerbread scenting the air, a cat purring in my lap, someone singing in another room.

I opened my eyes. The three remaining kittens were puddled in my lap, purring in their sleep. I was not imagining a Scholar's study at a great university, or even a study in a country house like Dart Hall or Arguty Manor. I was imagining myself in the winter sitting room of the Dower Cottage, with Violet singing out-of-tune and just out of sight.

***

We stopped at a crossroads inn that evening. Mr. Fancy had chosen it; Mr. Cartwright told us that it was where the Marchioness had always broken her journey.

We were at the top of Ederdale now, over the crest of its headwall in fact, on the bare heathland that bridged the uplands of Rondé and the Crook of Lind and the upper dales of Tarvenmoor.

"It's called Grightmire's Cross," Mr. Dart reported. I glanced at him; I was standing at the edge of the inn yard, contemplating the milestones on either side of the intersection. We were far from South Fiellan now, and the crossroads (however ancient-seeming the inn beside them) bore no ancient waystone. The huge blocks of stone comprising the highway continued on unbroken. No one would be burying anything here without destroying the road.

Nevertheless, I felt a superstitious unease at the building being at the crossroads rather than a decent furlong or more away. Superstition was one thing but tactical safety was another.

"Are you ready?" Mr. Dart asked after a further contemplative silence.

I sighed, then straightened my shoulders and my hat. Tonight would be the first time I ever introduced myself—or rather, permitted myself to be introduced as—the Viscount St-Noire. We had to explain the falarode somehow, and Mr. Dart thought I could perhaps do with some practice before we got to Orio City and its potential dangers.

***

Well, technically it could have gone worse, even if my efforts to project the suave confidence of the rightful Viscount St-Noire did not make it across the threshold. I tripped on a raised step, flailed my arms, hit one hand on the doorjamb, and landed hard against a table.

A female voice said, "Good sir!" in justified affront.

I pushed myself upright and brushed myself down, relieved that I had not spilled anything but a vase of winter greenery, although the women in front of me—two Charese gentlewomen of fashion from what I recalled of my visit to Stoneybridge—were less than pleased. They simultaneously gave me a haughty once-over followed by the cut direct.

Mr. Dart smirked at me in (I chose to presume) friendly incredulity, but was forestalled from any actual comment by the arrival of a stout woman in an apron I presumed was the innkeeper. She had, it appeared, met Mr. Fancy out the back, and was therefore decidedly more impressed with me.

She bobbed an exaggeratedly deep curtsy at me. I hastily turned my reflexive return bow into a stiff nod when she exclaimed, "Oh, my good lord, your man asked me to tell you he's gone to see to the room—not that he needs to do aught, my rooms are clean and fresh as a pinny—and he says the horses are well set for the night."

"Very good," I replied, trying to channel Hal, and not able to think what he'd do besides interrogate her about her kitchen garden. Mr. Dart grinned at me and wandered off towards the stairs, leaving me, the coward, to my fate.

Fortunately it seemed as if I didn't have to do much besides agree when the innkeeper took a breath. In short order I had agreed that the night was cruel damp, that the Kingsford road was a mire, that I hoped the influenza would not be bad this winter, that the inn was lovely, that supper for me and my companion would be well-received, that my coach was most splendid, a sight for sore eyes and hearts in these less-glamorous days since the Fall, and it was wonderful to think that the old titles were coming back, perhaps that boded well for the state of government as well, bless the Lady, that a good fire did more than anything else to put a soul in good heart, and wasn't it a right shame about that poor son of the Duke of Ronderell, truly, but how kind of the governor of Orio City to bring him there to see the best physicians, and wasn't it lovely that the King of Lind's oldest son, you know, the one betrothed to our King Roald's second daughter, had gone to the city already for the governor's wedding, it was supposed to be the most wonderful thing—but had I heard about the young man who'd slain a dragon, of all things, down in South Fiellan somewhere, of course they're all a bit strange down there but the Duke of Fillering Pool, you know, he's the sweetest lad, he said it was true—

At this point I managed to interrupt her. "Yes, we went to university together. Could you direct me to the parlour, please?"

She actually blushed, apparently at my saying 'please', for she muttered something about 'what delightful manners' and then, more loudly, "Of course, my lord," and promptly deputized a passing maid-servant to attend me and my guest.

My 'guest' was Mr. Dart, of course, who had somehow already found the parlour and was sitting before the fire with his feet on the fender and a bottle of wine at his side. I regarded his smug expression and could not help but huff a little in response when he merely indicated that a glass of fine Arcadian red had already been poured for me

CHAPTER SEVEN

First Glimpses of Orio City

Our planned sojourn in Orio City was to be three days, counting from our arrival on Sunday. We'd made our appointments for the Monday; we were to meet Mrs. and Miss Dart in the evening. I reckoned that the *New Salon* was published on Wednesdays, so even if it did reveal all the salacious gossip of Ragnor Bella—always and ever, it would seem, centering on my family affairs—we should be well on our way out of the Indrillines' immediate reach by the time the connection was made.

We were later arriving on Sunday than we'd anticipated, due to the shrines various members of our party had requested we stop at. Mr. Cartwright had an affinity for the shrine of the Green Lady at Oakhill Went; Mr. Dart had read about the history of the White Lady of Underlee Sound (and wasn't that a scramble getting back up from the seashore to the road before the tidal bore came in!); and Mr. Fancy had requested a stop at a stone circle he said honoured the Lady of the Green and White in her aspect of Peace. The megalith seemed ill-tended if that were truly the case, but I held my tongue and laid a handful of grain on the offering-stone. The closer we got to Orio City the less peace there seemed to be.

Indeed, as we rolled briskly down the long peninsula leading to Orio City, both land and sky seemed to rise into ominous masses. The high hills between Fiellan and Rondé had risen up into true mountains as we traversed the Crook of Lind. Even after we crossed into the long sloping dales on the other side of Grightmire's Cross, snow whitened the peaks and rattled around the carriage with a sound like stinging pebbles. After leaving Chrymdale to run along the coast the snow turned to rain and the low clouds came down.

On Sunday afternoon we dropped lower still, the road after Underlee Sound running along an old fault-line. "The Giants' Wall," Mr. Fancy called it, sniffing disdainfully. Mr. Dart was dozing, so after a moment I decided not to ask whether it were the idea of giants, the idea of giants building a wall, the idea of giants building a wall *there*, or some personal dislike of giants themselves that so offended him. The uncanny energy of the Ghiandor horses made me wary of assuming anything that might conceivably have to do with the Good Neighbours.

With the mountains on our left and the expanse of Oriolan Bay on our right, the journey should have been sublime, but the lowering clouds and the leaden water and the thin whining wind were instead oppressive. I sank against the tuffeted seats, playing with the remaining kittens, and worried at my thoughts without any result but a headache.

Hours of silence did not draw Mr. Dart out. He slouched beside me, stone arm propped on a cushion, sometimes reading and other times engrossed in the view through the window. I sometimes tried to engage in conversation, to which he always responded desultorily, usually with a comment from the guidebook. I found I could not quite bring myself to ask him outright about the wild magic or the sudden reversal in his inheritance, and so I sat there, hour upon hour, and found my thoughts dimming with the weather.

I had been looking forward to my first view of Orio City, which was supposed to be dramatic: poets and guidebooks alike extolled the black-basalt university on one horn, the white palace-prison on the other, the crescent of cheek-by-jowl houses fronting the harbour with tiled murals on their oldest walls. Perhaps fittingly—certainly with my mood—a grey fog rolled in from the sea even as we came round the flank of the last mountain before the city and we could see absolutely nothing past the walls bounding the road.

"Ugh," said Mr. Dart, peering out. Then, more cheerfully: "It could be the Outer Reaches, and full dark by three."

The dull gloaming of four o'clock was more than enough, I thought, thinking longingly of the open fields and bright mornings glittering with hoarfrost of home. I might have verbalized a question as to why Mr. Dart had any knowledge of the climactic conditions of the Outer Reaches, but Mr. Fancy suddenly swung us around a sharp corner and in the scrabble to reclaim the excited kittens I lost my train of thought.

***

Though much farther north than Ragnor Bella, the old provincial capital's proximity to the sea meant it had a considerably more temperate climate. Surveying dank grey buildings looming out of a thick drizzling fog, I was not immediately struck by the desirability of this.

Mr. Fancy had informed us that the Marchioness always stayed at the Red Lion when in the capital. It was a grand old hotel, he said, equally far from the riff-raff of the lower city along dockside and that hoi polloi which attended the university.

"We want to visit the university," I ventured.

Mr. Fancy sniffed. "Aye, so you shall. All the fine parents stayed at the Red Lion, ye ken."

Mr. Dart interrupted my instinctive protest against this egregious classism. "It sounds ideal for our purposes, then, Lord St-Noire."

"Ugh," I replied, subsiding gloomily into my seat as Mr. Fancy, satisfied, closed the communication window in the front wall of the carriage (a feature he had only showed us after Mr. Cartwright joined the party) and cracked his whip.

Mr. Dart grinned at me. I made a face at him and then returned to picking mindlessly at the tassels hanging from the window while doing my best to recall all the nuances of comportment, diction, and attitude Hal had been trying to teach me.

When we reached the hotel it was full blue dusk. The haloes of orange light around the torches placed at the doors were enough to show the grandeur of the building. The shabbiness that indicated its fortunes had diminished sharply in the years since the Fall only became evident once we'd disembarked and gone inside.

The front hall was designed to be opulent, with silk damask on the walls and gilding on the chandeliers, sconces, mirrors, and furniture. The candlelight was much dimmer and more variable than the mage-lights that had no doubt once illuminated the space. The flickering shadows mostly disguised the cracks and stains and general tiredness of a building no longer able to keep up with its own heritage.

"Well," I said, and straightened my shoulders. This was a form of grandeur I could more easily pretend to. I strode forward to the desk facing us, on which a brace of unlit candles stood. When no one came, I called out, "Ahoy the house!"

The thin man who eventually answered this summons contrasted unfavourably with Mr. White of the Bee at the Border back home. Thin and saturnine could have read as sardonic as Sir Hamish but instead came across as vaguely repellent. It was perhaps something in the way a bead of moisture hung trembling at the tip of his reddened nose.

I regarded him carefully, if not with the dismissiveness my grandmother would have shown. At Mr. Dart's warning glance I refrained from the attempt at cheerful conversation I would normally have begun. He'd said my best bet to be taken seriously as a Viscount was to speak as little as possible, thereby hiding most of my radical views as well as mitigating my occasional tendency to blurting out my thoughts.

(I thought this a trifle disingenuous, since Hal the Imperial Duke had no such gravity of mien, but I did have to grant the point that Hal had not been hiding either his dukedom or his politics when in Ragnor Bella.

"Remember," Mr. Dart had said just before we left coach, coachman, and Cartwright to go round to the servants' entrance. "We're trying not to let it be known you went to Morrowlea and are actually Jemis Greenwing, dragon-slayer and son of the infamous Jack Greenwing.")

"Right, right," said the innkeeper, bowing quite as if I'd said something scathing. "You be wanting rooms, then?"

His clear disbelief was not the most reassuring of welcomes.

***

We took our time over the bestowal of our belongings, though there was little enough to it besides trying our best to ensure that none of our clothing or books touched anything. It was then bare-ly past five, which would have been early in Ragnor Bella to find food, but Mr. Dart said the student pubs would be well underway. Morrowlea had been built on the ancient model of the self-sufficient university fiefdom, and it was a good three miles (and out-of-bounds) to the nearest public house. My visit to Mr. Dart in Stoneybridge had been eye-opening, to say the least, as to what students without strict curfews got up to.

We went to check on Messrs. Fancy and Cartwright first. We found them in the attic of the stables, deep in discussion about the ballad form. Once again, I bit my tongue when I heard Mr. Fancy allude to the Cave of Bright Sorrow, which was one of those legends around the Good Neighbours that my mother had told me not to talk about too loudly.

I might have fairy blood, as she had informed me in the letter I'd received so belatedly a fortnight ago, but every story she had told me insisted that one was never better off for confronting someone one suspected was of the Kingdom. I had half-imagined the problem of an ash-wife or a hollow man; I had not thought it would be so sim-ple, or so hard, as not talking about poetry with my grandmother's coachman.

The two men were sitting next to a ferociously hot potbellied stove, which was guarded by an old woman who inexorably present-ed herself to my mind as a 'crone'. She regarded Mr. Dart and my entrance with eyes as glittering-black as my grandmother's, but said nothing, merely puffing a disdainful billow out of her long-stemmed pipe. Blue smoke curled around her and made me sneeze.

At the sound Mr. Fancy interrupted himself to say, sharply, "This isn't the back country, young masters! We'll see to the horses and them kittens, and you to your own affairs."

Thus chastened, we both retreated. Mr. Dart was chuckling, murmuring something about tyrant retainers, but I had to control shudders at the smoke-wreathed room and the bright black eyes twinkling knowingly at me.

"Honestly, Jemis—Lord St-Noire, that is—hell and blast! I'm calling you St-Noire and won't worry about the rest, which will relieve you—you're seeing omens everywhere."

"I didn't say anything," I protested.

"As if I can't tell when you've fallen into a glum. Come now, all will be well, you'll see. We'll hie ourselves to a place Roald Ragnor told me. That'll cheer you."

***

Mr. Dart led me through a maze of ill-lit and narrow streets. He seemed to know his way; when I asked how, since he had never been to the city before, he shrugged and said that the Honourable Rag's directions had been sound. I raised my eyebrows at him, but he ignored my doubts as to that point. If he were utilizing some secret aspect of his wild magic, well, it was secret, and I was not so foolish as to ask him about it in the middle of the street.

Magic was not illegal in Orio City as it had been in Ghilousette, but from the accounts I'd heard it was even more suspect an activity there than in Ragnor Bella.

We had an openly practising witch, even if she were currently taking a prudently timed holiday, and my grandmother disdained hiding her skills, but no one else admitted to it—not after Dominus Gleason, or rather the person pretending to be the old Scholar-wizard, had been taken by the Magarran Strid in full flood while in the process of trying to sacrifice me to the Dark Kings—and people no longer used the everyday magic that had been such a part of life in the Empire and had failed so disastrously during the Fall.

It was obvious from even a mist-shrouded first sight that Orio City was closer to Ghilousette than Fiellan in its approach. There was something about the loss of magic that seemed related to a corresponding loss in civic pride.

Orio City, once the glory of the continent, was filthy.

We were picking our way through ordure in the middle of the street, and I did not want to know what were the contents of the piles of refuse in the corners and alleys. We passed a few people, all shrouded in voluminous dark capes and mufflers, all of them walking fast, mostly in pairs, and without greeting each other. About half openly wore swords, which I had never seen before, not even this past summer. Frankly extravagant hats were the only concession to individual whimsy I could see.

"Cheerful place," I murmured, sticking close to Mr. Dart.

"Very," he replied softly. "We must be getting close to the university district—keep an eye out for fire barrels."

"Meaning what, exactly?" I asked, but we came across them before Mr. Dart could answer.

"A barrel full of fire, obviously," he replied, grinning at me as we turned down the lane marked by a pair of massive stone urns blazing away. The fire seemed to be fed by coal, which explained the whiffs of brimstone and sulphur I'd caught in occasional breezes that stirred the mist without dispersing it. "They mark the area under the control of Tara. The university owns all the land here and many of the businesses."

"They seem to be better governors than in the main city," I observed, looking around at a street full of lights and crowds and colour.

"Shh!" he said, elbowing me. "Let's not get ourselves immediately lynched. Now, we're looking for the Bell-Tower …"

I followed him obediently, marvelling at the difference between the university district and the city proper. Here were students, obvious from the brilliantly-coloured robes peeking out from under the ubiquitous dark capes. They milled around in cheerful groups, chattering and laughing and greeting one another despite the drizzling rain. Merriment spilled out from half the doors we passed, and good smells, and the streets were everywhere illuminated and made tangibly warmer by the fire barrels (such an ugly name for a truly magnificent feature) positioned at regular intervals.

Some tension left my shoulders and I took a deep, relieved breath. Perhaps the situation was not so dire as the dark city and my darker fears had made me think. There was no magic here, no lights or toys or small wonders such as all the old accounts of visiting Tara had described, but there was still community, and fellowship, and fun.

"Right," said Mr. Dart. "Here we are. Roald said we shouldn't miss it. It seems busy, which is good."

"Is it?" I murmured, a little apprehensive at the thought of a room crowded with strangers, people the Honourable Rag (best known for his mad bets and madder jaunts hunting and drinking and poaching) felt at home with.

I wondered if the Honourable Rag had meant we *would not* miss it—which was true, as the whole frontage was lit by a series of cunningly mirrored candle-lanterns—or that we *ought not* to miss it, because of some other reason. I pressed my thumb to the ring on my right hand, a comforting ridge under the leather of the glove.

"No one's going to recognize you," Mr. Dart said in exasperation. "Would you please stop moping?"

I tried to rearrange my features into a pleasant smile. He rolled his eyes but spoke no criticism, and I followed him in.

CHAPTER EIGHT
Crimson Lake's Membership

We entered into a large room, rather like the parlour of the Old Arrow in Dartington, but rather brighter. The walls were some honeyed wood, as were the booths and bar that ran across the back of the room. There were rushes on the floor; an affectation, I thought at first, then wondered (given the state of the streets we had passed) if it might be more a necessity. A fireplace dominated each side wall, each roaring; one held a spitted lamb, the other a cauldron of hot spiced wine. I breathed in the mingled scents appreciatively, then sneezed when I caught perfume and smoke along with it.

In the middle of the room a potbellied stove, vaster than the one in the Red Lion's stables, provided even more heat. All the fittings were either blackened iron or polished brass; candles in glass chimneys were on every table and ensconced on the walls.

All this I saw in a marvelling second glance as I took off my cloak and gloves and unwrapped my muffler. My first glance was dazzled by the brightness, both of light and colour, and a stunning wall of noise.

At Morrowlea we wore a uniform of green robes trimmed with the colours of our disciplines once we had chosen them, while the Scholars wore black, of course. Mr. Dart had told me (and so I had seen on my visit to Stoneybridge) that he and his fellow students wore a less rigid uniform: their own garments underneath, with a light open robe thrown over, the robe grey with linings denoting faculties; his had been pale blue for History.

Tara was the oldest university of Alinor, and maintained its own idiosyncratic system in everything from pedagogy to dress. Instead of being divided by faculty or even by college (as was Stoneybridge), Taran students were apprenticed to their Masters, and wore robes denoting their status.

Mr. Dart had regaled me with these details in a less melancholic hour of our journey. I did not remember all the nuances, but white was for the newest students, various oranges and purples for the middle years, and the red and gold silks were for those nearing completion.

Mr. Dart and I, in our gentlemen's clothing (plum and grey for Mr. Dart, navy blue and brown for me) stood out in the rainbow of merrymaking students like pigeons among the songbirds. I checked instinctively as faces swivelled around to greet us and murmurs resulted when our foreignness was evident; and then I consciously lifted my chin and smiled.

Disastrous through other elements of my university career had been, I had been the Rondelan Scholar to Morrowlea and had come First in my cohort. Inveragory had sent me unsolicited invitations for a second degree. I had no reason at all to feel inadequate.

I followed Mr. Dart to the long bar at the back of the room. Most of the students turned back to their own parties and conversations, a little louder than before. Over by the fire with the mulled wine a group of four older students stared at our progress. Three wore gold silk and one a splendid royal blue; one of the gold-robed ones turned to his friend and whispered something behind his hand. Even from here the smirk on his face was visible. Mr. Dart showed no response to them, instead draping himself easily on a stool, one foot on the rail, good hand gesturing at the bartender for attention.

"You'd be in that blue if you decided to attend Tara, St-Noire," Mr. Dart said in a conversational voice, nodding in their direction as if absently, though the ease with which he said 'St-Noire' made it clear that he'd rehearsed the sentence in his mind before speaking.

"For the first year of a mastery, I presume? What of yourself?"

I assumed this was Mr. Dart's method of establishing our credentials. These sorts of games were not played at Morrowlea, where our isolation from other universities was combined with a principle of social equality achieved through intelligence and education.

Mr. Dart, like Hal, was good with everybody. I was only good with the ladies and gentlemen of the road, though I didn't really understand why.

"Ah, I don't see anyone here in the silver of a Fellow."

"Not too far off Stoneybridge," I commented. The barman set two goblets of wine before us, spiced steam rising up in fragrant coils. He had not, I noted, drawn them from the cauldron on the fire.

Mr. Dart flicked a coin across the bar but made no effort to draw the barman into conversation. I sipped my mulled wine and regarded the room with what I hoped was an aloof air. How I wanted Hal there beside us, undaunted by any situation high or low.

We drank quietly for a few minutes. The wine was sweet and well-spiced, and I felt my spirits lighten as I stood there, imagining myself into such society. Many snippets of conversation I overheard were familiar, arguments of literature and politics, the arcana of natural philosophy or linguistics. Others were less pleasing, bets being made, voices rising as drink loosened tongues, someone saying loudly, "The prince is too weak—" being shushed by his friends.

Eventually one of the gold-robed students got up to refill his goblet at the cauldron. This brought him within speaking distance of us. Not being much of a sociologist, I didn't really fancy holding up the observer's post all evening, so I let him catch my eye.

"You're a stranger here," he said, gesturing vaguely to incorporate Mr. Dart as well.

I had decided that my best effort at disguise would be to keep myself from rabbiting on about abstruse puzzle poets or classical symbolism, so I inclined my head silently and made a mocking salutation with my goblet. A flash of light drew his attention to my hand; his eyes widened when he saw my ring.

Now, I had received this ring in an unfinished game of Poacher I'd played with a Tarvenol duellist, my first weekend home in Ragnor Bella. Over the subsequent couple of months I'd determined that this somehow meant I'd joined a secret society called Crimson Lake. As far as I had learned, the society's aim was the restoration of magic in line with what had been the situation before the Fall of the Empire, and thus in support of the Lady rather than the Dark Kings.

As I'd nearly been sacrificed to the Dark Kings not even three weeks ago, I was feeling grumpy about them and had decided to wear the ring on this journey as a declaration of my allegiances.

I was nevertheless still rather leery of the fact that the only other person I knew was definitely part of Crimson Lake was the Honourable Roald Ragnor.

"What brings you here?" the student asked. "Not Tara," he hastened to add, sneering a little reflexively (or so I took it) at the idea that there could be any question of why one would come to Tara.

"It came recommended," Mr. Dart put in beside me, raising his eyebrows at our interlocutor. "Though I had heard there was company as well as drink here."

"Well, Mr. …"

I forcibly stopped myself from rolling my eyes at the student's tone. How could anyone sound so smug and condescending in the space of three syllables?

"Dart," said Mr. Dart, and, angling his head at me, "St-Noire."

"Well, Mr. Dart, why don't you two come over to our table and tell us what you might yet be a Fellow of, and make fellowship with us?"

"Certainly," he said without looking at me. I trailed after them, curious at the gold-robed student's game, and curious too as to what Mr. Dart was about. This was not to keep me from moping, or not solely, though that was likely a part of it. It might equally be to keep himself from moping. Or it could be something else entirely.

At the table I discovered both the mastery student and one of the gold robes were women. I looked around the room again and realized a good third were, something I hadn't seen before because they wore the same style of clothes as the men. One or two might be wearing skirts, but most were in breeches and brocade doublets, with the floating silk robes in luminous orange or glowing purple or white strewn everywhere. And everyone wore hats, not my stylish (in Fillering Pool and Ragnor Bella) tricorner but extravagant dinner-platters festooned with ostrich feathers, sometimes dyed to match the robes, sometimes in their natural white and black.

I wondered briefly where all the ostrich feathers came from, since I knew (via my late stepfather, the great merchant) that in Imperial days they'd been imported from Zunidh. Surely no one had been hoarding a warehouse full of them?

"We have visitors," the student who'd first greeted us announced grandly. "Dart of Stoneybridge, and St-Norell of—I didn't hear."

"Is it worth hearing?" the other male student said, with a bright bray of laughter and a deliberately insulting once-over of my outfit. "Once you have Stoneybridge and Tara, where else could you need?"

"Morrowlea, belike?" the one in a royal blue robe said.

I took a deep breath, caught Mr. Dart's warning frown, and then produced my best attempt at a sneer. While my suit was of unexceptional quality for a young gentleman in the country, it did not reflect city fashions or status, and would not immediately shout *Imperial Viscount who attended one of the Three Sisters*. Thank the Lady.

Spending most of my funds on the clothes had been my last, desperate attempt to maintain my identity as a gentleman, two months ago when only Mr. Dart's relentless optimism had kept me from despairing of ever being able to measure up to my parents.

Once I had actually received my inheritance from my stepfather I would be able to purchase more clothes, but with everything familial in total disarray I had been glad enough to agree when my father told me to borrow Sir Hamish's spare greatcoat for the journey.

"Don't bother," the obnoxious student said. "If you can't say yes, it doesn't really matter."

I snapped my teeth together. The insult in that! I was proud of going to Morrowlea, certainly, as Mr. Dart was of attending Stoneybridge, but to assume that no one else mattered?

"St-Noire," Mr. Dart said sharply, his tone making it sound 'St-Nore', which I actually liked better. "Stand down."

The arse brayed again, then started to choke on his own laughter and buried himself in his drink. I raised my eyebrows at the blue-robe, who grimaced apologetically and pushed a plate of chocolate biscuits towards me, as if that were sufficient grounds to ignore him.

"St-Norell is an unusual name," the female gold-robe said placatingly. "Charese, is it? Or no, there's a St-Norell over in Ronderell, isn't there?"

"That's St-Noire," the first male student said. "St-Norell's in Lind. Do keep up, Linda."

Linda, if that was her name, made a face. "St-Norell … good Emperor, that's a mouthful. Almost as bad as yours, Nury."

Nury appeared to be the one who'd invited us over, for he took off his hat in acknowledgement, thus revealing a head full of dark curly hair and mid-brown skin.

"We shall call you Snorry, then," the brayer said, "because I can't be arsed to add all those syllables in."

"You're very informal here," I said, ignoring his rudeness. Calling him out on a honour duel would do no good at all. We were here to make it through two days, find Mrs. and Miss Dart, fulfill our other errands, and leave again with no one the wiser to my presence.

Nury flicked his gaze meaningfully to my hand. I wished, not for the first time, that I knew more about Crimson Lake. "I'm Nury, as you heard. The ladies are Linda and Mistress May, and the donkey here is Artos."

Artos brayed again, taking the slight as a great jest. "Hey now, Nury, you know very well that a Taran ass is better than anyone else's racehorse."

Linda and Mistress May laughed heartily at this. I sat down, forcing a smile, and wondered if I'd made some great error already. If Roald Ragnor had made that joke I'd know it was deliberate, but famous though Jemis Swiftfoot was as a racehorse, surely there was no way for this group to have connected St-Noire (or St-Nore or St-Norell) of nowhere-in-particular to Jemis Greenwing of Ragnor Bella.

"We shall have to come up with something properly Taran for you, too," Mistress May said to Mr. Dart, leaning towards him with a sly smile that did not seem at all coquettish for all its intimacy. "If St-Norell is too long, then Dart is surely far too short. What's your field?"

"Astandalan History," he said, smiling genially when she gave a delighted cry in response.

"I have it! Javelin we shall christen you, with an unction of spice and spirits." She suited actions to words, dipping her fingers into Nury's goblet and flicking both of us with droplets of wine. I leaned back from the spattering, though Mr. Dart merely laughed.

Was there something wrong with me, I wondered, that I was so affronted by them? Why was I taking each action as condescending, each offer of welcome as calculated? Mr. Dart seemed to fall easily into their company, laughing already again at a jest I didn't even catch.

"Oh, he's a melancholic sort, never mind him," he said, when Artos the Ass made a crude joke and I shifted uncomfortably away.

After a few awkward minutes, in which I tried not to glower and Mr. Dart was more winsome than I'd ever be, a new person blew in in a flurry of royal blue robes and coppery ringlets under her plumed hat.

"Jullanar Maebh!" cried the group. Nury grabbed her knuckles for a kiss, but the newcomer's eyes were all for me and Mr. Dart.

"What's toward?" she asked meaningfully.

"The hunt's not yet begun, and we've already found us a fox," Nury said.

"Oh?"

"Aye, a Javelin of Stoneybridge and a Snorry of somewhere not worth mentioning."

She frowned at Artos, but left it. I wondered what they all saw in him, as it was neither brains nor courtesy. "And named them, eh?" she said, her voice taking on a lilting brogue I associated with the Outer Reaches. I wondered if I was right in guessing her second name was 'Maebh', like the great chieftainess, or if it was 'Maeve' as they'd spell it in Ghilousette. I liked Maebh better and decided to keep thinking of her in my mind that way, barring further developments.

"Christened them half into our company," Nury went on, lightly, his eyes entirely on Jullanar Maebh's.

"What do we need a commoner for, anyway?" Artos muttered.

"The hunt's afoot tonight," Linda said sharply, and shoved a re-filled tankard at him. "Now shut it. No one wants to hear your moan-ing."

"Western blighters," Artos said, then saw me looking at him and buried his face in his drink. I accepted my own refill absently, mind starting to turn for what felt like the first time in days.

What was his problem with me? The group accepted the equality of given names, which went against most of my ideas of Taran life. Their fashions of clothing were definitely Taran; my frock coat, white cravat, and blue waistcoat were all much soberer and plainer than anything anyone else in the room was wearing. Under the volumi-nous silk robes they wore hose, much tighter than my own close-fit-ting breeches, pantaloons and velvet doublets both puffed and slashed. There was, thankfully, no sign of the codpieces Mr. Dart had claimed were coming into fashion in Stoneybridge.

Many of the men were bearded, but not all; their hair was as long as the women's and equally curled, left loose instead of in the neat queue I sported. Perfume was very evident, tickling at my nose with primarily floral scents. Unlike those in the outer city none of these gallant students wore swords. Did the student robes convey some protection?

Yet I had seen no one in the bright silks outside the district marked by the fire barrels.

So much for the superficial differences. We—the two strangers, but more the upper-classmen we had joined—were being watched by the rest of the room. And half the room was focused on Jullanar Maebh, the senior student along with Mistress May and far more charismatic than she.

She was the queen, I thought; she was like Lark, though hopefully nowhere near so venal (or, truly, outright criminal). Nury, Mistress May, and Artos were her inner court, Linda was somewhere on the fringes, we were petitioners, and all the other hopeful courtiers watched to see whether were accepted or no.

I had only truly understood Lark's role when I had fallen out with her and consequently with everyone else except for the stalwart Hal and the quiet, moral, Marcan.

And so, if Jullanar Maebh were the queen, and Mistress May her chief attendant—the Violet to her Lark—then Artos was the jester, of course, a role played at Morrowlea by a variety of fellows who rarely lasted long, as Lark had even less of a sense of humour than Red Myrta. That left … well, that left me: the consort.

Nury was not scowling at Mr. Dart, though many others in the room were. That suggested the position was currently vacant, and in the space of perhaps ten minutes Mr. Dart had become a contender.

The situation need not be so suspicious as the noxious mess I had known. Jullanar Maebh was beginning a mastery, so it was possible, likely even, that her consort or even the king of this little court had simply graduated in the spring and gone off somewhere.

I thought vaguely that the Honourable Rag might well know such gossip, and then, more insightfully, that Roald had told Mr. Dart to come here. If anyone had the charisma and lack of self-doubt to be the natural king of a petty court, it was the tall, handsome, muscular, Honourable Rag.

"Do you know Roald Ragnor, by any chance?" I asked into the next lull, and regretted it instantly when Artos upended his tankard all over the table.

It was Nury who reacted most strongly, even as we all pushed away from Artos, who seemed to find his own clumsiness a great source of hilarity. Nury's face darkened dramatically. "Roald Ragnor! How do you know that bastard?"

Linda made a distressed noise, apparently at the profanity, since she did nothing but pass Artos a cloth napkin. I glanced at Mr. Dart, who looked as astonished as I felt; the Honourable Rag did not usually raise this sort of ire in anyone but occasionally myself.

I was a little chagrinned to think he was as deliberately annoying to other people.

But—why Nury? He was the one who had recognized my Crimson Lake ring and invited us over to his table.

"Oh, he's from near my home," Mr. Dart said while I was still scrambling to think of an answer that did not immediately reveal my identity. "He graduated from Tara this spring, so it didn't seem an impossible coincidence that you might know him."

Nury made an incoherent grumbling sort of noise. "Better not mention his name," Mistress May said, patting him on the arm in patently fake commiseration. "Nury's still annoyed he managed to pull off a first."

"Never studied," Nury said. "I think he was sleeping with the examiners."

"What, all of them?" said Mr. Dart.

"Nury!" Mistress May said, this time flicking him on the head with her fingers.

Linda mewled with distress again. Jullanar Maebh seemed to find this hilarious, though her expression belied some deeper emotion. I reckoned I was correct in thinking the Honourable Rag had been her consort, unless he'd been at the centre of some rival court, which was also a possibility if not something that had occurred at Morrowlea. It did not seem a particularly good idea to mention this, however.

I looked over at Artos, who was grinning foolishly while he carefully stuffed his wet cloths into his tankard. He lifted his head suddenly, but not to look at me: his eyes went to the door, and his face lit with a sly humour. "Well, well, well, speak of the devil."

Mr. Dart and I both twisted round, but it was not Roald Ragnor who'd entered. "That's not Roald," Mr. Dart pointed out once he recovered his voice sufficiently to speak.

The man who had entered was perhaps seven or eight years older than us, in his late twenties. He was dressed not in student's robes but in tight hose (yellow) and codpiece (black and white) and slashed doublet (blue and white). His hat was a tricorner with a vast profusion of black and yellow-dyed ostrich feathers, and he wore a voluminous cloak such as I'd seen on the streets of Orio City proper, but whereas most of those had been black or grey or brown, his was crimson lined with gold-and-white stripes.

After a few blinks I was able to take in his features, which were ordinary: mid-brown colouring, curling dark-brown hair worn down to his shoulders, dark eyes. He was fairly handsome, I supposed, and reasonably good-figured, but not to the extent to merit the adoring looks he was receiving from both male and female students in the room.

"Ooh, he did come," Linda said, her voice livening with animation for the first time that evening. She flicked her hair over her shoulder. "Is he truly coming over here, May? Tell me I don't look an awful fright with this humidity!"

"It's not as if he has eyes for anyone but his lady-fair," Artos said, though his voice was approving.

Linda sighed with extravagant disappointment. "It's so chivalric, how he dotes on her from afar."

"All words and no deeds," Nury muttered softly, then jerked, presumably (from the glare he was receiving from that direction) because Jullanar Maebh had kicked him under the table. "They are splendid words, I grant you."

"Who is he?" I asked, aiming at neutral. I really should not let myself make these snap judgments. Just because I thought him primped far beyond sense and arrogant beyond belief did not mean he was without any virtue whatsoever. "A ... professor?"

Nury snorted, good humour apparently restored by this question. "In his wildest dreams. He's a playwright."

"He's Jack Lindsary," Linda said in awed tones that fell into one of those unfortunate silences.

Unfortunate because the author of *Three Years Gone: The Tragicomedy of the Traitor of Loe*, that amazing hit of the year, performed to sold-out audiences in three kingdoms, heard her, gave her a glittering smile of thanks, saw Mr. Dart and I—obviously strangers from our foreign clothes and lack of student robes—and promptly made his way over.

Linda looked about to faint. She gripped Mistress May's arm with both hands, simpering (there was no other word for it) up into the playwright's face as he came to stand at our table.

He struck a pose, giving Mr. Dart and Jullanar Maebh direct

engagement with his codpiece (really? I thought disgustedly; then thought a little more happily that the Hunter in Green pulled off the costume significantly better), and smiled down at us with the air of one granting great favours.

"Ah," he said, "fans."

CHAPTER NINE
The Tragedy of Jemis Greenwing

Now, I was willing to admit that *Three Years Gone* was an excellent play according to the criteria of being entertaining and well-written.

Even deep in the throes of withdrawal from the wireweed addiction, even heart-broken, even in the midst of total disbelief that someone had written a play about my father, I could admire the poet's command of versification and character.

Just.

I sat there, staring up at Jack Lindsary, whose career had been made by a play spilling out all the shameful details of my father's reputed treason and return home in ignominy. He had written it as a melodrama, a tragicomedy indeed: the audience had been half in laughter, half in tears at any given moment.

I had promised myself, sitting there in stunned silence with the ducal party at the theatre in Fillering Pool, that if ever I met the author, I would punch him in the face for the slander to my dead father. And for listening to Lark, whom I was almost certain had commissioned the play from him and furnished details that could only have come from me.

My father wasn't dead, we were well on the way to restoring his name in legal terms, and I was supposed to be pretending to be someone other than Jack Greenwing's son.

He's Lark's pet playwright, I told myself. Artos might well be an informer too. You're in enemy territory—

Mr. Dart sank his boot-heel into my toes as hard as he could. I jerked and flushed and muttered an apology to no one in particular.

"Don't worry about it," Jack Lindsary said, waving his hand so that a wash of expensive perfume gusted my way. I sneezed, once, delicately, and saw Artos take note; he frowned suspiciously.

Had Lark furnished her minions with my description? Recurrent sneezing would be the most obvious point to anyone who had met me in the last three years.

"I often do overwhelm people on first meeting," the playwright went on, grandly. "But yes, yes, it is I, Jack Lindsary, author of *Three Years Gone*—and a sequel soon to be performed!"

Linda squealed and even Artos looked excited. "Oh!" Linda said, still gripping Mistress May's arm in a death grip but gazing up into the playwright's eyes. "Oh! Do tell us more!"

Jack Lindsary struck another pose, hands on his hips, hair tossed back, a brilliant and obviously practiced smile on his lips. "Well, you understand it is all still very much in the works," he said, as if confidingly but in a loud voice. "There will be announcements made in this week's *New Salon*—you will see the major lines of inspiration—but in general, I think I can tell you, that the tragicomic story of the Greenwings continues!"

"No!" gasped Linda.

"But yes!" cried Jack Lindsary. "The son of Mad Jack Greenwing, the traitor of Loe, has a history almost as convoluted as that of his father." His voice dropped into deep portentousness. "There may even be a *dragon* slain."

Everyone looked appropriately impressed by that, even Mr. Dart, whose foot was hard against mine. I was staring agape at the playwright, stunned into speechlessness. He went on, talking of inherited bravado and madness, a tragedy for the son fit for such a father, hinting that he had inside information, laughing with satisfaction at the eagerness and enthusiasm with which his audience listened to his words.

I managed to tear my eyes off him and look around the room. Everyone within hearing distance was listening, leaning towards us— towards *him*—engaged and attentive.

Here were half a hundred people who would go to his new play, I thought dismally, would laugh and cry and come back to this public house and debate the actions of the characters and the words of the playwright over the weeks and months to come.

And if it had not been a play about my family, about me (me!), I would probably have gladly joined them.

I sat there with my blood roaring in my ears. My hands were clenched around my goblet, grateful it was pewter, teeth gritted against an urge greater than I'd ever felt to respond, to speak back, to attack.

I couldn't attack. I couldn't respond, because I dared not respond in my own proper person and I was utterly certain I would be unable to keep my temper and my secrets if I tried to speak more neutrally.

Even Mr. Dart seemed unable to come up with a question, an objection, that did not sound overly partial. I could see him frowning a little as Jack Lindsary waxed poetic, arms waving, about the incredible success of the first play and the sure response to this second, which in his oh-so-humble opinion was even better.

"It'll be performed over the Twelve Nights," he said finally. "The first performance will be the evening of the prince's marriage-ball."

"A, uh, tragedy is appropriate?" Mr. Dart said skeptically.

The playwright gave him a once-over then smiled, apparently deciding Mr. Dart's clothing showed him of sufficient wealth and standing to talk to. "You're a stranger here, I take it? Thinking of coming to Tara for a second degree?"

Mr. Dart inclined his head.

"You've come from Stoneybridge, unless I miss my mark."

Mr. Dart inclined his head again.

"Then I fully understand," he proclaimed. "For one, this is a tragi-comedy, not a tragedy *simpliciter*—you will see, as I am sure you shall, that the audience will be laughing through their tears to the very end."

Wonderful. Simply wonderful.

"For another, my glorious lady, my dear patron, is the one to have commissioned the play, and I think she knows best what she wants!"

Lark.

I stared at the playwright wittering on about his splendid patron for a few minutes of braggadocio and trivialities, mind whirring with realizations. Undoubtedly I had made a lifelong enemy of Lark by refusing to die when she stopped giving me the wireweed, then compounded that crime by daring to disagree with her final paper. I had already suspected she was behind the writing of *Three Years Gone*, given certain details that I had only ever told her in confidence, before we fell out with each other.

But to learn that her vindictiveness went yet farther, that she had commissioned a sequel about me, that she would take any of the things I had achieved in the past six months and give them to a hack to turn them into a popular play—

To hate me so much that she would choose to have the premiere of said play at *her own wedding* to someone else—

I sat there frozen, so angry I couldn't think, couldn't move, could barely comprehend what anyone was saying. Jack Lindsary finally stopped speaking about his writing process and lauded his company of actors for their tireless work in getting the play together so quickly.

"So quickly?" Linda asked curiously.

"Ah yes, you see, many of these events have just happened."

Mr. Dart cleared his throat. "Don't you think it's a bit, ah, dangerous to write a play about someone living? He might not like it."

The playwright smiled down at him. "Not like it? My dear sir, this gives him fame!"

I recalled abruptly that Lark's final paper at Morrowlea, the one I had so thoroughly demolished on the grounds of its being unworthy of a Morrowlea student that the faculty had given me the distinction of coming First in our year, had been a philippic directed against the gods to the effect that Major Jack Greenwing did not deserve inclusion in the House of Fame.

I had not argued that he did, just that her arguments were false and her rhetoric flawed, but she had obviously decided my punishment was to be even more thoroughly humiliated and vilified by half the continent.

"But still, are you certain you have all the correct details?"

"My patron has all the details," the playwright said simply, waving his hands to brush off such niceties. "Are you a natural philosopher, sir?"

"An historian."

"Well then, you are in the business of ascertaining facts. I am in the business of entertaining, of making popular, of speaking to the people with what they want to hear. And what they want to hear, my dear historian, is the most salacious gossip wrapped up in splendid blank verse."

Even I blinked at that bald statement.

Jullanar Maebh covered her mouth to hide her expression.

Mr. Dart said, slowly, "That's very honest of you, Mr. Lindsary."

Mr. Lindsary beamed at him. "I do prefer my writing to come out of the truth, but I am not bound by it. Think of it this way: Jack Greenwing was a traitor and deserved what he got. His son—"

"Need hardly be a traitor."

"No, no, but his life was shaped by his father. You can see it in his actions, in his involvement with wicked cults and wild magic. Trust me when—"

"Wait a moment! Wicked cults?"

The playwright laughed as ears pricked up around the room. "Ah, ah, you'll have to wait until my play comes out! I can't go round telling all the secrets before-hand, can I? Look in this week's *New Salon* for hints, that's all I'll say."

Linda groaned. "No, no, please! You can't leave us there!"

He laughed again and actually patted her on the head. "Now then, my dear, you must leave me to my art. Just think! In a fortnight you'll know whether *The Runner Run* is better than *Three Years Gone*, as I suspect it is, for yourself!"

With that he flounced off to take congratulations and refuse eager questions from half the undergraduates in the room.

We sat in silence until he left, then Mr. Dart stirred. He drank down his mulled wine, made a face as if it had gone cold, and looked at me. "Well, shall we? I'm not sure anything can top hearing Jack Lindsary talk about his new play!"

"I know," Linda said dreamily, letting go (finally) of Mistress May's arm so she could twirl her hair in her fingers instead. "I think he's so … charismatic …"

"Indeed," Mr. Dart said, and stood up. I stood up mechanically next to him, as mechanically bowed to the table after he thanked them for their hospitality that evening, and as mechanically followed him back towards the Red Lion. When he gave me a hot baked potato from a street vendor I stared at the vegetable in my hands unseeingly.

"Eat it," he said softly, "you'll thank me for it later."

It was heavy in my stomach. I kept close behind him as he picked his way through the filthy streets, shying away from huddled lumps of beggars in doorways, the mangy dogs that seemed to have emerged out of the night gloom while we'd been in the university district. I ate half the potato, burning my tongue, tasting nothing, and finally dropped the rest for a dog that darted out of a shadow to follow us.

"I," I said numbly at one point.

Mr. Dart had finished his own potato and took me by the elbow with his good hand to steer me around a pile of refuse. "I know," he said softly. "Be quiet a little longer, till we get to the inn."

The rushing blank wind inside me was starting to pulse by the time we reached the courtyard of the Red Lion. It seemed to grow stronger with each pulse, each ebb only serving to show how very angry I was. Mr. Dart tugged me gently through the dilapidated halls to our revolting suite and sat me down, still dressed for outdoors, on the imperial-style couch. He prodded the coals in the fireplace with a poker until they glowed, then added kindling.

His valet, Mr. Cartwright, came in from the other door. Mr. Dart spoke to him softly for a minute; I was staring at the growing flames and did not hear what he said. After a moment the valet left out the main door, closing it firmly behind him. Mr. Dart unbuttoned his cape but did not remove it—the room was damp and chill—and sat down with a huff and a puff of dust in the chair opposite me.

"All right," he said. "Cartwright's gone to check no one's listening and get us some food and wine. We should be safe to talk now. I think—" He sighed. "You did very well not saying anything. Your expression could have been taken as star-struck."

"Wonderful," I muttered, and the dam broke.

Mr. Dart, bless him, just listened.

Monday morning was not quite as fogbound as the day before, though the air was saturated with a chill drizzle. Mizzling weather, Mr. Dart called it. We chose not to attempt surviving breakfast in the Red Lion—our late supper the night before had managed to penetrate even my mood in its awfulness—and instead wandered towards the university district and a coffeehouse Nury had recommended.

After expressing to Mr. Dart my unconflicted sentiments regarding Jack Lindsary last night, I was in a resolutely cheerful mood this morning, despite a slight headache from all the mulled wine. The fact that I could see slightly more than ten feet ahead of me helped.

I could find it in myself to be slightly amused at the fact that there was no hope of seeing the exterior of the Governor's Palace from afar. It was not the outside of that building, after all, that I had been interested in. And I had no desire to wander inside the halls of the palace-prison to assure myself of the validity of my literary analysis. Thankfully incontrovertible proof is not generally something required of scholars of literature.

I shied away from thinking about how proof was not required for playwrights, either. Perhaps Hal would know something about whether I could do something about libel and slander in another country. Being an Imperial Viscount was surely good for something.

I took a deep breath. There was nothing I could do, right this moment, about Jack Lindsary. It was very hard to push down my anger at the subject, but I did, and forced myself to puzzle over other small discoveries and mysteries of the night before. Mr. Dart was focused (I had no doubt) on the prospect of coffee, and left me to my riddling.

Jullanar Maebh and Mistress May had worn Crimson Lake's rings, but none of the gold-robed students had. Artos was no surprise there, and Linda seemed oblivious, but Nury, at least, had appeared more involved.

"Oh, of course!" I said aloud, making Mr. Dart grumble something about overly-cheerful morning people and walk faster.

I snickered. After he'd had coffee he would be interested in my thoughts, though he'd probably already been struck by the obvious point that only Jullanar Maebh and Mistress May had graduated and had the freedom of the city while under the protection of their masters. Undergraduate students were not permitted outside the precincts guarded by the fire barrels without passes from their masters, and female students were required to have another woman in attendance when meeting with male students outside of classes.

I had been wrong, as it turned out, with my assumption that Taran students did not have the strict curfews we'd had at Morrowlea. A student of the robes, as undergraduates were called, were bound by ancient enchantments placed upon the garments.

Artos, Linda, and even Nury had all looked uncomfortable when Jullanar Maebh had explained this, glancing quickly around to see if anyone had heard her mention the magic.

"Isn't there still a Faculty of Magic here?" I'd asked, making

Artos bray with derision and the rest hiss at me to be quiet. Eventually Jullanar Maebh, obviously the boldest of the group, told me that the faculty building was still physically present, but no one knew if there were any current students or even if the faculty would still be there a year from now.

Artos, curiously, shuddered, but when I asked him point-blank if he had any experience with the faculty, he said something incomprehensible but clearly rude about old bitches and disappeared off to the water closet, possibly to report in; I could not quite bring myself to disbelieve the possibility, though I tried to tell myself it was my instantaneous dislike of him speaking.

I contrasted their behaviour with Magistra Inoury from Oakhill talking about cursebreaking, with the tensions evident in a room full of students censoring themselves, and asked instead what were the penalties for being found out-of-bounds.

Nury answered. "It's not like that. Without a pass you can't go past the perimeter barrels—you can't even find the edge. Same with those coming in."

"We walked in easily enough."

"You're not students of the robes, so you'll be able to leave again, and you must have invitations to come to Tara?"

"We're speaking to Scholars tomorrow," Mr. Dart acknowledged.

"There you have it."

"And if you take off the robes?" I asked.

Mistress May snorted savagely. "Then you have none of the rights and freedoms of the university."

"The city—"

"The city is halfway to being a war zone," Jullanar Maebh said, quietly but fiercely. "During the Interim the university raised the old protections. Afterwards … the Chancellor and Senior Senate have not seen fit to lower them. And the city remembers."

"There was a power vacuum," Mr. Dart said slowly.

"Orio City has always been divided three ways, between the university, the governors, and the merchants, who control the local constables and harbour traffic. When the Empire Fell, and the university closed its doors …"

"The Indrillines," I whispered.

Nury savagely hushed me. Jullanar Maebh dropped her voice again.

"They kept themselves to the Rookeries and Dockside until a few years ago, when suddenly it became clear they owned half the city."

Owned literally, buildings and businesses, and perhaps people, secret slaves and those bribed or beguiled or bought with addictions.

"And the local authorities?"

Jullanar Maebh shrugged, her narrow face bitter. I wondered what the city was to her, daughter of the Outer Reaches as she was. Neither Linda nor Nury nor even Mistress May were so exercised with emotion; the other three were ostentatiously engaging in their own light conversation about someone who'd started courting someone else.

"Half of them or more are under their control, some of them since even before the Fall. The other half stayed loyal to authority, to the old governor, as he tried to maintain order. The balance of power has been uneasy, but the city was more or less safe so long as you kept out of the Rookeries."

"I note a distinct use of the past tense," Mr. Dart observed.

Jullanar Maebh leaned in, dropping her voice yet further. Her three friends raised their voices and shifted position to hide her from the view of the room. "The old governor hasn't been seen for months. His son is styling himself a prince and—"

"Artos is coming," Nury said softly.

I hastily said, "The Lady?"

"She hasn't been seen for four years."

I thought of the laughing woman at the Lady's Pools at the edge of the Coombe, several hundred miles away in Ragnor barony. And was that really the Lady of the Green and White, not the Lady of Alinor?

Mr. Dart said, "What happened?"

Jullanar Maebh sat upright with a sneer contorting her pretty features. "That's everyone's question, isn't it?"

***

We entered the enchanted precinct of the university district before the clocks had finished striking eight and both relaxed; I heard Mr. Dart sigh gently with clear relief. In the cold, if dank, light of day Jullanar Maebh's dire explanations should have seemed at least a little histrionic. It was disappointing that now that we were looking the tensions were visible in every person we passed.

After the untrustworthy Artos returned, looking worryingly pleased about something he declined to share, Mr. Dart had turned the conversation to distant history, and drawn Jullanar Maebh in deep. Her friends had smiled indulgently and asked after my own studies. I had fibbed, borrowing Violet's focus as my own, and bore up under Artos' lengthy interrogation of how little I knew about the ultra-modern poets of contemporary Orio City, before I brought up Roald Ragnor and the playwright came in.

At least, I thought, Artos clearly had no suspicion that I'd gone to

Morrowlea by the end of that little conversation.

It irked me to no end that I was pretending not to be any of things I was. Even swanning around as the Viscount St-Noire, assuming I could have held up the pose for more than half an hour at a stretch— and the evening at Grightmire's Cross suggested not—would have been more honest than this.

"I'm not cut out to be a spy," I muttered.

Mr. Dart snickered. "I'm pretty sure we established that after your night in pink satin at the Talgarths'."

"No one had any proof I was there!"

He laughed out loud, then buffeted me on the shoulder. "Your indignation is, as ever, endearing, Mr.—ahem."

"Yes, do stop there," I muttered, but I was grinning. "Is that the coffeehouse?"

"I do believe it is."

The Salon, as it was called, proclaimed itself the oldest coffee-house in the world. While Mr. Dart made up to the woman who was manning (so to speak) the counter, I investigated the informational plaque on the wall next to the entrance.

(Why did they have an informational plaque on the wall? I ap-proved, but was confused by its existence.)

From this I learned that in the time of the Empress Zangora VII— the one after the empress who had spearheaded the linguistic and script reform that had seen, among other things, official spelling of the empresses' names move from 'Dangora' to 'Zangora'—a governor of Northwest Alinor was a Zuni teetotaller by birth and culture and had taken it upon herself to proselytize coffee to the benighted Alinorel citizens under her rule.

"That was probably the most significant cultural exchange in the

Empire," Mr. Dart said from right behind me.

I jumped a little in surprise. He snickered gently and handed me a large cup and saucer. "Try this; it has warmed cream and dark chocolate in with the coffee."

"Thank you." I sipped the confection, which was sinfully rich, and returned to my perusal of the sign. After a few moments I recollected his comment. "What do you mean? About the cultural exchange?"

"Oh, in return for a workable bureaucracy and writing system we received coffee."

"Also the rule of law, surely?"

He made a disdainful gesture. "We had laws before the Empire came. Scattered, disparate, and sometimes contradictory ones—no, wait, that was under the Pax Astandalana."

"Go to, Mr. Dart."

"I'll grant the Empire brought peace and a great deal more trade."

I knew very well he was saying all this to wind me up, and made a face at him. He grinned back, obviously feeling more the thing now that he'd had coffee and (I noted) the remains of some sort of pastry, and ribbed me gently as I sipped my nearly solid drink and then moved to consider the other patrons in the building.

The clientele was predominantly students in their robes, most of them yawning and uninterested in conversation. Several were reading, with a fine disregard for the likely cost of their books; one or two were hunched over paper; no one, I was relieved to see, was reading this week's *New Salon*. I was fairly certain it wasn't published until Wednesdays, but I had not yet found any opportunity to ask. I might look like a foreigner, but I didn't really want to look like a total rural bumpkin, either.

I drifted over to the counter when the current customer left, and bought a cinnamon bun. It was nearly as good as what Mr. Inglesides back home in Ragnor Bella made.

The thought was so much the inverse of what I would have expected I actually paused in the act of taking a second bite. I had grown up chafing at being from a backwater; Mr. Dart and I had spent hours upon hours talking about how much more exciting the rest of the Empire must be. We had peace and good food and the legends of the Woods and the Forest to occupy us, but the romance of the Imperial Highway running past town on its way to Astandalas the Golden was always foremost in our thoughts.

After my mother had died, when I was fifteen, and my stepfather had remarried the year following, I had turned my thoughts to the only way I could see to escaping Ragnor Bella, the Entrance Examinations. I had focused as hard as I had ever done—the hardest, in fact—and studied everything I could think of, and as a result achieved second place in my year out of every student in the kingdom of Rondé. Thus I had won my seat at Morrowlea, and gone, and intended never to return to the little backwater town that Taddeo Toynbee's guidebook proclaimed the least interesting in all of Northwest Oriole.

"You're very pensive," Mr. Dart said, as I slowly finished my pastry and tried not to slurp draining the sweet sludge at the bottom of my cup. "Shall we continue to the university proper?"

"Let's," I agreed, and let him link arms with me once we were out of the store. "I was thinking."

"A dangerous propensity."

"I know." I smiled, glancing at the quiet street before us. This was still the semi-public precinct, outside the university's walls but within the fire barrels. There were people visible who were not students or Scholars: from their garments and activities I presumed most of them were shopkeepers and landladies, with a good sprinkling of servants both male and female. Very few students at Tara would be doing their own chores.

Unlike in the outer city, the streets here were clean and in good repair; there were no beggars slumped in corners, no dogs or rats skulking in the shadows. They could not, I supposed, help the damp and the fog and the faint drifting rain. It was not the days of the Empire, when a provincial capital hosted wizards who could manipulate the weather with relative ease.

"And what were you contemplating?" Mr. Dart went on.

I hesitated a little before putting my thoughts into spoken words. "I am coming to appreciate Ragnor Bella more than I used to."

My friend was silent for a few dozen paces. We turned a corner and saw in the distance ahead of us a grim wall of dark stone, tall and crenellated, with no obvious gate. There were bright spots of colour moving along to our right and disappearing, however, so I presumed there was some door there.

"And here I have been thinking that the world is wider than it had seemed," Mr. Dart murmured at last, and fell silent.

C H A P T E R   *E*L E V E N
At Tara

Coming up to the wall of Tara, the only thing I could think was how much it loomed.

"Cozy," Mr. Dart said, tipping his head back to look up. I did the same; the top of the wall disappeared into the mist.

"Quite."

The road terminated at a pair of stupendously magnificent ironwork gates, shaped into the pair of crowned stags that was the emblem of the university. There was some story Mr. Dart had once told me about how Tarazel, the historic founder, had followed a vision of a stag across half the continent to what was then a wild and lonely headland on the end of a peninsula stretching out into a near-mythic sea—Nên Corovel, the Rainbow-Girt Isle, had been home of the Lady since long before written records began—and there, to everyone's considerable astonishment, had founded a school.

It was said that the bell-tower of Tara was original to that founding. Peering through the ironwork gates, which were closed, I saw green grass and bare black trees and dour grey buildings whose gargoyles could not obscure the heaviness of their construction and design.

"Have you your letter, Mr.—Emperor, St-Noire?"

I patted my various pockets until I found the letter of introduction the Chancellor of Morrowlea had written for me. It would, I hoped, permit me to enter the gates and win me some sort of audience with the notable Scholars who resided within. I nodded; Mr. Dart grinned at me, flashing his own letter—the invitation to become a Fellow, a significantly more prestigious matter than my own half-hearted desire to pursue a Mastery—and with one accord we turned to the right to make our way to the sally port that was all the entry permitted nowadays.

It did not strike me as the most fortunate symbolism for a university.

At the sally port a porter sat behind a stout wooden counter. She was an older woman, severe as a chaperone, with iron-grey hair under a black scarf and an iron-hard expression on her face. She was well-wrapped in a marten-fur cape and had fine lambskin gloves, both of which seemed incongruous notes of luxury to her demeanour.

She surveyed us with a disdainful eye. Mr. Dart smiled without any pretension and presented her with his letter. "I've a letter of invitation to meet with Professor Hughrin today, ma'am," he said.

The heads of faculties at Tara were called Professor, to distinguish them from mere Scholars (who were, as elsewhere in the continent, referred to as Dominus or Domina according to an ancient and otherwise obsolete use of Old Shaian).

She perused the letter with magnificent disinterest. I was interested to see her face relax infinitesimally when she realized what Mr. Dart's invitation consisted of, and she folded the letter back into its envelope with more care than that with which she'd withdrawn it. "You are welcome to enter the hallowed grounds of the ancient and glorious University of Tara," she said, voice flat, and gestured him through the open wooden door.

He hesitated a moment, then went through when I made a chivvying gesture at him. I presented my letter in turn. "I don't have an appointment, ma'am, but I have a letter of introduction from the Chancellor of Morrowlea to Professor Minarey in Classical Languages and Literature."

The porter gave no indication of being impressed by the Chancellor of Morrowlea, but after a thorough reading of my letter she sighed and indicated with a jerk of her head that I could follow Mr. Dart into the sacred precincts.

"I didn't warrant a verbal invitation," I said once I'd joined him. He'd been loitering a few steps away from the gate, observing the area now open to us, and smiled with a bit of a distracted air. Well, it hadn't been all that good of a joke, really.

"Tara's seen off three sieges in its history," Mr. Dart said.

"It looks half-prepared to see off a fourth," I replied, seeing, as he had, the preparations for a more serious defense than I'd expected from the exterior. Barrels lay in neat stacks at intervals along the inner curtain wall; great cisterns stood at the corner of each building, filled by gutters channelled through gargoyle-bedecked spouts; and next to each stair leading up to the parapet was a sentry-box I would have bet a reasonable sum contained the basic components of weapons if not the weapons themselves. Putting spears and arrows into the hands of impressionable undergraduates without supervision was probably a bad idea, though having poles and ropes and the like in convenient locations was easy enough to manage.

"According to the guidebook, this is the Great Quadrangle of Tara. The Bell-Tower, which I know you want to see, should be directly across from us. We'll have to go around, though; I'm informed that one isn't permitted to walk on the grass."

Half a dozen white sheep were grazing on the lawn that filled the Great Quadrangle, but, indeed, all the students and Scholars we could see kept to the stone paths encircling it. Hal would probably know why its grass was still so green when ours wasn't.

I followed Mr. Dart as he set off widdershins, aiming at a massive structure with a decorative crust of ornamental details—mostly in the form of more gargoyles and statues of what were probably famous alumni or Scholars of the university.

Looking at the overall shape of the building, it was obvious it had been built for defense and not wholly compromised in the years since. The bottom floor had stoutly barred doors and narrow windows whose lower sills were a good ten feet from the ground. Upper floors had wider windows and more of them, but the corner towers had arrow-slits all the way up and, I was willing to bet, solid interior doors that could be barred and well defended.

"That's the main library," Mr. Dart said.

"Did you memorize that guidebook?"

"You're only sore because you didn't have the chance to. Ah—the Bell-Tower. Pity the door's locked."

I looked obediently at the Bell-Tower, which was pleasingly tall but disappointingly plain, and with a large padlock on its age-darkened wooden door. Four apertures at the top were filled with louvres, so we couldn't see the bells, and a stork had made a huge untidy nest on the very peak. I wondered if Tarazel would have approved.

"I like storks," Mr. Dart announced, and walked on.

I hastened after him. "Do you know where all our destinations are?"

"History is in the Rear Quad, according to my letter, as is Classics, according to the guidebook."

"And of course, Mr. Toynbee is noted for his unflinching devotion to the truth."

"He's not wrong in the architectural merits of the Talgarths' house, the speed of Jemis Swiftfoot, or even the strange and convoluted history of your family."

"Alas. Yet he claims with perfect seriousness that Ragnor Bella is the least interesting town in all of Northwest Oriole. I shudder to think what shenanigans he's experienced elsewhere to warrant that dismissal."

"Mrs. Etaris likes you, and your uncle doesn't."

"You say that as if that explains all the mysteries of the universe, Mr. Dart."

"It does the half of them you mentioned! Who do you think keeps all those secrets? The Embroidery Circle on the one hand and the Baron's circle on the other. The only reason any of those secrets started coming to light is because you came home and poked the hive with a stick."

"I seem to recall you were the one inviting me picking mushrooms ..."

"Hush, it'll not do to spoil my reputation here before I've even begun to decide on my future."

As that was the most I'd managed to get out of Mr. Dart on the subject, I subsided and tipped my hat to a passing student of the robes, who gave me a coy smile in return.

"Aim higher than the first years, Mr.—ugh."

"We've only till tomorrow," I said, soothingly, and with that we finally reached the far side of the Great Quadrangle and turned along a lane that ran between two grim buildings with no windows facing down. "More and more I miss Morrowlea."

"Spare me your punning!"

"Oh, and you are so grim and proper yourself, sir!"

He laughed aloud. I grinned back, glad to have lightened the air, and was even more glad withal to reach the end of the gloomy passageway and debouch into a smaller court, this one stone-paved, with six buildings of varying architectural periods arrayed along its sides, larger ones on each end and two pairs facing another across the middle. We'd entered between two of these, and Mr. Dart nodded in satisfaction. "History is that one on the north side," he said, "and Classics should be one of those two facing us. Shall we meet here again in an hour or so?"

"Let us," I agreed, and set off across the paved court, assuming I did not need to keep to the edges in this instance.

There was another porter at the entrance of the building, this one a yawning young man a little older than me. He regarded me with faint curiosity when I presented myself at his window.

"Well?"

"I have a letter of introduction from the Chancellor of Morrowlea to Professor Minarey," I said, refusing to feel daunted. "Is the Professor in?"

The porter yawned again. "You think I know?"

I raised my eyebrows in response. "You are sitting at the door, sir. Perhaps you could direct me to the Professor's office and I could see for myself?"

He considered this for a moment, then shrugged. "Her office isn't in this building."

"Is this not the location of Classics?"

"All sorts of dead languages," he agreed, "but she's over in the Lodge next to Magic. Not to put you off."

This struck me as being a far more fascinating conjunction of locations, so I smiled vaguely and waited expectantly. After a few moments of silent competition, the porter gave in with a sigh that turned into a yawn and gave me what I was quite sure were deliberately unclear instructions. Still, it was something of a quest, so I thanked him with a half-bow and took myself off.

The first part, traversing the building, was complicated enough. There didn't seem to be many people about, which struck me as odd, since as far as I knew term didn't end for another week, but perhaps they were all engaged in last-minute studying before end-of-term examinations. At any rate, I walked down the first corridor and through the heavy wooden door at the end. I noticed, with a kind of approval, that it had a heavy bar to lock it from the inside.

At this point my directions were 'outside, across the gardens, and out the Cherry Gate'. I hesitated at the hall I had now entered, looking left and right to see where the outside door might be. If the bar on the door I had just entered by was any indication, I was now in the inner portion of the building, not the outside.

Hasty footsteps followed by an unfortunately familiar bray of laughter indicated the arrival, from off to the right, of Artos the Taran ass. He was dressed sloppily under the bright silk robe, his clothes the same as the night before. So were mine, naturally, but I had changed undershirt and cravat; Artos had not. The disregard for what I had to admit were exquisite materials set my teeth on edge.

"Good morning," I said neutrally. I would have been glad to see Jullanar Maebh or Mistress May or Nury or even Linda, but Artos …! Well, it would be my luck. He made Roald Ragnor seem a dear friend and delightful company.

"Good morning, good morning!" he cried in return, clapping me fiercely on the shoulder. "What brings you into our hallowed halls this morning, lost as an ewe-lamb in the mountains?"

I couldn't say I was much pleased being described as a lost ewe-lamb, but I forced a smile. "I'm looking for Professor Minarey's office. The porter's directions were unclear."

"Joss is working off a delinquency," Artos said with complacent malice, and clapped me on the shoulder again. "Say no more! My little ewe-lamb, never fear, I will guide you through the maze, no matter the hazards! This way."

I reluctantly followed him. He led me back the way he'd come, up three steps and down four, through three doors (none of which the porter had mentioned), and finally out into a garden. It had more going on than I thought any garden this close to Winterturn should, including such spring flowers as snowdrops and something with a heady lily-of-the-valley fragrance I couldn't see. I resolved to write to Hal and enquire whether it was the close proximity of the Faculty of Magic or mere climate and gardening skill that saw these things in bloom.

"And over here," Artos said, giving the impression of skipping, as he led me to a gate with a pair of small trees next to it. One did, in fact, have cherry blossoms sprinkled along its branches. I eyed it a little askance, feeling that this was definitely not seasonable, but Artos ignored it in favour of opening the gate and ushering me through.

I did so, hoping I was not being led into an ambush, but all that happened was that we entered into a short passage lined with holly (the unnaturalness here confined to silver- and gold-variegated leaves and some yellow-berried specimens, but since I had been Hal's room-mate when he was in the throes of writing his paper on the genus *Ilex*,

I knew that these were indeed perfectly known variations; I made a mental note to add the presence of this garden to my forthcoming letter to him), and from thence into another courtyard. This one had a fountain in the middle of it, depicting three goddesses or nymphs performing a ring dance, with water arcing up and around them.

It would have looked magnificent in the sun; in the mist it was solemn and a little eerie. Artos gave it a dark look and then brayed nervously when I looked enquiringly at him.

"This courtyard gives me the willies," he said, a confession I found utterly astonishing and could only stare at him in response. He hurriedly gestured to the left, where a thatched-roof cottage sat incongruously. "That's the Professor's Lodge. I'll just leave you here—I must meet my tutor."

He patted me once more on the arm and then fairly scuttled back into the holly walk and out of sight. A moment later I heard the Cherry Gate bang shut.

"How odd," I murmured, turning back to the fountain, and was rewarded with a laugh as a woman appeared out of nowhere in front of me.

I looked at her: the skin as dark as Hal's, the hair like a smokey cloud, the eyes gold as an Astandalan crown, the crackle of magic filling the air. Only once before had I seen such a vision, when Mr. Dart and I had slid down a hill and fallen into one of the Lady's Pools.

She had laughed, too.

After a long moment of amazement I dropped to my knees.

"I'm not the Lady," she said immediately.

I rose up from my genuflection to regard her with a fair dose of skepticism.

"Truly, I'm not," she insisted.

Well, if she were, it was not my place to disobey—I was loyal to the Lady of Alinor under the Emperor, and a more-or-less practising communicant of the church of the Lady of the Green and White—and if she wasn't, well, it behoved me as a gentleman to at least pretend to believe a lady.

I bowed again, this time less deeply. "My apologies. You startled me."

"Magistra Aurelia Anyra," she said, indicating herself. "I prefer Magistra Aurelia."

I hesitated only a moment. Artos was long gone and I had no desire to fib before the Lady of Alinor, the Lady of the Green and White, or someone willing to admit they were a wizard-Scholar at Tara. "Jemis Greenwing, magistra."

"Were you looking for Professor Minarey or for Magic?"

"Both," I replied honestly, then felt myself flushing when she laughed again. "That is, I have a letter of introduction to Professor Minarey, but I am also ... I learned recently I have a small gift at magic and I ... that is, I had a curse recently lifted, and I was curious ..."

Magistra Aurelia listened to my stammered explanation with an increasingly amused expression. When I halted, embarrassed at my inarticulateness, she said briskly, "This sounds fascinating. Professor Minarey will be at the senate meeting today, I happen to know, so why don't you come have a cup of tea with me and tell me your story?"

"Er, thank you," I stammered back, and without further ado found myself led towards the once-fabled Faculty of Magic at the University of Tara.

Magistra Aurelia said, "The Faculty is even more eccentric than most of Tara's—" She stopped, laughed a little, and went on: "That is, both the faculty and the building itself. Or buildings, rather. What you see here," and here she gestured at the three frontages that were not the thatched-roof Lodge, "are the three primary wings of Magic. Theory, History, and Practice officially, though in reality almost everything is the History and Practice of Schooled Magic, with all other branches relegated to Theory. I'm in Theory with the great eccentrics."

It seemed rude to say, "Of course," so I said, "Oh?"

"You're very polite, Mr. Greenwing. It is Mr., is it?"

"It's technically Lord St-Noire, but I much prefer Mr. Greenwing."

"Oh, you're the one that slayed the dragon! How exciting. Professor Chilperic, the Chair of Theoretical Magic, will be sorry to have missed you. He's at the senate meeting, too. End of term, you know."

"I see. Er, how do you know about the dragon? It's not been in the *New Salon* yet ..."

"Oh, Miranda Inoury wrote as soon as she'd received the invitation to come examine the carcass. She studied here with me for a few years before she went to Oakhill. We're all jealous that Morrowlea gets the skeleton. There are plans to hold a symposium on dragons next year, assuming the political situation permits. Will you come and give your account?"

"I'd be honoured," I said, flabbergasted at this invitation.

"You could write a paper on it. Your experience, that is, with the dragon. Not on giving the talk. We have a journal, did you know? *Theoretical Magic*. The Lord of Ysthar is the most prolific contributor. He and the Last Emperor write half the articles, it seems like sometimes. Not that it's a very large field of study, alas. Never has been. In the Empire it wasn't considered quite correct to look too deeply at the whys and wherefores of magic outside of the Schooled system,

and the College of Wizards in Astandalas didn't like to share their secrets. Then there was the break in scholarship with the Fall."

"And in magic," I ventured, a little taken aback by this casual
throwing-around of names out of legend. Names from other worlds.
I didn't quite manage to continue my sentence to ask the question of
how they got articles from the Lord of Ysthar and the Last Emperor,
now Lord of Zunidh. 'Magic' only went so far in satisfying enquiry.

"Yes, in many places.—That reminds me." She stopped, both
walking and speaking, and looked meditatively at the door in front
of us. I looked at it, too. It didn't seem anything particularly special:
a wooden door, painted green, with a brass handle. The only unusual thing about it was the fact that it was perfectly round. I vaguely
recalled an account in some book I'd read at Morrowlea about the
'circle of the elements' theory of magic, once very much *au courant* at
Tara, and wondered if it could have been current at the moment the
doorway was designed.

Magistra Aurelia said, "We don't get many visitors to our building
now. In fact, you may be the first who hadn't also been here before
the Fall."

"You haven't had any new students?"

She gave me a considering glance. "How long has it been, for you,
in ... I can't remember where Miranda said you were from. Somewhere in Rondé, I think?"

"South Fiellan—Ragnor Bella. Uh, officially it's been twelve
years. The Interim, and then eight years since."

"I think your arrival suggests we're coming out of the Interim,"
Magistra Aurelia said brightly, and without further comment opened
the door.

CHAPTER TWELVE

The Faculty of Magic

The inside of the Faculty of Magic was as fantastic as I could have hoped. The entry hall soared up to a painted ceiling, the painting done in a style I didn't recognize except for being some instance of a version of the Baroque. High-piled clouds and fat cherubs in every skin tone abounded, as did a central image of a stylized Emperor of Astandalas encircled by the five lords magi of the worlds under his demesne. Magistra Aurelia waited patiently while I stared up at it and tried to decipher some of the symbolic elements.

"I used to play in here and make up stories about all the figures," she said after a bit. "My favourite was always that one up there, in the right-hand corner. He looks like he's about to pee on the Emperor, look." She pointed up to a cherub who did, indeed, seem unfortunately focused.

"Ah," I said faintly.

"Have I perturbed you? I'm sorry. I was raised here, you see."

I truly did not. "I beg your pardon?"

She was directing me towards a curving staircase on the other side of the hall. "Ben, Professor Chilperic that is, had been developing a theory about teaching magic to small children when he discovered me, a foundling in a basket at the gates. He decided to put his theories to the test and, lo, here I am!"

I trailed dumbfounded along behind her, not taking in any of the architectural merits or details of the halls we were now traversing. I had a blurred sense of stately whimsy, like the round green door in the ancient stone.

"Your reaction is very common, don't worry," she said with a distinct lack of perturbation. "People are usually fascinated, horrified, or both. Don't fret on my account. I had a lovely childhood. Magical in every sense."

"I'm glad," I managed.

She laughed. "It's also why I'm familiar with people mistaking me for Lady Jessamine on first sight. As I grew older I naturally became more curious about my parentage, but I was never able to find anything out. In those days Orio City was most cosmopolitan, you know—I was found early in the reign of the Emperor Artorin—and ships came from everywhere, other worlds included. The only hint I ever had was from people mistaking me for the Lady, but alas, when I went to see her before the Fall we could find out nothing but that it was a coincidence. She comes from a long line of only children, and her own were younger—your age."

"I'm sorry."

"I like to think of it as a piquant mystery in my life. One day, when I've finished my current project, I'll go on a quest and see if I can find anything more out. I suspect I'll have to do a ritual to increase serendipity, because I don't imagine I'll be able to succeed except by encountering someone who thinks I resemble someone else."

I was never so blasé about any of the 'piquant mysteries' of my life. Mind you, most of them were not so much mysteries as curious or appalling facts.

Though it was a mystery as to who had faked my father's death by suicide when he had actually been kidnapped by brigands and sold off to be a pirate's slave.

"Can you do that?" I asked weakly. "Increase serendipity?"

"I can," she said, with a faint emphasis on *I*. "I'll check, if you want, whether someone's cursed you with living in interesting times or something. Here we are!" She opened another door (this one arched) and gesturing me to precede her into a small sitting room. "Give me a moment to call up for some tea. Cook will be delighted to have someone new to serve."

She went over to a handbell that rested on a stand near the fireplace and rang it four times. It made a very soft chime, and I stared at it in amazement, realizing that it must ring a matching bell down in the kitchen.

"Magic," I murmured without meaning to.

The magistra smiled at me. "Indeed! They're still hard at work pretending it doesn't exist, are they? Miranda's mentioned the problem."

"It seems to be coming to a head," I said, trying not to stare as she gestured at the slumbering embers in the hearth and a bright flame leapt up. Another gesture saw several logs join the embers. A third collected papers and saw them stack themselves on a table against the wall, revealing two comfortable-looking armchairs.

"That's better," Magistra Aurelia said in satisfaction. "Do sit down, Mr. Greenwing."

I did so, slowly, a little intimidated by the way she leaned forward and fixed me with an intent eye.

"As I said, we haven't had many guests—no *new* guests. We don't even get many from the rest of the university. They think we're mad to still be using magic. I think they're mad not to be. Take that obnoxious young man who was leading you—you're not friends, are you?"

"No," I replied truthfully.

"Good. He is most uncouth, to say nothing of being a coward. He's been sniffing around the courtyard the last month or so. I came out once to get some water from the fountain—it has certain properties when the moon is full in the daytime—and had a most unpleasant altercation with him. He has no business being there unless to speak with the Professor in the Lodge, and to be honest she does not like undergraduate students bothering her at home. That's why she lives by us. Well, that and she's married to Dominus Fichte."

"Is Dominus Fichte a professor of magic?"

"If you can call geomancy magic, yes." She snickered, as at an inside joke; I didn't understand the humour, at any rate.

A soft tuneful chime drew Magistra Aurelia's attention (and perforce mine, as I felt nearly mesmerized by her dark eyes, which seemed to have flecks of amber-gold in them; hadn't they been gold outside?), over to a table set next to the wall. I blinked, astonished, at the appearance of a full silver service there. The magistra jumped up to collect the tray and place it on the low table between our seats, laughing complacently when she saw my expression.

"Not used to magic, are you?"

"Not anymore, no," I managed politely, attempting (poorly) not to stare. Even in the heyday of the Empire my family had never had such magic at our disposal.

My thoughts flickered to the visage of my terrifying witch of a grandmother. Perhaps in the Castle Noirell there had been such magic; not in the dower cottage at Arguty Manor.

"We've been working at stabilizing it," the magistra said. "I take it you have no preference for your tea? Try this to start," she went on without waiting for a response, pouring milk and tea with deft motions into bone-china cups so fine I could see the shadow of my fingers through the porcelain when I reached to cradle mine.

The magistra hummed with pleasure as she sipped her own drink. I tried mine apprehensively, knowing from a discussion once with Hal that a pot of tea cost approximately as much as my suit of clothes.

It tasted like faintly smokey, slightly fruity, and rather astringent hot milk. I confess I was disappointed. The second sip was better.

"Now," the magistra said, setting down her cup suddenly down in its saucer. I jumped a little at the abrupt motion. "Did I startle you? I apologize. I get very intrigued by new subjects, you see."

"What is your area of study, magistra?"

"Everyone's studying the effects of the Fall now, of course, but my own interests lie particularly in the human element." She leaned forward to stare directly into my eyes. I held my breath, the teacup precariously balanced on the edge of the saucer, unable to look away until she did.

"So! You're curious about the curse and, no doubt, what drew the dragon to you … And you reckon you have a gift of magic? What form has it taken?"

"I've lit candles," I said lamely, then, encouraged by her undaunted attention, described the scrying-spell Hal had performed and the results for both me and Mr. Dart. When I got to the point where I'd lost consciousness she said: "Sounds like a classic case of being caught in the backwash of great magic."

I'd thought the same, but couldn't reconcile it with what Mr. Dart had actually done. "All that happened was him reaching out to touch the items …"

"Probably his first conscious act of magic, from what you've said, which is always significant." She nodded. "And you said yourself he has the potential to be a great mage. It's a fundamentally different order of magic to your own."

"I don't suppose …

I trailed off, not entirely sure what I wanted to ask and a little dismayed by her sympathetic expression.

"I'll check for you, but your friend Hal sounds as if he performed the necessary tests in a most exemplary manner."

Somehow Hal always did everything in a most exemplary manner. It was possibly due to his early training as an Imperial Duke.

"Here," the professor said, passing me a covered bowl from the tray. "Eat that while I look at your magic. It's easier if you're distracted."

Easier for whom? I wondered, but lifted the ceramic lid off the bowl to reveal a revolting purple-and-white mess that at first was as disconcertingly alien as everything else.

"Blackcurrant fool," Magistra Aurelia said cheerfully. "Cousin to any number of syllabubs, trifles, and the celebrated Odd Mess— named for Odlington College, of course. You are lucky. Cook doesn't make it for everyone."

With that explanation the mass resolved itself into a more appetizing mixture. It certainly smelled delicious.

"Where do the ingredients come from, this time of year?"

"Oh, honey, it's never wise to ask a cook to reveal their secrets."

I obediently took up a spoon and tasted the fool. It was absolutely delicious: exactly the right mixture of tangy-tart and blandly sweet, the blackcurrant pulp and syrup swirled through thickly whipped cream. My mother used to make fools, gooseberry and rhubarb and, yes, blackcurrant too. I resolved that next summer I would make it. Perhaps my father would like it.

I ate the fool in small spoonfuls, trying to parse the flavours and ignore the fixity with which the magistra was staring at me. When I crunched down on something hard I flinched; she blinked several times, then laughed, less from humour than the abrupt shift in focus.

"Oh, did you find a prize? Go on, spit it out. Let's see what Cook has granted you."

Unable to believe I was doing this, I rolled the object around in my mouth until it seemed clean of blackcurrants and cream before spitting it out into my hand. At the magistra's eager interest I reluctantly opened my palm to reveal it.

It was an honest-to-goodness pearl.

"Most interesting," said the magistra. "It would appear Cook is giving you a benediction as well as a warning and perhaps even a clue."

The pearl was half the size of my thumbnail; the perfect size for, say, a ring. It was a strange but very lovely pale gold. "A clue for what?"

"Who knows?" She sounded unconcerned. "Think about pearls over, say, the next year, or perhaps three, or maybe even seven, and at some point Cook's meaning will come clear. Cook's never wrong. Ambiguous, naturally, but never wrong."

Right.

"Keep it safe, there's a good lad." She waited until I had wrapped the pearl tightly in a clean handkerchief and stowed it away in a pocket, then looked seriously at me.

"How long have you been addicted to wireweed?"

***

The second half of our conversation left me wandering in a daze through the labyrinthine halls of Classics. I was distantly grateful it was not the Labyrinth, the infamous maze created by the architect Irany, more properly Ihuranuë (who had also designed the palace-prison of Orio City, among a few other splendid buildings), who had trapped the Snow Fae in their own secrets and then, its work completed, had shrunken the complex magical artefact down and put it in her pocket, never to be seen again. The Snow Fae themselves had been delivered back to the Fairy Queen and a treaty made between the Kingdom Between the Worlds and the Empire of Astandalas.

The three years under Lark's beguilement had, it seemed, permanently damaged my magic. I would never be able to do much more than light a candle or shoo away flies. I might, with diligent study, develop more of my passive sensitivity to magic, but the active component had been crippled by the effect of the wireweed.

"You didn't lose that much," the magistra said, in what she apparently thought was a consoling tone of voice. "Your magic naturally cants more strongly towards the passive side of things. I doubt you'd ever have been able to achieve more than a second level rank under the old system."

"What are you?" I asked dully. It was rude but I felt a distant, despondent curiosity to know just how far removed we were.

Magistra Aurelia hesitated a moment. "I was seventh rank when I last tested, before the Fall. I'm a great mage by training, if not brute power. I'm not, after all, the Lady."

The lords magi under the emperor, she'd explained earlier, had been tenth degree wizards. The Last Emperor himself had never been tested but rumours suggested he was yet another level above that, as was the current Lord of Ysthar, who was quite possibly the most powerful magus in modern history.

I did not want that kind of power. I did not even want what Mr. Dart had, or where it might lead him. I had not thought I had magic, and then I learned I did but it had been stolen, and then here I was told Lark had damaged me permanently.

Permanently.

I eventually stumbled into the Rear Quad at the front of the Classics building, where I was physically accosted by an irate Mr. Dart.

"Where have you been?" he hissed. "You're over an hour late!"

"I was having tea with a wizard professor," I began.

He threw his arm into the air. "Oh, tea, he says. Of course, my lord, you must have tea! And did it not occur to you that we were to meet an *hour* ago?"

I stared at him. I couldn't recall the last time I'd seen Mr. Dart angry. "I'm sorry. I had no idea it had been so long."

He made a sort of grunt in reply, and turned to glare at the buildings opposite.

"Er, did your appointment not go as you'd hoped?"

He stalked off towards the front of the university. "It was fine," he bit out. "I can have the fellowship for the asking next year."

"And … did you? Ask?" I hastened to catch up. He showed no indication he wanted to link arms, as we often did walking, but I disliked this trailing-after.

He shook off my hand. "Leave off, will you? I explained I had to see my family situation settled first. I'm sure you understand."

"You needn't sound so nasty. I'm sorry, Mr. Dart—Perry. I didn't think—"

"No, you didn't!" He whirled around in the middle of the walk, causing a few passing students to have to dodge around us. He lowered his voice to an angry hiss, like a goose defending her nest. "You're only the one anxious about being discovered and captured by a notorious criminal organization! Do you not think I might be concerned when you don't show up as planned? That Artos came by to smirk."

"I saw him. Look—" I stopped as the sense of his words penetrated. It only took a few moments to imagine how worried I'd be in his place.

I took a deep breath to calm myself down. "Perry, I'm sorry. Ironically I spent most of the last half-hour talking about you—"

"Me?" He made a scoffing noise. "What could you possibly say about me to your tea-drinking wizard professor?"

I was struck forcibly by the idea that if Mr. Dart ever did follow his magic where it led he might become as eccentric as Magistra Aurelia in time. The books were fairly clear that great magi were rules unto themselves even when not literally lords of worlds.

"Oh, stop your smirking," he said bitterly. "I'm sorry if I care too much for your safety!"

"And I'm sorry if I care about yours! Mr. Dart, you need to gain control of your magic. Magistra Aurelia said that if you didn't, you ran the risk of your power flaring out with your emotions and turning destructive. She said—"

"*Stop it.*"

I stopped, the force of his words like a bludgeon, and stared wordlessly at him. His eyes were flat grey as the clouds.

He froze, face white, even as the wind gusted dead leaves about our feet.

After a long, long moment the oppressive weight of his power lifted. I started to speak, but before any words could form Mr. Dart said, "I don't want to hear it. Whatever it is, I don't want to talk about it."

"Mr. Dart—"

"No." And with that the leaves shot away from us like slung rocks. He whirled around, the edge of his coat flaring out, and stomped away from me, the wind between us solid as a wall.

CHAPTER THIRTEEN
In Orio City

Even though I'd been expecting, even attempting to provoke, such an outburst from Mr. Dart, now that it had happened I felt mostly numb and wondering why on earth I'd thought this a good idea. Mr. Dart had spent half the evening before commiserating with and consoling me for the scene with Jack Lindsary, and this was how I repaid him?

I sighed, watching him stalk across the fore-court of Tara's main academic quadrangle. I didn't know where he intended to go to work through his snit, but he knew my plans for the day and could find me when he was ready. He would not relish my following him now.

I was confident I could make it through a day in Orio City on my own without total disaster.

Mostly.

I cast one last anxious glance after him, straightened my hat, greatcoat, and shoulders, and made my way in the opposite direction. There was banking to be done.

The city was busier now, the shops open and the streets full of people chattering away. At first I relaxed, associating the bustle with pleasant experiences in Fillering Pool and Kingsbury this past summer. It had been exciting, spending time in the cities, after three years in Morrowlea and a lifetime where Ragnor Bella was the biggest community I'd ever seen. Despite the mist still cloaking most of the city from view, it was obvious Orio City was many times larger than even Kingsbury.

After sauntering out of the university precinct, I discovered the road I was on—which had led me straight from Tara's main gates—became what appeared to be the central thoroughfare of the city. A discreet enquiry of a woman Mrs. Etaris' age, sweeping her porch vigorously despite the damp, encouraged me that I was going in the correct direction for the central branch of the Imperial Bank of Commerce, Scholarship, and Trade.

"You can't miss it," she said, pointing straight down the road. "Half a mile or so down, past the Guildmarket Hall. It'll have the Astandalan flag out, you'll see."

Curious, I thought, and thanked her. The Guildmarket Hall was where the book fair was being held, Mrs. Etaris had told me, so that was convenient.

Half a mile in the city felt a lot longer than it did in the country. Ragnor Bella itself was perhaps a mile long at its greatest extent, from the humpback bridge over the Rag to the Boggle (some much earlier denizen's pride and joy, in the form of a bog garden showcasing numerous rare species; Hal had been incredulous when I told him the reason behind the name, and insisted he would come again in the spring to see what wonders might yet remain in its sloughs). There one would hardly walk briskly in a direct line, partly because the road system did not permit it but mostly because no one you met would let you pass with so little conversation.

A stranger in Ragnor Bella would attract even more attention than I, Jemis Greenwing, did—and given this autumn's events, that was saying something! A stranger in Orio City, on the other hand, garnered a few sly glances and muttered comments, and nothing else.

It did not relieve me to reflect that if I went around announcing I was Jemis Greenwing that I probably would have all the attention I'd ever received at home.

The road sloped down steeply from the university district, crossed a creek noisome with effluent, which I put behind me as quickly as possible, and led back up an even steeper incline to a sort of plateau. I reached the top and paused there, trying to see the logic of the geography. I had thought that there were two headlands, one occupied by Tara and the other by the governor's palace, between which was a low-lying crescent containing most of the city and the harbour.

I could barely see the bottom of the hill I had just come up, let alone the university, which had disappeared into mist as soon as the fire barrels were out of sight. I looked back in that direction, remembering Jullanar Maebh's comments about the university's protections. It was possible that it was not the weather that shrouded the university from sight, but ancient defensive magic.

Morrowlea stood proud and white-towered on its hill, pennons flapping and bells carolling, visible for miles around any day of the year I'd seen it from my long runs looping across its fields and woodlands and those of its neighbours.

No, I couldn't imagine coming to Tara, vaunted heart of scholarship or not. Even if there were not the situation with Lark and the Indrillines to deal with—and there was, obviously, that—I did not think I would last long in this grimy grey city and its suffocating fogs. No wonder the Honourable Rag had spent most of his time up in the hills with his noble friends, hunting.

No one accosted me to ask what I was doing, staring into the mist. They walked by, busy about their own concerns, in groups mostly of three or four, more than half of them girt with rapiers, almost all of them enveloped in heavy cloaks or capes in dark and somber colours. Bundled in Sir Hamish's greatcoat I did not feel quite so foreign as I had amongst all the silk-robed students, but I did wish for a sword.

Though of course I did not know the law in Orio City for carrying a sword, and after being accused of murder for slaying a dragon with a cake knife, I did not much like to think what I might be charged with on account of being armed, should anyone figure out who I really was.

After another ten minutes of walking I still hadn't found the bank, so I stopped at a cart selling roasted chestnuts to allay my hunger. As I waited in the short line, I looked around me, realized I was at the corner of a huge building that was probably the Guildmarket Hall, and then saw ... them.

Perhaps the only good result of my dislike of the architecture and the climate and the general sense of foreboding staining this whole trip was that it had not taken me long to become accustomed to the garbage everywhere.

At home in Ragnor Bella (how I had thought, not too long ago, that those were words I'd never say again!), we had Mr. Pinker and Mr. Garsom, who were paid by the council to pick up litter in public places. Fillering Pool had been quite clean, as well, though I hadn't asked Hal how he, as the local nobleman, ensured this. I remembered being quite disgusted at the state of things in Kingsbury, which I'd thought ought to be most resplendent, being the king's city, after all, but which had been much dingier and dirtier overall than home.

Orio City, once proud capital of Northwest Oriole, was filthy.

I collected my cone of chestnuts, paid the vendor, and moved a few yards further down, to a corner out of the drizzle. It was occupied by a pile of half-rotten cloths and something that stank dreadfully.

I moved on, picking my steps with care, noticing now how totally everyone around me was ignoring the situation. Everyone I saw had a hand free to pick up skirts or trailing edges of cloaks to avoid the ordure; no one displayed any awkwardness or disgust at having to do so. They continued their conversations about gossip and business as they parted to avoid a puddle of horse piss or a pile of something that was blown with sluggish flies.

They were so nonchalant, their actions so habitual, I nearly doubted my eyes. What had happened here for everyone to ignore this? Why was there no pride in their city? There were beggars everywhere—and that made my skin crawl, the hollow-eyed multitude, some with begging-bowls in front of them, most huddled into the rags, eyes closed, sleeping away their misery. Not many of the bowls held more than a few copper pfennigs.

They reminded me of Newbury in Ghilousette, where the good citizens of the town had ignored their own multitudes of beggars with grim anger. In the taverns I had gone into, desperate for company as my illness ravaged me (as I recovered, so slowly, from the withdrawal of the wireweed Lark had given me for the previous three years; from the curse that had risen fiercely when I broke free of Lark to protest her account of my father's infamy; from the broken heart and the broken gift of magic Lark had stolen from me; from Lark), people talked about the poor, the broken, those who *used magic*.

There was a blight of wireweed, Hal's great-uncle Ben had said soberly. All through the northern part of the continent, spreading out from its centres in Orio City—under the control of the Indrillines—

and Ghilousette, which was under control of the Indrillines' rivals, the Knockermen, more and more were turning to transform their dull or miserable lives with the hollow joy that the drug provided.

I stood there under the canopy of the Guildmarket Hall, watching the cheerful throngs of Orio City's citizens enter into the fair there, watching them ignore the poverty literally under their feet. The chestnuts grew cold in my hand.

People said that Ragnor Bella had been least affected, magically, by the Fall. I had not really understood what that meant until I went to Ghilousette and saw the fear of magic the Fall had given the people there. Other places I had been—South Erlingale around Morrowlea, the three duchies of Rondé (I had not gone into the Farry March)—had shown signs of the injuries that were there, but not like Ghilousette. Or like Orio City. I could not imagine that in the days of the Empire the provincial capital had looked like this.

While I stood there an altercation of sorts broke out a few yards from me. Someone was being evicted from the Guildmarket Hall, an old man with wild white hair. Unlike everyone else I could see he wore bright colours, a startling leaf-green cloak like the sight of spring after winter.

"Unhand me!" he cried to the guardsman who was propelling him out. The guard ignored him, stolidly dragging him by the arm down the steps of the Guildmarket Hall. He let go at the bottom, making the man stumble. I thought he'd catch himself, but his foot caught on a smear of fresh dung (of course) and he went flying.

No one else moved, so I went over to assist him. He might be making a scene, but he was old and I was not. I helped him up and held his shoulders as he brushed himself down since he seemed none too steady on his feet. He didn't smell of drink, and though his eyes were protuberant and oddly intense, they did not have the contracted pupils and excessive brilliance I had learned were signs of wireweed.

(My increasing preference for bright lights at Morrowlea—I always went through more candles than anyone else—now had a more depressing meaning behind it. The Bursar kept assigning me to candle-making duty in the hopes that if the tediousness of dipping candles didn't teach me not to waste them, well, at least I wasn't inconveniencing anyone else terribly. Lark had always laughed and said it was symbolic of my love of learning.)

"Thank you, thank you," the old man said eventually when he had determined that all of his parts were present and ready to his own satisfaction. "You're a stranger here."

"Er, yes," I admitted.

"This city has fallen to the dogs," he said, horking up a great lump of phlegm and spitting it down beside us.

I stared at him in total astonishment.

"And new to town to boot," he added, laughing thinly. "Kind to strangers and you've still got the manners your mother taught you. They won't last long in this dump."

"I'm not here long."

"Good, good," he said vaguely, and spat again, this time in the direction of the Guildmarket Hall entrance. The guardsman had gone back inside, and the passersby were once again passing by with nothing more than the now-familiar sidelong glances and muttered comments. "Idiots. A world's wealth of books in there, and where do you think they're all going?"

"Er, where?"

"There's a bear-baiting round the back at noon. Can you believe it? Can you?" He sneered. I took a step back, wary he was going to spit again in my specific direction. He stepped forward, breathing heavily up at me, his hair wilder than before. "This was a great city once, you know."

His breath smelled incongruously of mint. I felt a faint tremor running through his hand, conveying his alarm and making my neck prickle. I couldn't deny any of his words. Everything I had seen said the same.

"Before the Fall," I ventured.

"Aye," he said, "though we were falling before then, and are falling farther now. If nothing changes the city will tear itself to pieces."

"The university …"

"Pah! They've closed themselves off from the rest of us in their mists. The Lady's not doing anything; probably can't, given what happened with the magic, and her navy's almost overrun by the pirates. The governor—excuse me, prince—" He spat again; some of the spittle landed on my boot. I had to resist the urge to wipe it on my other leg. My boots had tracked through the streets and were as filthy as everything else now. "The prince is making his deal with the devils in the Rookeries before he loses his head."

I began to see why he'd been thrown out of the Guildmarket Hall. I edged a step back again, trying to get him to release my arm without actually pulling away too harshly, and kicked my heels into something that emitted a low, inhuman groan.

I looked down in horror to see that the pile of rags next me was shifting. I expected a rat or a stray dog to come out, but after a moment spent quivering, the pile subsided again into stillness. An indefinable sense of emptiness settled around us. My mouth went completely dry.

"Ah," the old man said sadly. "There's another Sleeper gone. May the Lady of the Green grant him spring in the hereafter."

"Amen," I said automatically, trying to process what had happened. "Is that—was that—what—"

"A stranger from far away," the old man said, not entirely unkindly. "Best leave the city before you're caught by the madness, lad. It'll take all of us sooner or later, you'll see." He sighed. "It's hard to know whether it's better to go that way, or stay awake through to the end …"

I forced my eyes away from the rag-pile—from the *corpse*—to meet his boring into my face.

"The flower is sweet in the bloom," he intoned, "though it fades all too quickly, and the heart and spirit and mind with it. And once those are gone, why, the body is jealous, and follows soon after. Yes," he said, sighing again, "who's to say they don't have the right of it? A bright summer, a quick fall, a winter's slumber, and the Lady's Spring to wake you on the other side."

"I," I said, with utterly nothing to say to this.

He patted me on the arm and then straightened my coat collar for me. "Go on your way, stranger-lad, and leave this city before it's too late. You don't want to be caught here, and soon enough the gates will open for nobody."

He patted me again and left me with a handful of cold roasted chestnuts, a dead body at my feet, and a street full of totally uninterested passersby making their various ways to the bear-baiting, the book sale, or the bank.

I put the chestnuts in the next begging-bowl I saw and strode as quickly as I could to the bank. The green-garbed old man himself had disappeared into the mist by the time I thought to look after him.

Mr. Vandray, the banker, looked like a jolly country innkeeper.

The bank itself looked like a temple.

I walked in, wishing my hand didn't feel so greasy from the paper cone of chestnuts, wondering sardonically a moment later whether anyone in this benighted city would even notice. Though to be honest, despite the exterior filth, the interiors I had seen were all clean, even sweet-smelling, and people themselves spotless. The rushes on the floor of the student tavern now made sense, and even seemed a little quaint, if one had never heard of the state of things under the Empire.

My garments were of sufficient quality that no one in the bank sneered at the idea that I should enter; they were of sufficiently low style and material that no one approached to see what I needed, either. I took myself over to the side while I delved in the pockets of Sir Hamish's greatcoat to find the letter I had received, by way of the Kingsford lawyers, requesting me to present myself to Mr. Ned Vandray at my earliest convenience.

I had originally intended to announce myself, by title at least, and request an interview with Mr. Vandray, but given the hints dropped by Jack Lindsary the night before, I was beginning to worry that even 'St-Noire' was a trifle dangerous to speak too loudly in public, and certainly not with the addition of 'Imperial Viscount', which would cause a nine-days-wonder almost anywhere, let alone somewhere where half the people I met might be compromised one way or another. It was disheartening to think how little trust there could be in this city, with the criminal kings of the seaboard coming into open power.

I therefore wrote a note on the back of the letter I'd received from Mr. Vandray, asking if he was available. I regretted my continuing lack of my good fountain pen; the replacement I had acquired from Mrs. Etaris' store was nothing like so fine an instrument. I had so little of sentimental value from my stepfather, and it would have been pleasant, waiting there to hear what exactly he had left me, to use it. At some point I would confront the Honourable Rag about it.

After a moment I chose a junior-looking person and asked him to deliver the letter to Mr. Vandray. He gave me a scathing once-over, decided that I was likely a secretary or junior steward from someone important, and condescended to take the missive to the back.

I watched a dozen people come and go, all of them much more eagerly attended to than I. I kept myself out of the way, watching their interactions and considering their clothing, making a game of guessing what they might do or who they might be. This man was a merchant, I decided idly, worried to thinness over his ships, what with all the pirates out in the North Sea; that woman was the celebrated patron of a musical troupe; this one—

This one was Jemis Greenwing, Viscount St-Noire, and *very* distinguished patron of the bank, apparently. Mr. Vandray came out for me personally.

He shook my hand, greeted me exuberantly if not by name, and took my arm to lead me to an office in the back. I had a fleeting glimpse of marble walls and gold-gilt fixtures, thick carpets in rich colours, a seemingly endless array of portraits of a seemingly endless number of distinguished bankers and their patrons. Across from a portrait of the Emperor Artorin was a door of carved mahogany, and it was through this Mr. Vandray led me.

He ushered me to a comfortable seat across the desk from his own, bowed, and then took his seat when I bowed back, trying not to show my uncertainty.

"Mr. Greenwing," he said at last, "thank you for coming."

"Thank you for seeing me," I replied, a little confused at his heartiness. We regarded each other for a few moments. I knew he saw a young gentleman, a little short, fairly lean, undistinguished of feature; pale of skin, darker brown of hair and eyes; dressed in clothing of Fiellanese cut, equally undistinguished.

Mr. Vandray himself was portly, swarthier than me but still noticeably rubicund. His dark brown hair seemed to be shorter than what I'd seen among the students, and his hat was a plain black beaver. He wore a waistcoat and breeches similar to my own, but his coat was looser and longer, the sleeves puffed and slashed to show the silk lining. It was nowhere near so dramatic as what the students had been wearing, especially as the coat and lining both were a deep dark green, only the change in materials showing the decorative features; I did like the silver and lighter green embroidery of leaves on his waistcoat.

He tapped the letter I had just sent to him. "I understand your discretion, Mr. Greenwing—you do prefer that address, do you not? Mr. Morres was quite emphatic in his report to me that you did."

"Yes, sir," I replied. "The, er, viscountcy is very new."

"It will sit better with time," he said soothingly. "These things always do."

"Indeed, sir," I said neutrally, making him laugh.

"You're a canny one, aren't you! Tell me, Mr. Greenwing, why you are here."

I raised my eyebrows at him and did not say the obvious line of, *Because you asked me to come.*

I had thought, ever since the reading of my stepfather's will, about what I should do with what he had left me. I had spoken with my father about it, though he had admitted, with a wry smile, that he had never been that keen on financial administration even before his years as a pirate slave; apparently my mother had been the one to manage their combined estate; and longer with Hal before my friend had left Ragnor Bella. Hal had been managing the single largest private estate in Northwest Oriole since he was fourteen.

("Well, I do have help," Hal had said self-deprecatingly, and then proceeded to demonstrate that he knew exactly what each of his employees, from chief steward to goose-girl, did.)

"Mr. Vandray," I said slowly, "the last time I saw my stepfather was last spring in Morrowlea. He asked me what I intended to do when I graduated."

"Yes," he said encouragingly.

"At that time I had hopes that I would marry one of my fellow students and that we would return to her home—which is, in fact, here, Orio City—and make our way together. I had no clear idea of what form that would take, due to some of the eccentricities of Morrowlea's charter. Mr. Buchance informed me that he would see that I had enough of a competency not to starve."

I paused a moment, gathering my thoughts. Even though I'd decided to tell him the outlines of my story—my stepfather had trusted him and so did Hal, who was one of his other clients—it was still very hard to put it into words to a stranger. Mr. Vandray steepled his fingers before him.

"Ben, Mr. Buchance, came to see me shortly after that trip," he said. "It was his practice, as I'm sure you heard at the will-reading, to update everything after the birth of a child. He told me that it was a doubly blessed spring, for he had a new daughter and a son setting forth into the world. He was very proud of you."

I looked down at the table, working to keep my composure. I had been proud, disclaiming any need for his assistance, refusing always to take his name and follow him into his business. It was hard to have lost him without ever being able to know him as an adult, hard to feel that I'd never been able to settle my feelings for him, let alone tell him how much I had come to admire and (say it) love him over the years he had been my stepfather. I had been so angry that he was there, in my father's place, when my father came home the first time.

Now both mother and stepfather were dead, and my father had come home again, entering a space left cavernous by their passing. I thought now that my father and stepfather would have liked each other, and wished I could have Mr. Buchance's advice for what to do with the broken estates of the Woods Noirell and Arguty Manor. Having only his money was a poor second.

"Thank you," I said eventually, once I felt able to speak calmly again. "I'm not sure whether he would have told you—"

I wasn't in fact sure what I had told *him*; I had been in no fit state, last spring, to be coherent explaining something I could not myself well understand— "But my final term at Morrowlea was in many ways disastrous. I was very ill, and the woman I was in love with be-trayed my confidence severely."

Even if it had been induced by drugs and maintained by magic, in my mind and heart I had loved Lark; there was no other word for what I had felt.

"Oh?" Mr. Vandray said softly.

"You have, I trust, heard of the play *Three Years Gone: the Tragicomedy of the Traitor of Loe.*"

"Oh," he said, eyes widening. "I had not—oh no."

I smiled involuntarily despite not feeling at all amused. "Oh yes. The outlines of events were unfortunately quite true, even if the motivations ascribed were false to the point of slander. My father did return home to Ragnor Bella three years after the disaster at Loe, to be reviled as the traitor, and find his wife married to another man."

"Mr. Buchance died before he could reply to my letter enquiring about the play," Mr. Vandray said mournfully, "and no one seemed to know where you were. In the absence of instruction I could legally do nothing ..."

"You're not a lawyer on retainer to my family," I said. "I'm not sure what you could have done."

"You're kind to say so."

"I was travelling alone after I saw the play in Fillering Pool; I was in Ghilousette when Mrs. Buchance's letters eventually reached me. By the time I got home the Midsomer Assizes were long over."

"And so you come now," Mr. Vandray said, nodding. He then fixed me with a piercing glance. "You are very free with your story to a stranger, Mr. Greenwing."

I laughed unmirthfully. "My family's doings are the talk of three kingdoms, Mr. Vandray. Last night I encountered Jack Lindsary, and it appears there is a sequel to *Three Years Gone* in the works. My former ... friend ... is vindictive."

"You think this is her doing?"

"I know it," I replied simply. "The name she used at Morrowlea was Lark. I have since been informed she is one of the Indrillines, and am nearly certain she is the one about to marry the governor-prince of Orio City."

And hadn't that been a pleasant revelation last night. We had not been able to get so drunk, last night in our rooms at the Red Lion, to hide Mr. Dart's realization of what Jack Lindsary's comments about his patron had meant. I only wished I could doubt it.

"Damme," whispered Mr. Vandray, and rubbed his temples. He shook himself a moment later. "We have gone far afield, Mr. Greenwing. I apologize."

"I wished you to be clear what my situation is." I realized I was worrying my lip with my teeth and grimaced at this lack of subtlety. "There is more, I'm afraid."

"More?"

"You know how I recently became Viscount St-Noire?"

"Yes, Mr. Morres wrote immediately following the reading of the will, to inform me it had been done—I'd asked him to do so—and to let me know that that had also happened." He smiled. "He might have mentioned something about you slaying a dragon."

I waved that off as a distraction. "Did he happen to mention that my father—Jakory Greenwing, that is—had returned from the reputed dead a second time?"

"Yes ..."

"And that my uncle, my father's younger brother, had illegally claimed the family estate?"

"Yes."

"So I find myself, then, with a formerly cursed village with no resources for the winter, an estate that was only not run entirely into the ground because of my aunt's various illegal dealings, and a vindictive ex-lover with the might of the most notorious criminal gang in the continent behind her."

And that wasn't mentioning the cult to the Dark Kings that had tried to sacrifice me on the Fallowday of the Autumn, my grandmother the Marchioness' sudden interest in my marriageability, the fact that the *New Salon* was likely to announce all of these things within the week, and my own uncertainties as to my future career.

"You are very trusting, Mr. Greenwing, to tell me all this," Mr. Vandray said thoughtfully.

I sat back and regarded him equally intently, then smiled. "You already know most of it, sir. Besides, my stepfather was a very canny man, and he trusted you. So did his Charese business partners, Mr. Palaion and Mr. Zuraine; I did ask them, before they left Ragnor Bella after the will was read. I'm sure they would have told me had they had any reservations."

"I'm glad to see you did your due diligence," Mr. Vandray said with a smile.

"Moreover," I went on, "my best friend from Morrowlea is the Imperial Duke of Fillering Pool, and he tells me you are also his banker, and that I could trust you with these details. Two more different men than Mr. Buchance and Hal I could not imagine, and if they both have trusted you for many years with their dealings, I think I am able to do so as well."

Mr. Vandray chuckled. "Ah, you have the young duke at your side? Then you will go far."

"He is a good friend."

"Very well, we have laid out the lines of your situation. I take it you will want to know the details of what you have been left now?"

"Yes," I said, nodding. "I know from the will that I was left the residue of Mr. Buchance's fortune after the specific bequests were made."

Those specific bequests had totalled a great fortune in their own right, given to my stepfather's wife and daughters, so after due reflection I did not expect my portion to be that great, all things told. Although undoubtedly it was still more than I'd ever seen in my life before, or had expected from the words 'competency'.

"I am hoping that I will be able to draw enough to see the village of St-Noire through the winter without touching the capital, and in the spring start making investments to the end of making both St-Noire and Arguty profitable again."

Mr. Vandray actually stared at me for a moment. "Mr. Greenwing, do you not have any idea what Mr. Buchance left you?"

I shrank back a little. "Is there not enough? I've made a budget—" I passed him the paper I'd prepared, with Mr. Dart's help, after finding out from Mr. White in the Woods just how bad the situation was for the villagers.

The banker glanced down at it but did not seem to actually read it. "Mr. Greenwing ..." He sighed. "Ben left you half his fortune. You're the twenty-fourth richest man in Northwest Oriole."

***

Mr. Vandray and I spoke for almost an hour before he sighed and said I'd gotten the gist of everything he could do at the moment and that my budget was not entirely absurd.

I was most grateful for Hal's crash course in the administration of a great lord's estate; at Morrowlea we had learned the basics of personal finance, how to manage money and think about investments and small businesses, but nothing on this scale.

"The basic principles are the same," Mr. Vandray assured me. "Spend less than you earn, and you will increase your wealth."

Well, yes, that was clear enough, but there were many, many other parts to it when one had a fortune even half the size of my stepfather's. I was struck, over and over again, with gratitude and wonder for how well he'd managed his affairs. The house in Ragnor Bella he'd bought for the second Mrs. Buchance, which had been the talk of the town (or so I had been informed; I'd been away at Morrowlea by then), was extremely modest for a merchant of Mr. Buchance's stature.

"I knew he was wealthy, but not … this," I murmured, stacking the documents Mr. Vandray had given me together neatly.

"Everyone uses his containers, and he kept the most important features of the seals proprietary. His wife will earn far more than you have now over time."

That made me feel better, knowing that neither Mrs. Buchance nor my sisters would lose out by Mr. Buchance leaving me the half of his fortune.

"By the time your sisters are your age they will be great heiresses many times over," Mr. Vandray went on, smiling happily at the thought.

I smiled back, a little less reluctant than I had been a month ago when I had first learned I was to be Viscount St-Noire. "I will have to work hard to reclaim the reputation and standing of the marquisate, then, and assist my father with Arguty, so that when they are of age I can help launch them into society."

Mr. Vandray looked pleased at this thought. "That connection will do them very well indeed, Mr. Greenwing. Now, I believe that's everything we can do today. I will make arrangements to have the funds we discussed available to you at the branch in Yrchester; you should be able to access what you need for supplies by this time next week, and the rest will come soon after. I think you are quite correct to prefer not to use the branch in Ragnor Bella itself. I know Mr. Hurry at Yrchester will assist you well."

"Thank you, Mr. Vandray. I hope the next time we meet the political situation is a bit less fraught."

He huffed a sigh. "I doubt we'll be seriously affected—both the law-abiding and the criminal need their funds kept safe, after all. Nevertheless, if things continue as they are, send me a letter and we'll make arrangements to meet in a more neutral location. Perhaps Fillering Pool, since as you say you know the duke."

"That would be most appreciated."

He smiled crookedly at me. "It's most appreciated that you continue to patronize our establishment, Mr. Greenwing. Now, I'll walk you out and see that you get the ready cash you've requested."

This had been his idea, in fact, so that I could (as he said) refresh my wardrobe as well as get the immediate stores needed by the villagers on my way back. I nodded and stood, tucking the papers carefully into my waistcoat pocket, then shrugging back into the great-coat and straightening my hat.

"Very dashing," Mr. Vandray said. "I think I prefer your fashions to those currently sported by the young here in Tara."

"We'll probably get there in a year or two," I replied, privately certain I was never going to wear a codpiece in public (or in private, for that matter). Mr. Vandray held the door for me and led me back down the gorgeous hallway and into the main foyer of the bank, whereupon we immediately encountered Hal.

I forestalled his surprised greeting (no need for him to shout "Jemis!" in the midst of the hall) by reaching out for his extended hand, clasping my left to his shoulder, and whispering into his ear, "Don't say my name!"

"How intriguing," he murmured back very quietly, then stood back to smile cheerfully at me and Mr. Vandray. "What a surprise to see you, sir! I had no idea we should see each other again so soon; I would have waited to accompany you here had I known."

"Mr. Dart was unexpectedly required to make the journey, and I accompanied him in the hopes of speaking to Mr. Vandray, here." I gestured at the banker, who was smiling jovially but could not hide his bemusement. Perhaps he had not quite believed me when I said I was friends with Hal?

It occurred to me that probably there were many who pretended to be friends with the wealthy and titled, and that Hal probably had to foist them off with sticks.

"And have you finished your banking?" Hal asked courteously, prompting Mr. Vandray to whisper something to an attentive flunky, who whispered in turn to a teller, who promptly counted out a sum into a leather wallet. The teller handed this to the flunky, who handed it to Mr. Vandray, who presented it to me with a nod halfway to a bow.

The gossips were going to be buzzing with this, I realized, catching a few patrons of the bank leaning to discuss this development. Hal was dressed as befit an Imperial Duke, and I … was not.

"Yes, for today," I said simply, putting the wallet inside my waistcoat pocket.

"Shall we meet after my business is concluded?"

I nodded. "I understand there is a book fair under way in the Guildmarket Hall …"

"Say no more!" Hal laughed. "I'm sure you will be well occupied, no matter how long I am here." He clapped me on the back. "Good searching. Now, Mr. Vandray, if you're amenable?"

"Always, your grace," replied the banker, and I left them to their meeting.

The street outside seemed brighter merely for having met Hal. I smiled generally at people, receiving startled and suspicious glances in return. This made me sigh, for the city had not, actually, changed in the past hour. I picked my way past the piles of ordure with less grace and more attention than the citizens did, but nevertheless arrived at the Guildmarket Hall without any further adventure.

It was, it appeared, free to enter. I went past the guardsman on duty, in a uniform relict of the Fourth Division of the Fifth Imperial Army, unless I missed my guess (and I probably did not, my father having spent much time teaching me the different uniforms when I was a child and he was home from his campaigns). He glowered a little at me, perhaps because of the encounter with the odd old man earlier, but said nothing.

There was a steady stream of people moving through the building. Mindful of the warning about the bear baiting, I pushed my way to a corner to see where I should go. After a few minutes of observation I noted that several of an obviously academic bent—a tall, willowy man in the royal-blue robes of a mastery student, another man in a Scholar's black robes—had broken away from the main crowd to enter a door down the hall from me.

I followed them and was rewarded by the book fair.

CHAPTER FIFTEEN
The Book Fair

I was engrossed in a book of engravings depicting the floral emblems of Voonran houses when Hal found me. It took me a moment to realize he was there, standing at my shoulder and grinning steadily at me.

"Only three books?" Hal said when I looked at him, nodding at the small stack in the crook of my arm.

"My boxes are over by the tellers," I said vaguely. "You pay each vendor separately."

"Do you need longer to fulfill your commission?"

Spending an hour (or two; I hadn't been counting) investigating the book fair was a salve to my spirits, and I felt much less unsettled than earlier. I considered Hal's question as we joined the short queue before the bookseller's table.

"Mrs. Etaris said to take a portion of the funds for transportation, which I don't really need to do, given the falarode."

"Unless you want to ferry all these up to your accommodations yourself, I'd suggest hiring a porter with a wagon."

"I would have thought of that eventually."

He chuckled; we both shuffled forward a few steps. I shifted the books in my arms slightly. "In that case, while I'm sure I could spend many more hours here, I've spent most of Mrs. Etaris's budget and all of mine for myself."

"Excellent. In that case, may I take you to my club for a sup of lunch? You may tell me about your book purchases."

We shuffled forward another spot. "You have a club here? I'd have thought Kingsford?"

Hal smiled easily. "Oh, I have one there as well, which I expect to use more frequently now that I'm home, but this is still the cultural and economic capital of Northwest Oriole, you know."

"I suppose so," I replied. That made sense for why both Mr. Buchance from Chare (and living in South Fiellan) and Hal, Duke of Fillering Pool in northern Ronderell, did their banking here.

"It is so," Hal assured me. We stepped up to the counter and I started laying out my books so they could be tallied by the seller. One partway down was the botanical illustrations I'd thought Hal would appreciate. I was gratified to see his attention immediately diverted upon seeing it.

The seller looked at me. "Alongside your other boxes, that'll be a gold emperor and seven wheatears, six bees, young sir."

I pulled out my wallet and counted out the money with care. I was sharply reminded of Mr. Buchance as I did so, recalling a lesson in the etiquette of merchanting. He'd said that while everyone respected what money could do, few showed that respect in their transactions with those who dealt in it. Recalling my own experiences working at the bookstore in Ragnor Bella, I realized what he meant. Counting the money in front of the merchant, so both he and I could see no shenanigans were involved, was not the sign of distrust or miserliness I would once have taken it for.

"Starting a library are you, young sir?" the merchant asked genially as he accepted the coins and began re-packing the books into some
wooden crates that had been behind him.

I chuckled dutifully, even as Hal laughed his whooping laugh outright—no doubt thinking of my small flat above the store.

It was rather thrilling to realize that I *could* start a library, now.
Arguty Manor's was very good on fish and artificial waterworks (my
uncle) and pre-Imperial Alinorel history (my aunt), but held almost
nothing else but the sort of books ordered by the yard for effect. My
grandfather had run through the estate and it was only my elder uncle
Sir Rinald's hard work that had seen it even begin to recuperate. Sir
Rinald had not been able to keep much of the once-excellent library,
unfortunately.

"Some of it's coming to me," I said agreeably. "The greater part is
a commission from Mrs. Etaris, who is—"

But the merchant's eyes had lit up with recognition. "Mrs. Etaris
of Ragnor Bella! I should have known from your subjects of choice,
sir. Do give her my regards—Jack Jospian, she'll know me, she once
did me a very good turn. Oh yes, I know her."

"How did that come about?" I asked curiously.

Jack Jospian rubbed his balding head in some embarrassment,
then winked at me. "Not something to talk about in public, but it
saved my marriage, it did. Now, if I give you a book for the lady herself, will you see it reaches her?"

"I shall," I said, confused at the earnestness of this question. Was I
not already taking half a cartload of books to her?

Jack Jospian reached into the small strongbox on the floor next to
him before pulling out a plain-covered book with no title or author's
name visible. He wrapped it efficiently in brown paper, tied off with

string, and set in on my last crate.

"And there you are, young sir."

"Thank you. Now … do you know where I might hire a porter with a cart?"

The merchant gave me a series of directions I found about as clear as those I'd received in Tara, but Hal was nodding along, so I put the crates with those containing my earlier purchases, promised the urchin watching them another bee to wait an additional few minutes, and let Hal guide me to a stand of hansom cabs drawn by single horses I would never have found on my own. He glanced at me, smiled, and let me negotiate what I thought was an exorbitant price for haulage but which seemed, from everyone else's reactions, to be a hard bargain.

We showed the driver my piles, paid the urchin generously to assist in the loading, and, on Hal's unspoken advice—in fact, he just climbed into the seat without comment once we'd finished the loading—accompanied my books to the Red Lion.

Mr. Fancy and Mr. Cartwright were both there. They efficiently took over the job of unloading the crates, leaving me to pay the driver, thank them for their work, and finally take a deep breath as I returned to Hal. He had, I discovered, held back the hansom cab.

"Swordage's," he said to the driver, whose eyes widened. Hal ignored his mutter and barely let me seat myself next to him before rapping on the window to indicate we should depart.

"You shouldn't let all your purchases out of your sight," Hal said quietly.

I brought my attention back from fruitless examination of the foggy streets. "I beg your pardon?"

He smiled. "I should say theft probably isn't a problem in Ragnor Bella, outside of your numerous highwaymen."

I snickered, not quite embarrassed at my naivete, but not happy about it either. Still, we were both men of Alinor, and Hal a good enough friend to let me tell him about the literary treasures I'd just acquired all the way back down to a building approximately thirty yards from the cab stand.

The cab driver dropped us off with a nearly incomprehensible mutter about mad rich nobs, accompanied by a servile leer when I paid him generously for his trouble. Leaving him to join the other hansom cabs at the stand, Hal led me back around the Guildmarket Hall to the front.

We stopped very nearly at the same corner where I'd had the unpleasant interaction with the old man, though in the intervening few hours someone had removed the beggar's corpse, thank the Lady.

Hal caught my distraction. "What is it?"

"Someone died here earlier," I began, and told him about the incident. He looked troubled by more than the events, but when I started to ask him why, said quietly, "Not here—once we're in the club. This is the old centre of Orio City," he went on more loudly, gesturing at the Guildmarket Hall and the other grand buildings, which displayed most of four centuries of Imperial architecture (the Hall being by far the oldest, probably pre-Astandalan in origin though its facade was of later manufacture).

"The main street here runs from the governor's palace to the university, though the old city proper stopped at the Loughan Gates, just past the bank, where the cattle market used to be held."

"Which way is the harbour?" I enquired, taking his arm as he began to stroll in the direction he'd said held the palace.

"Ahead and to our right. On a clear day you'd see it."

"Not all that common, this time of year, as I understand."

"Indeed, not this year. Come, we turn in here." He indicated an old limestone building in Early Bastard Decadent style, far less elaborated than the flamboyant Grange of the Talgarths back home. Hal tugged my arm gently, and I followed hastily, trying to shake my thoughts free of the distractions occasioned by the architecture and thought of wireweed. (For the Talgarths, as Mr. Dart and I had discovered my first weekend home, had been growing wireweed on their estate all summer for the Knockermen.)

"I'd like to see the harbourfront one day," I murmured.

"The mosaics are remarkable," Hal agreed. We strode up the steps to the covered portico, where a doorman in scarlet and gold nodded deferentially to Hal opened the door.

"Your grace."

"Eamon."

It warmed me that Hal remembered the doorman's name, though I wasn't surprised.

Inside the club was all muted luxury, mostly in shades of dark green velvet, old oak, and gold accents. A few ancient tapestries representing the Lady, mostly amidst unicorns or holding court to her chivalrous knights, provided some leavening.

The first room was something of a parlour where mostly old and distinguished men sat with respectable women, complete with chaperones. "The Members' Guestroom," Hal said softly, nodding at a few people but not stopping to greet any as he led me across the room to an unremarkable door at the back of the room.

"We're not eating here?"

He smiled. "In the private dining chamber. I thought I'd sponsor you for membership. It'll please your grandmother."

Because that wasn't a daunting prospect in the least.

That it was not exactly common for the Duke of Fillering Pool to be ushering a young man of modest demeanour to be sponsored was evident by the reactions of many of the distinguished old men in the room, whose soft murmurs of conversation sharpened with interest and curiosity once we had passed. I was reminded of far too many situations in Ragnor Bella where my appearance had elicited a similar response.

Like on those occasions, I straightened my shoulders, lifted my chin, and otherwise ignored them as best as I could pretend.

Hal, of course, appeared entirely comfortable in himself and utterly oblivious of the stir.

The unremarkable door opened onto a small antechamber. Once the door shut behind us, all the noise of conversation was entirely cut off.

"This is all a little mysterious," I said. I tried for suavity—it was always good to practise—but doubted I achieved it.

Hal smirked at me. "It's not the Unicorn, don't worry."

The Unicorn—gambling hell and club for gentlemen of, let us say, diverse tastes—had been mentioned at the student tavern the night before. I decided not to engage with that (and damn my fair skin's telltale blush). "Hal, do you you think this is a good idea? I'm trying to be inconspicuous, you know. We're worrisomely close to the Indrillines here."

"Not in here," he replied easily. "This is the bastion of the old aristocracy. The current governor's an upstart compared to my family or yours. Lark can hardly know your title yet, can she?"

"She—" I stopped. Hal had not been there at the student tavern. "Jack Lindsary's writing a sequel to *Three Years Gone*, commissioned by and for Lark, to be performed at her wedding this Winterturn.

It's about Mad Jack Greenwing's son's return home from university. Complete with rumours of dragons."

Hal stared at me. "How do you know? I haven't heard that gossip."

"I met him last night at a student pub recommended to Mr. Dart by Roald Ragnor. The general response suggested it was his first announcement."

"I haven't heard anything about this!"

I blinked at Hal, then realized he meant about my reaction to Lindsary's announcement. "The conversation prior had made it clear that there were those present who might bear tales. I held my tongue."

Hal paused a moment, then smiled grimly. "Good show."

I bowed ironically. "Thank you."

He glanced at the door uncertainly. "I confess I was thinking more about the longer term than your current contretemps with Lark. Like it or not, you're a new player in the game of courts."

"It's a nearly empty title," I protested. "There's the Woods, and the village, but it's not as if the road goes to Astandalas any more."

"Things are happening in the wider game, Jemis. Alliances are shifting—people are less and less likely to wish Astandalas back again. They're looking now to what we can build on our own. You know the power the anti-magic faction has—and how their fears are permitting the unscrupulous who use magic to take more and more power."

"I do know," I replied bitterly, thinking about my aunt and uncle, about the cult to the Dark Kings, about poor Miss Shipston the mermaid from Ghilousette, about all those poor souls sleeping away their wireweed addiction on the streets of Orio City.

"You see, then? I'm not on that side—"

"Nor am I. You know that, Hal."

"I need allies. Jemis, I've spent the last few months taking up my full responsibilities. Something's going on—half my traditional allies have backed away in the past month. I returned home from visiting you to find my sister half-frantic about the situation. People who staunchly agreed that they would support my positions on magic are abruptly declaring neutrality or, even worse, turning to open support of the governor here. These are people whose families have support-ed mine for generations. Something—or someone—is persuading them to change sides."

"So why, when we're half a mile from said governor, in the heart of his territory, do you think this a good idea? Aren't you worried you'll be … persuaded?"

Hal scoffed. "I have magic and many protections. The situation with active magic is not anywhere so dire as it was—it's fear that keeps the practice out of fashion, not necessity."

"Terrible things happened in the Fall and the Interim."

"Don't I know it," he replied grimly.

I stared at the closed door by which we'd entered. No sound came through at all. I hoped our conversation was equally inaudible.

"You think, then, that I would be a useful ally to you? I agree with you, Hal, you know that, and I'll stand beside you as you've stood be-side me, but you must know I don't know who you're talking about or even where these 'decisions' are being made!"

"They're made in places like this, in conversations like this," Hal said, gesturing at the door we had not come through. "In the quiet private rooms of aristocratic clubs, at salons and balls, and ultimately in parliaments and royal courts. But by the time the subjects are spo-ken of openly, the decisions have almost always already been made."

I made a face at this. "That is so entirely unfair."

Hal regarded me for a long moment. "I promise you I'll support your democratic revolution in the future if you'll support me against the so-called prince of Orio City now."

"You needn't mock."

"I'm not."

I glanced aside, taking in the understated expensiveness of this antechamber. I was never going to be any sort of great mage, and certainly would not be attending Tara for a second degree any time soon. And … much as I had no desire to be a lord, let alone a politician, I *was* a lord, and therefore a politician. I knew well enough from Mr. Dart's history lessons that if I did not decide on my position others would do it for me.

"Very well," I said at last. "But I don't want to …" I faltered, not sure how to express my many reservations.

Hal clapped me on the arm, grinning not at all like an Imperial Duke making alliances. "Jemis, you need only be yourself to make all your politics and mine abundantly clear. All you need to do is stand beside me."

I thought of Hal, unflinchingly standing beside me though all the students of Morrowlea threw stones.

"As you have stood with me, so shall I keep faith with you," I said formally, not knowing that I thereby formed an alliance the Dukes of Fillering Pool and the Marches of the Woods Noirell had been dancing around for three and a half centuries of acrimony and embattled pride.

Not that that would have stopped me in the least.

CHAPTER SIXTEEN
The Bear Baited

To my surprise, nothing untoward at all happened. Hal brought me to a man he called The Secretary, who wore gold-rimmed pince-nez that went most incongruously with his velvet doublet and pantaloons. These were of rich black velvet, with bronze satin peeking out the slashed gussets, matching the bronze stockings clocked with winged items.

The Secretary caught me trying to determine what the items were and gave me a tight smile. "Winged swords, sir, the Club's sign."

"Very good, Mr. Secretary. I like the colour."

His smile loosened marginally and he nodded gravely before turning to Hal. "Your Grace is sponsoring this gentleman to the Club?"

"Yes. He is my friend from Morrowlea, where he was the Rondelan Scholar on entry and came First in our year upon graduation. He was recently instated as Viscount St-Noire, heir to the Imperial Marquisate of Noirell."

"A most illustrious peerage, and a most encouraging beginning," The Secretary said in approval. "Your Grace does not, of course, require a second to sponsor a fellow holder of an Imperial title. Welcome to Swordage's, Lord St-Noire. I am sure his Grace will tell you all salient points, but if you have any questions I will be *always* available to you."

I bowed politely and murmured my thanks. Hal led me deeper into the club, into what seemed to be the private dining room, where he ordered a bottle of wine and a sumptuous meal from a quickly-appearing waiter.

"The Secretary liked you," he said one this was done. "He sets hours if he doesn't, but you may call on him quite literally at any time."

"I can't imagine needing a club secretary at two in the morning, but I thank you."

Hal laughed. "You never know. If not this year, then five years from hence."

"I confess I haven't given much thought to where I might be five years from hence. The last six months have been too chaotic. I doubt it'll be here or at Tara, however. This city is far too grim for my tastes."

"It's better in the summer."

"Most places are."

"True." Hal fiddled with his wine glass, a blown crystal affair of probably absurd expense. "Are you thinking … What are you thinking, now that you've seen Vandray?"

I shrugged. "Restoring the fortunes of the Woods Noirell and assisting my father with the Arguty estate. There's such a lot of work to be done."

"I'll keep an eye out for someone who might be able to assist. A steward or a competent secretary would be a great help, I expect."

I stared at him. It honestly hadn't occurred to me that I could hire help. While I was still gobsmacked at the thought we were interrupted by the waiter arriving with the first course (they were following the

Late Astandalan style of many separate courses), a clear soup. When he'd gone I gathered my thoughts and asked Hal what sort of employees he had, a topic which occupied us through the rest of lunch.

* * *

Exiting the—our—club, we discovered that the weather had improved marginally. Although certainly not clear, the sun was shining brightly somewhere above us and the omnipresent fog was lit golden.

"See, it's not always grim," Hal said, nudging me as if I wouldn't have noticed this on my own.

"Still a bit grimy," I replied, gesturing at the now glittering piles and the way the white limestone buildings had black tracks like tears trailing down from the corners of windows, pediments, and waterspouts.

Hal chuffed in response to this sally. At his direction I turned left at the bottom of the stairs, ending up entering an alley a little out of the way of the passersby emerging out of the golden fog and disappearing, like souls to the afterlife, back into it.

"It occurs to me that you are missing your bear-baiter."

"That's behind the Guildmarket Hall. You didn't want—"

"No, no, I mean your Mr. Dart."

I ran the words over again in my mind, but they still made no sense. "Whatever do you mean?"

Hal glanced sidelong at me. "This is not intended to be a criticism, but you're not really an *initiator*, are you? Oh, you chose Morrowlea, but in general you react to rather than initiate events."

My initial—hah—reaction was to contest this, but even as the denial rose to my lips my father's earnest request that I stop launching myself headlong into danger came to mind. It was not that I went out seeking danger, after all—quite the opposite, at least in theory. In practice, however … well, one invitation from Mr. Dart to go 'picking mushrooms' on a stormy autumn evening, and three months later I had—

"I'd never thought about it that way," I said. "Hold up, I have a stone in my boot."

Hal watched as I tugged at the offending boot. "It's no aspersion on your character," he went on.

I tipped the boot upside down and then was puzzled when nothing fell out but a piece of lint. "No?"

"No. You told me once you'd always wanted to be a soldier, like your father."

Back in those halcyon days at Morrowlea, when he was just Hal and I was just Jemis, and Lark lovely, witty, and—well, never kind. I stuck my hand into the boot, heedful of the hidden knife, and began to feel my way to the toe. "This is true."

"And what are the excellent qualities of a soldier? An officer? Courage, strength, fortitude, intelligence, and—"

My father the reputed traitor made this one all too easy. "Loyalty."

Hal nodded. "Precisely. Not blind loyalty, not for an officer, but the willingness to follow a respected person's order, no matter what? Jemis, your father single-handedly held the Bloodwater Pass against an invading army for long enough that my great-uncle and his party could escape down the other side, knowing there would be no relief or rescue."

I still hadn't heard the full story of what had happened there, for my father to come home that first time. I found the offending pebble, caught in a fold of leather where the foot bends into toes, and stood there rubbing it back and forth across my fingers, boot dangling from the other hand, posed there with my foot lifted out of the muck.

"But he wanted to—it might even have been his idea—"

"I believe it was, but the order came from Uncle Ben. He's spent years grieving the necessity of it and honouring the courage Jack showed in obeying that order. It's no shame to be able to listen and be led. Nor to lead," he added after a moment, with a wry smile. "It occurs to me that you begrudge your 'promotion' to viscount."

"Oh, really?" I huffed a bit of a laugh to show I did not mean my sarcasm to be quite so sharp. "Very well. Upon further reflection I can understand that I will indeed follow Mr. Dart where he leads, though I'll also state that I am not always so sanguine following others."

Roald Ragnor came to mind, for one.

"Discretion in all its meanings is a most useful trait."

I bent at last to replace my boot. "Nonetheless, I find your phrasing peculiar. Of a bear-leader I have heard tell in such a context, but a bear-baiter, no."

Hal stared at me blankly. "A bear-leader is a tutor or perhaps a governess, if both she and her charge are of a certain ilk. A bear-baiter is—well, as I have said. The one in a group who initiates the adventures. Have you really never heard the phrase?"

"Only in context of the actual sport."

"Perhaps it's an Odlington oddity."

"Like the Odd Mess."

He grimaced. "Ugh, don't remind me of school food. We only had desserts other than stewed prunes and custard on Parents' Days and the Emperor's Birthday. Are you going to put that boot on, or shall I leave you to it and go fetch Mr. Dart from the Guildmarket Hall myself?"

"What makes you think he's there?"

"Where else would he think to find you?"

I flushed and finished re-settling the knife, whose sheath had shifted to an uncomfortable degree. I looked up again only to see that Mr. Dart was a bare ten yards away from us, at the other end of the alley. I called his name but he was entirely focused forward, good hand clenched into a fist.

I cast a wary glance around. The air in the alleyway—duller by the minute, as the sun disappeared into unseen clouds above the mist— was starting to move, the mist almost naturally and the shadows definitely not.

Hal put his hand on my arm. "Quietly now, Jemis. No sense in making a fuss."

I wanted to shake him off. Every instinct screamed danger, the need to move, to act, to fight against the threat Mr. Dart was facing. But with our conversation so fresh I instead permitted him to take my arm—with a probably necessary tight grip, though I could have slipped out of it easily enough—and lead me at a brisk pace forward.

Thus we were still several feet back when there was a loud roar and a huge brown shape rushed past the alley mouth. Someone screamed, someone else shouted, a dog began to bark relentlessly—and then Mr. Dart's shoulders loosened, his hand unclenched, and he turned his head with a smile to see us.

I saw first that the shadows were still swirling, the mist still eddying. And second, in the open court beyond the alley a crowd was clustering, faces eager with bloodlust.

"The bear escaped," Mr. Dart said, nodding his chin in the crowd's direction. "I'm surprised you didn't come flying past me, Jemis."

If I had run when I first realized Mr. Dart was raising magic against a threat, I would have been in time to interfere.

"Just as well," Hal said, with a meaningful nudge for me.

"Indeed!" cried Mr. Dart, the morning's quarrel apparently forgotten. "It would no doubt have been nearly as spectacular as the dragon, but much more disastrous. And a good afternoon to you, your grace. Thank you for taking care of our friend. He's been indiscreet already today, it would be best to contain it to the university."

Or not forgotten.

I was glad my two closest friends got on so well, really I was.

***

We passed the afternoon completing my various commissions to the best of our collective ability. Since we had Hal, who knew Orio City surprisingly well ("Oh, we had to come every year for the spring Season growing up"), we were able to find everything from the grains-of-paradise for Fogerty the Fish to two bottles of a specific Lesser Arcadian vintage for Sir Hamish without egregious difficulty. The only true failure was at the Post Office, and even there I could admire the architecture of the central postal facility of Northwest Oriole.

I was also given a list of all the habitations, old and new, with a name even remotely close to "St-Noire," including—keeping Artos the Ass' sneers in mind—variations without the Saint. It would be difficult to travel to all of them, and the post officials hemmed and hawed about how regular their service was to a few more remote and recondite villages (my St-Noire being one of them; I explained about the curse, more or less). Still, at least we could write to enquire after misdirected letters for Mr. White.

The romance of the situation—falling in love with a woman from another world, staying to learn her family's business, wondering always about those left behind—had caught my imagination. Hal sniffed and said he expected writing to the Ambassador of Zunidh at the Lady's court on Nên Corovel would probably prove more effective.

I thought about stories of the traditional hierarchy of Zuni society, the fact that Mr. White had said his family was thoroughly bourgeois and, moreover, from a very remote province, and the likely rank of those chosen to be intermundial ambassadors on behalf of the Last Emperor of Astandalas, and resolved to write to all thirty-two possible communities once I was home.

CHAPTER SEVENTEEN
Meeting Miss Dart

It was still foggy that evening. Mr. Dart and I made our way from the Red Lion (where we'd detailed Messrs. Fancy and Cartwright to deal with our many and manifold acquisitions) to the public house where we were to meet the mysterious relations.

I glanced around, alert for danger, but the prickling unease of being in narrow roads with no prospects or knowledge of escape routes did not diminish with the realization that we'd moved into a wealthier neighbourhood. There were more torches lit here against the fog and falling dusk, and fewer beggars lying in the doorways, but the damp air held dank whiffs of corruption and sulphur, and there was refuse in every corner of mew and courtyard.

"It's such an ugly city," I murmured, picking my way through tangled skeins of rotting leaves mixed with horse dung. I'd spent enough time in the Morrowlea vegetable plots to know the piles would make excellent compost, and could only deplore the apathy that left them on the street as noxious waste instead.

"Yes," Mr. Dart said thoughtfully. "The university itself wasn't bad."

I drew my coat closer about me, once again grateful my father had cut off any prideful rejection of Sir Hamish's offer of it. "I think I was spoiled by Morrowlea's architecture."

"Here I would've thought you'd appreciate a university fully able to withstand a siege."

"I haven't much desire to be in the position to sit one out. My father doesn't have much good to say of his sieges, either as besieger or besieged."

"His last one was Loe, so I should think not."

We came to a crossroads then and Mr. Dart frowned. "Can you see a fountain? The directions I got yesterday said to take the road next to the fountain."

I peered obediently through the gloom. The dark stone of the city dissolved in the fog, shadows uncertain but deeper than normal. "There's a sound of water over here," I began, taking a step in that direction, then recoiled when a clear smell of piss wafted back.

I bumbled against Mr. Dart and gave him a wry smile I hoped disguised my nerves. The city put me on edge; everything about it seemed just slightly *off*. There were people hidden in the fog, at the edge of hearing and just past the edge of sight, and any of them might be an Indrilline spy, or a more ordinary sort of criminal, or, for all I knew, the Red Company and the Lady's angels besides. Though if the latter were there they must have a lot of cares besides the two of us, in Orio City.

"Let's try that side," Mr. Dart said, going away from the invisible pisser. We edged around a rough patch of broken cobbles and nearly walked into a huge barrel turned on its side and full of noisome rags. Heavy breathing indicated that there was a person there. The odd sickly-floral scent mixed into the putrefaction made it clear this was one of the Sleepers.

I shuddered involuntarily, gripping my greatcoat ever more tightly. How close had I come to that fate? If Lark and I had not fallen out in the spring, if I had followed her here to Orio City, beguiled and adoring still, would I have lasted out the summer before the wireweed stole everything but my most basic vegetable life?

It was all too easy to see that Lark had been amoral enough to believe her own personal good outweighed every other consideration. She was brilliant, beautiful, utterly disengaged from others' emotions except to manipulate them. I had seen it play out over and over again from my favoured seat at her side, as other students—our friends, I had thought—were brought into the charmed circle, used and enjoyed for their conversation or wit or petty favours, until use and enjoyment failed, and then were cast out again into the mass of the unconsidered, baffled and left wondering, always, what they had done wrong.

The only person who'd ever expressed the opinion that Lark herself might be the one at fault was Hal. Lark had left him alone, perhaps aware of his actual rank, perhaps because of his hidden magic. (Hidden, yes, but crucially, and unlike mine, trained.) She had encouraged me in our friendship, an encouragement that seemed increasingly sinister the more I came to understand her games, though I had always felt an undercurrent of displeasure that there was someone I turned to outside of herself. Hal had kept me from being entirely consumed by my drug-fueled passion for her.

Well, Hal and Violet.

I sighed. Violet might be in the same city as me—*might* being the operable word—but I could not, absolutely could not forget the fact that she was Lark's confidante and right hand; that she had told me not to trust her; that whatever game she was playing was deeper than my knowledge.

I hoped she was playing a game. The idea that Violet was acting entirely of her own volition, that she was such a moral coward that she entered into Lark's schemes without resistance—no. That I could not believe. Whatever thrall she was under, there was one. Blackmail, beguilement, or something else, surely.

"It's this way, I think," Mr. Dart said, linking his good arm in mine. I stumbled after him, away from the barrel and the Sleeper slowly sleeping his way to death.

I was glad when we reached the Pear Tree a few moments later. It stood fifty yards or so from the fire barrels marking the edge of the university district, and I presumed was a place intended for those who were not invited within the precinct to meet with those who were.

It was warm and well-lit within, clean, cheerful, pleasantly noisy. It was such a contrast to the city outside that I felt nearly dumbfounded, fumbling with the clasps of my greatcoat. Everywhere we went in Orio City the streets were dim and dirty, conversations hushed and sinister, encounters wary and brief. Inside—or inside everywhere except for the Red Lion—all the wariness and reserve vanished. Voices raised in song and argument, liquor flowed in rivers, and strangers such as Mr. Dart and I were drawn into conversations heady with philosophy and politics.

And yet ... the city was seen by some as a war zone. It was not open war, but the lines were becoming clearer, and people were waiting for what blows would fall once the Indrillines took open control by marrying one of their own to the governor-prince.

Someone was waving at us. Mr. Dart tugged me along towards the thin young man with an extravagant hat—no; I blinked, catching a glimpse of copper curls. It was Jullanar Maebh from the night before, still in her royal blue robes.

Mr. Dart lifted his hand in greeting and led me along. She sat near a fireplace, in a seat that let her see who came in the door. Mr. Dart was not so far gone in his flirtation that he did not forget to sit in the seat across the fire from her, which gave him the same view. I, therefore, was left to the one with my back to the door, which made my skin crawl but which I could not justly protest. It was Mr. Dart's sister-in-law and niece we were meeting, after all.

I smiled mechanically, as if I were one of the automata I'd seen in Ghilousette. There they'd whispered of magic, not of drugs, had cast sidelong glances at one another when speaking of witches, of those who had gone back to the old ways from before the Empire. After events in Ragnor Bella this autumn I had understood better what the Ghilousettens so feared. There was power there, given to those who gave their allegiance to the Dark Kings, but I had seen nothing but twisted results come of it.

I brushed hair back from my face and scowled when my hand came back wet. "This infernal fog," I muttered. "Does it ever lift?"

Jullanar Maebh snorted. "Sometime around the spring spur weeks, usually, before the sea fogs come in."

"The record is three months straight," Mr. Dart chimed in.

"I'm going to cast that guidebook from the carriage on our return journey if you bring it out to regale me again," I warned.

Mr. Dart laughed. "No chance of seeing the governor's palace, then, for you."

"Nor yet Nên Corovel."

Jullanar Maebh shook her head. "The mists there haven't lifted since the Fall." She lowered her voice to add, "You'd be better served not mentioning either."

"Why not?" Mr. Dart asked, still smiling with splendid unconcern.

She glanced at the door. I couldn't stand having my back to it, especially if they were going to keep looking behind me, and shuffled my chair over so I was a little closer to Mr. Dart and could see the room side-on, at least. Jullanar Maebh had stiffened at the sight of an older man who stood by the door, unwinding his muffler, but relaxed when he turned away to a table in the corner with two other old men at it.

"The governor—excuse me, the 'prince', is getting married soon. Had you heard?"

I did not feel like stating I'd received an invitation. "Yes," I said, "it was mentioned last night."

Jullanar Maebh looked at the door again, tensing (again) when a man my father's age looked at us. She subsided when he shook his head and went to the bar instead. "The bride … let me say that's she's from an old family in the city. They've become much more prominent since the Fall."

"And?"

"And they don't like the Lady, not the goddess nor the mage, and now that the old governor's died, the new one styles himself a prince and is making it clear he's not on the Lady's side."

"But what is the Lady doing?" Mr. Dart asked, equally softly. "Why isn't she asking?"

"Why has she let the mists hide the Isle?" Jullanar Maebh shrugged, through her expression was dour. "Once the prince is married in law he'll have the whole weight of the city behind him."

I pretended to have only just realized what she meant. "You don't mean the bride is one of the Indrillines, do you."

She darted a glance to the door, where a couple had entered, the man removing the woman's fur cloak with a flirtatious gesture. "Hush! Do you want to attract attention?"

"You're the one looking suspiciously at the door every time it opens," I retorted.

"I'm waiting for someone, you dolt. And yes, The Indrilline—that's the head of the family—has chosen his successor, and she's the one pushing for open power. Not that anyone can go against them directly anymore, not with their witchcraft added to their economic control. Add in the constabulary and political legitimacy ... It's not a good time to be on the other side."

My mind was as foggy as the city, I thought irritably. In Ghilousette, the Dark Kings were acting in secret while wholesome wizardry was outright banned. In Fiellan certain parties sought to ban all magic to stop the perceived infection, but the other duchies and earldom of the kingdom were split, and Hal, at least, did not think the edict would stand even if it were passed.

In Ragnor Bella, the cult to the Dark Kings had made a nearly successful bid to seize power in the community, though why there and to what end I did not know. It was possibly simply that Ragnor Bella was convenient and vulnerable, but there seemed to be more to it than that. Certainly the events around the Fallowday of the Autumn had suggested that vengeance against my father for his actions at Loe was involved.

There were also the strange magics of the Woods Noirell and the many mysteries of the Arguty Forest to take into consideration; not to mention the fact that Ragnor Bella was reputed to have been the place least magically affected by the Fall, but no one knew why.

And that perhaps was connected to the events my first weekend back in town, when the Knockermen and the Indrillines alike had sought to take control of the wireweed crop grown there, and also the stone the Black Priest had called the Heart of the Moon ...

Then there was Orio City, former capital of our province of the Empire, still centre of commerce and fashion, with the ancient university on one horn and the governor-prince's palace-prison on the other; in sight, on a clear day, of Nên Corovel the Lady's Isle ... but there were no clear days, and though the people cried out in confusion and need for the good government and stable magic the Lady represented, the Lady of Alinor did not answer.

In all these places, or at least in Orio City and in Ragnor Bella, there was a secret society dedicated to the restoration of magic under the Lady.

And in the Arguty Forest was someone claiming to the be the Hunter in the Green, summer consort of the Lady of the Green and White.

I rubbed my temples, wishing any of this made sense, and opened my eyes to hear Mr. Dart say with dawning horror, "Are you waiting for Mr. Dart of Dartington?"

CHAPTER EIGHTEEN
"*Cousins*"

"Oh, by all the gods!" Jullanar Maebh cried, then flinched and lowered her voice again when half the room glared at us. "Please tell me you're not my brother."

"It's almost as bad," Mr. Dart said miserably. "I'm technically your uncle."

Jullanar Maebh digested this for a moment. Her disgusted expression gradually softened, until she started to snicker softly. "By all the gods indeed! I thought I felt oddly comfortable with you."

Mr. Dart glanced at me, then firmly down at the table, face flushed with embarrassment. They had been flirting shamelessly, I reflected, then reflected further that at least it could not have gone any further than flirtation given the time and opportunities they'd had.

"Well," I said, when neither of them spoke further, "moving on: Miss Dart, may I introduce you to your uncle, Mr. Perry Dart?"

He cast me a grateful look, she an amused one, and they nodded courteously at each other over the table.

"And may I ask my uncle for a proper introduction to his friend?"

Mr. Dart took a moment to consider the room. No one seemed particularly interested in us, but Jullanar Maebh's exclamation—and the fact that we were by far the youngest people in there—did mean we were not being entirely ignored, either.

"I think full formal introductions are better left until we've left the city. Mr.—Snorry here is avoiding attracting the notice of a lady with whom he'd at one point had an understanding."

"A misunderstanding the whole time," I muttered darkly.

Jullanar Maebh gave me a rather disdainful crook of her eyebrows. "That seems a trifle cowardly, sir," she said.

Mr. Dart breathed in sharply. I felt an immediate wash of fury, but I forced myself to take several long, deep breaths. I had not responded as I wanted to Jack Lindsary; I could hold my temper for this.

"Miss Dart, I might say the same of you, as you seem to be running away in fear to throw yourself on the mercy of a family you do not know in the least. I do you the honour of presuming there is more to the matter than the face of it, and that this is prudence, not poltroonry. I ask you to leave your judgment of me until you know more of the facts."

I was proud I managed to keep my voice relatively even, albeit cold. Jullanar Maebh blushed hard, eyes bright with shame.

"That was out of line of me," she said after a moment. "I apologize. I am sorry, sir, I am most on edge from my situation and this new discovery—"

I cut her off. "I do understand, and I accept your apology. Once we both know the truths of each other's actions we can decide if we wish to call the other out."

She stared at me open-mouthed. "You … you truly would grant me that equality?"

I was coming to hate Tara. That would never been an acceptable response at Morrowlea. "Yes; why not? If you have not studied the art of defence …" I trailed off, then smiled at her. "I should be very surprised. Nevertheless, I'm sure we could come to an adequate resolution."

"I am a woman."

"And so?"

She opened her mouth again, then closed it, shook her head, and turned to a smugly smiling (why?) Mr. Dart. "I'm not sure if I can call you *uncle* without laughing at the absurdity given the parity of our ages, sir."

"Ah! Call me cousin, then, if you will. Close, if not exact, but close enough to answer most questions of propriety."

"Cousin, then," she said gratefully. "May I ask about my father? Why did he not come himself?"

"He's the Chief Magistrate for the Winterturn Assizes," Mr. Dart replied easily. "He asked me to come in his stead, and Mr.—my friend, here, came along on a few errands of his own and because his grandmother would loan only him her coach."

"Speaking of which, we should make plans," I interjected.

"Yes …" Jullanar Maebh said uncomfortably.

I smiled at her. "It seems as if it'd suit all of us to leave soon?'

"I've an appointment at the university in the morning. Can you be ready to leave by noon, cousin?"

"Yes—yes. I … yes."

Jullanar Maebh seemed rather flustered suddenly. I eyed her curiously, but did not question her behaviour.

"Do you have a maid?" Mr. Dart went on.

"No, not—no."

"Do we need someone else as a chaperone?" I asked thoughtfully, thinking of the good gossips of Ragnor barony. "Usually an uncle would be sufficient, but under the circumstances ..."

"We thought your mother would be joining us," Mr. Dart added by way of explanation.

"That's a matter to discuss later," she said firmly. "Mr. Snorry—gods, that's absurd—please say that's not truly your name?"

"No, thank goodness."

"Good. Sir, you'll grant me full capacity in all respects to fight an honour duel with a gentleman, but not to travel alone with my uncle—or my cousin—and his friend?"

"Touché. If you don't yourself object ... it's only the gossips of the barony, truly. They find my affairs deeply intriguing, and I did not wish to subject you to more than you will already receive by your sudden appearance."

"We can look for a maid or a chaperone in Yrchester, when we stop so you can collect all those supplies," Mr. Dart said practically. "Perhaps we can persuade Magistra Bellamy back home with us. I still want her to look at my arm. I don't want to chance the physickers here."

I raised my eyebrows at him at the idea that our local witch would be considered an appropriate chaperone for the Acting Magistrate's newly-discovered daughter; he grinned unrepentantly at me and turned to Jullanar Maebh, touching his sling lightly. "That's another matter to discuss once we've all the time in the carriage to fill."

She accepted the demurral with good humour, if obvious curiosity. "On to practical matters, then: I have a small trunk, that's all. If you have a carriage, I take it that will not be a problem?"

"Even with the number of books Mr.—ugh, he bought yesterday, no."

"They were a commission," I protested.

"You bought out half the fair, I am sure of it," he said blandly. "Mrs. Etaris will be well pleased. Where are your lodgings, cousin?"

I found it puzzling he was less awkward saying St-Noire to me than Jullanar Maebh to her, but said nothing of it. He could retort with great reasonableness that I wavered considerably in how I addressed my father.

"In the university district, but you cannot bring a carriage within the fire barrels without formal permission from the Chancellor."

"Which we do not have and cannot easily get," I said, ignoring Mr. Dart's suggestive expression that the Viscount St-Noire might be able to make this happen. "How close can we bring a carriage to the edge nearest you?"

"It shouldn't be a problem, as you saw," Jullanar Maebh replied, gesturing outside. "This is the closest."

I considered the width of the street and winced. "That's never going to work."

She laughed, taking this as a joke. "Really? What on earth did you bring?"

"A coach-and-six," Mr. Dart informed her, grinning. "A falarode, to be exact."

I could see Jullanar Maebh's impression of my wealth and social standing rise sharply at this revelation of our conveyance. "A falarode? I've only seen one of those at an imperial procession."

"Yes, well, my grandmother is somewhat eccentric," I replied briskly. "We can discuss my family later. We're staying at the Red Lion."

"A most interesting choice."

"It was the coachman's. He seemed to feel it answered our dignity."

"He hadn't been here since the Fall, had he?" she said brightly.

I snorted. "No. Very well, Mr. Dart's appointment is at nine, in History. Shall we meet you here afterwards?"

"I can meet you there," she said, thinking it through. "We can then cut across the Commons to the Picklegate, which will cut the route to the Red Lion considerably."

"The Picklegate?"

"You're a linguist, aren't you?" she replied.

I worked through it in my mind and eventually realized it might be a corruption of the Old Shaian *pekili*, northeast; though it could as easily have been some ancient student's idea of a joke on posterity.

"Right, we have a plan," Mr. Dart said. "If you don't object, cousin, we'll leave you to your evening so we can make our own arrangements at the inn."

Jullanar Maebh nodded, face sober, and picked up her hat. We stood together and made our way out (realizing from the glare cast us by the waiter that we'd never actually ordered anything in the restaurant; I felt bad and was a little relieved we wouldn't be returning), whereupon I sketched a bow. Jullanar Maebh curtsied to me and to Mr. Dart, who bowed back and then took a breath and said, "Miss Dart, I have been remiss; please forgive me. I welcome you to our family."

She dropped down instinctively, it seemed to me, into another curtsy. Her face when she rose up was intent. "Thank you, sir," she replied quietly. "I thank you for your welcome. Until the morrow."

We doffed our hats again and she watched as she turned and walked back into the area marked by the fire barrels. We stood there a moment longer, watching until she disappeared into the gloom, and then Mr. Dart sighed.

"Why do we always fall for the entirely unsuitable ladies, Jemis?"

"I think the Lady must be playing tricks with us," I said, taking his good arm in mine and tugging him back towards the Red Lion. "Come now, my friend, not even the decrepitude of the building can destroy potent alcohol."

"We can hope," he muttered, and changed the subject back to the linguistic puzzle of 'Picklegate'.

The next morning was, at long last, that of our departure. I was packed and pacing long before the church on the square opposite the Red Lion had rung eight o'clock.

On the prowl for a cup of coffee before the crack of dawn (which was, to be fair to Mr. Dart, some time after half past eight), I had encountered Mr. Cartwright. When I asked after Mr. Dart, his valet frowned, then waved away the chambermaid he'd been speaking to with the injunction to fetch both the young sirs their coffee.

When we were alone, I said, "Is something amiss, Mr. Cartwright?"

He whuffled into his moustache and hesitated.

I'd been up since something like half past five, staring out into what of the gloomy, grimy, fogbound cityscape I could see out my window. My sleep had been decidedly interrupted. Pleasant dreams of Violet and Lark, Hal and Mr. Dart (present at Morrowlea, my dreams apparently being catholic regarding my friendships) all gradually became limned with a creeping dread made worse by my dream-self's blithe ignorance.

I woke over and over again to wonder if these were dreams or memories (notwithstanding the presence of Mr. Dart) or those strange true dreams my mother's fairy lineage granted me.

At some point around midnight I fell asleep and dreamed one of those dreams, the fairy dreams, making all others seem mere prelude and preface.

In that dream I encountered Mr. Dart at a dark and dreary cross-roads. The waystone in the middle was South Fiellanese, with an offering-stone beside it large enough for even the human-sized bundle laid out upon it.

In my dream I both desired and dreaded my definite need to see what—or who—that bundle was. I hesitated at the edge of the paved area around the stones, unable to cross to see if what I feared was true.

Then Mr. Dart was there, an older Mr. Dart, weary and hard. He held a sword in his left hand and what looked like a magic wand in his right. I felt intensely relieved that at some point in the next ten or fifteen years he would manage to disenchant his stone arm, and resolved even in my dream to tell him so in the morning.

In the dream I stepped forward to greet him, cheerfully and with great pleasure at this apparently unexpected encounter. He whirled, shifted into a classic defensive posture—one foot forward, one back, torso twisted to present less of a target, sword forward and wand back and up like a dagger.

I smiled. His face, intent, went grim.

"Jemis! You're dead."

And then the shadows moved.

****

Mr. Cartwright's slow words broke me out of my maundering.

"He's not been sleeping well, the young master."

I considered this. "Since we arrived in the city?"

The valet whuffled into his moustache some more. "Since he came home this summer, like. Worse since he came to hurt his arm."

"I'm sorry to hear that," I said, as I was, but I also couldn't see any way I could assist Mr. Dart with this, any more than he could help me with my dreams whether true, false, or prophetic.

Mr. Cartwright peered around, cocking his head as if to listen for the chambermaid's return. He beckoned me closer so he could whisper right into my ear.

"The shadows move when he dreams, sir. I'm sore afraid."

Well.

"I, er, will see what I can do, Mr. Cartwright," I said at last. "I'm not sure there's much, alas."

"You're a true Southerner, m'lud Jemis. I don't reckon with all them superstitions, but then that dragon came." He shook his head. "Never seen a sight like you slaying it. Straight out of a book of tales. Surely you can help the young master."

My bear-baiter, Hal had called Mr. Dart: the one who led where I followed. I sighed, grateful that I could hear footsteps coming up the stairs. "I'll do my best, Mr. Cartwright."

"Here's tha coffee, sir," he said, as if in thanks.

***

Mr. Dart and I considered, and rejected, the offer of breakfast (though we were later informed that this was the one meal the Red Lion did indisputably well; its kippers were highly regarded; but as I disliked kippers in most formats I was not overly distraught at our decision to wait for the Salon). The coffee, however revolting, was at least strong enough to waken even Mr. Dart for the morning's jaunt to the university district.

After we'd finished packing our remaining possessions and handed our bags over to Mr. Cartwright's care, with the instructions for him and Mr. Fancy to meet us as close to the Picklegate as possible with the falarode, we headed out to meet Miss Dart and the Faculty of History.

"I shall be well glad to be quit of this city," said Mr. Dart as we paced past the fountain, startling me considerably.

"Oh? Really?"

"You sound most surprised for someone who's been valiantly refraining from his multitude of complaints."

I flushed. "I have, yes."

"Though less vocal, I am not in total disagreement, Mr.—Well. There's a peculiar distress to a place once beautiful and now bereft."

"Very true, Mr. Dart." We turned in past the fire barrels and both breathed easier. "What is your appointment this morning?"

"I asked for some recommendations, books and Scholars, about the current state of affairs."

"Risky," I murmured.

Mr. Dart flushed this time. "How do you do that? Fine: I am curious about the role of the Lady, how it changed with the Conquest and how it might be changing now. If the Dark Kings are returning, to say nothing of dragons, who knows what else may come?"

If he wasn't going to address his magic directly, this was certainly a positive step. I had not forgotten that Hal's little identification ritual had identified Mr. Dart as a wild mage and prospectively a great one, if he ever trained his power to its extent.

"I shall be interested to know what you discover."

He quirked his eyebrows at me. "I have hopes you'll assist in the research."

"I can help with the acquisition of the books, at any rate. I suspect Mrs. Etaris has a widespread network of fellow bibliophiles at her disposal."

"Oh?"

Mr. Dart had not been there for Jack Jospian's rhapsody of praise. I told him the story, and we amused ourselves the rest of the way to the Salon by thinking up all the "good deeds" by which Mrs. Etaris might have saved the man's marriage.

I resolutely did not enquire why Mr. Dart, that infamously not-a-morning-person, was so alert and cheerful at dawn.

***

We dined on Tarvenol pastries both sweet and savoury. Only the cheese and apricot was more delectable than what Mr. Inglesides produced at home; but that was truly delicious. I was so taken with the apricot pastry that I left Mr. Dart sipping his chocolate to see if I could finagle a recipe out of the cook. Said cook, a young woman barely older than I, refused to say more than that a grating of fresh nutmeg always appealed.

"It's not as if we can't get nutmegs at home," I muttered, though they had been on the list of several of Ragnor Bella's citizens for us to acquire in 'the city'.

"Nutmeg's an aphrodisiac," Mr. Dart commented blithely.

"I wasn't flirting!"

"You might have gotten on better if you had."

I protested this, he laughed merrily, and we continued on through the sally port of the Gates of Knowledge (Mr. Dart, once again, receiving a much warmer welcome than I). We skirted the grassy field, observed the immaculate piles of proto-weaponry in their places, and eventually passed into the Rear Quad, which was empty.

"I'll wait here for Miss Dart," I said, though the words were drowned out by the commencement of the university bells striking nine.

As the final one echoed away into silence Mr. Dart doffed his hat to me. "Very good. I expect to find you here, mind you, when I return, which should be within the hour."

"I promise."

"Indeed."

I planted myself ostentatiously on a plinth supporting a statue of a constipated-looking Scholar of some indeterminate Imperial period (for both Scholar and sculpture) and let lines of *On Being Incarcerated in Orio Prison* run through my mind in all their sonorous Shaian to while away the time.

***

After a few minutes my enthusiasm for silent recitation waned. I looked around in hopes of more interesting fare. Sadly, apart from a small flock of pigeons, nothing was on offer. The doors in the Classics building, some thirty yards across the open plaza from me, remained firmly shut on whatever intrigues they held. The rest of the quadrangle remained empty of people.

I got up from the plinth and studied the statue. The sculptor had been of that sort of skill that could convey the individuality of his or her subject without truly displaying personality.

"It's Sir Toma of Goldlake and Varra," a voice said behind me.

I jumped, whirling to see that Jullanar Maebh had arrived.

She smirked slightly and went on. "Chancellor of Tara at some point in that run of the seven Empress Zangoras."

Jullanar Maebh still wore her student robes, the royal blue even more intense in the dull light of the day, her copper hair frizzled by the humidity despite being pulled back into a high braid.

"No hat?" I enquired foolishly, removing mine so I could giver her a polite bow.

"I removed it coming through Halls," Jullanar Maebh replied, lifting her right hand to display her ostrich-feather-bedecked platter of a hat and making a gesture in the direction of the east end of the Classics building. "Good morning, sir."

"Miss Dart. Your, ah, cousin has bid me make you welcome and assure you he will join us soon."

"I give you thanks," she replied demurely, placing her hat on her head a moment before I did the same with mine. She looked around, then sank gracefully onto the curved top of her trunk, an attractive brass-chased wooden thing of the sort I imagined seasoned travellers taking to sea.

I cast around for subjects of conversation, but couldn't find anything beyond the weather (dull) and our destination (dangerous). Jullanar Maebh, for her part, seemed also to be wishing she'd thought to provide herself with an easily accessible book.

We contemplated the pigeons in silence.

When the bell struck half-past nine Jullanar Maebh stood. I had gone back to sitting on the plinth. At her movement, I stood upright, expecting to see Mr. Dart come out of History.

Jullanar Maebh was frowning the other way, however, towards Classics. Her face was set, jaw firm; then she smiled brightly and greeted Artos the Ass as he angled around a cluster of Scholars, who had just exited the door to our right, and headed straight to us.

"Fiery Miss Jullanar Maebh of the Blue!" he cried, seizing her hand to give it a sloppy kiss. He brayed at me when I took a hesitant step forward in case Jullanar Maebh desired my assistance. "And the noble Snorry of nowhere-in-particular! You did not lose yourself in Magic after all, I see."

"No thanks to you," I muttered, then bowed as shallowly as I dared. "Artos, if I recall correctly."

He ignored me in favour of leering dramatically at Jullanar Maebh. "What are you doing here this fine morning? You have a trunk, but no Mistress May to accompany you—does Nury know you're eloping?"

Artos brayed at his own wit, sounding as mindless as the animal, but I noticed his eyes were intent.

Did everyone have a secret life?

Jullanar Maebh affected unconcern fairly well, but couldn't seem to think of anything to say. As the silence stretched on and Artos showed no sign of moving, I sighed lightly. "I'm waiting on my friend. What brings you here, Artos?"

"Oh, ferreting out the gossip," he said, with an expansive gesture that slapped against once of the Scholars, who had drifted towards us in the course of their conversation.

Artos's face darkened in a sneer. "Watch yourself—oh! My apologies, Magistra. I didn't see you were there."

Magistra Aurelia gave him a distinctly unimpressed glance. She then smiled at me, and gestured her companion to step forward. I was conscious of my heart sinking even as Artos's eyes widened.

"Domina Ashridge, this is the young man I was telling you about, the—Viscount, wasn't it? Of St-Noire down in South Fiellan."

I bowed. Everyone had heard of Domina Ashridge, professor emerita of Tara, probably the foremost Scholar of Classics in the Nine Worlds.

"St-Noire, St-Noire …" Domina Ashridge murmured, twinkling happily at me as she did so. She was a dumpy woman of medium height, with her grey hair braided into a poufy sort of coronet, her robes of very good quality and considerable age. I liked her immediately and wished miserably that Artos was not standing there beside me with his entire being alert as a hound on a scent.

I did not have the luck that would have made my name noted only as the First in my year at Morrowlea. No, it was—

Domina Ashridge made a happy exclamation. "Oh, you're the young man who slayed a dragon last month! The son of Jack Greenwing, aren't you?"

***

"Half an hour!" Mr. Dart hissed. "I left you alone for *half an hour!*"

"It was closer to forty minutes," I muttered truculently. We'd already had this conversation over several times, and I did not feel that Mr. Dart's criticism was entirely fair. "Did I do anything to provoke this?" I said rhetorically. "Did I move from the statue? No. Everyone came to me."

"Your fame is excessive."

"It's not my fault my ex-lover is a vindictive bitch who hires people to write plays about me!" I retorted, causing Mr. Dart to stop abruptly, Jullanar Maebh to crash into us, and several uninvolved passersby to stop and stare.

Mr. Dart spoke through gritted teeth. "Will you just stop talking, please?"

Out of the corner of my eye I saw a thin man go slinking off round a corner. I nodded tightly, hot with misery and embarrassment. I really should not have said that so loudly, or at all.

Being introduced to the greatest scholar in my field should have been a matter of great satisfaction and much rejoicing. It should not have been an endless and endlessly awkward conversation about the dragon and the play and the burden of being Jack Greenwing's only son, nor the polite disbelief when I argued for the rehabilitation of his character, all the while ever more aware that Artos the Ass had excused himself two minutes in with a look of unconcealed glee.

Mr. Dart had arrived before I'd been able to finish the conversation and had understood the problem as soon as I'd introduced him and mentioned that he'd just missed 'our acquaintance Artos'.

His arrival had delayed our departure, for Magistra Aurelia had been intrigued by his magical aura and wanted him to stay so that she could study it and discuss the questions I'd raised on his behalf with her. Mr. Dart had given her a remarkably polite smile and promised another time, as we really did not want to cause his cousin to miss her conveyance home.

For her part Jullanar Maebh was staring at me every chance she got, her expression moving between horror, speculation, and amusement as her thoughts shifted. I wasn't sure whether she was aware of the gravity of my problem and consequently hers and Mr. Dart's, but did suggest we take a shortcut she knew to the street past Picklegate where we'd told Mr. Fancy et al. to meet us.

And so here we were, lugging her trunk through narrow, twisting alleyways just outside the university district, trying to keep out of sight and out of the way of any of the people Artos might have chosen to tell about us.

About me. It was, after all, due to me that we were in danger.

I sighed and took better hold of my end of the trunk, which was quite heavy. I was impressed Jullanar Maebh had managed to bring it to meet us on her own.

"There's Mr. Cartwright,' I said in relief, spotting the valet starting down the alley towards us.

"And there's Hal," Mr. Dart added, nodding in the direction of said duke, who was some dozen feet closer to us than Mr. Cartwright. He was gesturing stiffly, but the mist had thickened again and in this warren of tall buildings not much light reached us.

I squinted, trying to make out his expression. About half a minute too late I realized he was indicating the presence of an ambush.

With my hands bound behind me I felt remarkably helpless. I had to concentrate not to stumble, and was concerned particularly for Mr. Dart, who seemed woozy from the blow he'd taken when the ambuscade poured out each cross alley.

I could only see him from the corner of my eye, and Hal and Jullanar Maebh not at all. When I turned my head to look for them my captor barked at me to keep my eyes front, giving me a clout with his truncheon to underline the order.

I complied, seething but not seeing any recourse but to do what they said for now. My heart was beating too fast, and I was a little afraid the truncheon might have cracked my shoulder blade. My left arm felt worryingly numb. I could only hope the others were in better shape.

No one interfered as we were 'arrested'. People watched with only vaguely engaged expressions, as if this were a common and not particularly interesting entertainment. Mind you, they had shown barely more reaction to the bear.

We were thrust down the side alley to a covered wagon and bundled summarily inside without so much as a by-your-leave. Unable to catch myself, I tripped forward and banged my chin on the splintery wooden bench opposite.

Someone laughed coarsely, hauling me up to sit on the bench beside them. Before I could quite catch my balance they put a sack over my head. I sneezed immediately at the mustiness and the surprise; was racked with sneezes such as I had not experienced for, oh, a good fortnight.

I blinked to find myself unable to see anything but a dim brownness. My eyes were watering, from dust and whatever grit had been in the sack before this re-use. Thumps and bumps and various curses suggested my friends had the same greeting given them. Mr. Dart started to say something, only to break off with a yelp.

"No yabbering, you lot," a man with a growling, gravelly voice said. "No one will care so long as you're alive at t'other end."

This threat effectively silenced all of us. Whatever the end of this abduction, it would not be made easier for us being beaten bloody beforehand.

I sneezed again, trying to suppress the sound. The truncheon cracked down on my already-damaged shoulder, and I could not stop the whimper that escaped.

"Quiet," the growling voice said, utterly flatly.

I shrank back against my seat as the wagon lurched into motion. My pulse was elevated, my breath coming faster, more shallowly, and bright threads of pain were radiating out from my collarbone.

And had I really slain a dragon, a month and a half ago?

A fortnight ago I had been stuffed into a barrel and conveyed to what was intended to be my death by human sacrifice.

I did not like these parallels.

I was not alone in the dark with my enemies, this time. This time my friends were there, my two best friends in all the world and Mr. Dart's new relation. I could not panic.

Mr. Dart's wild magic had saved me from the Magarran Strid, but even though he was mostly used to his dominant arm being stone, he had not regained his ability at fencing and had never loved violent action as I (to my occasional shame) did. Hal was not at all a fighter, though he had saved me from the near-total physical and emotional ruin of the end of the final examinations at Morrowlea, and was perhaps the most morally courageous person of my acquaintance, with the exception of my father.

(And who, really, could stand in the same league as Major Jack Greenwing? He had once held a border of the Empire all by himself, and for that won the Heart of Glory from the hands of the Emperor; he had come home a second time from the dead, though the first had seen him and his family undeservedly disgraced).

As for Jullanar Maebh, the newly-known Miss Dart … well, she did remind me quite a lot of Violet, but that didn't necessarily mean she was quite so lethal as the former friends we were undoubtedly now on our way to see.

I forced myself to slow down my breathing, counting up and down to five over and over again. The cart rumbled and rattled over rough cobbles and disturbingly soft bumps; the air grew close and warm and stank from whatever the bags had last been used for.

The grit and dust seemed half-familiar.

One … two … three … four … five …

I swayed around a corner, bumping shoulders with someone; both of us flinched and murmured in pain, though I wasn't sure who the other was.

Five … four … three … two … one

Something in the dust and the stench reminded me of that wild first weekend back in Ragnor Bella, when Mr. Dart had taken me for what I thought would be poaching but which turned out to be spying on a cult sacrificing a cow to the Dark Kings.

Mrs. Etaris had been right, when she said that if they had started on the sacrifices that they would not long rest content with the cows. Not even a month later I had been prepared, in some way that had left a blank in my memory and a lingering dread of small, enclosed, dark spaces, to be sacrificed on the turning-day of the Magarran Strid, on the Fallowday of the Fall.

One … two … three … four … five …

Unlike in Ragnor Bella or Ghilousette there was no evidence of the cults to the Dark Kings.

Five … four … three … two … one …

Not that I actually knew what to look for, when they weren't in the midst of obscene rites. For all I knew the dark cloaks worn by half the population of Orio City proclaimed their allegiance.

In the dark, in the must and dust and grit, I caught my breath and caught thereby a faint sickly-sweet odour in the back of my throat, and knew with a sudden certainty what these sacks had been used to convey. Wireweed.

One … two … three … four … five …

It could even have been the wireweed that had been harvested this summer from the Talgarths' estate in Ragnor Bella. Violet had come to town to oversee the theft of the harvest from the Knocker-men, if I had understood her oblique comments properly.

All that was truly clear from that weekend were the discoveries that Lark had been drugging me with wireweed and using the drug to boost her ability to steal my magic for her own purposes, and that

I should not, regardless of my instincts or desire, trust Violet.

Five … four … three … two … one …

We had run straight into some of the last vines, Mr. Dart and I, running away from the cult. We had met the Lady (one of the Ladies: I thought it was Lady Jessamine of Alinor, Mr. Dart still maintained it was the Lady of the Green and White; Magistra Aurelia Anyra had been no help). Mr. Dart had saved me from a perilous fascination and lost his arm to petrification in so doing, and we had run into the Talgarths' gardens before falling into their moat.

One … two … three … four … five …

After an interminable length of time my shoulder subsided to an angry throbbing. I concentrated on my breathing and my counting until I could force my hands to relax, though neither my nerves nor the bindings would let me entirely unlace my fingers. I settled for flexing them against each other as best as I could. My left hand was not responding well.

One … two … three … four … five …

Five … four … three … two … one …

As had become my practice when this fear of enclosures struck, I started to recite poetry to myself. After a few stanzas of Ariadne nev Lingarel's *On Being Incarcerated in Orio Prison* I faltered mentally, bit my lip, and then resolutely turned my thoughts to Fitzroy Angursell's *Aurora*. There was only so much dramatic irony I could take at one time.

***

I felt sick and dizzy (and disinclined, even more, to appreciate the irony that my first in-person encounter with the governor's palace of Orio City was as a prisoner) when the cart eventually jerked to a halt. We were man-handled out. Clearly, from the muttered comments of the guards, I was not the only one whose limbs were numb and unresponsive. They took no care of us, which meant I, at least, could look forward to several new bruises come the morning.

With the sack over my head little but sounds indicated where we might be. We began in an enclosed yard of some sort; a trickle of cold air made its way through a seam. We were then pushed through a doorway. I fell, tripping on the threshold, and slammed my chin into a hard stone floor. My captor sniggered and yanked me upright by grabbing hold of the back of my coat, making my cravat catch tightly around my throat. I gasped as silently as I could for air, like a stranded fish.

Our boots echoed sharply after that as we must have been led along long bare stone halls, up stairs and down them, and around and around a long coiling ramp. I lost track of our possible height after the fifth staircase up and third down. The coiled ramp made me think of the long, angst-ridden passage in the middle of *On Being Incarcerated* where the fair Ariadne spoke of the invidious spiral of despair.

Some part of me refused to give into the agonizingly slow build-up to sneezing. I held my breath and counted my footsteps and pressed my tongue to the roof of my mouth and thought of my father, who never gave up no matter what happened. He'd laughed at my tales of how I had basically sneezed my way through Morrowlea, and revealed that my paternal grandfather had been known to have hayfever. Something I could share with a man I'd never met besides a propensity to addictive tendencies, I supposed.

I sneezed, nevertheless, when the sack was ripped off my head, and the dust and grit of the dried remnants of the wireweed mixed with an all-too-familiar scent of smoke and perfume.

I sneezed, eyes streaming, bent over as my shoulder cramped and spiked with pain. At length I was able to stand, breathless and begrimed, unable to wipe my face but at least able to lift my head. A blur of colour resolved itself into a dozen people in jewel-toned velvets, all grouped around a pair of thrones.

On my left lounged a young man a little older than me. He was dressed more richly than I'd ever seen anyone in real life, and in a style again more fantastic and less practical than the students. His hose was a sort of dull gold colour with an odd greenish sheen to it; his codpiece (of course he wore a codpiece) literally gilded. His doublet was red velvet with white satin puffed through its slashed sleeves; the sword at his hip was a fantasy of gold and rubies. Over this he wore a voluminous robe of thick velvet the colour of orange marigolds, which was lined with white satin and trimmed with ermine. He wore high-heeled shoes the same orange as his outer robe, with gold and ruby buckles.

All this I saw in one glance before the woman sitting in the throne next to him trilled out a laugh even more familiar to me than the smoke whirling through the room.

I looked at her, at her oval face and dark amber eyes, her wickedly curving eyebrows and the extravagantly curled and braided dark hair. She wore the pale blue she had always favoured, this one an iridescent shot silk over creamy underskirts. Corseting exaggerated her curves and narrowed her waist; seed pearls dotted with tiny sparkling diamonds accentuated every line, especially around a scandalously low décolletage. She wore a sort of diaphanous veil draped around her neck that did nothing but draw attention to her attributes.

My first thought was that she had surely not been quite that beautiful when I had last seen her, nor looked quite that mature; my second that she wore thin silk in a room where everyone else was robed in velvets, and why was she not cold?

"Oh, Jemis," said Lark, lifting an elegant hand with her elegant ivory pipe to her lips and blowing a smoke ring into the space between us, "how simply marvellous of you to join us."

CHAPTER TWENTY-ONE
And the Prison

"Lark," I said, inclining my head curtly. "I can't say it's entirely a surprise to see you."

She smiled; several people tittered. Lark leaned against the padded back of her throne, blowing smoke rings and watching me. I could feel a strange pressure building, making me want to keep my eyes on her, and her alone.

Memories passed through my mind in a bright pageant: Lark in her huge straw hat in the garden; Lark curled up beside me as we read together next to the fire; Lark at the centre of the table in the refectory, regal as any queen holding court.

The smoke was sweet-scented, cutting through the thick perfume in the air like a breath of freshness, full of the more innocent years at Morrowlea, where we had laughed and loved and learned and made merry without heed of the outside world. I stood there, watching her, the memories crowding faster the longer I looked at her once-so-beloved face, those melting amber eyes, that smile.

The first time I had noticed her had been the first Winterturn Ball. She'd been wearing pale blue that evening, too, and I'd thought she looked like the Lady of Winter, with black ivy-berries and white hellebores and red holly in her hair. I'd crossed the dancing floor to meet her, to ask her to dance, and she had turned those laughing eyes up at me and blew a ring of smoke around my head and I was hers.

She was smiling down at me now, the smoke wreathing her, reaching me. I was close but not close enough, aching to reach out to her, unable to move my hands, barely able to move feet or head. Surely her skin had never been so flawless, her eyes so large and brilliant, her hair so lustrous? Surely her lips had never been quite that full, her proportions quite that perfect, her waist quite that small?

I shook my head at those niggling criticisms. Lark had never liked criticism, not of any sort. She would sulk … How prettily she sulked, I remembered, remembering afternoons spent cajoling her back into good humour, the rewards of kisses and caresses I received for my patience …

"It's been far too long," said Lark, and then looked over to one side and smiled. "Hasn't it, my dear? Look who has come to visit us!"

I turned, annoyed that she should smile at someone else, and felt as if I'd been doused with cold water.

"V—V—" I started, then stammered to a halt when I recalled I had not properly greeted Lark, and then, as I saw Violet pause in her approach, then continue on to stand at the side of the throne, my mind started to clear under the influence of a rising anger.

It was no grand conflagration, or not yet, but it was enough, this fanning ember, to keep my mind my own. I was able to stare coldly at Violet, to remember the presence of the richly garbed young man on the throne, to remember that I was bound and injured and captive all because Lark did not handle jealousy well.

It had, after all, been Violet whom I had crossed that dance floor to meet.

Violet was wearing a gown of similar design to Lark's, though hers was not so generous in its revelations and was, moreover, of a rich emerald green. Over this she wore open robes similar to those of the students or the other members of this court; hers was velvet of a green so dark as to be nearly black. Her hair was up in a less fancy version of Lark's style; a gold pin held a sheer black veil in place. She did not have the pearls or diamonds embroidered on her bodice, but instead faint gold patterns I could not read from this distance.

All told she looked like a dimmer, duller version of the woman beside her, who in close comparison fairly crackled with energy.

"I see you remember Violet, Jemis," Lark said smugly, caressing Violet's arm with the hand that did not hold the ivory pipe. Lark wore easily a dozen rings on each hand, each of them set with an opal that caught the light in rainbow flashes.

I could feel a hum of magic around them, and wondered what exactly they represented. I had never investigated gemstones, could not remember what Hope—the only student in our year who studied them—had had to say about their magical properties. It was not something people spent a lot of time on, even at Morrowlea, these days. None of my poets had used more than the commonest for their symbolism.

Though now I thought that I wondered if I had missed something in Ariadne nev Lingarel's poem ...

"Jemis," said Violet in a cool voice, curtseying very slightly. When she lifted her skirts to perform the gesture I saw her one of her shoes, a silk slipper in a lovely lavender embroidered with green to match her dress.

It was odd she'd choose to wear any garments that showed the Lady's colours, I thought idly even as I stared between Lark and Violet and wondered why it was Violet's entrance that had broken Lark's pervasive beguilement. I could feel the magic humming in the air, along threads that stretched from her rings out past my line of sight, as if she were the spider in the centre of her web.

My eyes turned involuntarily to the man in the orange robes. Lark saw the direction of my gaze and trilled out her laugh again. He turned his head at the sound, smiling up at her with such a besotted expression I nearly vomited.

Lark caressed his face with the bowl of her pipe, then when he leaned into its touch, eyes half-closed with obvious pleasure, she tilted his head back with the stem and gave him a deep, slow, kiss. When Lark released him he slouched back into his cushions and smiled dazedly at her.

"My betrothed," she said, in a low, sultry voice. She was looking at me as she said it, as if I were supposed to respond with jealous anger. I could feel some distant echo of the emotion, but was mostly preoccupied with outrage and a sick desire to know whether I had looked so utterly mindless when I had been with her.

Please say I had never looked at her with *quite* that abject devotion.

"My love," said the man.

His voice was disappointingly good, as mellifluous as his face was symmetrical. He was of Shaian descent, though not quite so dark as Hal, his wiry hair trimmed close. If his posture had been better and his face not so vacant he would have cut a very fine figure, not unworthy of being called a prince.

So this was the new governor of Orio City, who was stealing all Hal's allies away from him.

"My dear," Lark cooed. One of the assembled courtiers sighed with something very like appreciation.

I cast a wary glance around the room. There were only half a dozen courtiers in truth; the rest were guards. Four of the courtiers were in their forties or older, distinguished in their appearance, seeming as if they ought to have been sober sensible counsellors for the former governor. They gazed indulgently at their prince and his lady, their eyes as doting as a senile grandparent's. (Not that I had ever had such a look directed at me. My grandmother was a terrifying virago fully in control of her intelligence, even if she seemed half-mad in other respects.)

The other two were even younger than we were, barely adolescent. They had very different skin tones and features, so I assumed were unrelated, though their expressions were equally vacuous, the visual equivalent of tittering.

All six wore necklaces set with opals.

Lark drew my eye back to her with an imperious gesture. I tensed, but it was Violet who responded by walking over to a table a few feet away, where she picked up a plate of chocolate truffles to bring back to the thrones.

I blinked at the surreality of this, especially as Lark then proceeded to feed one to her betrothed, laughing and smiling as if no one else were in the room when he mock-snatched the plate out of her hands and half-turned as if to guard them from her. I felt deeply uncomfortable at the whole scene, knowing just how many times it had played out at Morrowlea with me in the position of the consort. They were even the same damned chocolates! She must have had them sent from home, quite against the rules.

I'd probably known they were against the rules when she gave them to me, but any reaction beyond pleasure was buried deep in the fog of advanced wireweed addiction.

"There, that's sorted," Lark said once the governor-prince was thoroughly occupied with the chocolates. I watched him in sick fascination as he ate each with enormous, even disturbing, gusto.

"Don't mind him, Jemis," Lark said brightly, drawing my attention back to her. She smiled at me; I could feel the magic pulsing against whatever protection Violet had placed on me. (Had it been Violet? Or had Hal or even Mr. Dart used the interruption of her entrance to cast something?) I did not quite want to demonstrate I was so protected, so I smiled back at her; if it was not so adoring or so witless as it might have been in the past, well, she did not seem unduly concerned.

"Jemis," Hal said from behind me, followed by a heartfelt *oof.*

"Hal!" Lark cried, "How could I have neglected to greet you? What a wonderful surprise to have you here as well. I've been hoping Jemis would show up, but I never expected *you* to come along with him. No, don't try to speak yet—the guards can be a little protective, you know."

I lifted my eyes to meet Violet's. She was watching us with her face vaguely attentive, as disengaged as any of the citizenry to our apprehension. Her body language was calm, her eyes tranquil, her hands still.

And yet …

Lark was talking again, praising herself for her own cleverness in catching us. Apparently she had been sure Jack Lindsary's play would be bring me to Orio City for vengeance sooner or later, and was very pleased with herself for the idea of commissioning him.

I listened desultorily, much more interested in the enigma that was Violet. For all her beauty and her surface brilliance Lark's depths were hollow: she used what must have been a potent gift at magic to steal other's power for her own use, used rhetoric instead of truth to convince; seemed, indeed, to have fallen into the trap that historical figure after historical figure had fallen into, of believing power worth any cost.

I wondered how she avoided the consequences of wireweed herself. Perhaps that was why she needed to steal other's magic? Wireweed had given me a kind of borrowed brilliance (a false summer, the old man outside the Guildmarket Hall had called it), the sensation of elevated wit and insightfulness, as well as an incredible soaring delight focused, always, on Lark's company. If the drug acted the same for her, but she was able to siphon other's magic for it to burn instead, then … well, I could understand why someone might pursue such a path.

If one were totally uncaring of moral rectitude, then yes, sacrificing their lives to your own personal gain—and Lark had gained from it, had gained beauty and power both magical and now political—made perfect sense.

At length she stopped congratulating herself on the catch and turned to the more pressing matter of what she was planning to do now that she had me. The governor-prince had finished his chocolates and was now playing with a small hand mirror. Lark smiled at him and switched her pipe to her other hand so she could card her fingers through his hair. He looked up at her for a moment in melting adoration and then, when she shifted position to face me, tilted the mirror until he could see her profile in it, whereupon he settled contentedly into meditating on it.

I could take small comfort in the fact that I knew I had never fallen that far, at least.

Lark said, "Now, Jemis, I know you will take particular joy in being my guest here. I did not expect to have Hal as well, let alone your other friends, but I'm sure they will be glad to keep you company."

She paused, so I said, "And how long do you expect us to stay?"

She trilled. "Oh, my darling Jemis, how you make me laugh! I have missed your company so these last months. Can you believe it has been over half a year since we last saw each other? You cannot imagine I will let you go so easily now that I have you back again!"

"It seems a lot of effort for a broken relationship."

There was a faint stir in the audience. Apparently I was not supposed to be able to be so snarky to Lark. Her face hardened into a cold and cruel smile. I did not like the knowledge that I had once found that smile attractive.

"My dear Jemis, we will not discuss all the reasons I have for wanting you here. Suffice it to say that your fate will ensure that no one ever thinks to speak, let alone act, against me."

I felt, finally, the first stirrings of the cold clear world of mortal danger come closing in. I should not welcome it so, I knew, it was as dangerous an addiction and quite potentially as fatal as the wireweed. But oh, for whatever reason it was I had inherited my father's love of dire circumstances.

In that mode I could slay a dragon with a cake knife or cross a seventy-foot chasm on a narrow tree-trunk. My eyes flicked around the room, assessing possibilities and pitfalls. My hands were bound, my left shoulder badly bruised—I could feel it, but no longer seemed bound by the pain, in this state of mind—my friends behind me were equally compromised. There were a dozen guards, each armed with sword and knife and halberd, each wearing chain-mail surcoats and light helms. There were the half-dozen courtiers, almost certainly bound by enchantments through those opal jewelry.

This was quite possibly the worst situation I had ever found myself in. Every other time I'd at least had my hands free.

Well, except for that horrible night spent in the barrel. That time I'd had to wait until the situation changed before I could begin to rescue myself, before Red Myrta and the Chancellor of Morrowlea had arrived to assist.

Violet's expression closed off, became guarded, when I looked intently at her. No help there, I deduced, disappointed even through the cool disinterest of my current state. She dropped her gaze away from mine, shifted position so that her lavender slipper peeped out again.

Or—no direct help.

"Always so defiant," Lark murmured, that cold, cruel smile turned full on me. She rose from her throne, hand trailing down the side of her betrothed's face as it fell. He lifted his gaze from the mirror to watch her, his eyes on how her hips swayed as she stepped lightly past Violet to the table with the chocolates. There was something electric about her, like a thunderstorm about to break, though all she was doing was choosing a bonbon. The ivory pipe emitted a thin stream of smoke that coiled and became impossibly thick as it slowly settled.

At last she chose a truffle and sashayed over to me. The smoke wreathed around her, smelling of flowers; the magic gathered thickly about her. There was no way I could have moved from her path even if I could have come up with some way of escaping.

"That's better," she said softly, stopping beside me. She took the pipe in the hand with the truffle and used the other to caress my face as she had so often before. With the example of the governor-prince in front of me I tried to resist my habitual and unintentional physical response, but even without the wireweed—and I did not trust that smoke in the least—my body knew hers, and reacted accordingly.

"Yes, that's right," she said, her too-large eyes unblinking on mine. "I know how you have missed me, Jemis. I know how deep your hunger goes, how hollow your heart is, how thirsty you are. There is nothing that will satisfy it but what I can offer, you know, nothing that will ever truly please you save for what I alone can give."

"There are other pleasures," I said with effort, willing myself ineffectually to step back, turn my head, close my eyes. Willpower did nothing. I stayed staring at her.

"Food, for instance?" she said mockingly, lifting the truffle to my lips. Its scent was heady and seductive, as well-remembered and as well-loved as Lark herself had been, less tainted by memory than the smoke. I could still like chocolate, without Lark, though she had laughed at me for being addicted to her confections.

I would have resisted longer but she brushed her fingers down my nose, across my lips.

"Lark," I said involuntarily, half a groan as my body responded eagerly.

She pushed the chocolate into my mouth. It felt intimate, arousing, the chocolate melting against my tongue, a bright burst of flavour that warmed through all my extremities.

It was easily the best chocolate I had ever eaten.

I shivered, mind warring with my body, trying desperately to keep my thoughts my own even as I could feel the magic humming around me, sinking into my skin. Whatever protection whoever had cast on me was too subtle for this crass assault.

When I was breathing too fast, only pride keeping me from begging her to stop, she lifted up the pipe to draw a deep mouthful of smoke. She blew it directly in my face, where it got in my eyes and nose and mouth. I breathed in the familiar scent, more incense than ash, as my eyes blinked hard against the irritation. When I opened them again Lark's appearance wavered with wasting shadows, then solidified into something inhumanly beautiful and cold.

"You hurt me, Jemis," she said, her voice still sultry and seductive. "You humiliated me. You broke my faith. For these things you will pay."

I could not utter anything intelligible. When I opened my mouth she pressed her finger against my lips and my words stuttered into a low moan I could not believe came from me.

"You will pay with your magic and your mind and your body, Jemis Greenwing, until when I am done with you not even the monsters in the sea will take your corpse. You think you have friends who can help you? I have your friends here as hostages, and if you think I will not use them, think again on why it is the Lady in Nên Corovel does not leave her isle to aid those fools who think she is theirs. You think you have courage, wit, strength?"

I stared at her, feeling every inch of me helpless and stupid and weak.

"You know, I think, that this palace can be a prison that no one has ever escaped. I will give you some time to think over your situation, and decide how you want to die."

"I … what?"

"Come now, my darling, we have only just begun playing. You have seen the unfortunates on the street, I am sure?" She waited, so I nodded, not wanting to say anything, not sure if I could manage anything better than "What?" again.

She trilled again. "Had you not realized that you're, oh, two or maybe even three doses away from that fate? My dear Jemis, do not make me think you are stupid!"

I could not say anything at all to this. Was I truly that close to the fatal sleep?

"Yes," she said, stepping closer again, but my ardour had cooled abruptly with this revelation and her proximity did not warm it again. My limbs felt heavy and sluggish, but my thoughts were beginning to move more swiftly.

"Or is it one dose, now?" she murmured, licking the smears of chocolate from her fingers. "Perhaps still two. It's hard to say in your case. There haven't been many who have lasted so long as you under the influence, on the one hand, and on the other, you've had a bit of a break, haven't you? The scholar in me is curious. Are the effects slower or quicker, stronger or weaker, longer-lasting or the same or shorter?"

The chocolate. The smoke was a camouflage, or perhaps what mitigated the effects for herself; the chocolates were where the drug was concealed.

Just how many people had she taken a trickle of magic from? I was the only one given leave (given encouragement ... hell, subtly forced ...) to eat the chocolates regularly; everyone else received them as a benison for some favour won.

"Quicker, it would seem, and likely stronger as well," she said, humming happily. "Remember, Jemis, as you wait for the next audience I grant you, that this is the easy way to go. Be careful you do not give me cause to choose the hard way. You won't like it nearly so much."

CHAPTER TWENTY-TWO
I Formulate a Plan

The sacks were put back on our heads and we were led as roughly as before out of the room and back into the echoing stone halls. Despite the fact that clearly nothing about our situation had changed, I could feel my mood lifting. By the time we reached our destination—or at least the room into which we were unceremoniously thrust and locked, if the slam and clicks and dire echoing clangs were any indication—I was downright ecstatic.

Everything seemed so *easy*.

I was even whistling as I set my thoughts to the problem of releasing my bound wrists. I could not really feel my left shoulder, which was an improvement, though I reckoned I would have to find a sling to match Mr. Dart's if I wished to get anything done. The question of whether I felt the need to colour-coordinate such an accessory, as Mr. Dart did, occupied me for a few moments even as I wriggled around on the floor until I could bump into someone.

"Hello, Jemis," Hal said in a tired voice. "What can I do for you?"

"How did you know it was me?" I asked even as I manoeuvred myself until my right boot was somewhere on him.

"You only whistled like that for most of three months last year," he said, sounding even more tired. "Also, and I realize you're probably not in the best state to care about such social niceties, but you've just stuck your foot in my lap."

I snickered at the thought. "Oh, sorry. Where are your hands?"

"Not in my lap, I'm afraid. Though your boot—oof—still is, I notice."

"Yes, yes, I'm moving it," I said, rolling over to my good elbow to gain a little leverage. "I want you to tell me when you can feel my boot with your hands."

"That sounds incredibly rude," Jullanar Maebh said thoughtfully from somewhere across the room.

I burst out into a full, hearty laugh. It felt splendid. "I do apologize, Miss Dart. It's only that I have a knife in my boot, and if Hal can reach it—"

"You could have led with that, honestly," Hal muttered. After a moment of us both squirming around I felt firm fingers digging around the top of my boot. "Right," he said, "I've got the knife. Um … I'm not sure I can cut my own bonds without slashing my wrists in the process. Any volunteers to go first?"

I swivelled around until we bumped our backs against each other. Then it was a simple matter of inching my hand over, ignoring the shooting pains coming from my shoulder, and guiding my fingers down Hal's arm to reach the leather-wrapped hilt of my knife. "Here we go," I said. "You hold it still, Hal, and I'll move my wrists up and down until the rope splits."

"The Emperor," Hal said flatly.

"You always call on the Emperor when you feel put-upon, did you realize?" I said, smiling into the dim brown murkiness of the sack. "When you're truly moved you call on the Lady."

He merely grunted. I grinned, even though he couldn't see it, and kept on with the rope-cutting.

"You're not bleeding out over there, are you?" Mr. Dart called. "We're perishing of curiosity on this side of the room."

"Haven't cut myself yet," I replied. "Aha! There's the trick. One moment, Hal, while I get this sack off my head, then I'll do yours."

I fumbled a few times as the blood started circulating properly in my arms again. I decided that it would be better to wait a moment to use the knife—no sense in being too hasty and hurting someone—and used the time to remove the sacks from my friends' heads. "There," I said, helping Mr. Dart to a more upright position, since his stone arm seemed to have unbalanced him, and carefully straightening Jullanar Maebh's skirts from where they'd rucked up.

"In your own time," Hal said.

"I'm coming," I said, smiling at his familiar sardonic tone. "Where did the knife go?"

"I think you knocked it under the chair, there," Mr. Dart said.

"Thank you." I found the knife under a spindly but exceedingly decorative chair in the Middle Eletanyrian style. It was a little awkward getting Hal's hands into position without using my left hand, but I managed in the end. As I cut carefully at the ropes I said, "I must admit I was already admiring of how you have learned to accommodate your stone arm, Mr. Dart, but I am finding a greater appreciation now that I seem to have injured mine, and it's not even my dominant hand."

"Your stone arm?" Jullanar Maebh said faintly as I went over to her, leaving Hal to shake out his hands and shoulders.

"I do apologize, Miss Dart," I said to her, "I should have come to you first, as a lady, though Hal does take formal precedence and was more proximate to the knife."

"Proximate?" Hal said. "Jemis …"

"There you go," I said to Jullanar Maebh, and turned to Mr. Dart, who was staring at me in quiet perturbation. "Mr. Dart, if you don't mind twisting a little to the side … thank you."

"You're welcome," he said, in a voice nearly as sardonic as Hal's. I grinned at him as I cut the last of his bonds, then slid the knife back into the sheath in my boot. "That was very cunning of you."

"My father gave me the knife before we left," I said by way of explanation, and then turned around in a circle to look more carefully at the room we were imprisoned in.

It matched the spindly Middle Eletanyrian chair, which suggested the furnishings were original. The ceiling was high and plastered, the plaster worked into elaborate rondels and borders. The walls were covered in silvery-grey slubbed silk with the exception of a formidable white-limestone fireplace surround.

A spotted silvered-glass mirror with an elaborate silver-gilt plasterwork frame took up most of the space over the mantle. I tried it experimentally, but it refused to budge so much as an inch from its place. The fireplace itself was closed off by a fine ornamental metal grille that seemed soldered in place. Behind the grille a white-gold flame burned on a single log that did not seem to create ash or be consumed. It threw a good heat into the room.

The visible part of the floor was tiled in tiny mosaic pieces that depicted a series of linked squares in blue and grey. Most of the centre of the room was occupied by a thick if dusty wool and silk carpet, again in blue and grey with silver thread, which must have been made specially for the room since it matched the linked square motif.

The furnishings consisted of three chairs with curved legs and lyre-shaped backs, their upholstery matching the rug, and two equally spindly side tables inlaid with mother-of-pearl and silver wire. On one of these was a silver ewer of water and three handleless cups in white bone china.

No doubt all this was Lark's idea of a joke. Someone would have to sit on the floor and share a cup or go without.

"It's not much of a prison cell," I said.

"Except for the fact it has no windows and no doors," said Hal.

"Except for that," I agreed, and could not help but laugh aloud at the thought that of all the rooms in the palace Lark could have decided to lock us in, she'd chosen this one.

"I fail to understand why you're laughing," Jullanar Maebh said snippily. "Or why you're suddenly in such a good mood, for that matter. We are now hostages to your good behaviour in the most notorious prison in Northwest Oriole!"

"He's high on wireweed," Mr. Dart said. "The Lady knows what's going through his head right now."

"I'm right here," I said, "and just because I feel good for once doesn't mean my mind has stopped working."

Jullanar Maebh raised her eyebrows at me. "All you're doing is staring at the room."

"I'm identifying it," I replied haughtily, to their obvious confusion. "It seems like it's the Silver-Square Room, but I am wondering if it might not be the Hearth. What do you think this design is supposed to be, Hal, on this grille, here?"

He heaved a great sigh and left off massaging his hands to come look at the fireplace with me. "I suppose I might as well, given that there's no way out of here unless they un-magic the door," he said.

"Does your magic help?" Mr. Dart asked him, helping Jullanar

Maebh to her feet and drawing her to stand next to us.

"Do you think this pattern here looks like ivy?" I asked Hal, pointing at the sinuous shape to the right of the screen.

"Not really, no. To either of you." Hal looked at Mr. Dart, smiling apologetically. "Sorry. I don't mean to be so short. There's something in here that dampens my abilities … I can feel that there's magic all around, but not … I can't touch it."

"It's a prison," I said. "What do you think that is, then?"

"A snake, maybe?" Jullanar Maebh suggested.

"If that's a snake, does that look like a bird to you?"

"A dove, maybe."

"Perfect," I said, confirming that it was actually the Silver-Square Room and not the Hearth (which would have ivy and hawthorn for the Lady of the Green and White, as well as being disappointing for a room that was the occasion for that famous, soaring, splendid lyrical passage), and crossed the room to look at the corner diagonally opposite.

Yes, there was a place where the pattern of tiles in the mosaic changed from blue and grey to one single line of white. I followed the white from the corner as it wove its way through the squares, careful to always keep to my original line and not stray into any of the other palest-grey or white tiles that made up other sections of the pattern.

"Roll up the carpet, would you, please?" I called to my friends, who were still grouped by the fireplace.

"What? Why?" said Jullanar Maebh. Hal and Mr. Dart exchanged a glance. I smiled at them.

"Please?'

"We really don't have anything else to do," Mr. Dart said after a moment.

"Conserve our strength?" said Hal, dryly.

"I thought you wanted to escape?" I said in exasperation, keeping my finger on the correct line so I didn't lose it. "Will you please roll the carpet up out of my way?"

"Escape? What do you mean?" said Mr. Dart, moving the chairs out of the way even as Jullanar Maebh and Hal bent over the edge of the carpet and started to roll it up.

"Hal should understand," I said, following the line into the centre of the pattern. Each time it came to another link one had to notice whether my line went 'under' or 'over' the other; after thirteen of these intersections my line came to an end in a 'T' shape, and I took the right-hand branch. After twelve I took the left; after another eleven I was back over by the fireplace and took the right again, and so on around the room until at last I came down to the last four interchanges. At length the last line led me out of the floor and back over to the fireplace to finish the pattern at the corner of one specific stone in the surround.

"All right, you can lay the carpet back down and put the chairs back," I said, counting upwards and over according to the number of syllables in the haiku sequence set into the middle of the stanzas describing the Silver-Square Room. This led me to a stone that appeared no different from any of the rest. I laid my palm on it, heart beating with excitement.

"Right," said Mr. Dart kicking the last corner of the carpet down. "Will you explain now?"

"Certainly," I replied. "Hal, what did I write my final paper at Morrowlea on?"

He made a face. "Some damnably boring poem about architecture. Jemis, I'm sorry, no one read your final paper—not even Lark!"

"Violet did," I retorted, but forgave him. I couldn't give details of his final paper on all the many, many things to be learned about the genus *Ilex*.

"Jemis," said Mr. Dart warningly.

"Yes, yes. I studied Classical puzzle poetry, Miss Dart," I explained to her; she seemed unimpressed. "I focused in particular on a subgenre known as architectural poetry, which can be either poetry about architecture or poetry that uses architectural principles for its own purposes, usually to make some esoteric point."

"And your point now is?" she said.

"My final paper argued, admittedly in a hypothetical fashion, that one particular poet had used her poem both to describe the building in which she was held as an allegory of her emotional and spiritual state and—this being my particular insight—to give a full blueprint as to the actual physical layout of the prison."

They all stared at me. I grinned at them and tapped the stone I was touching seven times, short and long and long and short and short and long and long, the rhythm of the metre the poet used for this stanza. The stone grew briefly warm under my fingers and then subsided as a faint click from the direction of the fireplace made itself known.

I grinned at them as I took two steps over and lifted the bottom of the mirror up to reveal a passage stretching back into the stonework that had not been there before.

"The poet was Ariadne nev Lingarel, and her poem was *On Being Incarcerated in Orio Prison*, and it would seem as if my hypothesis is quite provably correct."

CHAPTER TWENTY-THREE
A Coat of Claret Velvet

The passage was rather awkward to get up into, given that neither Mr. Dart nor I were able to use one of our arms, but Hal and Jullanar Maebh hoisted us up (none of us being very sanguine about the structural integrity of the Middle Eletanyrian chairs, and I rather liked the idea of Lark's minions, or even Lark herself, being totally puzzled about our disappearance from a room with no doors or windows or furniture moved out of place). We had to crawl for the first few yards, which my shoulder and developing bruises certainly did not like, but it was not long, for all that, before we came to a vaulted room where we could all stand and contemplate things.

At least, I did. The others stood and stared at me.

"Well," I said, smiling happily at them. "Isn't this fun! It's not every day you get to prove a literary theory."

"Yes, yes, you can write it up for *The Annals of Classical Literature*," Jullanar Maebh said. "*After* we've escaped the inescapable prison."

"Not that I wish to put a damper on your enthusiasm, Jemis, but I seem to recall you saying that Ariadne nev Lingarel died here," Mr. Dart said.

I frowned. "Yes, that is a bit of a puzzle, but then again I didn't finish working out the entire poem. There is a section at the heart of the Spiral of Despair that I think hides deeper meaning …"

"The Emperor," Hal said.

"No, no, Ariadne was definitely against the Emperor of the day. That was why she was in prison."

"The Lady," Mr. Dart said, and then turned to Hal. "Was he like this all through Morrowlea?"

"Towards the end, yes," replied Hal, in a slightly constrained voice.

I raised my eyebrows at them and then turned my back on them to peruse the chamber. A row of skylights some ten feet above our heads let in daylight and illuminated a space of stark simplicity. The five ribs came together in a gothic-arched point; a five-petalled flower not dissimilar from the one on my Crimson Lake ring was carved on the boss.

We had come out of an entrance that had faded back into stone as soon as we stopped paying attention to it. I thought for a few minutes about the poem, sifting through what I had spent half a year trying to disentangle of its interconnections.

"Right," Jullanar Maebh said. "Where next?"

"Next we need Violet," I said, finding the ammonite without any difficulty (this section of the poem, near the beginning, was very nearly obvious; but then finding the room with no doors in the first place was not) and twisting it first one way and then the next. ("Crescent and re-crescent shadows …")

Hal spluttered. "Violet! Why?"

"I don't have the entire poem memorized," I said reasonably. "She'll have a copy. Also, I believe she's on our side. She was wearing the Lady's colours just now."

***

Despite their vigorous protests, I was the only one who had the slightest idea how to go anywhere, and so they perforce had to follow me. I was glad that the numerous enchantments on the building undoubtedly hid our voices. Historical records suggested the prison's magic made it so no one in the palace was ever aware of what happened on the other side unless they were keyed into one of the two ways to cross between. Once the guards had left us behind and sealed the doors against us, we were, according to all accounts, stuck.

"The Palace was built in the reign of the Empress Dangora III," I said, following a trail of scallop shapes through what seemed ordinary, if extraordinarily cold, corridors. It was winter outside, I reminded myself, kicking at a thin layer of glittering dust that rose up at our passage and fell again in undisturbed layers as if we had never passed by. There would be no telling if our paths crossed or re-crossed, or indeed if there were anyone else in here.

"There were three primary architects in the first ten years, but eventually the construction was taken over by an architect from Zunidh called Ihuranuë, whose name is usually abbreviated to Irany."

Mr. Dart lifted his head from a whispered discussion with Hal to stare at me. "Not Irany who designed the mythical Labyrinth of Dreams to trap the Snow Fae?"

"The very same," I said, pleased. "Though it's not actually Snow—remember our discussion of *ebraöni*? That meant *mountain*, or *cloud*, or the *wool pulled over your eyes* …"

"Back on subject, Jemis," Hal said sternly, though his eyes were twinkling at this reminder of the many evenings at Morrowlea spent meandering through every subject under the sun.

"It's relevant," I protested, as I had so often back then.

"Explain, then."

"'Snow' is one translation, certainly, but it also means 'starfall' or 'diamond'. The Neighbours who invaded the Empire came in the winter, but they claimed they were looking for a sacred diamond that had been stolen by Damar the Bold, back when the Empire was first expanding. They claimed it was hidden—"

"Unless you think it's hidden here, I don't see how this is relevant."

I frowned at the thought, some very distant connecting ringing in my mind. "No … I don't think … though now you mention it, I wonder if that stone the cultists wanted …"

"Jemis."

I shook myself, eyes on the rising and falling glitter. Diamond, starfall, snow. And on the walls, ivy for binding. Not real ivy, but wonderful mosaics. I wished I knew more of magic; I was sure each stone was set with sigils for arcane purpose. "Right. Once we're out of here. Anyway, yes, Ihuranuë was the architect of the Labyrinth used to trap the Snow Fae and thereby turn back the fifth of the great Terrors of Astandalas. After the war with the Kingdom was over the Labyrinth was reportedly dismantled and lost to legend."

"But? I sense there's a 'but' coming," Hal said.

"But in her extreme old age—she lived to be over a hundred and twenty, which everyone reckoned was a curse from the Good Neighbours because it was a terrible lingering death—"

"Jemis."

"I'm getting there. In her old age, Ihuranuë had some sort of falling out with the Imperial University in Astandalas and in a fit of pique left all her possessions to Morrowlea. By then she had mostly been forgotten, the Labyrinth having passed into legendary status and the wars with the Kingdom forgotten but for the tithe the Queen sent to the Emperor. Architecture was not in vogue at Morrowlea at the time, and her papers were stacked in boxes and set in a back room of the Archives, and left there, unopened and uninvestigated, until I spent one winter cataloguing them. Whereupon I discovered that she had had all of the earlier construction torn down and rebuilt according to her plans. This was her last great design."

"Don't tell us," said Mr. Dart.

I grinned at him. "It's hard not to see why it's always been called an inescapable prison, isn't it? And might go a long way to explaining why Ariadne nev Lingarel decided to spend her entire lifetime studying it. She was Alinorel, you know."

"Even granting all that, how do you expect to find Violet? She's not going to be on this side."

"She was wearing the Lady's colours," I said.

"So you say. Green, white …"

"Lavender on her slippers."

"Sounds like the folk song," Jullanar Maebh said, humming a few bars.

> *Green in the spring, hey dill dilly O!*
> *Lavender's blue, O down dilly O!*
> *White in the winter, hey dill dilly O!*
> *Lavender's grey, O down dilly O!*

"Exactly. She'll be in the Imperial Reception Room for use in the summer. That, for your information, is the only place prisoners were ever able to meet with visitors or officials. We turn right here," I added, seeing a sprig of holly tucked into the mosaic near the ceiling.

(And hadn't that been fun, figuring out that the intensity of colours described in the poem referred to directions: paler meant look down, darker look up, warmer to the front, cooler to the rear, primaries to the left, secondaries to the right, and metals, rainbows, and wood colours suggested three entirely different sets of rules.)

After a long few minutes where I recited the stanzas in my head to be sure I wouldn't miss a turn, we came to a sharp left turn. I turned right, where the mosaic formed a border around a tall oval mirror set in the wall. This one was bronze, and did not reflect us, but instead a room that seemed to be inverted over us.

A person dressed in red sat in it with a book in her hand.

"And there she is," Mr. Dart said, shaking his head. "She told you not to trust her, Jemis."

"I think she's playing a deep game."

"You're high on wireweed!"

"That doesn't mean my mind is totally compromised," I said. "Have I not brought you here?"

That silenced them. I frowned, turning over the description of Ariadne nev Lingarel meeting her brother for the last time. I had not been able to decipher any deeper meanings from this section, and had tentatively concluded that it was one of the few passages in the poem that actually described the process openly.

I therefore knocked on the mirror three times.

The image wavered, verdigris crawling over the surface as if the ivy had decided to take over. This was in the poem, I reminded myself, though I felt my heart beating steadily. *Look through the mirror, knock, wait while the green comes and then the white—*

Frost chased the verdigris in veins like the veins of a leaf or the ramifications of an oak tree. Once the bronze was entirely obscured I leaned forward, breathed on the centre, and watched in amazement as the whole metal melted away to form an oval door. I moved my hand tentatively, but that rule held good: we could see, but not cross, from this side.

Violet was standing on the other side, a bag over her shoulder and a sword at her side. She had changed into men's clothing, closer to Mr. Dart's style than what we'd seen in Tara: she wore a coat of claret velvet, her breeches brown leather, and a foaming cravat at her throat. Her boots were up to her knees, and her sword looked as if it meant business.

"I don't get it," Jullanar Maebh said after a moment. "How can there be all these passages no one knows about?"

"From the outside it seems as if the magic is hiding nothing but a set of cells." Violet showed her empty hands to us, then looked past me at Hal and Mr. Dart. "May I join you on that side?"

I stepped back immediately. Mr. Dart frowned at me, as did Hal; Jullanar Maebh seemed discontent.

"Will you grant us some indication that you are to be trusted?" Hal said at last. "Jemis' opinions on the matter are not currently sufficient, as I'm sure you understand better than I."

Violet did not wince, merely nodded gravely. "I would be impressed that you let him persuade you to meet me at all, if I were not entirely aware he is the only one who understands this building. You have known me for three and a half years, Hal, but ..." She turned her head suddenly, at something we could not see, and suddenly added with urgency, "We do not have time for me to persuade you properly. Let me through so Jemis can close the mirror-door."

"You're invited to join us," I said promptly, just before Mr. Dart's hand closed over my mouth. It was too late; Violet stepped gracefully over the threshold. I laid my hand on the middle pair of three sets of mourning doves, bowed my head, and said, "I thank the Lady for her gift."

Just as it had for Ariadne nev Lingarel, the bronze oval reformed slowly out thin air. This time it bore a pattern in its metal, ivy and hawthorn interlaced together.

"There is no one left on that side for whom we can open the mirror," I said in astonishment. "That's what this means … For Ariadne it was because all of her family was dead, but for us—"

"It's geographically limited," Violet said quickly. "Everyone who could visit within the ancient bounds of Orio City is either dead or already on this side. I—Wait."

I turned to see that Hal had disarmed her and Jullanar Maebh held her arms behind her back. "No," Hal said firmly. "We've been caught in too many traps. Give us one reason to trust that you won't hand us back over to Lark or any of the rest."

Violet closed her eyes, an expression of great weariness crossing her features. She relaxed in Jullanar Maebh's hold, shaking a little with the sort of silent laughter that might turn any moment into sobs.

"I'm sorry," she said at length. "I shouldn't … You have no idea what …" She shook her head sharply as if to clear it. "Forgive me. I cannot fully explain while we are not yet free, but … Hal, when you were ten you and your sister went to Nên Corovel to see the Lady. Do you remember?"

He frowned. "Yes."

Violet looked intently at him, her brown eyes earnest. "While you were there you escaped one afternoon from your minders and found your way into a private garden. The irises were blooming and you became angry with your sister for picking one that was nearly true red."

"How do you know that?"

She swallowed, face twisting. "My brother and I were there, in that garden. He … blew bubbles at you, gold and silver ones, that nearly swept you away in the flood."

Hal's face was still with shock. "Your brother—Do you mean to say *you're*—"

"Don't," she pleaded, "not yet."

"What are you doing here?" he growled.

"You said you ran away from an arranged marriage at fourteen," Mr. Dart said politely. "I take it that was not entirely correct?"

Her eyes were brimming, but the tears did not quite fall, and her voice was almost level when she went on. "It was the story I gave. Here. Everywhere. My brother … he is older than I … he was captured by their agents. I was sixteen but looked younger, and there was no one else, not then, not who could go. They never accept anyone from outside the Family as an adult. No one's ever infiltrated as far as I did."

"You *are* a spy!" I blurted out. "For the Lady!"

Her face twisted again. "Oh, Jemis. I am so deep in I have almost forgotten who I am."

"I know who you are," Hal said, and nodded at Jullanar Maebh to release her. He presented Violet's sword back to her, hilt-first. She did not yet reach out for it.

"You will trust me?"

"I am somewhat aghast that Jemis was correct that your choice of footwear was significant. I thought he was seeing symbols everywhere in some vast conspiracy of omens."

They all looked at me. I blinked back at them. "What? I'm right, aren't I?"

"Sadly, yes," Mr. Dart sighed. "Miss … Redshank, I suppose we might as well keep calling you, Jemis seemed to be of the opinion that you would have a copy of Ariadne nev Lingarel's poem with you, as for some reason he neglected to memorize the entire thing in Old

Shaian. I can't think what he's been doing this past month."

She reached into her bag and pulled out a volume covered in blue leather. "I've been studying it all year, ever since I read Jemis's thesis. I haven't been able to unravel all the layers—your final paper was almost incomprehensible, I'm afraid."

"Latter stages of wireweed poisoning," I agreed, probably a little too cheerfully given how they all looked at me.

"Thank you for trusting me," she added, a little faintly.

"He's been in love with you since the first month at Morrowlea," Hal said dryly. "He's spent half the autumn trying to convince himself your warnings were not what they seemed."

"Which they weren't," I said, smiling at Violet and not even minding too much that Hal had just revealed my emotions. The wireweed made my thoughts faster and my heart seem whole and joyous for the first time in literally months, and I had a grand puzzle to unravel, my friends by my side, and the world of clear mortal danger tickling at the edges.

"Right. Now to figure out how to find an exit."

Violet cleared her throat. "Actually, first we need to find the Oubliette."

"That's why the Lady's not been acting," Hal breathed.

"I'm missing something," Jullanar Maebh said. I was, too, but my mind was too focused on the book to fully attend to what Violet was saying, or not saying, as the case might be.

"My brother's been a hostage here for six years," Violet explained. "We need to find him first."

"A rescue and then an escape from the inescapable prison!" I said, once this fully registered. "How absolutely splendid."

CHAPTER *TWENTY-FOUR*
The Hearth

I flipped through the text a little aimlessly, frowning as I tried to think through the various incidents of the poem. "Did you get far enough to figure out what passage might be referring to the Oubliette?" I asked Violet.

She took a deep breath, then released it in a huff. "I only figured out that there *is* an Oubliette this autumn, after I came back from Ragnor Bella. I'd proven myself on that trip, you see, according to their lights."

"Stole the whole harvest from under the noses of the Knocker-men and the Dark Kings and the authorities, then?" Mr. Dart said.

She eyed him. "Just so. Warned those I was supposed to warn, was not seen fraternizing with those I ought not to be, and … well, there were a few other tasks I completed to The Indrilline's satisfaction. He was worried I'd been compromised while away at Morrowlea, you see. The end of Lark's degree of study was not how it was supposed to go."

I looked up from the book. "Am I supposed to feel bad about that? Because I really don't."

"How are you not back to your slavering obsession with Lark?"

Mr. Dart asked, then shivered involuntarily. "This is bloody cold."

"Snow, starfall, diamonds," I murmured, pages falling open to the account of the Hearth and its ever-burning fire.

They ignored me. Violet said, "I was bound to Lark as her serving-maid; that was the payment for their protection. They really don't understand loyalty unless it is within their own ranks and blood. There's something off about all the true Indrillines."

"There was always something off about Lark," Hal said.

"I think they made some sort of dealing with the old gods, during the Interim. From what I've learned they were nowhere near so vile before the Fall. They were criminals, yes, and feared for their ruthlessness and violence, but they took care of those under them, in their own way, and had a notion of honour that was not entirely ludicrous."

Violet paused there in her explanation as Jullanar Maebh coughed and drew her coat a little more closely about herself.

"I am most remiss," I said, and gestured to the two women. "Violet, this is Miss Jullanar Maebh Dart; Jullanar Maebh, Miss Violet Redshank. Which is obviously not her real name, but it doesn't sound like we're going to get that any time soon. Let's go this way; I think I can get us to a room where we'll be warm and dry so I can study the book properly."

"Warm and dry would be good," Mr. Dart admitted. "Some food wouldn't go amiss, either."

"There won't be any," Violet said with a sigh. "Hunger, yes, but the magics in this place keep it ever becoming true starvation. It is the same with thirst. The makers did not want anyone to escape their punishment."

I shook my head and started to hunt for any ivy-berries in the mosaic that had one green berry amongst the black. "Come along this way, but keep your eye open for anything that looks like a bird. Or perhaps a bird. Yes, a bird."

"In the mosaic?" Hal asked, running his fingers along the tiles and then jerking his hand away as if stung.

"Anywhere."

We walked a few dozen yards along the straight hallway, not seeing where we had initially come in, me counting not tiles or ivy-bunches but the apertures along the ceiling that gave a dim light into the space. The diamond-dust rose up and fell undisturbed behind us; I held the book in my good hand and murmured the lines of the next set of stanzas after the Bronze Mirror until Jullanar Maebh said, "There's a carving of a sparrow up here, will that do?"

This coincided with my landing on the line, *The curving fire warm and endless as my conscience*—the fair Ariadne had not, in point of fact, ever really regretted the actions that had led to her life imprisonment—so I thought that this was very likely the correct interpretation of the passage.

> *The   curving   fire   warm   and   endless   as   my   conscience*
> > *(my mind speaks guilt my heart does not hear)*
> *Nestled into a hearth ever-burning,*
> *Down-feathered with the white ashes of unfathomable woods*
> *Where the birds call one to another*
> > *Home-under-the-sky*

I recited these lines aloud, complete with my haphazard translation into Modern Shaian, and was met with resounding silence.

"Well?" Violet said eventually. "I read the twenty-five pages you spent explaining every association you could find for that passage, of which there were an intolerable number. Nowhere did you say, 'this is how you get into the room it is theoretically describing'."

"Well, how could I when I didn't know what any of the physical parallels actually are?" I asked her. "There are only that number of associations because she's alluding to Kidnor's *Sengeriad* with that bit about the unfathomable woods and the home-under-the-sky."

"Yes," Violet said in a dangerous voice.

I smiled at her, knowing that she had focused on the great epic poets, including Kidnor.

Hal sneezed meaningfully.

"The Lady bless you," I intoned. "Right, here's how it works, at least here: the birds calling tell us to look for a bird as the symbol for entering the room—Ariadne's 'home', you see? Since we know it's referring to Kidnor's *Sengeriad* we can presume that the birds in question are sparrows." I pointed up at the statuette tucked into the edge of a decorative stone border that had started to run along the top of the mosaic at some point I hadn't quite noticed. "Now, the question is: how do we get in?"

"There being no visible door," said Hal, nodding with a good semblance of encouragement.

"The intensity of the colour tells us whether to look up or down; in this case, white means all the way down, on the floor. Warmer colours are in front, cooler behind; white is a neutral, so we are straight down, and since it is neither a primary colour nor a secondary, neither right nor left of where we stand."

"A trap door," Mr. Dart said, understanding dawning. We all looked down, but there was nothing apparent under our feet.

"I'm just getting started," I said. "There's a lot more to pull out of this passage."

Hal sighed impatiently. "Twenty-five pages of allusions, yes, we heard Violet. Please can you just open the door? Miss Dart landed in a puddle when we were captured and is undoubtedly freezing."

"Not to mention that you still have most of the poem to decipher," Violet added.

"Very well," I said, not able to be truly annoyed at these exceedingly practical requests, and therefore reached up to the branch the little sparrow was carved sitting on and twisted it three times, thinking to myself that it was good I'd spent half of spring term teasing out the numerical significances of the various adjectives Ariadne nev Lingarel had used to describe fire.

"Should we back away, if there's a trapdoor?" Hal asked.

"Not if you want to come through it with me." I smiled at them and used my hand to swirl the dust up and keep it from falling and then, when we were all starting to cough, stamped my foot down hard on the flagstone upon which we were all standing. Once, twice, three times, four—

All the diamond-dust froze in its swirls and then started to spin back the other way. I felt a moment of great dizziness, as if the world had turned upside down around me, and then suddenly the dust fell and we were no longer standing on the flagstones in a freezing-cold hallway but instead clustered together on a richly coloured carpet in front of a blazing fire.

"The Hearth," I said happily, "the poet's home."

"What an extraordinary room," Jullanar Maebh said, turning around slowly. I followed suit, eager to see the room that was the setting, and the occasion, for one of the most soaring passages in the entire poem, and, indeed, in the entire Classical Shaian canon, the reason that anyone besides me ever read any part of the *Ode*.

It was odd how much bare descriptions had made the Silver-Square Room seem like it could be this; in actuality, the difference was like a room lit by many candles and by the noonday sun. Both illuminated, yes, but how differently.

The same high ceilings with embossed plasterwork, the same slubbed-silk walls in silvery-grey, the same mosaic floor in grey and blue and silver interlinked squares, even the same limestone chimney breast for the fireplace.

"The chairs look rather sturdier," Mr. Dart said, sinking in a vast leather armchair with some relief. I slid into the one next to him and smiled sympathetically at him as I was finally able to relieve some of the pressure on my shoulder by resting my forearm on the chair's arm. "Actually, I like this room."

"I like that it has windows," Hal said. "Too bad the fog's still thick."

"It'll be thick until past the solstice," Violet muttered, then sat down in another chair.

Apart from the leather armchairs (of which there were five, curiously enough; I wondered briefly if the number changed depending on how many people entered), there was a fine oak table, the fire blazing away (on five ever-burning logs) behind a grille that definitely did have emblems of ivy and holly on it, the aforementioned windows, and a door.

"Shall I try the door?" said Jullanar Maebh, gesturing from where she stood huddled by the fire.

"It should lead to the facilities," I said, "and a bedchamber through the other side. What? This is one of the open descriptions in the poem. Anybody who's read it would know that."

"There are two people in this room who've read that poem," said Hal with some actual amusement in his voice, "and probably only one or two more outside of it."

"They certainly weren't very interested at Tara," I agreed,

gratified when both Violet and Jullanar Maebh frowned at this, though for different reasons.

"Well, I shall explore," Jullanar Maebh declared, and opened the door with unnecessary vigour.

I smiled at Violet, who rolled her eyes at me. "Jemis, I know you're finding this all a grand lark, but would you please put your mind to your task? You're the only one who can find my brother and get us out of here."

Chastened, as she knew I would be, by both the reprimand and the allusion to Lark, I focused on the familiar text in my hands.

***

I found it very difficult to sink into the analytical mode at first. My friends talked amongst themselves and made use of the facilities once Jullanar Maebh returned safely from her expedition. They found an ewer of water and goblets and after lengthy conferral with Violet decided it was safe to drink.

Some time later, restlessly exploring the rooms, Mr. Dart returned triumphantly with three bottles of wine of a label that had gone under at least a century before the Fall. Apparently it was still delicious.

I knew I could blame my distractedness on the wireweed, and sought to fan the anger in my belly that it was there; though I knew at the same time (or thought I knew; it might have been the drug speaking) that I was not, truly, this quick of thought and intuition when in my right mind. I had realized the hidden secrets of the poem only after my body had started breaking down under the wireweed, been able to make the vast jumps of logic to unravel its mysteries only as my mind blazed in a futile effort to save itself from the ruination of the drug.

I persevered.

My friends drank the wine and were giddy and melancholy by turns. I surfaced every now and then to hear them talking softly, stories of Morrowlea and Tara and Stoneybridge. Here were the rival Three Sisters in one room, I thought briefly, dazed with the gorgeousness of the Classical Shaian (so much better than any of my translations), working together.

Deeper and deeper I went into the poem, catching on the smallest phrases, the tiniest word choices, that were the keys to something deeper. What seemed to be rocks at the surface of the Magarran Strid were actually the tips of pinnacles that dropped down seventy or a hundred feet or more. This mention of an obscure flower, that old-fashioned adjective for sheep wool, the five places where Ariadne's superlative grasp of her metres faltered ... all these were my clues.

The commonly excerpted passages showed Ariadne's lyric genius. Her skill at layering meaning, at using allusions to other poems to describe something she could not in her own words, the numerical games ... those were the markers not of a young poet, but of someone who had spent a long lifetime working and reworking one poem.

Commentators and scholars decried her stubbornness in polishing a poem that would never be more than the masterpiece of a minor poet. Critics from her own day onwards had bemoaned her choice not to pursue short-form poetry, even though her best forms had lost favour in the wake of the Gainsgooding Conspiracy.

It was incredible to think that somewhere between the wireweed and the puzzles Violet and I set for each other I should realize that the lyric heights were camouflage for a description of terrifying thoroughness. Ariadne nev Lingarel had spent thirty years walking these hidden passages and learning the ways into and out of rooms with no doors or windows, delving deep into the genius of the Labyrinth of Ihuranuë, which had caught an army of the Fair Folk in their own cleverness.

I fell asleep at one point and woke to find the window outside dark. The room was reflected in its glass; the hearth blazed as fiercely as it had on our entry, as it had for Ariadne, as it had when Ihuranuë lit the flame that would never die.

The ramp that we had spiralled up, in the palace that occupied the same space we did; it was key to something.

For my final paper I had only just begun mapping the poem onto the notes Ihuranuë had left of her design. The magic was so far beyond my skill I could only now begin to realize that much of what she'd been describing had been for the use of the wizard-engineers who had constructed and enchanted the rooms. (She had trusted no one but herself to make the linking passages, she wrote at one point, not when the Snow Fae had a creeping frost that could numb any wariness into indiscretion.) My understanding, such as it was, was that the prison occupied the inversions of the spaces in the palace. What exactly that meant I did not know.

We had climbed up a ramp; Ariadne wrote of the Spiral of Despair.

Violet said that what she had learned was that her brother was kept in an Oubliette. No one but The Indrilline himself knew where it was. Lark might have been told, as she was quickly becoming acknowledged as The Indrilline's successor, but she had not shared that confidence with Violet.

I fell asleep again as I read about the Spiral for the seventeenth time and woke at dawn with the utter certainty that I was going about this entirely the wrong way.

Violet had a sack of slightly stale scones in her bag. They tasted ambrosial.

"I have some dried fruit and nuts as well," she said as we each ate our scone and tried not to be too greedy for another. "We should probably keep the rest of the scones for later."

"Though we won't starve, you said," Mr. Dart commented.

"We'll still be weaker than we would be if properly fed. Less inclined to escape."

Hal snorted. "Fortunately we have Jemis here to decipher the riddle of this prison for us."

"Well, now that I've established that my interpretation is correct, I believe I can unfold the rest of the poem's layers of meaning using more normal methods of literary analysis."

"Does that mean you want to go to Tara, after all?"

I stared at Mr. Dart, nonplussed. "No. I hate this city."

Mr. Dart frowned at me. "You're not reacting quite as I'd been told people on wireweed do."

"That's because he's built up a resistance over the years, what with how Lark was experimenting with the dosages and what she could do with … er, her magic," Violet said, regarding me seriously but seeming a little flustered by her own words. I smiled encouragingly at her, but she merely shook her head and continued on to Mr. Dart, "Pretty well no one has been in his situation. I'd be inclined to write up an account of it for the medical journals if all my knowledge didn't come from being a criminal."

"You're a spy," Jullanar Maebh said. "I'm confused by most of this but I definitely understood that part."

"And just how much authority does the Lady have at present?" Violet responded unhappily.

"If we rescue your brother, that situation will improve," Hal said, and looked expectantly at me. "Have you worked out where the Oubliette is, Jemis?"

"I believe I've worked out how to get to where we can find it, yes."

"The distinction being …?"

"You don't know how to open the door?" Mr. Dart guessed.

I traced the inlaid gilt symbol on the front of the book, ironically and most misleadingly the Imperial Sun-in-Glory. "Do you know what an oubliette is?"

Mr. Dart made an abortive gesture as if he were looking for his pipe. "Historically? The famous example was in the Kirkhailo Fortress on Voonra. They had what they called bottle dungeons—the only way in or out was through a trapdoor in the ceiling. The Astandalan forces who conquered the place called one of them the oubliette, because they'd put a piece of furniture over the trapdoor and forgotten all about it."

Jullanar Maebh shuddered violently. "How can people do these things?"

"He's not dead," Violet said fiercely. "I know he's not dead."

"It's been five years," Hal said softly.

"Six," she muttered, fisting her hands on the brim of her hat, which she held in her lap. "The enchantments on this prison are cruel."

"I've been wondering about that," Mr. Dart said, and at Violet's encouraging look went on: "Why haven't these enchantments failed? Jemis is using a book from, what, four hundred years ago? More? How did this place come through the Fall?"

There was a silence. We all looked at each other, even me feeling sobered by the thought. Then I said, "Look, everything's been accurate so far. If we find evidence of things being compromised, then we'll reassess. We'll hardly be in a worse spot than we are now."

They all stared at me, and then Mr. Dart gave a twisted sort of smile. "Fair enough, Mr. Greenwing. Do continue with your analysis."

I knew the others thought the wireweed Lark had given me had entirely compromised my emotions and deleteriously affected my judgment, but that was not how I felt. I felt as if the hollow aching hunger in me, the emptiness that risk and games of hazard masked so briefly, was finally filled. The first euphoria of that relief had settled into something more like contentment.

I had forgotten how *content* I had been at Morrowlea, until the end.

There was nothing terrible about this state, really, I thought. My thoughts were faster, my intuition stronger, my emotions positive for once, inclining towards trust and kindness and gladness and courage. The pleasant fizzing in the back of my mind, the warming buzz in my veins, was, I knew intellectually, the drug consuming my magic and providing me with these gifts in return.

It did not seem an ill exchange. What had I ever done with my magic besides light a few candles? It wasn't as if I were Mr. Dart, with the gifts of a wild mage and the potential power to be truly great, if only he reached out to learn his gift.

I shifted position, feeling an itch I could not explain, and focused back on the conversation. They'd moved on to debating what to do once we'd rescued Violet's brother.

"Perhaps we shouldn't get ahead of ourselves," Mr. Dart said, noticing me looking at him. "What did you mean, Jemis? About knowing where we can find the Oubliette, if not knowing where it is."

"Oh … yes." I rallied myself. "We cannot access the Oubliette the way The Indrilline can—it will be tied into their blood or magic or something like that. They must be descendants of the caretakers—"

"Mr. Greenwing."

"Mr. Dart." I smiled at him, and turned to the side. "Violet, what exactly were you told about this Oubliette?"

She worried at her lip. "I overheard a conversation I wasn't supposed to, between Lark and The Indrilline."

"What exactly is their relationship?" Hal asked curiously.

"I believe the current Indrilline is her grandfather, but you must understand that they do not speak about the Family outside their ranks. Those underneath them are taught to treat each member of the Family as one. Once the younger ones are inducted into the Family Council they do not go about in public without wearing the mask of The Indrilline. The idea is that you never know if you are speaking to The Indrilline or not; whatever the Family's internal politics, and there are many, in public they are one."

"Lark won't like that," Hal murmured.

Violet smirked for a moment, then sobered. "They're moving

into the open. Lark was sent to Morrowlea to learn how to comport herself in any society, so she could be accepted as a true lady by the governor's court here. They can't drug the entire administration of the city if they want to build a power base."

"That's their goal, then."

Mr. Dart had found his pipe and with a sidelong glance at me lit it. I didn't mind his pipe smoke, found it rather homely and comforting, in fact. At Hal's words he blew a series of smoke circles to hover above his head.

I eyed them, wondering just how he didn't think his magic was becoming an issue, and returned my attention to Violet and Hal.

Violet was saying, "They've been the notorious criminals for centuries, never quite eradicated by the government even in the days of the Empire. The power vacuum since the Fall has given them the opportunity to seize control of the city, and from here, I know Lark intends to be Empress of her own petty empire before she's through."

"Everyone bowing down in adoration and worship," I said, feeling faintly sick.

"Exactly. Her vanity knows no bounds."

"She must be stopped," Hal said flatly. "They must be stopped. We cannot let them continue. If they were bringing anything like good government to pass it would be one thing, but it's obvious from the state of the city that that is not their goal. We must stop them."

"Us?" Jullanar Maebh said doubtfully.

"You're part of Crimson Lake," Mr. Dart said, glancing meaningfully down at her hand. "What's that for, if not this?"

"That's for—" She flushed, redder than Mr. Dart ever got, her freckles standing out lividly. "That's about magic, not politics."

"Magic *is* politics, nowadays," Mr. Dart returned. "Here as much as in Rondé."

Jullanar Maebh started to say something, but Hal spoke over her. "My apologies, Miss Dart, but my question has led us far off-topic. Violet, you were saying that you overheard a conversation you weren't supposed to?"

She sighed. "Yes. I was preparing Lark's bath—I'd done something that annoyed her, so she had me doing more menial tasks than usual for a week as punishment. Usually the Family use mute slaves for that; they have a custom of having important conversations in the bath or boudoir."

"Urgh," Mr. Dart said, making a face.

"That's fairly common in the north, actually," Jullanar Maebh said. "In the Outer Reaches everyone is in the sauna—that's a sort of steam-room—together, and it's a good time to have serious conversations, because everyone's relaxed."

"We don't do that in Fiellan," Mr. Dart said after a moment.

"Saunas are wonderful!"

"Perhaps you can install one," I suggested.

"Anyhow," Violet said, "I was in a storage room collecting everything that would be needed when they came in, Lark and The Indrilline. They were talking about what responsibilities Lark would be taking on once she was married, and The Indrilline said she'd get primary access to the hostages."

Violet looked disgusted. "She's had secondary access to the prisoners for years, under her Mistress—that is, the senior wizard she's been studying with, the one who taught her what to do with the wireweed—and since we came back this year has been taking more and more power. There was some sort of duel at the summer solstice, and the senior wizard lost, so Lark has been allowed to take the majority of the power drawn from the addicts."

We all shuddered at the thought. There was the downside to wireweed: you were addicted to a substance controlled by unscrupulous wizards who ran a major criminal empire.

I shivered again at how near a miss I'd had with Lark. Had she miss-stepped, or overreached her ambition, or had it been what the cursebreaker from Oakhill had said, that my love for my father could break through the curse Dominus Gleason had placed on me and the enchantment Lark had woven around my addiction?

"So Lark asked about the hostages. She sounded so hungry ... I was sure someone had to be a very powerful source of magic for her to sound so eager about having access. She's addicted to the power as badly as anyone to the wireweed, but in her case it's this vicious cycle where each piece of magic she steals permits her to expand her reach."

"Historically that's exactly the model most expanding governments use," Mr. Dart said. "You conquer your neighbour and use the resources there to permit you to conquer the next."

"It's deeply disturbing seeing a single individual doing that. I keep hoping she'll bite off more than she can chew, but ... not yet. She hasn't declared it openly, but I'm sure her goal is to have a power base sufficient to challenge the Lady directly."

"And if there was a hint of good government involved in this, I'd be less inclined to worry," Hal said. "As it stands, my statement from earlier does: we must stop her."

I shivered again, glad I still wore Sir Hamish's greatcoat so I could huddle into it for comfort. Lark as the founder of a new empire was all too easily imagined. I wondered if the people around Yr the Conqueror, founder of Astandalas, had been wary or excited or terrified by him.

"Which starts with rescuing my brother. I'm giving you the whole story in the hopes you see something I missed."

Mr. Dart nodded. "So: they spoke of the prisoners, and then the hostages. There are many?"

"I have no idea how many, but enough that none of the countries this side of the continent have been willing to form alliances against the Indrilline threat. Of the prominent countries in the northwest only Rondé and the Outer Reaches are still standing strong against them. And with Hal here as a hostage, I'm sure they're all busy thinking how they can use him to cripple the Rondelan economy and power base. Aren't you cousins with the King of Rondé?"

Hal sighed. "Yes. As well as being the single largest landowner in the continent."

"You're the obvious leader for the pro-Imperial contingent, you know," she said, looking intently at him. "People have been talking about how you've finished university now and are fully taking up your responsibilities. You have the highest title left in Northwest Oriole …"

"Not even to stop Lark am I setting myself up as a petty emperor," Hal said firmly.

"It's how history works," Mr. Dart said encouragingly.

I laughed slightly at Hal's offended expression, though the laughter turned into a long coughing fit. "Thanks," I said once I could, accepting the glass of water Jullanar Maebh handed to me. I managed to drink it without spilling all of it, though it was a near thing. "Sorry," I added breathlessly. "I'm feeling chilled. Let's—let's leave aside how we're going to destroy the Indrillines until after we've escaped, shall we?"

Violet gave me a long searching look. "Let me know when you start to have a headache."

"Surely you mean 'if'?" I asked with a pathetic attempt at levity.

"No," she said gravely, then turned to the others. "They negotiated Lark's access to the hostages and who else should be granted the privilege, and finally Lark asked about 'the last one'. She had that smug tone to her voice, you know the one, Hal, when she knows something you don't think she does."

"Emperor, yes, I know exactly that smirk."

"The Indrilline runs his family like a tyrant, but he still admires a certain spunk and push against his power. Not a big push, of course, but for Lark, who's proving herself as his successor, this was a victory. He asked her what she meant, obviously trying to see whether she knew more than the words. I'd never heard the phrase so I guessed it was an internal secret from the upper council of the Family. And of course, in the context I was all ears.

"Lark said she knew there was 'one more hostage: the centrepiece', and she felt that she's at the position, now, where her power and skill are sufficient to 'tap' even that well." Violet scrunched up her face. "I hate how they talk about other people, as if they are objects to use as they will. The idea that a person is only considered in terms of what value they have, and is disposable once that value is fully extracted, is deplorable. The idea that they've held my brother all these years so that they can draw out his magic … It's disgusting."

"What did The Indrilline say?"

"He laughed at Lark and said that she was not as ready as she thought she was, and that the 'last hostage' was in a special place, which requires certain sacrifices and conditions to enter. Lark said, 'Not the Oubliette?' The Indrilline said, 'The Oubliette is a ghost story for children, my dear.' And Lark replied, 'So is the Well, but we know better.' And the Indrilline replied, and I quote, 'Well, you are not entirely wrong, my dear, but neither am I.' And that was the end of the conversation."

I was sure there was something vital in that exchange, but I couldn't quite make it come into focus. I frowned, rubbing my forehead hard as if the pressure on the outside could relieve the inside.

"Jemis, are you all right?" Hal asked suddenly.

I looked up at him, squinting against the too-bright room. They were all outlined with strange haloes of colour, wavering in a room no longer calm greys and silver-blues but stabbing shadows. I winced and closed my eyes, pressing against them with both hands.

"Jemis, say something," Hal ordered.

I tried to laugh away his concern, but found myself panting for breath. "Sorry," I said, slurring the sounds. "That scone must have disagreed with me."

"It wasn't the scone," Violet said grimly.

"This seems a lot faster than before," Hal said, voice worried.

"I told you, no one's been in this situation. His reactions are all over the place."

There was a pause. I drew my knees up so I could rest my head on them. Everything was aching, and the pressure in my head was fantastic, as if my brain were growing larger with every passing moment. I could hear my friends' voices coming in and out of focus, having an urgent discussion. I was sure they were discussing me but couldn't bring the words into sense.

A touch on my hand startled me into jumping. I lifted my head, trying to stifle a whimper from the pain in my head and shoulder. "I'm sorry," I whispered, realizing tears were streaming out of my eyes. "I don't know what's come over me."

"A severe reaction to the wireweed," Violet said, her touch on my hand anchoring me to her voice. "I'm sorry, Jemis, but you're the only one who knows how to interpret the poem."

"I … I don't understand …"

She put on gentle hand under my chin and lifted my head up so she could look directly into my eyes. Or so I assumed she was doing; the bright haloes obscured everything but the dark oval of her face not far from mine.

"Open your mouth, Jemis," she said calmly and authoritatively.

Someone from behind said something about sleeping, but I couldn't focus past her. I would have laughed otherwise, at the thought that anything would let me sleep in this state except for one of the fabled sleeping potions of an Imperial apothecary.

"That's right. Open your mouth."

I complied easily, trusting Violet to know what she was doing, and a moment later tasted rich chocolate dissolving on my tongue.

It was quite amazing how quickly I felt better.

CHAPTER TWENTY-SIX

The Riddle of Ariadne nev Lingarel

"Why haven't we run into any of the other hostages?" Jullanar Maebh was asking when I resurfaced from a particularly knotted passage, frowning at the play of meanings in the word *vhailor*. Wonder, and poetry, and a sacred altar, and sacrifice, and—

Violet said, "They stay where they're put, I'm afraid."

Hal shuddered, face limned with an atavistic horror quite at odds with his usual urbanity. "In rooms with no doors or windows, no absolute *need* to eat …"

I let them talk, turning over ideas, hearing snippets, my mind going back to what I could recall of Ihuranuë's notes. How I wished I'd finished reading them, even (for how could one finish studying such a thing?), but I'd been sidetracked by finding her few written accounts of the Labyrinth, and I had been so taken with her offhand reference to it in the context of how her last three buildings were—

I stopped, all my thoughts ringing with triumphant certainty.

"This *is* the Labyrinth."

My friends looked up from their conversation with expressions ranging from polite bafflement (Jullanar Maebh) through elaborate patience (Hal) to two nicely graded variants of false amazement (Violet and Mr. Dart).

"No, really, it all fits. I can't imagine why I didn't see it before."

"Is this relevant, or just interesting?" Hal asked with even more elaborate patience, a familiar expression from the last year at Morrowlea.

That reminded me I'd wanted to tell him about the holly walk I'd seen at Tara. "Hal, did you know there's a little walkway between the main Classics building and the Faculty of Magic at Tara that's lined with all these varieties of holly—"

"And that's definitely irrelevant," Mr. Dart interjected. "Go back to the Labyrinth, Mr. Greenwing."

"It explains everything, don't you see? The mystery of what happened to Irany's Labyrinth in the first place. The eyewitness accounts claim she miniaturized it and put it in her pocket, never to be seen again. In her papers—I only read some of them …" I frowned again at that unfortunate realization. "I'll have to go back and do a proper investigation."

"Mr. Greenwing."

"Mr. Dart. This is relevant. In her last letter, Irany made a reference to her legacy, stating that her last works—the palace here and the Great Hall at Lornwood and—"Their faces indicated I should not follow these side tangents. I forced myself not to explain why they were all most relevant to the situation at hand. They would see soon enough. "Anyway, she wrote that her 'last works were built on the greatest', that is, her Labyrinth."

After a moment of appreciative silence, Violet said, "That does not seem definite proof, Jemis. It's the sort of metaphor anyone might make."

"Irany loved physical metaphors," I explained. "Look at this building! Even if it weren't the Labyrinth, it's a palace that's literally also a prison! How many poems have you read about the tyranny of wealth and status? It was the most clichéd trope of the period."

"That is true, actually," Violet said, sounding oddly reluctant to agree with me.

"Exactly. So when she wrote that about the last being built on the greatest—or—oh, yes!" I stopped in amazement at my own insight, as the phrase in Old Shaian on the page in front of me caught my eye and I realized something I'd never noticed before. "Even better, she used *elvai* with the ablative, so she might mean even more literally that it was built *out of*—I can't see how I didn't figure this all out before. It's so obvious."

"It's possible that your near-collapse from advanced wireweed poisoning might have had something to do with it," Mr. Dart suggested. I could only nod judiciously in agreement. It was hard to think about the wireweed when I had so much else to consider.

"All right," Jullanar Maebh said, "I'm still confused about this whole situation, so although I am naturally very pleased for you that you've had an insight into your scholarship, how does it help us now? We need to find this Oubliette, rescue Miss Redshank's brother, and escape without being recaptured by the Indrillines who, let me remind you, are in physical control of this half of the city including the port."

"That's the genius of this discovery," I said, beaming at her and patting the book. "Ariadne nev Lingarel never had to escape to be free."

"The Emperor," Violet cried, and I turned to her, glad she'd caught my gist, to find her obviously mocking me. "It's all there in the Early Syncretic philosophers, isn't it? Freedom is an illusion of the spirit!"

"You don't have to make fun," I said, a little hurt. "I meant it literally. After the Labyrinth Irany designed three more buildings on Alinor: the governor's palace-prison here, the Great Hall of the University of Lornwood, and the hunting lodge of the kings of Lind. Which were built on, or out of, the Labyrinth."

"You think they're all connected?" Violet said, more seriously.

I turned to Hal. "What's the famous story of Lornwood? We heard it when were in Tiffledale."

"Their great hall is supposedly haunted," Mr. Dart said, then added when I looked at him: "What? I had a period of reading travel guides, you know that."

"Bloody Taddeo Toynbee," I muttered automatically.

"Yes, yes, may he rot in hell along with Jack Lindsary."

"What have you got against Taddeo Toynbee?" Jullanar Maebh asked. "I quite understand now why you might dislike Jack Lindsary."

"Mr. Greenwing doesn't like that his family's in the guidebook."

"And what did we learn from Marcan about that hunting lodge?" I went on, glaring at Mr. Dart to stop talking about side topics.

Hal shook his head, less at my elegant analysis and more at the fact that I actually had a point, I was sure. "Marcan didn't want to go there because he said there were strange noises in his room, like someone crying or whimpering."

"Lornwood's ghost is supposed to be a woman in antique dress," Mr. Dart put in.

"What does Marcan have to do with the king of Lind's hunting lodge?" Violet asked.

"He's the second son of the king." At her disbelieving look I snorted. "I know! He's actually the Count of Westmoor."

"I was sure he was an archbishop's byblow," Violet said mournfully.

"We're lucky he's not a hostage here with us," Hal said. "Right-ho, Jemis, what do we do now? You think the Labyrinth connects these three buildings somehow?"

"And the ghost of the woman in antique dress is probably a story of people seeing Ariadne nev Lingarel. She has a few 'dream sequences' in here where she describes visions of wandering through a small university town and being free to be an ordinary woman."

"But she never escaped?"

I looked down at the book. "I think she found her calling late in life. She wasn't a very good governor, you know, even apart from the treason, but this is a magnificent poem. Far greater than anyone's ever given her credit for. I think she understood what a masterpiece Irany's architecture was and this was her response. A poem as full of secrets and hidden meanings as the building itself."

"Lornwood's not that far from here," Violet said. "And I know for a certainty both university and civic authorities are fully under the thumb of the Indrillines. We might escape, but I doubt we'd get far."

"It's also on the obvious route for us to take, towards Fillering Pool," Hal added. "If we could reach Fillering Pool, that would be one thing, but the whole Tarvenol peninsula is compromised. As soon as the Indrillines put up the alarm ..."

"How long do you think we have?" Mr. Dart asked Violet. "Before Lark comes back to check on us, I mean."

She sighed. "She was planning on leaving Jemis for long enough that the wireweed dose had faded and he'd be desperate. It also depends if she's realized I've gone. I didn't have permission to leave the palace, unfortunately."

"So any moment now the alarm could be raised," Mr. Dart said.

Jullanar Maebh frowned. "Surely they won't think we'll already have escaped the city?"

"They won't take the risk,"Violet assured her grimly. "As soon as there's any concern they'll flood the streets with agents and alert the surroundings."

"I wonder if your coachman will have made it out," Jullanar Maebh said thoughtfully.

"I hope he collected your trunk," I said.

They ignored me. Violet went on: "They have means of communication, and their agents are everywhere in the courts of their sycophants. Uncanny crows, and other magic."

"Mr. Fancy was driving six Ghiandor horses, which drew us from Ragnor Bella to Orio City in two days without being changed," Mr. Dart said. "Nevertheless, it behoves us to rescue ourselves, I believe. Mr. Greenwing? Can you get us to this hunting lodge in Lind? We should be able to make it over the pass down into the Coombe before the snows close it if we can get to the Linder mountains."

I considered the poem and the dreams of the high white mountains with their clear air and ice-cold streams. "Yes," I said, "I think I can get us out. Moreover, I'm fairly certain that's where the Oubliette is."

"What, in a pocket dimension of Marcan's bedroom?" Hal said incredulously.

"Yes," I replied solemnly, "something very like that."

"How do we get there?"

I opened the book to that central spiral. Lark had mentioned the Well that was a childhood tale that she and The Indrilline knew to be true. The fair Ariadne spoke of a well, too.

"'Through the invidious spiral of despair,' I quoted, "'I found my way to the savage air.'"

"Sounds splendid fun," said Mr. Dart. "How do we join in?"

I stared at him for a moment, then turned with resignation back to the book.

***

"So there you have it," I proclaimed proudly, laying my notes down on the table. A dozen lines of poetry, each word, metre, image, allusion, rhyme teased out, expanded into a dozen pages of notes (and would be much further expanded once I had access to proper reference books; there were things I was missing, I was sure, and cross-connections within the poem), collapsed down again into a single page of directions.

Violet had the most experience reading my hand in the throes of literary analysis. She picked up the final sheet and read it over silently.

"Well?" Mr. Dart asked finally, when she set it down again and massaged her eyes in lieu of saying anything.

Hal picked up the pages and cleared his throat before reading it aloud.

> *To escape the inescapable:*
>
> *First, collect the key to freedom: it lies under the feet of tyranny.*
>
> *Second, acquire the necessary supplies: a silver ewer of water that never knew the sun; fine white bread made without yeast; a fruit of next year's crop; a coin never minted but everywhere accepted.*
>
> *Third, prepare yourself for the journey: Vest yourself in threads unspun by human hands; bathe in water that has not touched the ground; crown yourself with honesty and thrift.*
>
> *Fourth, find the door: from the salten well there is an invisible bridge that leads to an island built neither by man nor nature. On the*

island there is a garden neither of romance nor of wonder, but in a box of uncommon girth will you find both.

Ask the one who knows darkness without end for the means of light, and the one cast outside for the joy that lies within, and the one cursed for a blessing.

Be courteous, and accept what doom you are offered. You are clever enough to have deciphered this, and foolish enough to have needed to: by any door, you will find wisdom, though it be your death.

Hal put the paper down as wearily as Violet had.

"Why is it always a riddle?" Mr. Dart asked. "This is impossible. Unless you have any more brilliant insights, Mr. Greenwing?"

I was miffed at their disregard for what I had achieved. "No, but the five of us are graduates of the Three Sisters. Surely to the Lady we can figure out this."

"I hate riddles," proclaimed Jullanar Maebh, which seemed to be the consensus, but as there was nothing else to do, we sat down and started to talk out what it could mean, though it wasn't until Violet brought out the remaining scones that we had anything resembling a breakthrough.

CHAPTER TWENTY-SEVEN

The Well of Despair

"Wait!" Jullanar Maebh cried suddenly, grabbing Hal by the hand before he could bite into the last remaining scone.

"I do beg your pardon," he said more courteously than I could have managed, lowering it and presenting it to her. "Did you want it?"

She waved his courtesy away. "No—well—no, don't eat it! We need it for the riddle—look." She stabbed her finger at the first set of instructions. "A fine white bread without yeast."

We all looked at the scones. Hal said slowly, "Of course. One uses baking soda and, er, cream of tartar as leavening agents, not yeast, if I recall correctly."

"And water that has never touched the ground … rain?"

We looked out the window at the mizzle. "Or mist, potentially," I agreed.

With these two revelations, we turned back to the riddle more eagerly. Jullanar Maebh said, "Next: What sort of thread is unspun by human hands?"

"Spiderwebs," Mr. Dart suggested, shuddering a little. I wondered if he was remembering the cobwebs in the Castle Noirell, or the ones in the woods when we'd run from the cult, or the ones—well, we seemed to have spent a fair amount of time getting tangled up in the things, all told.

"I'm not wearing cobwebs and nothing else," Jullanar Maebh proclaimed. "I'd almost rather be stuck here than escape naked and grotty."

Mr. Dart blushed, and Hal and I tried not to follow suit, while Violet and Jullanar Maebh both smirked at us. "Er," I said, trying to keep my voice level (and definitely not imagining the two women in the nude), "what other natural threads are there?"

"Linen, cotton, wool," Hal said, ticking them off on his fingers.

"They all need to be spun," Violet noted, grimacing. I nodded agreement with her.

I'd actually quite liked the sartorial arts classes we'd had at Morrowlea. My most important lesson was probably the deep appreciation I'd gained for the generations of mostly female ancestors who'd spent the majority of their waking hours making cloth from scratch. Seeing students diligently trying to spin thread from wool roving with drop spindles was a very common sight at Morrowlea.

"Leather—"

"Not exactly threads."

"What else are clothes made of? Hemp, satin, velvet, muslin."

"Muslin's cotton," I murmured; it came from the fields of southern East Oriole, along with rice and jute and silk. "Silk!"

"Of course!" Violet said. "Spun as long single threads by silkworms."

"Eurgh, really?" asked Jullanar Maebh, then appeared embarrassed when we all looked at her. "I don't know much about how cloth is made. I'm interested in the scientific properties of water."

"Which is fascinating, but not precisely relevant," Hal said, with an apologetic grimace. "I can't believe I'm saying that to anyone but Jemis. How are you feeling, by the way?"

"Me?" I said, surprised. "I'm fine. A little headache, I suppose, but nothing bad."

"You're not cold?"

I smiled at him. "No, I'm fine. Look, that's the second point nearly done."

Mr. Dart sighed. "Apart from the scone, we haven't actually got any of this."

"We're in a room with a window, at least, so we can 'bathe' in the mist. We have a scone. We have a silver ewer—" I waved vaguely at the table with the goblets, and then at the wall for good measure. "The walls are covered with silk cloth. If we can't find anything in the back rooms here we can pull down the wall-coverings and use those as, er, garments."

"Charming," Violet muttered, then grinned at Jullanar Maebh. "But better than cobwebs."

"Moving on," Mr. Dart said.

Hal tapped his finger on the first section. "A fruit of next year's crop. I wonder … Are there fig trees anywhere in here?"

"There's an ancient one espaliered in the front court. Didn't you see it as you came in?"

We all stared at Violet in amazement. "We had our heads covered by sacks, so no," Mr. Dart said. "But I seem to recall that being noted in the guidebook, thinking about it. Why?"

"Figs have two crops," Hal explained. "The one in the autumn is the most well known, but there's a spring one, called the breba, which consists of fruits that overwinter in immature form on the branches."

"So if you pick one now, that's a fruit from next year's crop."

"This is not as difficult as I'd expected," Jullanar Maebh murmured. "This is the sort of riddle you hear about in old stories and fairy tales."

Hal, who didn't have much truck with fairy tales even after the events in the Woods Noirell, said, "Note that Jemis had to analyze the entire poem to get to this point."

"Riddles always seem easy once you start to unravel them," Violet added.

***

I must confess that I let my friends work at solving the riddle. I felt mentally exhausted from the effort involved in my feat of analysis. I had not worked so intently, I was sure, since that not-exactly-halcyon summer I'd studied for the entrance examinations.

Instead I sat there, sipping water (a mouthful of the ancient wine had been both ambrosial and, in my current state, perilous) and watching Hal and Violet fashioning garments out of the wall-hangings. Our initial idea of togas had been frustrated by the way the cloth had been affixed to the wall with some sort of glue, so the silk tore in long strips. My two friends from Morrowlea were currently weaving and knotting the strips together with what would undoubtedly be a most original effect.

I dozed off, waking when the two Darts returned from the back rooms.

"Well, we're just going to have to hope that the water in here comes from a well rather than a cistern," Jullanar Maebh reported. "Unless we find an actual well-head it's going to be impossible to tell."

I struggled to sit upright, hoping the better posture would ensure better clarity of thought. "Is there a well—sorry, I keep yawning—in the garden courtyard?"

"The garden's on the island, isn't it?" Mr. Dart returned, frowning.

"No, the one with the—sorry—fig tree."

We all looked at Violet, who was sitting on the floor in her crimson suit, silver-grey silk puddled all around her. She looked like a figure in some Middle Shaian allegory. Possibly the anthropomorphization of Vengeance. Her shrug, however, was entirely modern. "I've never noticed, I'm afraid."

"No care for your surroundings at all," Hal said with a mocking tut. Violet turned to stare at him for a brief moment, then relaxed and grinned back. It was nice to see that at some point in the night they'd mended their fences.

"So the figs and the water in the courtyard," I said, resolutely forcing down another yawn. "What about bathing?"

Mr. Dart and Jullanar Maebh seemed to be avoiding each other's eyes while still trying to communicate silently. Eventually Jullanar Maebh won, and Mr. Dart, flushing lightly, said, "There's a balcony off the back room; we forced open the door, which was stuck but not locked. It looks out over the ocean, so we should be able to, er, bathe in the mist."

"Mizzle," I murmured, but they ignored me.

There was a long discussion of what it could possibly mean to crown yourself with honesty and thrift. Mr. Dart was of the opinion that since we were gathering all the requisite accoutrements from our surroundings, we were showing great thriftiness, and perhaps we could resolve to speak with total honesty to one another.

There was a pause when he said that, as we all looked around the room and thought about our various secrets. Only Hal did not seem overly bothered by the idea.

"I can promise not to lie to you," Jullanar Maebh offered eventually.

"Lies of omission do count against honesty," Hal said sternly. I glanced down at the sheet of paper with the riddle on it, trying not to smile at his tone. He, after all, had kept quite as much to himself as any of the rest of us at Morrowlea.

"What about secrets? Not all of them are mine."

"That's it," I said, my eyes catching on a line. "That's the coin never minted but everywhere accepted."

"What is?" Mr. Dart said cautiously.

"Secrets. If you have the right secret, any door is open to you."

"Moligny, *Discourse on Government,*" Violet identified, smiling at me.

"Do we have a secret big enough to open any door?" Mr. Dart said. We all turned to look at Violet again, though I noticed that Jullanar Maebh sighed with relief when we did not focus on her. Not that it was a total surprise that she had some secret she'd not yet revealed to us; we were almost total strangers, after all, and had embroiled her escape in our own disasters.

"That might be sufficient honesty," Mr. Dart said. "Any insights into the key to freedom, which lies under the feet of tyranny?"

"That sounds like Violet, too," said Hal. The two of them exchanged a look both meaningful and merry, such as I'd not seen between them for a year, at least.

My heart swooped somewhere down by my stomach. Hal had learned something about Violet to completely invert his view of her; also she was related to someone important, evidently, from their discussion at the bronze mirror. And she had seen ... well, he was an Imperial Duke, smart, handsome, funny, the largest landowner in Northwest Oriole, with a loving family and no whiff of scandal. And he had told me last month it was time for him to look for a bride, and that while he had no expectation of marrying for love he did want someone who liked him for himself.

I told myself there was no reason to think their thoughts were moving in that direction, but the same cascade of intuitive leaps that had unravelled the riddle out of the poem wove together a hundred little interactions at Morrowlea and in the past day. He had been as angry as myself at Violet's siding with Lark in our little contretemps in the spring.

I closed my eyes against the sight of them smiling and turning back to their work with the silk, but that just gave me images of the past to worry over. Violet and Hal working together in the gardens; a glimpse I had seen of them walking together from refectory to dormitory, heads bent together and strides matching; Hal standing over Violet's shoulder watching her play cards. Violet looking past me and Lark with an ironic eye to Hal …

I did not recall falling asleep, but must have, for when I was shaken gently awake the puddles of silk were gone. Below the wall-coverings the walls were off-white plaster, striped with the frayed pieces that had kept to the glue. The room seemed dimmer without them, the shadows in the corners heavier. I blinked up at Mr. Dart.

He frowned and seemed about to speak, then shook his head and said instead, "It's your turn to bathe in the mist."

"Mizzle," I retorted, making him smile crookedly.

"If you insist, Mr. Greenwing."

"I intend to, Mr. Dart."

I pushed myself upright. The lack of food in the past day made itself known by a wash of dizziness, but I gripped the back of the chair until it passed. The faint headache in the corner of my eye did not want to go away, alas, but I shuffled after Mr. Dart to the back room, where he showed me my silken garment and gave me a sort of bag to put my proper clothes in.

The cold damp mizzle did much to wake me up. I stripped fully, something I had never actually done in anything like so exposed a location before, and stood shivering on the balcony as the air swirled around. This was not a very proper activity. I told myself to be grateful it was the beginning of winter, not the frozen heart of it; and that if we'd been here in the summer there would have been flies and Lady knew what else from those noxious streets.

Hal and Violet had fashioned a sort of knee-length smock out of the silk, with a hole for the head and two for the arms and a straight fall of wide-woven bands. There was no mirror, but when I came back out with my bag of clothes, my hat in hand, I saw how utterly ridiculous we all looked, and couldn't help but laugh.

"You don't look any better," Mr. Dart muttered. "Now, wake up, Jemis—are you awake?"

I covered my mouth to hide another yawn. "Yes, yes, I'm listening."

"We need you to focus—Jemis, pay attention."

"I do apologize for my tendency to yawn. It could be sneezing, you know."

Hal said, "I'd rather it were sneezing, given the circumstances."

"Perhaps we should hurry up," Violet said. "Between Jemis's state of mind and Lark's …"

"Right-ho," Mr. Dart agreed, and turned back to me. I leaned against my perch on the back of a chair and smiled at him to show my readiness. "We need you, Jemis, to get us first to the courtyard, and then to wherever you think this passage is. Can you do that?"

"You don't need to keep saying my name. I do know who you're talking to."

"Mr. Greenwing."

"Mr. Dart." I could see he was getting truly irritated, so I turned to Violet. "Could you pass me the book, please? Thank you." I flipped through the pages to the sections I'd vaguely marked as dealing with the entrance of the palace-prison. Or rather the exit. "All right," I said eventually, finding the passage in question. "I'm not sure that we can enter the physical space of the courtyard without needing to cross over to the palace proper. Except—"

I stopped as a few lines re-oriented themselves in my mind.

"Except?" said Violet, sighing.

I ignored her, staring at the same passage in *On Being Incarcerated* for long enough that the others broke off their conversation to ask me about it.

"Where are you stuck?" Violet asked. "Perhaps there's a word, or an allusion, I might know?"

I showed her the passage. She read it over, lips pursed in the familiar way she had. I watched her, feeling none of the ecstasy and exhilaration I'd once known in the company of Lark. I had been as dependent on Lark as on her drug; emotionally and physically twisted around her desires and ability to play me like a fiddle.

My feelings for Violet, by contrast, were like a banked fire being stirred into wakefulness.

She looked up suddenly from the page to catch me staring. For a moment tenderness softened her eyes and her mouth, before she shook her head and smiled wryly. Perhaps she reciprocated my feelings, but if she did they were not anything like a primary motivation in her life. I might not have understood everything about her response to Hal's challenge, but I was certain that Violet would sacrifice, had sacrificed, her own desires in order to achieve her chosen goals. She had stood next to Lark, been an Indrilline spy, done who knew what else, all to rescue her brother.

"'The new-Moon shadows wax and wane and wax again,'" she said huskily, "'as the Sun in his fullness meets the Moon in hers, casting half-shadows in the court of a throneless king.'"

I had translated it as 'crescent and re-crescent shadows'. It was a passage I loved greatly.

"It refers to the solar eclipse, literally, the commentators say," I said.

"'Here in the hearth-room, my heart's blood I spill, that there in the well of salt water I might shed my salt tears, not for the city I have betrayed but for the bright isle I have never owned.'"

"That's a very famous poem," Jullanar Maebh said.

"This part is often excerpted," Violet agreed. "It's beautiful."

"Yes," I murmured, staring at her, until Mr. Dart elbowed me hard. I coughed, flushed, spluttered, and desperately changed the subject to how Violet's translation had given me the keys to our escape.

(I wondered, briefly, how she could be the key to freedom that lies under the tyrant's feet for us; then I realized that this was a work of high magic we had wandered into, and like the dragon's riddle would always have more than one answer.)

Other passages cross-referencing this one—some of my dozens of pages had listed them—gave me the second part of each key.

Nine drops of blood, flicked onto the everlasting fire in the hearth of the Heart, and the wall that led to the back chambers opened a new door for us. When we walked through it, bearing our clothes in tight bundles and our necessary preparations as well, we found ourselves in another vaulted antechamber, this one with nine walls each holding a niche in which hovered a sphere representing a globe of the world, and in the centre a great golden light. It took a moment longer to find the hovering white alabaster sphere representing the Moon.

Seven turns around the chamber, each time twisting one of the enamelled spheres of the Nine Worlds and the alabaster Moon to a new position relative to each other and yet in line with the central light so that each time we made of the Sun and the Moon an eclipse visible on the sphere representing our own Alinor.

On the seventh turn a trapdoor appeared, opened, showed a tight spiral leading down. We followed the stairs and ended climbing up into a stone courtyard with nothing but high blank walls and an enormous fig tree espaliered halfway to the sky.

Hal plucked his breba fig, a fruit of next year's crop, and turned expectantly to me.

"We climb the tree next," I said. Mr. Dart eyed me, then rolled back his shoulders.

"To any particular point?"

"There," I said, pointing up where the leading truck forked in two. "There is a hollow there we must enter."

The passage came easily to my tongue: "'The mouth of the green lover whose fruit is known to secret lovers encircles me, envelops me, draws me down that dark spiral, through the', ah—"

"Through the crotch between north and south,'" Violet finished for me, smiling at my blush.

"I always thought that was a reference to the story of the Hunter in Green meeting the Lady disguised as a milkmaid," said Jullanar Maebh.

"It's also about that," I agreed, and set up the trunk. My thoughts drifted to the Honourable Rag flirting with milkmaids at market day back home, quoting liberally from a few folk ballads on the subject.

Behind the fork was a stork's nest, half within a hole that looked too small to enter but permitted me entry when I hesitantly bent my head to try. I tried not to think of all the ribald interpretations of this particular passage.

We tumbled down a steep spiralling pipe, landing with muffled thumps on a mound of fig leaves that might have spent four hundred years piling up but for the evidence on the walls that the sea came this high on rare occasions.

We were in a sort of sea cave; grey light streamed in from a jagged mouth, illuminating our dirty skin and strange smocks. I helped Jullanar Maebh and Mr. Dart up, Hal already having assisted Violet, and turned to what I hoped I would find.

At the back of the cave steps led down into a circular basin. It was decorated with tiny black and white tiles in a pattern I could not quite make out.

"Very early Tarvenol mosaic," Mr. Dart said softly. "Showing Fell-tree runes, no less." He ran his fingers along a border of angular markings. From somewhere all around us a deep resonant sound came forth.

"Perhaps we shouldn't," Jullanar Maebh whispered.

Mr. Dart's hand fell but his eyes were shining with something I could not recognize. The sound faded.

I felt suddenly inordinately tired, and sat down hard on the ground.

"Seven—sorry—seven tears," I said, fighting to get the words out. "Into the water."

They looked at one another, or I thought they did. I listened, eyes half-closed, to a deep vibration coming out of the stone, the well, the sea.

Ariadne had written of the whale-road, and the birds she could see, and many, many allusions to the kraken she had never seen but her poet's fancy put there. In some moods she embraced it, the dark coils of its tentacles, its sea-borne shadows; other times she fought it, as a daughter of the Lady ought.

From where I sat on the ground I could imagine the tiles showed great snaking tentacles rising out of the water.

Mr. Dart touched the tiles one last time, and the noise sounded again, like a great bell struck and holding its note.

If my magic had called forth a dragon, now that the old bindings were gone, what might Mr. Dart's?

But I was not left long to wonder, for Violet had managed to raise tears and let seven of them drip from her fingers to the utterly still salt-water well.

"'Sorrow fell like snow,'" she whispered, "'and all the world was silent.'"

It was a line from her beloved *Segneriad* and fit perfectly to the moment when Ariadne nev Lingarel's words about incarceration and sorrow unfolded into a bridge made of thin air illuminated with sunlight that was not shining outside the cave.

CHAPTER *TWENTY-EIGHT*
The Island

I stepped off the invisible bridge and fell to the ground, gasping, as my entire body flooded with energy.

When I struggled to sit up it was to squint at the brilliant sunlight. I took deep breaths, as if I could swallow the light, or the fresh, clean air, or the pins-and-needles feeling that had suddenly surged to the tips of my fingers and toes.

"Welcome back," Hal said, smiling, though I could see his face was still shadowed with concern. He reached down and offered me a hand; I took it, grateful for the assistance in getting upright. Once standing, I could look around and see where we had landed.

"A garden on an island …" I murmured, turning around in a circle. Mr. Dart, Jullanar Maebh, and Violet stood slightly apart from each other, all of them alternating between looking at me and looking at our surroundings. I smiled, still weary but inexpressibly more awake and aware than I had been.

"There must be a lot of magic here," Hal said.

"Do you think that's what it is?" I asked him, gesturing vaguely at myself. "The wireweed burns up one's native magic."

"You were awfully close to falling asleep."

I shuddered, the image of the piles of rags in mucky corners of Orio City seared in my brain. Hal clapped me on the shoulder. "Don't let's think about it right now, Jemis. We still have to further our escape."

"Indeed! Rescue Violet's brother from the Oubliette, figure out how to get from Oubliette to hunting lodge, and then it's just a hop, skip, and a jump over a mountain range with winter coming on. Easy as pie."

"As a stargazy pie, perhaps," Mr. Dart said, with a sly glance at Violet, who started and then laughed.

"I still can't tell you everything," she said. "Now, then, which way do you think we should go?"

We stood on a sort of paved wharf at the edge of a lapping sea. Two stone pillars carved with oak leaves presumably marked where the invisible bridge leading to the now-invisible palace-prison started. Ariadne nev Lingarel, or rather whoever Irany had intended this for, had presumably needed a way back to where they were supposed to be. I looked through the pillars, but all I could see was a calm blue sea under a calm blue sky. The quality of the light suggested it was very early morning.

After a moment I turned my back on the sea and looked at the land. The wharf was made of the shelly limestone of the palace, brilliant white against the green sward that ran level to it. To the right and the left a pebbled shingle swept out in a gentle arc.

"Not much sign of a tide," Jullanar Maebh said. "We must be far south."

Hal shook his head in polite disagreement. "The plants are temperate-climate."

"It's early summer here," Violet said, touching the terrifically scented white blooms of a shrub that grew next to the end of the dock. "This is philadelphus, isn't it?"

In the middle distance clumps of trees and shrubs hid the actual size of the island. Many seemed to be blooming, and there were birds and butterflies and bees everywhere. The honeybees were huge and reminded me of nothing so much as the ones in the Woods Noirell, which were said to be descended from the fairy bees of Melmúsion.

That made me wonder. I looked up and around more carefully, hunting for some indication that we were still on Alinor, and found the contrary.

"There's no sun," I said. "We've left Alinor."

"Ah," said Jullanar Maebh, and dumped the ewer out on the ground so she could re-fill it with water from beyond the world's end.

***

We made our way slowly towards the centre of the garden and, presumably, the island. It was very level, perhaps a foot or two above the sea. We could hear the soft lapping of the waves for quite some time, though as we drew nearer the copse of trees before us the bird-song drowned it out.

I had thought the Tillarny limes of the Woods Noirell in their autumn bloom, thunderous with the hum of the bees, had been magical almost unto a fairy tale. Walking along that springy lawn, the grass cool and welcoming to our bare feet, the air redolent with light, the sky always limpid and lucid as early dawn, the birdsong like true music, I realized two things.

First, that the Woods Noirell were indeed akin to this.

Secondly, that it felt like home. Every moment I expected my mother to come tripping out from behind a shrub, her hair and her hands full of flowers, her mouth and her eyes laughing, her gown green and white for the Lady she had loved so much.

I walked beside Mr. Dart, whose face (when I sneaked glances at him) showed that he was responding to some other element of the air, the light, the garden. I felt relaxed and welcomed, as if all my cares and concerns had lifted from me, as if I were a young child safe in my mother's arms. He looked as if he had caught the scent of adventure, and his eyes were as lucid and light-filled as the sky.

I watched his face, the yearning and the wonder on it, the way that the auburn of his hair and beard seemed richer in colour, almost as coppery as Jullanar Maebh's curls. Barefoot and bareheaded, in the silvery-grey silk tunic, he looked like an ancient priest leading us to the sacred grove.

I wished suddenly that I knew more of the old ways that pertained to the Lady. The churches of Northwest Oriole had come quite late, adopted in parallel with the institutions of the Empire. The religion of the Lady was much older, of course. In the old *old* days she had been worshipped in the circles of hawthorn and holly and, sometimes, stone. The Lady had been protecting us against the Dark Kings for longer than any written record. The idea of using buildings had been the innovation of a sect out of Lind: the oldest church was supposed to be the one in Markpfen, Lind's capital.

In the half-century before the coming of the Empire the Church of Lind had been increasing in power and influence under the guidance of a series of extremely charismatic archbishops and abbesses with close ties to the Kings of Lind. Mr. Dart would know all the details, no doubt, but I seemed to recall something about a series of sets of siblings who had between them held all the important positions; and who had decided, on meeting the early envoys of the Empire, that they could see which way the wind was blowing. They had assisted in the conquest, and saw their sect rise dominant over most of the continent.

The Dukes of Fiellan, like the Earls of the Farry March, had not been so eager to welcome the foreign invaders, and had held out for nearly thirty years before succumbing. The Imperial Highway punching down the length of Fiellan, crossed at Yrchester with the main east-west highway, had been both statement and enactment of the superiority of Imperial power. Once the road (with all of its magic, and all of the non-magical influences that soon followed along) was laid, Fiellan boasted of being on the way to Astandalas. But I had already learned to my cost that there were those who had never quite forgiven the dukes for falling to the Empire, and who had maintained worship of the Dark Kings in secret even unto our own days, this side of the Fall of Astandalas.

"Oh," said Hal softly, but it was so quiet that we all stopped immediately to look at him.

He ducked his head as if a tad embarrassed, but soon lifted it to gesture at the flowers growing beside us. "Honesty and thrift," he said; "they're names for these flowers. It's odd," he added. "They don't normally grow together quite like this."

I looked down. While I'd been pondering the history of the Church of Lind, we had crossed the wide lawn and entered into an area where the grasses had been left to grow into a knee-high flowering meadow.

There were even more bees here. I could feel their hum in my bones, my blood, in the faint tingle I felt when I came close to magic. These bees might be the fabled bees of Melmúsion, or they might not, but they were kin, certainly, to those of my maternal inheritance.

"Well then," Violet said, "let us crown ourselves with virtues. Which are the ones we want, Hal?"

Hal showed us the pink and white pompoms of the thrift, which grew on naked stalks about half a foot high from a tussock of wiry leaves, and the deep magenta honesty, which was taller and leafier.

We set down our bags and collected armfuls of flowers, then sat there in the grass, trying not to stare unbecomingly at each others' bare legs and feet, though I'm sure everyone felt, as I did, the faint thrill of breaking a social taboo.

"I can tell you don't have any sisters," Hal said after a moment, watching Mr. Dart's attempts. "Start with the honesty, and add thrift after."

"Seems most sound advice," Mr. Dart commented, obediently starting over again with the long stalks of the honesty. I thought he was doing very well, given that he had only one hand to be using.

"This is called money-plant where I'm from," Jullanar Maebh offered. "The seedpods are all silvery when they dry."

Mr. Dart snorted. "Start with honesty, add thrift, and one ends up with silver coin? 'Twould be an excellent sermon of a Sunday. Why are you so good at this, Mr. Greenwing?"

"I helped my mother make coronets for holy days," I said after a moment. "When we danced the Lady in."

Hal looked up from his own rather neat effort. "Like you did for the bees, in the autumn?"

I nodded, trying on my wreath of honesty to see if it would hold, and commencing to poke in thrift pompoms once it seemed as if it would. "Hawthorn in the spring, and holly and wayfaring-tree in the autumn."

"Your mother followed the old ways, then?" Violet asked, as if it was all one to her, but when I glanced at her her eyes seemed just a little too intent.

It seemed poor form to make a crown of honesty and then speak a falsehood, however polite, and so I said, "I don't truly know, but I believe so. I have recently learned that her family line has fairy blood, and certainly the Woods Noirell are full of very old magic. I should like to learn more about the history of her family."

"So far you've called forth a dragon to test your suitability as an heir," Mr. Dart said, regarding his final product with vague dissatisfaction. "Well, it's a little lopsided, but I don't think it's going to fall apart entirely immediately."

"Can we ask for much more?" I said, intending humour but realizing, from the way he jerked and frowned at me, that it had probably sounded much more snide. "Mr. Dart—"

He waved me off with a curt gesture and put on his circlet. For a moment his eyes flashed green, and I shivered as a wave of something curled over and through us. I was not sure if it had come from my friend or in reaction to something he or we had done, but it was powerful and not entirely benign.

"Everyone finished?" Violet asked, brushing bits of leaf and stalk off her garments. "Then shall we continue?"

I could have sat there forever, I thought a bit forlornly, if only I had not put my foot in my mouth.

The grass path led straight towards the largest clump of trees. As we drew closer a familiar heady fragrance reached us, and the bee-song thrummed even louder.

"Now this feels like the Woods Noirell over again," Mr. Dart murmured, obviously recognizing scent and sound as well.

The others said nothing. I relaxed even further, letting the sound and scent soothe me, smoothing ragged edges in my heart and soul. I wondered whether this balm was sufficient to mend the damage done by the wireweed, or if it were all as temporary as our tenure here hopefully would be.

The trees seemed *more* than the trees in the Woods Noirell. The heart-shaped leaves glittered like faceted emeralds, the trunks shone like polished silver, the bracts and powder-puff flowers like so many hundreds of thousands of tiny golden bells. And the bees, when we came closer to them, were not the old-gold and black of the bees of the Woods, but new-minted gold and ruby, and half the length of my thumb.

"The bees of Melmúsion," I breathed as we approached the ring of trees. No one replied, because as soon as we tried to pass through the gap our way was blocked.

The man standing foursquare in the path was dark-skinned and dressed in an extravagant costume of cloth-of-gold and blue-green silk embroidered with diamonds; he wore a diamond-and-sapphire coronet, and four layers of necklaces, the most dramatic one made of rubies the size of quail eggs.

It took me a long moment to recognize the outfit from the portraits at Morrowlea as the Astandalan court costume of a very high ranking nobleman; and even longer to recognize the man as Hal.

Real Hal stood stock-still, eyes fixed on his gorgeously dressed double, face stricken. Not-Hal stared back, expression cool and collected. A fragment of a description of the imperial court floated through my mind, unattached to context: *The marble countenances of the Starry Court stood guard …*

After a brief further hesitation Hal stepped forward. Not close enough to touch his double, but foremost out of our instinctive huddle.

"So now is when we pay with our coin of secrets, is it?'" he asked, his voice barely wavering.

Hal was one of the most morally courageous people I'd ever met, as brave in many ways as my father.

The double inclined his head slowly, expression unchanging. A subtle movement lower down caught my eye. Real Hal was clenching his hands into fists.

It took him a long moment of staring down his double before he lifted his chin and, in a voice that no longer wavered, spoke forth the uttermost secret of his heart.

"My father died falling down the stairs. I pushed him. It wasn't on purpose, I was foolishly angry as a foolish child can be, but it was my doing. He lost his balance and fell, and broke his neck. He died instantly, with my name on his lips."

And made Hal the Imperial Duke of Fillering Pool as a result, I finished silently.

The double smiled gently and stepped aside to let us pass. We filed past him without looking, attention on the quiet green lawn before us and the hedge that faced us; but when I turned to look back the figure had disappeared and so too had the gap in the trees.

The grass lawn gave way to a carefully laid and perfectly circular hawthorn hedge in full bloom. I was reassured by the choice of plant; like the trees all this seemed of a piece with my mother's family magic. I wondered, if I looked more carefully at Ihuranuë's notes and asked my grandmother to look at the library at the Castle Noirell, if I would find some connection. It seemed as if it could hardly be coincidental, though it was coincidence that I had chosen to study Ariadne nev Lingarel's poem.

Magistra Aurelia's comments about performing a ritual to increase serendipity came to mind. I pondered the idea as we approached the arch in the hawthorn hedge, the scent of the may overwhelming for an instant the heady perfume exhaled by the trees, and found before us another velvet-smooth lawn, this one studded with daisies and some incredibly deep blue flower Hal identified as a stemless mountain gentian. They looked like puddles of the sky scattered across the sward.

Violet's double came next.

She was easier to recognize, both because we had an idea now of what to expect and because she was wearing the same gown she had when we first saw her in Lark's court. The dark green gown, the lavender slippers, the veil over her hair were all the same. Only her expression was different: not the calm the real Violet had shown (as marble a countenance as Hal's courtly double), but a much darker and crueler smile that made her look disquietingly like Lark.

It took the real Violet longer, it felt, than it had Hal to decide to speak forth her secret. She locked eyes with her double, who smiled with a clear enjoyment of real-Violet's distress. When at last she spoke, however, her voice was clear; though tears ran freely down her face.

"It was my fault my brother was captured. I was jealous of his magic and our mother's preference for him, but I swear I intended it only as a prank. I had no idea that he would be made captive for real …"

Not-Violet's smile slid into a pitiless sneer at real-Violet's trailing-off, but she stepped aside and let us pass.

Walking across the next lawn I thought that I had no secrets of such moment as Hal's or Violet's, but when we reached the holly hedge and I saw who waited for us there I discovered how little I truly knew myself, or wanted to.

I met my own brown eyes and was conscious I had begun trembling.

My double was garbed in my ordinary clothes, over which was cast the hooded black robes the Black Priest of the Dark Kings had worn. Instead of the polished mask, however, the face that hid my own was … mine.

The mask's expression was affable and friendly. It seemed as if it were simply my own face, by how it moved, but I knew, with an absolute certainty, that the apparent visage was only a front.

The longer I looked the heavier my unspoken secret was.

My father was decorated by the Emperor for his bravery. He'd expressed amazement that I tried to hold myself to the standard of the Heart of Glory, but how could I not? A man was supposed to follow his father, if his father were anything worth imitating.

Hal had just confessed he'd accidentally killed his own father, Violet that some ill-spirited prank had gone terribly wrong. Mr. Dart and Jullanar Maebh had their own secrets yet to face.

I had to try several times before any words would come out. I had been utterly unable to explain to my father what I feared, what I wanted, what I yearned for with respect to him. It was ironic that to escape the Labyrinth of Irany I had to vocalize that deep and shameful truth to a false double of myself.

Behind the mask my double's eyes were terrified. I wondered what my own real ones looked like. Much the same, probably, though my expression was undoubtedly not so affable or friendly or calm.

I started and discarded half-a-dozen near-truths before I metaphorically kicked myself and made the leap: "I don't know who I am without the wireweed."

My double regarded me, and I swallowed hard, and added: "I've been under curses and enchantments since I was fifteen. I don't know who I am if you strip all that away. I don't know if I want to know

… I think it will be a great disappointment to everyone. I think my father will be sorry he came home for me."

And that was the truth, the secret I had never quite articulated to myself, let alone to anyone else.

My double performed one of the elaborate bows I'd developed as response to all the snubs of the last summer, complete down to the heel-click (which looked less silly than I'd feared), and let us through.

Like Hal and Violet I could not bear to look at anyone else.

***

At the centre of the next circle was a low lavender hedge, the purple blossoms surprising after all the green and white but yet satisfying in their simplicity, and satisfying, too, in the indication that perhaps we had not strayed entirely away from Alinor and our lady mage. Violet and Jullanar Maebh both looked pleased to see the lavender, at any rate. Hal muttered something about it blooming early. Mr. Dart was pressing ahead in his eagerness.

There was some magic that kept us from looking too far forward. Though the lavender hedge was hardly more than waist high, we could not see what lay beyond until we came up to the entrance and met Jullanar Maebh's double.

Her double was dressed in a simple white shift; her copper hair, twice as long as it was now, fell loose well past her waist in heavy ringlets. The lowest tendrils brushed against the tips of the lavender flowers. She wore a crown of periwinkle and white jasmine, and she was smiling.

The real Jullanar Maebh gasped a little on seeing her. The double continued to smile, her face luminous and full of a solemnity that seemed an emotion beyond joy, not sorrow.

Jullanar Maebh's voice shook not with grief or guilt or fear, but the revelation of a deeply private joy.

"Before I left for Tara I met the Lady of the Green and White in the sacred grove near my home. She blessed me and said I should see her Hunter before the end ..."

I was more relieved than I should have been that someone, at least, had a happy secret to hold close to her heart. I wondered despite my good resolutions whether that made the whole of life happier, that its secret core was such a joy, as my own doubts shadowed all the minor happinesses of my own life.

The next hedge was of beech decked in autumn gold. The Mr. Dart who met us there looked exactly like the real Mr. Dart, down to the stone arm and the lucent eyes and the plum-and-grey clothes.

My Mr. Dart met his double's eyes calmly, before something seemed to go out of him, and he said, a hint of rueful laughter in his voice (how could he laugh, I thought in an internal exclamation, before his words penetrated):

"In general I am very happy with myself and who I am, but ... I have also been deeply jealous of Jemis Greenwing for most of my life."

CHAPTER TWENTY-NINE
The Oubliette

On the other side of the beech hedge was the centre of the garden, or nearly.

The path finished at another grass circle, this one girding a large and nearly perfectly spherical shrub.

We all looked at it and then at each other, the incongruity of the topiary breaking through the embarrassment of our various confessions, and then Hal started to laugh. "A box of uncommon girth, indeed! Your riddle-master was fond of her horticultural puns, Jemis. What was the next line? We're supposed to find something in the box?"

Violet dug around in her bag and pulled out the piece of paper with the riddle on it. "On the island there is a garden neither of romance nor of wonder, but in a box of uncommon girth will you find both."

"*In* a box … You're sure of the preposition, Jemis?"

Unravelling the poem felt a hundred years and a lifetime ago. It was hard to think back across the unexpected revelation that Mr. Dart was jealous of me to the mad heights of ecstasy of the wireweed burning up my magic nearly to the bitter end.

"I think so," I said hesitantly. "I wonder … I hope I didn't miss anything …"

"The rest of your interpretation was correct,"Violet said, but absently; she was frowning down at the paper, and soon added, in a lower voice, "*Ask the one who knows darkness without end for the means of light, and the one cast outside for the secret that lies within, and the one cursed for a blessing. Be courteous, and accept what doom you are offered.You are clever enough to have deciphered this, and foolish enough to have needed to: by any door, you will find wisdom, though it be your death.*"

"Perhaps I missed something," I said helplessly. Hal studied the box sphere and then, with an actual spoken apology to the plant, pressed forward into it.

"My brother was born blind,"Violet said, even as Hal managed to wriggle his way between the branches.

I was watching Hal's progress, but said, "Irany was noted to be a very eccentric wizard, but that's well beyond eccentricity and into the stuff of legend."

The leaves sprang back with a concerted rustle, making it look disturbingly as if the topiary had eaten him.

"Er, Hal," I began, only to be interrupted by his exclamation.

"The Emperor!"Then, in a much different voice, Hal said, "I do beg your pardon. Er, may I call my friends?"

We were already hastening to follow him into the shrub, which rustled in seeming aggravation before letting us pass. I realized even as I pushed branches aside that I was ascribing sentience and sapience to a topiary, but could not but believe it to be the case.

The topiary had seemed perhaps twenty feet in diameter when we were on the outside. Once through the clutching branches I burst into a dim green space, very still and solemn, with grey-brown branches curving out and upwards overhead to form a hollow centre much, much larger than twenty feet.

At the exact centre of the hollow four trunks rose up, gnarled in their bark but straight in their direction, until they forked overhead to cross into a four-way arch and then fork again to form the understructure of the sphere. I wondered for a brief moment whether there were three other paths leading to three other bridges, but my attention was soon absorbed, as Hal's had been and so too the others', by the gryphon that lay couchant under the arches.

It had a falcon's head, with dark streaks under its golden eyes. It was slate-blue and fawn, like a peregrine, the feathers shading smoothly into soft dun fur at the withers. A tufted tail curled neatly around the lion's hind legs, the tuft flicking every now and again as it regarded us.

"This wasn't in your riddle," Mr. Dart murmured to me.

"Perhaps it is the guardian of the way, who will offer us our doom?" I returned as quietly.

Violet stepped forward and curtsied deeply to the gryphon, with a grace I remembered from Morrowlea but an inflection to the gesture that I had not before seen.

"Lady," said the gryphon, inclining its head to her. Its voice was smooth, alto, ambiguously gendered. Did gryphons have genders? They were as mythical, as legendary, I had thought, as a dragon or a giant or a mermaid. Well, I had yet to meet a giant.

Violet said, "We seek my brother, captive in the Oubliette of the prison of Orio City, and safe passage through to the building known as the hunting lodge of the King of Lind."

The gryphon considered this, tilting its head back and forth to regard us with first one eye and then the other. Its tail twitched a little more vigorously.

"And who," it said at last, "is your clever riddle-master?"

I stepped forward to perform the bow I had been taught to use before great lords. "I deciphered the riddle, but it was all five of us who unravelled its sense and made our way here. I could not have done it alone."

"And so you seek to find your way together. What offering do you bring?"

Mr. Dart said, "We cleansed ourselves in water that did not touch the ground, and garbed ourselves in threads unspun by human hands. We crowned ourselves with honesty and thrift, and bring to you fine white bread made without yeast, water that has never seen the sun, and a fruit of next year's crop."

Violet laid down the scone in its napkin. Jullanar Maebh had been carrying the silver ewer this whole time, and now, with a curtsey of her own, she placed it on the grass next to the scone. Hal placed the unripe figs of the breba crop next to the scone, and that left me.

I said, "The coin that is never minted and everywhere accepted is a secret, which we have disburdened to those who met us at each of the gates through the hedges coming here."

The gryphon's front talons, which were more a falcon's foot than a lion's, dug deep into the grass. We watched it warily, knowing that that beak and those claws could do untold damage to us; though of course it didn't need physical violence to leave us trapped here as long as it pleased.

It said, "Your offerings are acceptable to me. You may pass by the fourfold gate into the places that you seek."

And with that it disappeared and our offerings with it.

We stared at the empty space where it had been, and then at the natural arches of the fourfold gate. "How do you think we pass through?" Jullanar Maebh asked at last.

"I think we should hold hands," Hal said. "We don't want to get separated at this point."

"Good idea," Violet decided, and so we spent a few moments arranging ourselves. Mr. Dart, having only one good arm, had to be at the end. He held Jullanar Maebh's right hand with his left; she held mine, and I Violet's, and then came Hal at the forefront.

"Well?" said Hal, looking at the scuffed ground, bare of growth but scattered with dead leaves from the great box sphere around us.

"In the box you will find both romance and wonder," I paraphrased from my riddle, hoping desperately I had not missed something important, sure that neither romance nor wonder were the only meanings of those particular Old Shaian words.

"To the Oubliette and the Hunting Lodge of the King of Lind!" he cried, and walked through the arch that faced us, disappearing before Violet had more than begun to move herself.

***

We found ourselves in darkness, in close quarters, and back in the mortal world, but that was all I knew at first as a roiling wave of pain started somewhere near my toes and rolled inexorably up my body to crest in my head.

I cried out despite myself, gripping Jullanar Maebh's and Violet's hands convulsively. They gripped back, and with that comfort I was eventually able to focus on my breathing. At last I was able to relax my grip somewhat, though I did not let go. Neither did they.

It was still dark, and still close quarters. The pain subsided to a bearable steady state, but thin shivers of anxiety at the darkness and suffocating closeness started to run up and down my body. I was conscious of a deep shame, but it felt distant, far removed from the physical panic.

"Who comes?" a voice said out of the darkness. I was not the only one who jumped, each motion rippling through our linked hands.

After a moment Mr. Dart whispered, "What did he say? Did anyone understand it?"

I turned my head towards the sound of his voice. "He said, 'Who comes?'" I said, my voice cracking. I coughed, turning my head into my shoulder, and took a long time to realize the voice had spoken in Old Shaian, not modern.

This must be the one who knows darkness without end, the guardian of our doom. I tried to capture the other parts of the riddle's end, the questions we were supposed to ask, but every time my thoughts were scattered by the sensation of the dark pressing ever closer. The tremors were constant now, and my heart beat high and rapidly in my throat. My hands were clammy and cold; Violet's were, too, but Jullanar Maebh's seemed burning-hot.

Hal said, "Violet? Jemis? Can you ask him our questions?"

"I don't remember them," I confessed, my voice only a step up from a whimper. I bit my tongue in humiliation, but could not do anything but stand there. Where was the familiar courage? Where was the cool, clear, world of mortal danger? Surely we were in great peril; but all I could feel was panic fear.

"Ask the one in endless darkness for the means of light," Mr. Dart said softly.

"Ask the one cast outside for the joy that lies within," Jullanar Maebh added.

"And the one cursed for a blessing," Hal finished.

Violet's hand clenched harder on mine. I stood there, trembling, unable to bring forth words in Shaian whether old or modern. My mind felt as if it were roaring like the Magarran Strid at the Turning of the Waters.

Wherever we were was quiet but for a faint whispering sound, like a distant watercourse. The air was cool and stale: indoor air, which did not make me feel any better about the situation. We were in the Oubliette of the prison-palace of Orio City, potentially in a magically folded space somehow bridging the hundred or more miles between Orio City and the hunting lodge of the Kings of Lind, trapped in the end of a riddle.

A slow shuffling noise came towards us. The echoes made it seem as if it came from everywhere at once. The hairs on the back of my neck rose. It sounded like something dragging, and my mind filled with images of serpents and hideous monsters out of fairy tales. We had just encountered a gryphon: what might await us here?

The same voice as before spoke, this time in modern Shaian: "You are not from the far past! But you do not come by the door my captors use. Who are you? How did you come here? Are you here to kill me?"

The eagerness with which he asked this last question was perhaps the most horrifying thing I had ever heard. Mr. Dart cried a wordless denial, and Hal exclaimed, "No! We are—I think we are—Violet?"

"Violet," murmured the voice, and the shuffling came closer. "I … I seem to know that name … From long ago … It was a … a joke, a nickname … from the summer …"

Nên Corovel, the Rainbow-Girt Isle, the Summer Country.

Violet spoke barely above a whisper. "Ru … Rory …"

I clung desperately to their words, refusing to let the dark swallow me up no matter how much I trembled or sweated or lost my breath. Something about the way she said Rory was odd. Jullanar Maebh stirred next to me, her hand clenching mine almost as hard as Violet's for a moment, and I thought of her name and the idiosyncratic spellings of Outer Reaches names. *Ru* could well be short for *Ruaridh*.

Ruaridh. Ruaridh of Nên Corovel, where Hal had gone as a child to meet the Lady.

Ruaridh, as everyone had been taught at the kingschool, was the name of the son and heir of the Lady of Alinor.

***

The revelations came crowding fast, almost as fast as the crashing waves of the headache. I couldn't see anything clearly, the forms of my friends and our captive-to-be-rescued haloed in strange colours like the ones you see when your eyes are closed. Mr. Dart and Ruaridh wavered brightest, then Hal, then Jullanar Maebh, then Violet. Each time one of them shifted position my eyes stabbed into my head.

"Jemis," Hal said in an urgent whisper, even as Violet kept speaking to her brother, her voice shifting accents to something at once more upper-class, like Hal's, and more of a brogue, like Jullanar Maebh's.

I shook my head, gripping whoever's hands I was holding tight.

"I can't," I said, my voice hoarse. "I can't …"

Mr. Dart cleared his throat as if that would help mine. "Jemis, we need you to think. How do we get away from here?"

I turned my eyes to the brightest of the two haloes. One green backlit with gold, the other a kind of dim orange. Somehow I knew that the dimness was not how it should be; that the years a captive had broken something fundamental about Ruaridh's magic.

"On the island there is a garden neither of romance nor of wonder, but in a box of uncommon girth will you find both," I said in a near-whimper, for I remembered that niggling sense that I'd missed something, and knew that it had to do with that word for wonder, *vhailor*, which in Old Shaian meant *wonder*, yes, but also *poetry*, and a *sacred altar*, and *sacrifice*, and a certain sort of death.

As for *heür*, which was usually translated as *romance*, its primary meaning was actually *path*, with the connotation of wilderness; and thus adventure; and, more oddly, the kind of high-hearted chivalry that was understood in the ancient days to be a form of charity.

"What, then?" said Mr. Dart. "We have entered the box of uncommon girth."

I swallowed, feeling the motion shudder through all through my body. My extremities were tingling, fingers and toes as full of pins-and-needles as the mermaid who had given up the sea. The haloes brightened, until I could feel them on my skin, thrumming louder than my heartbeat.

One dose, perhaps two, away from the final sleep, Lark had said, and I had had how many?

"Ruaridh," I said once I thought I could speak calmly.

"Yes?" came the strange voice, shuffling closer. I closed my eyes but the haloes still burned in my vision.

Ask the one who knows darkness without end for the means of light
And the one cast outside for the secret that lies within
And the one cursed for a blessing.

Three questions, it sounded like, and three answers. Except that was never how these things worked.

Be courteous, and accept what doom you are offered. You are clever enough to have deciphered this, and foolish enough to have needed to: by any door, you will find wisdom, though it be your death.

"Did you have a question for me?" came the voice, eager, doubting, hopeful, anxious. He sounded much younger than he must be.

I hesitated, images and allusions chiming off each other in my mind without quite sounding out clearly.

"Hold our hands, so we form a circle," I said at last.

"Jemis," said Mr. Dart, even as we all shuffled around until Hal, on one end, and Mr. Dart, on the other, bracketed the blazing but broken halo that was Ruaridh of Nên Corovel.

But Ruaridh said nothing but a murmured, "Ah, there is your hand, and yours as well," and something snicked into place inside my mind.

Nine drops of blood offered to the everlasting fire had been our means of leaving the Hearth and finding the great fig tree in its court-yard. Seven tears dropped into a silent pool within the uncut stone of a cliff had given us a bridge through thin air to an island beyond the world's end. Five secrets had given us access to the Oubliette, last and most terrible of the prison cells of the palace.

Three questions to form a doorway, and one true sacrifice to open it.

I opened my eyes to the endless darkness and the bright haloes, facing inwards to a circle I would not get to stay within, body failing me from the cruelty and carelessness of someone I had once loved.

Vhailor sae heür: wonder and romance, poetry and adventure, altar and path, sacrifice and chivalry.

We did not have to move to find the doorway, any more than we had in order to enter the Hearth, the heart of the prison.

I called up my magic, as Hal had taught me, and I thought of my mother dancing with the bees, and my father coming home no matter how far and how hard the journey, and how much I wanted to see Mr. Dart come into his power, and then I said, in a clear and confident voice:

"*Norima,*" and there was the first slash of light, a vertical line drawn in fire the colour of a candle flame;

"*Norimai,*" and there was the second slash, three feet from the first; and

"*Enorimaso,*" and there was the third, a horizontal slash above our heads.

The space between was black as anything. I looked at it, and gripped my friends' hands tightly. Jullanar Maebh was on my left, and Violet on my right.

A wind began to blow from the doorway I had created, a soft and welcome zephyr. I could hear a sound like thousands of wings rustling along it, as if invisible birds flew past us. They were scented of something sweet and wild and fragrant.

Ruaridh said softly, "*Norima.* Hope. Be hopeful. I had forgotten what it was like."

The wind blew, the thousands of invisible birds flew past, the scent grew stronger and stronger, and my heart swelled with all the possible futures that doorway could give me.

Be courteous, and accept what doom you are offered. You are clever enough to have deciphered this, and foolish enough to have needed to: by any door, you will find wisdom, though it be your death.

The wind moved our hair, tugged at our makeshift silk tunics, scoured away the grime, presented image after image of potential lives only to whirl them away again after the merest glimpse.

I grasped one, where Violet and I sat next to each other, reading, a cat on her lap and a child on mine, my father lying back in a chair beside us, happily asleep, a sense of coziness and protection and freedom encircling us with a wild green wind no less peaceful for its wildness.

"*Malaso,*" I whispered, the ancient word for abnegation, for abdication, for loss.

All the lights went out at once.

CHAPTER *THIRTY*
The Wood of Spiritual Refreshment

I had endeavoured, at various times in my life, not to succumb to morbidity, but the fact that I could point without difficulty to those times indicated just how frequent a visitor the thoughts had been. No doubt my father's twice-reported first death, his second by apparent suicide, and then my mother's subsequent death of the influenza had made the subject the more pressing.

The homilies offered by the priests of Ragnor Bella had never really given me a clear picture of what happened after, except to indicate that the Lady of the Green and White would claim those who followed her and bring the worthy to her feasting-hall and garden. There were, of course, many injunctions as to what made one worthy.

When I rolled over and sat up and looked about me, I discovered I had walked sideways out of my life and into—well, not a dream, exactly, but rather what my daydreams and poor attempts at poetry had been trying to imagine.

At length I discovered I felt better: far better than I had in months, in fact, or even years. I was breathing easily, and the strange smouldering buzz that the wireweed had given me was gone, with a bright effervescent sense of health and wellness in its place. I felt more alive than I ever had; it was this realization that led me to the discovery that I had, in point of fact, died.

I was sitting on a fine lawn, much sprinkled with pink and white daisies, yellow buttercups, and something prostrate and clear blue with little furry leaves that might have been Hal's blue-eyed Veronica. I smiled at the thought, and continued smiling with delight as I took in the wider surroundings.

Over to my left was a stream, very clear and seemingly quite shallow, with jewel-like stones in its bed and festoons of greenery dotted with little white flowers swaying in its current. The far side of the stream was wooded, with very tall trees of a rough reddish bark, and long drooping branches with multitudes of short fine branchlets giving the effect of fern leaves. There was less grass on that side of the stream but even more flowers.

There were trees on my side of the stream as well, set back a little from the mead I had found myself in. These bore flowers and fruits of luminous colours and scents both very rich and sweet and yet invigorating, even exalting.

I breathed deeply, as if I could swallow the light and the air, and rejoiced in the fact that I did not even want to sneeze. The island in the heart of the labyrinth had been a dim shadow of this place. Here there was a sun, brilliant but yet not uncomfortable.

I stood up and brushed myself off a bit. I was no longer wearing the makeshift silk tunic, but rather a splendid version of my favourite suit of clothes. The dark blue and tan seemed richer and lovelier, my cravat more comfortable, my boots more resplendently polished and yet better fitting. My head was bare, but when I thought that and looked around there was my beloved Fillering Pool tricorner, its feather curling more extravagantly than it ever had before.

I had always rather assumed that one would be met with a guide of some form. This solitary arrival in a lonely wood was not something any priest had ever mentioned.

As I settled my hat on my head and looked about to decide what direction I should go, a shift in the breeze brought me the sound of conversation and merriment. I turned, tilting my head to hear it better and be sure of the direction, and heard Mr. Dart say, "Jemis."

I spun around, delighted and rueful in equal measure that he should be joining me here so soon, but no matter where I looked I could see no sign of him, and though I waited, listening, I could hear nothing further.

At length I decided to head towards the voices. I had only taken one or two steps when I discovered that someone was there, standing next to a rock and observing me, her chin lifting in acknowledgement as I looked at her in enquiry.

I had, I supposed, always assumed that it would be my father or my mother who would greet me, or failing that an angel of the Lady. This woman might have been an angel in the technical sense of being an agent of the divine, but her face and demeanour seemed entirely human.

Ethnically Shaian, she wore her black hair up in narrow braids twisted into a kind of coronet, with creamy flowers woven into the design. Her dress was a simple cream-coloured silk with a leaf-green lace overgown, both gathered high under her bosom to fall down like a column. It was a very lovely style, I thought, and wished vaguely that it had been the fashion when I was in university and when (and here I faltered a little) I was alive, I supposed.

Her face would probably not have been considered beautiful, but here the light and the air and the emotion behind the expression all conspired to make her luminous and rare as a lily. She was neither young nor old, though her eyes were full of knowledge and memory.

There did not seem to be any reason to be embarrassed that I was looking my fill: she regarded me as calmly and with as much interest, until I finally met her gaze and essayed a polite bow.

"Are you Ariadne nev Lingarel?" I asked, not quite certain but seeing in her posture and her jaw something of that magisterial portrait in the Morrowlea collection.

"I am," she said, in what might have been Classical Shaian and might have been Modern. It didn't seem to matter, there.

"I am honoured, ma'am," I said, bowing more deeply. "I am Jemis Greenwing. I have studied your poem; it is a masterpiece."

She inclined her head, though I could see her lips twitching with amusement at this. "It has brought you here."

"Have I died?"

"Down there—back there—in that other place: yes."

"I see," I said.

She did smile. "You died well, Jemis Greenwing."

I confess I stared at her for a moment, before looking at the wider surroundings, and then I bowed again to her. "Thank you, ma'am."

"Will you walk with me a while?" she asked, reaching to take my arm when I (somewhat flabbergasted, I admit) nodded. "You doubt me."

"Not that I died," I assured her. There was some settled certainty in me that this place was not part of the mortal worlds, nor yet some part of the Kingdom between the Worlds. Perhaps it was that my body, for the first time in my memory, felt wholly and utterly well.

"Then that you died well? Be assured, your sacrifice was not in vain: your friends arrived at their destination safely and without further injury."

"Except for my dying on them," I said, though there was something about the air of that place that softened that rue.

She smiled and gently directed me to start walking away from the stream. I complied, feeling a zephyr in my face that brought with it a scent that lifted my heart and seemed to break up any megrims I was still, somehow, clinging to. We walked into the woods, though ahead I could see a kind of brightness that suggested an opening in the trees.

"Do not fret," Ariadne nev Lingarel murmured. "It does not come immediately for all, the refreshment of the soul. Some of us take longer to be ready to go on."

"On?" I said, but even as I turned my head to look at her she was using her free hand to indicate I should look ahead. Turning back, I saw that we had come to the edge of the woods.

We stood on a kind of bluff. Below us the land opened up into a wide valley, wooded in parts and full of flowering meadows in others; everywhere there were birds, and the scent of good things, and in the distance cattle and deer and horses and other, stranger creatures. I glanced at them, but my eyes were inexorably drawn to the mountains in the blue distance, and the sunrise dawning behind them.

Time really didn't seem to mean much there. I stood for a long time, gazing at those distant mountains, feeling some aching emptiness inside of me start to be—not filled, exactly, but transformed, so that I realized that the twisted hunger I had felt was untwisting, unclenching, becoming cleansed, becoming properly directed.

All from the sight of distant mountains, white-crowned and splendid, rising up at the edge of wherever we were to hide whatever it was that was on the other side, that I knew with an instinct deeper than anything else I had ever felt before was *home*.

At long length I took a deep breath, and wiped my face—I had been weeping—and turned to Ariadne nev Lingarel, who was gazing at the Mountains herself with a patient yearning. In the light streaming towards us between the shoulders of the peaks she looked youthful and anciently wise, her dark eyes happy, and my mind suddenly thundered with that soaring ode to the hearth and heart of the palace-prison she had spent so long in.

She turned her head to me, her eyes still glad, and I knew that somehow she understood exactly what her poem had been to me.

"Yes," she said softly, answering the unspoken thought. "Is it time for you to go to the Mountains?"

I looked again at them, and felt the yearning to go rise up in me, immediately to be tempered with a desire to explore the woods a little more, to spend some time by the stream, to speak to whoever was laughing and talking just out of sight.

"Not yet," I said, unsure suddenly whether I had just spoken my own damnation.

The poet placed her hand on my arm. "Do not fret. You would not long for the Mountains if you could not go to them."

It was a simple statement, but the truth of it echoed in the woods with absolute finality. "Why then do I not want to go now that I have seen them?"

"You have seen them long since," she said, guiding me back away from the edge of the bluff and into the woods again. "Your soul cries out for refreshment before it undertakes the next journey. There is no shame, nor concern, that you are not yet ready for the next stage. I myself have been waiting here for many years."

Four hundred or so. "What keeps you—us—here?"

She actually laughed. "Nothing! Or nothing but ourselves. Do you not yet understand, my friend? Our lives as we lived them bring us here. Our Lady knows that we come tired and weary and sore of spirit; few are those who arrive whole-hearted and without any un-finished business."

"The saints?" I asked, vague stories from church coming to mind.

"They are sometimes among that number, yes."

She had been a politician, I supposed. I smiled at her, then turned my gaze back to the woods around us. We had returned to the stream, though away from our first meeting-place; the trees were closer to-gether here, and ran more to ones with multitudes of four-petalled white or pink flowers.

"Speak your questions without fear or shame," the poet said.

"It is not yet a question," I said. "I don't quite understand … I can see why I would want to meet you, because of your poem, but I don't—are you delaying your journey to wait for me? Why would you do that?"

"Why do you think I did not need to meet you?" she countered.

I stopped beneath a waterfall of blossoms, discovering that below the tree was a carpet of lily-of-the-valley in full fragrant bloom. "You lived hundreds of years before me. How could you be waiting for me?"

She smiled at me, unperturbed. "It is a mystery, but not so great a one, perhaps. In this wood time does not have the meaning it does back there, back then. We are each here as long as we need to be to be refreshed, for our souls to be healed of the wounds inflicted on them. I have waited for those whose souls were stirred into exaltation from my writing, because they taught me what I wrote."

A little away from us was a cluster of waist-high arching stems, pairs of waxy white bells hanging down from each leaf node all along the curve. There was something about their grace, the elegant and simple line of the plant, that reminded me of the 'boring' passages of

On Being Incarcerated in Orio Prison, the ones that turned out to be the key to escape.

"There," Ariadne nev Lingarel said, and when I turned to her her face was alight. "My friend, when your heart is stirred you think of my poem: can you not realize what a gift that is to me? What *grace* that is to me?"

I stared dumbly at her, my only answer, foolishly, that line of the poem about crescent and re-crescent shadows.

She patted me on the arm. "I was not a good person, Jemis Greenwing, in my life. I was often angry, often envious, often bitter, always greedy, and I committed treason, broke solemn promises, for personal gain. When I was caught and sentenced to my imprisonment, I was angry, and it took me many years before I even began to think of anything outside of my own anger."

"The Spiral of Despair," I said, and then, a little unsurely, "which turned out to be the way to salvation …"

"Exactly. I discovered that there were secrets below the apparent surfaces of the prison, and as I explored them, my soul started to slough off its hardened and unresponsive parts, and I came to waken to beauty and eventually to write my own response to it."

We walked on, away from the arching plants, towards the mossy bank of the stream, where we turned to go up against its current. I thought I could hear Mr. Dart calling my name again, but Ariadne nev Lingarel did not seem to hear anything and I didn't know quite how to ask after that distant echo.

"In investigating and exploring Ihuranuë's masterpiece of architecture, and then in shaping my own poetical response to it, I slowly began to see what I had been missing, became able to see the divine— to learn to hear the call of those Mountains yonder. When it was my time to pass here, that work continued. I have met those who found in my poem a glimpse of the way to the Mountains, and their souls, echoing mine, have helped me heal."

"It's reciprocal, then?" I asked.

She smiled at me, gently but full of a deep-seated delight. "It is. And you, my friend, for I feel you are my friend, read my poem more carefully and understood it more fully than anyone else, and by it was able to rescue your friends and yourself from your imprisonment."

"I'm not sure if I can say I rescued myself," I pointed out, "since I died."

She actually laughed, not at all meanly. "Yet you died *well!* You did not succumb to the drug that was consuming you; you did not fall into despair; you made the clear and conscious decision to sacrifice your magic and thereby your life to ensure that your friends were able to make it out. You were imprisoned in more ways than one."

I looked at the calm and verdant wood around us and knew that this was true. I tucked her arm into mine. "I believe you, but I think I will have a while yet in this wood to understand what you mean."

"That is as it should be," Ariadne nev Lingarel replied. "The reciprocity of souls across time and space is a great mystery. We await those whose souls speak to us, those we need and those who need us. You needed my poem to show you your way hither; I needed your reading to show me my way hence."

We had walked a few more yards, towards the sound of the voices in merriment, before I quite parsed her words. "Are you ready, then, to continue on your way to the Mountains?"

"Do you need me any longer?"

I hesitated, trying to turn my attention inwards, towards the secret workings of my soul. But I could feel a certain settling in myself, a kind of certainty, that however much her poem had been to me—however much it had, as its author said, shown me my way hither—this encounter had been perhaps even more for her than it was for me.

The realization filled me with gladness and a deep unfurling of wonder. That I, who had done so little with his life, but had recognized in that poem something magnificent; who had become a better person for reading it, for studying it, for working to disentangle sign and sense and significance; that I by my studiousness and love had somehow helped the long-dead poet come to her own peace ...

"Thank you," I said, as we came to the edge of the clearing.

"There will be time enough to converse, on the other side of the Mountains," Ariadne nev Lingarel promised, and kissed me on the cheek. "Thank you, Jemis Greenwing, for your love and care of my work. Love is never lost, in the end."

And with that she gently removed her arm from the crook of mine, curtsied politely in an antique fashion—I responded with my most elaborated bow—and she laughed in delight before turning herself to enter the woods and seek out her way to the Mountains.

I watched her go, and when she had disappeared behind the trees I straightened my hat and took a breath and turned around to see what waited me in the clearing.

The first person I saw was my mother, and the second was Mr. Buchance.

CHAPTER THIRTY-ONE
Those Who Wait

My mother was in a white and green dress; like Ariadne nev Ling-arel she looked younger than I'd ever seen her, but her eyes were full of her lived experience. She was sitting on a chair next to her second husband, conversing with the quick gestures and frequent laughter I remembered. Mr. Buchance did not look so young, but he did seem fitter than he had: sleek and comfortable instead of a little too fat for health, settled in himself, dignified without strain.

I stayed where I was, drinking in the sight of both of them, coming to realize as I watched them talking to each other that they were the ages they felt themselves most, my mother a young woman apparently not much older than I was myself, Mr. Buchance more solidly middle-aged. It made me feel indescribably pleased to know that there were those who were happiest, most themselves, as forty-year-olds. It had always seemed hard to me to imagine that everyone lived the better part of their lives wishing they were decades younger.

After a while I became ready to speak to them. I started to walk towards them, across the smooth flower-bedecked sward that covered the ground of this clearing. I'd not gone far when a soft chime began ringing. As it started all conversation stopped, and the various people looked up and around to smile at each other with delight and triumph and wonder. The chime grew louder and louder, until it rang in the air like the bells underfoot when Hal and I had spent that night on the campanile at Morrowlea. Finally with a triumphant clarion-call like a thunderclap and a thousand trumpets it faded away again into silence.

The crowd cheered, and I heard someone say, "Ariadne's gone to the Mountains!" in the way that he might have cried out the winner of a great race.

My mother and stepfather looked at each other, and I saw the hope and rising joy on their faces, and then they both rose and turned to search the edge of the woods with their gazes. I stepped forward hesitantly, my eagerness to see them tempered not with fear so much as a longing so forceful it made my limbs weak, and that drew their attention.

"Jemis," said my mother, her arms opening wide.

I ran towards her, my hat falling off in my haste, and enfolded myself in her familiar embrace. "Oh Mama, Mama," I said, unable to stop smiling, finally pushing back so I could look at her face, as beautiful as I remembered it, yet so much more real, more peaceful, more alive than I recalled. She had been so sick, that last year, and so worn by the Interim, the situation with my father, the difficulties with our extended family.

"Hush," she said, reaching out to brush her hand across my cheek. "That is all gone into the past now, my love. We have all the time we need to talk."

What Ariadne nev Lingarel had said about taking the time the soul needed floated into my mind, and I wondered if perhaps this was why it had not been my mother first, but someone I had never met and did not know (except for the communion of our souls through the medium of her poem, which I had never imagined reciprocal un-til she told me it was through the Lady's grace), so that I could learn the first few items of importance to this new adventure.

All the time we need … I turned next to my stepfather, who was smiling down at me. I smiled uncertainly up at him, and said, "Mr. Buchance, sir," and held out my hand as we always had.

He held out his hand in return, and said, "Always so formal, Jemis?" but as I grasped his hand something in his tone, his smile, the whole atmosphere of that wood touched me, and a flake of something hard and crusty seemed to detach itself from inside me, and I let go of his hand so I could embrace him round his firm middle and start sobbing into his chest.

"Jemis," he said softly, patting my back.

The words tumbled out, inarticulate and broken, even as I tried to stop sobbing. "You said all those nice things about me and left me all that money and all your colleagues were so kind, and I never once told you I loved you!"

"Oh, Jemis, I knew."

We stood there for a while, my head against his chest, his arms around me. I knew I would normally have felt deeply embarrassed, showing such emotion and especially showing such emotion in front of other people, but there, in that garden, I felt nothing except a strong sense of consolation.

When I at last lifted my head and stepped back, I felt tender and yet whole. My mother was smiling, her eyes shining, as lucent as Mr. Dart's had been as we crossed that island between worlds.

I wondered how I knew, with such utter certainty, that this was not such another in-between place, but rather *the* in-between place, between our mortal life and what came after.

"Come and sit, love," my mother said, patting what was now not a chair but a bench wide enough for the both of us. I felt Mr. Buchance clasp me firmly on the shoulder as I turned to obey, a benediction I could now take as it was offered.

We sat there and simply—talked. Mr. Buchance knew my life up till the spring, of course, or as much as I'd ever told him, but they both seemed to know quite a bit of what had happened since as well.

"I still can't believe you slew a dragon with a cake knife," Mr. Buchance exclaimed at one point, laughing heartily.

I could just barely hear the echo of what he might have said, when he was alive, about my foolishness and my desire to show off and what danger I had put myself and my sisters in; but back then I would not have been able to hear the pride, and the love, that also spoke forth in those words.

My mother put her hand on my knee. I had picked up my hat (or rather, Mr. Buchance had picked up my hat and handed it to me), and I sat there fiddling with the brim. How could I be so brimful of joy and yet …

I had no ideas for what that *and yet* was. Healing, perhaps.

"I was very proud how you solved the riddle and resolved the curse on the Woods," my mother said. "I'm sorry that my letter came so late to you."

"Who had it? I—events got away from me, and I forgot to look into it."

She shook her head fondly. "I gave it to Roddy Kulfield, to pass on to Magistra Bellamy or, failing that, his mother, but he sprained his ankle before he could hand it over and forgot afterwards. Such a sweet lad but not the most reliable for such things, but he was the one who was there."

"Hopefully a sea journey will help him," I replied, and then had to explain Hal's expedition and Roddy's adventure.

This led to a question I had been wondering about, though when there came a pause I wasn't sure how to phrase it without sounding insane.

"Ask, my son. Your desires are wholesome, here."

I flushed at her bright-eyed smile, the way Mr. Buchance put his hand gently on her shoulder without any sort of claim but also without embarrassment.

"How … how much do you know of what passes … back there? And how?"

My mother smiled with a flash of sorrow from which the poison had all been drawn. "Our hearts know whom they follow, Jemis, and we hear the prayers sent to us."

I thought of my angry grief this summer, how I had been unable to pray, my mouth seizing when I sought to mend what had never quite been whole between myself and my stepfather. He watched me gravely, not saying anything. I knew that this was part of why he was here, in this glade, waiting until I was ready to speak and to listen.

I was not ready to speak, not to him. I swallowed, turning my head apologetically, but he made no show of impatience or disapproval that I was not so decisive and forthright as he.

I cleared my throat and changed the subject. "Is that why I can hear Mr. Dart?"

"You can hear Mr. Dart? Now?"

My mother was not quite frowning. I felt immediately unsure. "Not right this moment, but every now and again I can hear him call my name. Just as if he's in another room or behind a tree. But then I can't see him."

"And all he's saying is your name?"

"Yes. Is—is that wrong?"

She smiled reassuringly. "No, my love, there are no wrong things here. Some making right, to be true, but no *new* wrongs. There is time enough here to resolve all knots and show the way to answer all mysteries save the very greatest."

"The way to the Mountains."

"Exactly. Now, my son, when did you first hear your friend call?"

"From my first arrival. Even before I met Ariadne nev Lingarel."

My mother pondered. I glanced at Mr. Buchance, who shrugged apologetically. "I am not so wise in the mysteries as Lady Olive, Jemis."

I felt a genuine smile lift my heart. I was glad, so glad, that I had this opportunity and all the time necessary to unravel the knots of our relationship. Another crusty piece of something seemed to flake off and float away. Mr. Buchance smiled at me, gently, and I was aware I was staring. I turned my head, whereupon I discovered a man and a woman had approached, arm in arm, and were waiting politely to be noticed.

I had seen, on entering the glade, that there were other people there, but had recognized—tried to recognize—none but my mother and stepfather. I wondered now, but without any urgency, just who they all were. Surely not all those who had died to the world in Alinor, or even Northwest Oriole, could be present; but had death undone so many in Ragnor Bella?

"Hello," I said tentatively to the pair in front of me. He was a man in robust middle age, hair roan, eyes blue, tall and broad-shouldered. He had a face that seemed to have relaxed away from sternness into good humour. Something about the set of his mouth was familiar, but I was sure I did not know him as he was now. I tried to imagine him an old man, perhaps, white of hair and wrinkled of mien. It didn't serve to identify him, so I turned to the woman.

She was younger than he, but older than my mother's apparent age: in her thirties, perhaps, with cheerful crow-feet wrinkles at her eyes and a settled sort of maturity to her face. Her hair was red, too, a deep familiar auburn. And her smile I knew I recognized.

I looked hastily back at the man, and saw now how much he resembled Mr. Dart's brother—or rather how much Torquin Dart resembled him.

"Mistress Dart? Master Dart? I—I'm sorry, but I don't know your given names. I'm Jemis Greenwing—Mr. Dart, Perry, that is, is my closest friend."

Mistress Dart laughed at my stammered introduction and came forward to embrace me. She smelled of flowers, not the jasmine and sweet pea I'd always associated with my mother but a heady lilac scent that made me think of sun-drenched afternoons at Dart Hall.

"My dear Jemis," said she, "you have been a good friend to my dear Peregrine."

Any number of incidents over the past few months crowded to mind: I blushed. "He has been a much better friend to me, ma'am."

"It's Petronelle, and my husband's name is Ricard."

"You must have chosen your sons' names," I blurted, and both she and my mother burst out laughing. Master Ricard and my stepfather made a kind of pro-forma grumble before agreeing in mock regret.

My mother gave me a brilliant smile. "I'll have you know, Jemis, that your name is a perfectly ordinary one in Pfaschen and Harktree."

"Oh, I am glad to hear it!" I replied; and indeed I was, though naturally it was never going to overshadow the fact that it was also the name of my grandfather's favourite racehorse, for whom I had actually been named.

"Both Torquin and Peregrine are noble names," Mistress Petronelle protested laughingly. "Torquin was the name of the first lawgiver of the Empire, and Peregrine the name of the second son of Tarazel—your distant ancestor, husband!"

"I didn't know she'd had a son by the Bard," I said, intrigued by this glimpse into ancient history.

"I look forward to seeing them on the other side of the Mountains," Master Ricard said, patting his wife on her hand. She gave him a meaningful smile and I chuckled at this evidence that our ordinary, earthly concerns were not ignored, not wholly destroyed. They seemed themselves, more than anyone else I had ever met: distinctly whole.

"Now, my dear Jemis, you have been hearing our son calling you?"

I opened my mouth to explain again when Mr. Dart's sounded forth. "There! Did you hear him?"

His parents and mine all regarded me solemnly. Finally Master Ricard said, sadly, "No."

At my expression my mother hastily said, "Do not fret, Jemis, we will confer with the others and pray that the Lady come to explain if no one else can."

CHAPTER THIRTY-TWO
The Lady's Table

I was deep in a description of the Magarran Strid at the Turning of the Waters—leached of the horror and terror, now seeming a great adventure—to a man I had hardly recognized as my Uncle Sir Rinald and another I did not know at all but quickly identified as my maternal grandfather Udo, whom I truly did resemble—when the Lady came.

Her approach was heralded by a sudden flock of white birds. At first I thought they were doves, and perhaps they were, but there was something about them that suggested they were *other*. While I was still pondering them a gentle breeze swirled around us, full of the scent of good things.

Conversations faded away as face after face turned in a direction I knew instinctively was towards the Mountains.

A flush of colour ran through the assembly, as if the sun had come out from behind a cloud, or as if our souls were blossoms opening to a radiance beyond even that. For my own part I felt myself turning, my heart both calming and quickening, as if I drank deeply of the most refreshing draught there could be. Even my first arrival into that country had not been so exhilarating.

And then there She was, the Lady of the Green and White.

She walked across the meadow gently, stopping to greet some, smiling at others. I stood, as I had always stood when a lady entered the room, and removed my hat.

She did not look as I had pictured her. She had long dark hair, brown rather than black, and a complexion much more carnations-and-cream than the Shaian brown or black I had always imagined. She looked at me, smiling, and I realized that of course She was far older an inhabitant of Alinor than the Astandalans or their mythologies. Her eyes were no colour I could describe: blue, perhaps, like the sky, or maybe a wise grey, or even a deep forest green.

I was reminded of Mr. Dart's eyes when his magic moved.

She came to a stop before me, her green overgrown and white petticoats dancing in the breeze attending Her. I realized I was staring into Her smile, Her eyes, and bowed deeply. Every church service I had missed, every ceremony I had dozed through, every prayer I had not spoken or meant filled my mind.

"I'm sorry," I said, feeling entirely unworthy of Her presence.

She said: "This is where you come to be cleansed, my son, to unknot your soul and to ease your mind. You have heard the call to the Mountains, and I turn no one away who longs for my Table, my Garden."

She smiled, and now I recalled every kind word and good deed, every true prayer, my stubborn defense and even more stubborn love of my father, my endless engagement with Ariadne's poem.

I bowed again, because that was always the appropriate response. I was not expecting Her to laugh with enough true mirth that all the trees set about the glade shook themselves into blossoms pink and white.

I didn't quite feel embarrassed—I didn't think it was possible to feel embarrassed, in that place—but I truly did not how to respond to this. Fortunately—and oh, how wonderful it was to have her there, whole and healthy and her own person—my mother spoke on my behalf.

"Lady," she said, "my son is hearing his friend calling his name."

The Lady's face went solemn, though the merriment did not leave her eyes and the blossoms did not fall. "Ah, my dear Champion is coming into his power at last."

I couldn't think that Mr. Dart had any great desire to waken the dead. From this side of the veil, the whole idea was utterly abhorrent. Reaching back for a moment, as my mother had when I had woken the bees and she had joined the dance to break the curse, was one thing; being *called* back, away from this Wood and the path to the Mountains, was almost literally damnable.

The Lady turned to me. "Your thoughts are correct as far as your knowledge permits. My Champion's gifts are not for the dead, but for the living."

"Why then do I hear him calling, Lady?"

"He guards the passages against the shadows. It is his calling and he has answered that call. Your mortal body lays in the darkness between midnight and dawn, in the dark of the moon on a night when there are no stars. He is guarding the passage that remains after your leave-taking of the once-living world."

I frowned, trying to recall what I knew of theology, though I had the feeling I had never paid enough attention to know what was true and what in error. Mr. Dart and the Hunter's conversation about the distinctions between Hunter in Green and Hunter in the Green, which I had forgone in favour of staring out the window, were a case in point.

"There are the prayers for the dead," I said finally, remembering as if through a haze the endless prayers that we'd performed for what we thought was my father's corpse. The dead by suicide or murder had to have special rituals to ensure that nothing … came through … the passageway thus opened by violence.

"But I didn't commit suicide." I looked from the Lady to my mother and back, pleading. "I knew if I gave up my magic I would probably die, but that's not … surely I didn't … I didn't *want* to die."

Suicide was damnation, the priests were very clear about that. Suicides were buried under crossroads in the middle of the night with a stake through their heart so they could not come back.

The Lady laid a hand on my shoulder. "My son, are you not here, at my Table, in My company? Have you not seen the Mountains? You are new here, but you need not fear you will be cast out. Your sacrifice was true."

My panic seemed foolish in the wake of Her reassurance. I discovered you *could* feel embarrassed in the Wood of Spiritual Refreshment; though, thankfully, not for very long. The Lady clasped my shoulder gently. "There. Cease your fretting, child."

I nodded shakily. After a moment Mistress Petronelle spoke. "My Lady, nevertheless Jemis can hear my Peregrine, when no one else can. What is the cause?"

The Lady actually sighed. "Between that place and this is the realm of the Shades. You do not need to know of their origins; suffice it to say that they cast themselves out of the Bright Countries in their pride and envy, and that they have ever sought since to wage war on that which they lost. They cannot come into the Bright Countries by their old doors, for those were barred to them, and so instead they ever seek to force entrance through the once-living lands."

I was conscious of a sinking feeling, despite Her presence, despite the nature of that Wood, despite everything. I cleared my throat. "A fortnight ago the Black Priest did something to prepare me to be made sacrifice and host for the Dark Kings."

The Lady nodded gravely. To my surprise it was not my mother but Mr. Buchance who came over to me and enfolded me in an embrace.

I could count on one hand the number of times we'd ever hugged each other like that, and two of the occasions had been since I'd died. I still felt better for his sturdy strength and comforting arms, and wished I had not been quite so stubborn or quite so confused about the nature of love. We could have so much better a relationship, so much better a life, had I ever understood what he was offering, or that in loving him I did not negate or deny my love for my father.

The Lady waited until I was able to focus my attention on Her again. Then She spoke. "You are, once again, correct so far as your knowledge reaches. The passing from there to here is always a time of vulnerability. The ceremonies and prayers of wakes and funerals generally protect the living against the danger. My Champion is learning, has spent his life learning, to listen to the warnings I can give him and to fight when necessary. I may only act in the living world directly under certain conditions."

Miracles, I thought, but whispered, "The voices of the inanimate."

The Lady inclined Her head in a way that suggested this was another partial truth but one She didn't intend to clarify at present. "The perverted ritual that was performed on you, Jemis, made of the vulnerability—a crack, let us say, in the walls protecting the world—a gaping hole."

"And my son is guarding this?"

"He is."

"I named him well," Mistress Petronelle said proudly. "As fierce as a falcon, and as courageous as your Knight."

Of course. Sir Peregrine of Nên Corovel, who had rescued the unicorn that became the symbol of Alinor …

"But why can I hear him?" I asked, even as Mr. Dart's voice called Jemis softly but clearly through the air. "Why does he keep calling my name?"

"He is your friend, and he mourns you," the Lady said simply. "Your hearing him … ah, that is more complicated. The manner of your death—a true self-sacrifice while you crossed between worlds—is so completely the inverse of the death the false priests had intended for you that the passage stands open both ways. They seek to enter; but My hand may act."

A miracle, reaching through from here, the beginning of the Bright Countries, to there, what I had always thought of as the living world. I looked at the Lady's eyes, grey now as a cloud, and swallowed dryly. And was I my father's son?

"How may the passage be closed, Lady?"

"Oh, Jemis," said my mother, reaching out to take my hand. Mr. Buchance, arm still over my shoulders, squeezed tightly. Master Ricard looked even more like Torquin Dart than ever, magisterial, grave, and respectful.

The Lady said, "My Champion guards the way against those who would pass. By sacrifice did you leave the world, and by sacrifice may you return."

I hesitated a long time, though my thoughts were not more than impressions of emotions and wishes and inchoate falling images. But half a dozen lines echoed clearly:

The curving fire warm and endless as my conscience
    (my mind speaks guilt my heart does not hear)
Nestled into a hearth ever-burning,
Down-feathered with the white ashes of unfathomable woods
Where the birds call one to another
    Home-under-the-sky

I looked at the Lady. "I shall not lose the way to the Mountains?"

The Lady shook her head. "There is always all the time you need here, child."

Back there it would have been laughable to think that death was more desirable than life, but in that Wood, in the Presence of the Lady, with the promise of the Mountains—oh, the living world was a shadow I did not want to return to.

But I was my father's son, and I could not leave Mr. Dart to fight the Dark Kings alone when it was through me they might find entry to the world.

"Walk with Me," said the Lady, offering Her arm to me. "There are things you must know if you are to return whole and hale to your body."

CHAPTER THIRTY-THREE

The Grim Cross

The doorway had disappeared behind me, leaving me in a sort of open area with rocks and cliffs half-visible through the fog. In the centre of this space was a megalith in the familiar combination of the Lady's ancient stones, an upright standing stone with a flat offering-stone at its foot. Both were larger than the usual run of stones in South Fiellan; large enough that the cloth-covered object on the offering-stone could be human-sized.

Mr. Dart was standing next to the stone, looking down at the object, even in the distance and through the mist obviously dejected. He did not seem to hear me as I walked closer.

"Why are you so jealous of me?" I asked Mr. Dart, which was probably not the first question I should have been asking.

Mr. Dart jumped violently and whirled around to stare at me. "Jemis!"

"The same," I replied, smiling, as I bowed. "It's good to see you."

"You're dead," he said sharply.

"At the moment, yes."

He stared at me for a long moment, body tense. I looked him up and down, curious to see what he looked like in this strange limbo at the edge of life and death. He was wearing his usual style of clothes, though instead of plum and grey they were green and white, a reassuring choice in the circumstances.

As a champion ought, he bore weapons, though I couldn't think that I had ever seen Mr. Dart actually bear either in life: in his left hand he held a foot-long stick, and in his right—not stone, I noted with some surprise—a one-handed sword.

"What's the stick for?" I asked, nodding at it.

"It's a magic wand," he said, as if this was perfectly obvious, and looked around the space cautiously. His eyes kept straying down to the offering-stone. "What are you doing here, Jemis?"

"Coming back with you."

His face twisted. "You're in my dream. Why are you in my dream? You're dead. You died."

"Yes, I know," I said, not as empathetically, perhaps, as I should have been, but the calm joy of the Wood of Spiritual Refreshment was still filling me and it was hard to be worried, even in sympathy. I looked around at the space again. The gloomy mist was swirling, revealing that we stood in a kind of blighted and burned stone amphitheatre. "Where are we?"

"In my dream," he said blankly.

"How fascinating. It's a little gloomy, isn't it?"

He settled his shoulders, rolling them with a practiced motion I'd never seen him use. This Mr. Dart was more heavily muscular than the one I was familiar with, and he looked older, more mature; a warrior, in fact. I looked at his chosen weapons again. A sword and a magic wand.

"You use magic in your dream?" I asked.

He gave me an exasperated glance, so familiar I startled to

chuckle. "What are you laughing at?" he asked suspiciously.

"It *is* you," I said, which didn't really answer the question.

"This is my dream," he said, and circled around me with light feet. I had learned enough from my father and the arms master at Morrowlea to know that he was showing every indication of being both skilled and well-practiced.

The way he said *my dream* triggered an idea. "Do you have this dream often, then?"

"Every week or two," he said. "What are you doing here?"

"Every week or two? What happens in it?"

"What I'm guarding isn't usually so talkative," he muttered, more to himself than to me, then he sighed and spoke with the exaggerated patience he had hitherto only shown me when I was deep under the thrall of the wireweed. "If you're really Jemis, you know I hear the voices of the inanimate."

"Yes, like the cigar your brother was going to take ..."

He started, as if he hadn't expected me to actually know that, and peered intently at me. "You look older than Jemis should ..."

"How curious. I suppose my soul has had its tribulations, and they've left their mark. I expect once I get back to my body it will be as it used to."

He shuddered, glance falling down to the offering-stone. "Can we not talk about that right now?"

"What do you mean?"

"Jemis, you're my best friend, and you died! If it's really you, your spirit or whatever, come to visit me, why are you tormenting me? Aren't you supposed to console me? It's all my fault you died— don't—don't tell me you're going to come back! People don't come back—not when they're really dead—and I saw you, I saw you die—"

I winced. "Perry, Mr. Dart, I'm not here to torment you, nor really to console you."

He snorted. "Just as well, given the hash you're making of it."

"I'm sorry." I tried to collect what I'd been told, though some of the finer details of my sojourn at the Lady's Table were starting to fade into feelings and sensations I could not put into words. "I don't know why it's taking the form of a recurrent dream of yours, but I could … hear you, I guess is the best way to say it, on the other side. You were calling to me …"

"You can't say I called you back?"

He sounded so horrified I hastened to reassure him. "No, no, or not exactly. The Lady explained it to me. You know how I was prepared to be a sacrifice to the Dark Kings, so that their avatar could possess my body?"

He shuddered again, the horror not leaving his expression at all.

"Well, because of what they did, and I think because of your, er, ability to hear the inanimate, the way back was kept open."

"The way back," he said flatly.

"My way back," I clarified, as the faint scrabbling noise that had been surrounding us started to get noticeably louder. "*Their* way in."

He stared at me for a long moment and then jerked his head over to the side. "There's another sword over there. You're going to need it."

I did as he bid, finding a rapier leaning up against one of the boulders. I picked it up and was unsurprised to discover it was a very fine blade, very similar to—perhaps, in the way of dreams, *the same as*—the sword I had been given by the Hunter in Green that time in the Forest before I had learned my father was alive.

"So what happens in this dream of yours?" I asked when I

returned to find him grim-faced and attentive to whatever was coming out of the shadows and mist.

"I fight the monsters," he said simply, and then they were upon us.

***

They were made of shadow and mist and had the distinct wrongness of a nightmare. A tentacle came snaking towards us, to be stabbed by Mr. Dart; something like the talons of a raptor came plunging out of the sky, attached to a gigantic moth, which Mr. Dart fended off with an arcing flick of his wand.

Up until being dosed with wireweed in the palace-prison I had, on encountering mortal danger, found myself in a world of clear and simple certainties. Facing the dragon, I had known exactly what to do (courtesy of a month of lessons and a lifetime of daydreams) and had all the apparent time necessary to do it in; crawling across a tree as the Magarran river dropped away from me to reveal a canyon full of spiked limestone, I had been able to leave aside my natural fear and move.

Standing there in Mr. Dart's dream, I was (metaphorically) petrified with terror.

He moved with the ease of long and hard practice, sword and wand working in concert. I'd never known him to be ambidextrous until the (literally) petrified arm had forced him to use his left hand instead of his right, but he had, I'd thought, seemed unusually able to make that switch once it became necessary. Watching him fight the monsters, while I stood there like a proverbial damsel in distress, mouth agape and rapier drooping, I could see where he had learned it.

He stabbed and sliced and parried with the sword, while the wand jabbed and flicked and sent controlled waves of magic at the monsters.

They did not like the sword, but it was the wand, and the gold-white-and-green magic that came out of it, that they abhorred.

***

The monsters came.

At first I had very little to do. Mr. Dart fought expertly, wand and sword moving in concert. I stood in guard position, eyes straining in the shadows and mist, but nothing got past my friend.

I recalled, as from a long time ago, Mr. Cartwright talking about Mr. Dart's restless sleep, his many dreams. In how many of them did he fight the monsters, guarding the Lady's flock?

After a while the onslaught eased, then ebbed, until Mr. Dart was able to lower his sword a trifle and take several deep, slow breaths.

He then did a slow perimeter circuit, pacing a wide arc around where I stood next to the standing stone. The monsters had collapsed into shadows that puddled on the stone of the crossroads.

Finally he came to the centre, standing beside me but facing the opposite direction, so that we were shoulder-to-shoulder and between us could watch the approaches.

"Where do the roads lead?" I asked at last. My voice fell oddly into the space.

"You came down one; I from another," Mr. Dart said, gesturing with his wand to the paths to our respective rights. "The other two … this is the Grim Crossroads."

"The Shadow Realms …"

He lifted the sword, pointed it down the road directly before him, as if in challenge and defiance. I had turned my head to look; motion out of the corner of my other eye made me swing back to the road before me, sword raising automatically.

It was a bird, a white bird, flying hard.

"That way is Faerie," said Mr. Dart, "or so the legends tell."

The bird flew straight towards us. I lifted my sword uncertainly. "It looks like the birds that came before the Lady."

The white bird was gleaming in no light I could see a source for, brilliant as a sudden reflection. It circled once over us, then landed on the top of the standing stone with a soft mournful coo.

Mr. Dart regarded it intently for a moment. "I think it's a prayer. Keep an eye on it in case it attacks."

"Certainly," I replied, shifting position so I could watch bird and roads. My bear-baiter, Hal had called Mr. Dart, leading where I followed. But that had rarely bothered me at home, and it did not bother me here, where he was the Lady's Champion against the monsters that came out of the shadows.

The white bird was joined by another and then a third. They clustered at the top of the standing stone, jostling against each other and cooing as doves or pigeons do.

A fourth white bird came sweeping towards us, accompanied this time by something darker. I watched warily, hoping the darker bird was not a curse or a monster, and was staring up into the sky as it resolved into a crimson dove when Mr. Dart hissed in alarm and pressed his back into mine.

"The shadows are rising," he sais swiftly, lowly. I could feel the breadth of his shoulders against mine, the muscles playing as he lifted wand and sword in readiness. "They are coming, You will have to fight—we cannot let them touch your body."

"I understand." And so I did: if I were lost here, I was lost indeed until the Hunter sent his hounds to harry out of the Shadow Realms all those who had fallen from the Lady's grace but had not, for all that, lost sight of Her entirely. So long as I held true and remembered the Mountains, She had promised, I would not be lost though I could not go back either to that world or the old through my death's portal. Miracles were, by their nature, singular.

I glanced up at the white birds and the crimson one. Prayers, were they? That suggested my friends were praying over me even now, while Mr. Dart slept and dreamed and fought.

Even as I thought this a rich purple—violet—bird joined the rest, and another white one, and then I could only hope they were the prayers sent up by Hal and Violet and perhaps Jullanar Maebh in her pity, for *they* were coming.

The mist thickened, scudding unnaturally about us, outside the perimeter Mr. Dart had walked. The puddled shadows of his earlier triumphs seeped backwards, as if draining not through the cracks between paving-stones but between the wisps of fog.

And behind the mist, out of the dark voids that stretched into infinite shadows, *they* came.

Each road was a pale line leading into the invisible distance. From the crossroads I could see nothing to distinguish them, nothing to say this one led to heaven and that one to hell, this one to Fairyland and that one home. Each traversed that blasted and blighted land, between cracked rocks and black pools that might have been water and might have been something else, and between each broken stone and from each black hole *they* came.

They seemed to come slowly, like a tide such as I'd seen in Ghilousette, but tides were deceptive there, and all too soon the rivers of darkness were upon us.

Mr. Dart's back tensed, so it seemed I could feel each curve of a muscle in his shoulders, each flexed rib as he breathed.

"For the Lady," I said, lifting my sword. He lit a glimmering light along the length of his wand, a soft gold edged with emerald green, like light shining through leaves. Above us the prayer-birds cooed and shifted restlessly on the standing stone.

My sacrifice had been true, the Lady said. I no longer had any of the active part of my magic, only what naturally belonged to a living soul and a lingering passive sensitivity to magical energies. I could not call light in that darkness, against those shadows.

But I was my father's son, for good and for ill, and by the Lady I would fight.

Back to back, beside the offering-stone containing my own shrouded corpse, Mr. Dart and I fought against what we knew as the Dark Kings, and the prayers for the dead fought with us.

The world shrank, and shrank again, to the heavy coils of darkness that snaked out of the fog, and the silver flash of my sword, and the white and crimson and violet of the birds. My eyes could not focus on whatever they were; I stabbed blindly at any dark movement.

At my back Mr. Dart fought, wand and sword flashing in my peripheral vision, fireworks of gold and green. More birds joined us, white and crimson and white and violet and white—who was praying so urgently, so relentlessly, so *well*? None of my friends but Mr. Dart were deeply pious, but perhaps that was something else Violet had been hiding, or perhaps it was Jullanar Maebh, whose deepest secret had been a vision of meeting the Lady in the mortal woods …

"*Ivailo ivaro ivo!*" cried Mr. Dart suddenly, the Old Shaian words to command light, and with a concussion like a thunderclap light kindled.

The dark coils writhed in the mist as the light fell on them. I could feel Mr. Dart straining, muscles quivering with the effort, and without thinking I set my feet and pushed back, shoulder to shoulder. All the gifts of his friendship to me fell through my mind in a cataract of gratitude and grace.

The light grew: from a pinprick to a candle to a lantern, from a lantern to a light like the lighthouses I'd seen up along the northern coast.

The shadows bubbled and boiled as they retreated in the face of that light. Mr. Dart was trembling now but my mind was full of the many times he'd saved me, from his magic at the Magarran Strid to his unwavering friendship no matter what melodrama I fell into.

I knew with an absolute and utter certainty that Mr. Dart would never see me lost in the Shadow Realms: and I knew with the same utter surety that even as my father had held a border when General Ben commanded him to, and held the Bloodwater Pass so General Ben could escape, and came home after the Fall, after his disgrace, after seven years a pirate slave, with General Ben his companion, friend, and support, so too would I keep faith with my bear-baiter and best friend.

Somewhere in the quarter between the roads to Heaven and Faërie I saw a great mound of darkness rising. I slid my free hand back to grasp Mr. Dart's upper arm, the one holding the wand, the one that in our waking, ordinary life was stone.

I did not know what to say, but perhaps I did not need to, for with an effort I felt to the soles of my feet Mr. Dart raised his arm that bit higher. I prayed for the Lady to grant us her aid, here in the dark between the living and the dead.

With a noise like a windstorm the light exploded.

I crouched down, sword above my head, free hand still on Mr. Dart's arm.

I blinked away the afterimages until I could see clearly. His eyes were blue, and grey, and green, and flecked with the same golden light he had just cast across that sunless land.

We were now facing each other across the offering-stone. The shrouded body was hidden beneath a blanket of the prayer-birds, white and crimson and violet and green and gold.

I touched one of the green birds with a trembling finger. It let me stroke its back before shifting over.

"It is done,'" said Mr. Dart, sheathing his sword, though he still held the wand. "By the Lady's grace we have made it to sunrise, and the danger is passed for this night."

I looked around. The land around us was a grim and blighted as before, the mist as grey. But there were no shadows deeper than the dimness, and one of the roads glimmered as if it were touched by a sunrise that reached nowhere else.

"Thank you," Mr. Dart went on, nodding gravely to the birds. They cooed and jostled and hid my body. Then he turned to me and smiled tiredly. "And thank you, Jemis. I've never had the soul of anything I was guarding come to my assistance before, but I am glad for it."

He reached out his hand for me to shake, in that Charese custom he'd picked up at Stoneybridge, but I could only stare at him, heart still thundering.

And then I knew what I should do, a hundred of my father's tales, my mother's songs, Mr. Dart's own beloved histories, coming to mind.

I knelt down and laid my sword at his feet. Then I looked up at him and used the ancient words to swear my sword and my heart and my hand in fealty to him, who had saved my life and my sanity and my soul.

It was a very ancient ceremony and one that could not be undone save by betrayal of loyalty either given or received, and for that one would wander these dark wastes.

"Mr. Greenwing," said Mr. Dart.

"Mr. Dart," I replied, as we so often did, smiling as I permitted him to draw me up, hands clasped around mine.

"Why are you grinning? You shouldn't be grinning."

I knew better that to say, We just fought off—*you* just fought off—the Dark Kings—not when they might yet hear—and so I instead took his arm, as if we were walking down the high street of Ragnor Bella, and turned our steps to the one sunlit road.

CHAPTER THIRTY-FOUR
Not a Dream

I felt a tide of joy run through my body as I settled back into it. A little distantly I could feel a stiffness to my muscles and a lingering unwholesomeness from the wireweed, but the Lady's assurances that I had burned the drug from my system by means of sacrificing my magic made me acknowledge the truth of that sensation. It was akin to the stage of a bad cold when one was still full of the sneezing and general malaise but could tell, inwardly and in secret, that the threat had passed. In times past I would have immediately feared the worst, but I knew, now, that though I would still have to be careful, I was no longer in the drug's thrall.

I wriggled my fingers and toes experimentally, pleased beyond words that everything was working as it ought. I took a deep breath, and then another, and then, naturally, sneezed, at which point someone screamed.

I sat up, curious rather than alarmed. The peace of the Wood of Spiritual Refreshment still enveloped me, leaving little room for actual distress.

Alas, none of the other people within hearing distance could say the same.

I blinked as my eyes adjusted to the light level around me. I was in a room, plainly furnished at first glimpse, illuminated by several guttering candles and one newly lit one. A waft of incense made me sneeze again, which in turn made me smile, my hand at my face.

Tumbled over on his rear and staring at me in utter shock was a young man I recognized a moment later as Marcan, Hal's and my friend from Morrowlea.

"Oh, we did make it to the hunting lodge, then!" I said happily.

Marcan made a noise I could only describe as *gibbering*.

"You remind me of when my uncle's factor saw my father and thought he was a ghost," I said.

Marcan stammered something incomprehensible. I watched him with amusement. Some rational part of my mind acknowledged that it was perfectly understandable that he should be shocked, but on the whole I felt far too pleased to be back in the world to respond.

Before he had collected himself, or I could say anything else true but perhaps unfortunate, the door to the room crashed open and Mr. Dart, Violet, and Hal all burst in.

Hal cried, "Marcan! What is it? What happened?"

Marcan was unable to articulate anything intelligible, and instead pointed shakily at me.

Hal and the others, who'd all been focused on Marcan, swivelled to look.

Violet said, "Eeep!" and blushed furiously. Hal said, "The Lady!" and Mr. Dart simply stared.

"Greetings," I said, smiling with a glad heart at them, and especially at Mr. Dart.

"J-Jemis?" Violet managed.

"The very same," I replied, then bowed slightly in Mr. Dart's direction. "Thanks to Mr. Dart here."

"Necromancy!" Marcan spluttered.

"No, no, quite the opposite: the Lady granted me leave to return because Mr. Dart was holding the way—"

"Necromancy!" Marcan cried again, pushing away from Mr. Dart in revulsion.

"No!" I stood up, but they all shifted back, horror and hope wavering on their faces. I sank back down on the bed, then had a thought and brought my hands to rest in plain sight on my knees.

Hal swallowed. "How do we know—are you really Jemis?"

I couldn't help myself, and laughed. Despite it being a perfectly normal, even merry laugh—I heard the echo of the Lady's Table in it, and from the wavering sort of wonder in his eyes, so too did Mr. Dart—it did not seem to reassure either Hal or Violet very much; Marcan was now muttering about necromancy and what *would* his father think.

"I do apologize," I said. "It is the opposite of necromancy, in fact—rather a miracle."

"From Marcan's prayers?" Hal asked, rather skeptically, after a short but pregnant pause.

"His prayers certainly were of assistance," I replied, thinking of the multitude of white birds that had come out of the shadows to help us fight against the monsters. "But it was really Mr. Dart—"

"Necromancer!"

"No," I repeated. "Marcan, will you listen to me? I died—yes, died!—I sacrificed my magic so that we could free ourselves from the Labyrinth of Ihuranuë. Violet, did you manage to get your brother to safety? And Miss Dart?"

Violet nodded stiffly. "They're both sleeping, though I don't know how Jullanar Maebh didn't rouse for that scream."

Relief rippled through me and a tension I had not quite acknowledged relaxed. "Splendid. Well, since I was experiencing the effects of an excess of wireweed—"

I paused again as Marcan grumbled something else, but as he was frowning mightily at the floor, and refused to look up, I decided he would have to wait.

"Because of that, my body couldn't handle the abnegation of my magical gift, such as it is, and so I died."

"We had worked that out," Violet said, her voice sharp. "It's how you *came back to life* that's the question."

"We were witnesses to your death, after all," Hal added. He glanced down at Marcan, who had pulled out a rosary. "Marcan was not very happy when we tumbled out of thin air into his bedroom in the middle of the night with your corpse in tow."

"I can understand that," I said, and then leaned forward to catch Marcan's attention. "Thank you for your prayers."

He dropped his rosary in utter astonishment. "Demons—thanking—me—"

Hal leaned down to put a hand on his shoulder, as he still sat on the floor. "Marcan, get hold of yourself. Either this is Jemis and you're witness to a miracle, or it's some foul art we need to guard against."

"You're not doing a very good job of the latter," I observed.

At this Violet suddenly let out a choked laugh and, to my astonishment, began to cry. I moved instinctively to comfort her, only for Mr. Dart to make a gesture I recognized from his dream-warrior self. I subsided on the bed, and it was Hal who put one arm around her.

"Continue," the duke said firmly.

"I found myself on the other side, in a wood—*the* wood—of

spiritual refreshment. Ariadne nev Lingarel, the poet, came to meet me, and she told me about the reciprocity of love and the woods and the way to the Mountains."

My voice was full of longing. I was glad to be back in the world, truly I was; but I would yearn for those Mountains all the days of my life.

"Not your mother?" Mr. Dart said softly.

I turned to him with an eager smile. "I saw her later, and my step-father too, but only after Ariadne had spoken with me. I think it was so emotions didn't overwhelm everything. And because she needed to talk with me, too, I suppose—that's the bit about the reciprocity of love—it was—"

"Jemis," said Violet, in familiar tones.

"Violet!" I laughed. "Oh, I am glad to be here again. I didn't mind when I was *there*—that is our homeland, of course, or our way thither, where our souls long to be—but I am happy to be back here with you as well."

"Your courtesy is astonishing. *How?*"

"It was a miracle. I could hear Mr. Dart calling, you see, every once in a while, and it kept reminding me of this place. More than it seems … I don't know quite how to explain … I wasn't there very long, I don't think. They seemed to know a good deal of what we were doing, but I don't know how." I considered. "Perhaps that is one of the things I am not permitted to remember now that I am here again. The Lady said there would be some."

"You met the Lady?" Violet spoke softly.

"You heard me?" Mr. Dart spoke even more softly.

Marcan was still fingering his beads but apart from a huff did not interrupt again.

"Yes—just as if you were calling my name from another room. After I spoke to my mother and Mr. Buchance, the Lady came, and I asked her what it meant. She said that I could hear you because of the rituals the priests of the Dark Kings had done."

That caused a stir. Marcan jumped to his feet, white as anything, to point a shaking hand at me. "Necromancy and black magic! I can't believe I was starting to listen to you!"

I retorted, "It wasn't my choice. I was captured and, er, prepared to be made a vessel of the Dark Kings, but we—" for his and Violet's benefit I gestured to Hal and Mr. Dart—"managed to flout them. But between the fact that I died of wireweed overdose and loss of magic while crossing through a fey artefact—the Labyrinth and the island— meant that the way in was … open."

"Ugh," said Hal, before catching that he had said that aloud, whereupon he immediately looked mortified.

"Exactly," I said, smiling at him. "Which is why it was quite liter- ally miraculous that my oldest friend, Mr. Dart here, has been fighting against the monsters for years, and was able to guard my body—with the assistance of your prayers—" (for there had been the crimson and violet birds too) "against the incursion of the Dark Kings, so that I, and not one of them, could return to my body. The Lady was of the opinion that if I were willing to return it would be better than having to deal with all that."

"You might not have?" Hal said, as if snatching at a straw of sense.

"I *died*, Hal," I replied patiently. "How many people come back? Once one is there, one is desirous of the Mountains, and on preparing to make the journey there. That's the whole point. This life is—pre- amble, rehearsal, shadow—my mother said that this life is like the plant that grows according to its nature and circumstances, and our souls are the seeds which seem to die to this life, only in reality they are transformed and grow into the new life ..."

I saw their confusion and gestured grandly, silently asking their forgiveness for my inarticulate blundering. I knew, with a certainty I had never felt before, that I would spend the rest of my life unfolding the meaning of that glimpse of the Mountains.

After several minutes of silence, Mr. Dart spoke slowly. "I am glad that I do not have to tell your father that you died two weeks after he returned."

I grinned. "You can still tell him. It's yet another way in which I can only begin to emulate him; I won't be given the opportunity to return from the dead a second time. Now, is it acceptable to you that I get up? I'm thirsty, and I have messages for you."

"M-messages?" Violet said, paling a little.

"You don't think all your loved ones waiting for you at the Lady's Table wouldn't want to take advantage of a return traveller?"

"By the Emperor," Hal said flatly, though I saw his eyes start to shine brilliantly, "it is you, Jemis!"

"Of course," I said, and went to embrace the uncharacteristically quiet Mr. Dart. "Dying just seems to have smoothed off the rough edges a trifle. Come now, *Peregrine*, your mother wants to know why you don't like your name."

"Only a trifle," said Violet; but she reached out and squeezed my shoulder with her hand.

Note

Blackcurrant Fool is the fourth book of Greenwing & Dart. Book Five, *Love-in-a-Mist*, finds Mr. Greenwing, Mr. Dart, and their various companions endeavouring to return home to Ragnor Bella. Given the circumstances, it is no surprise at all that this is complicated by more than simply the weather.